THE ADVENTURES OF CLEMENTINE LEMONS

& THE LOST STONES OF DOHI

THE EARTH STONE

IRELAND VON MUELLER

EMB
ERIN MILLER BOOKS

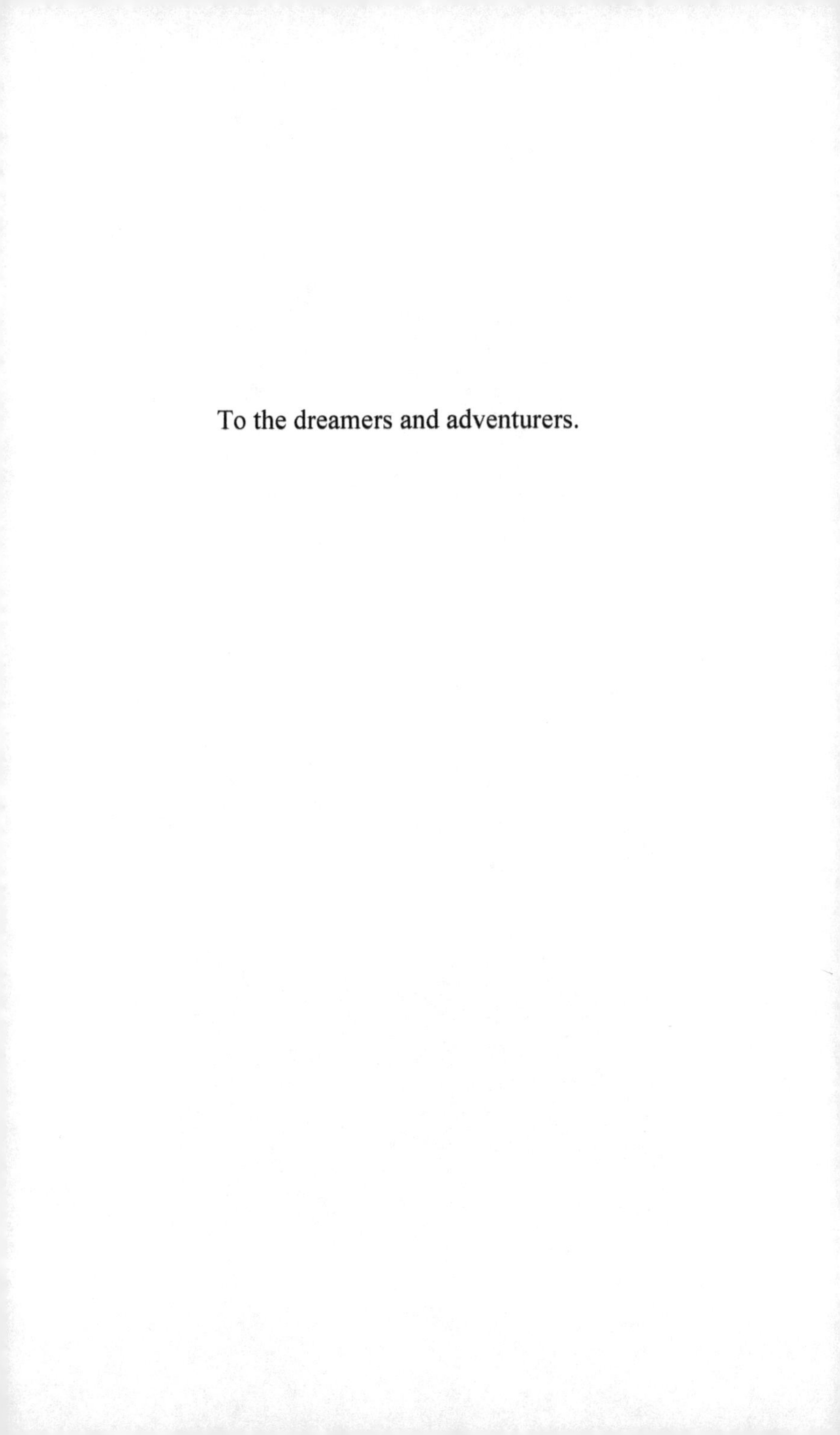

To the dreamers and adventurers.

PART ONE

CHAPTER 1

Clementine Lemons sat alone at the Pandora Avenue bus stop, completely and utterly lost in the pages of the mystery novel wedged against her knees. Now and then, she'd run her fingers through her long dark hair or casually fidget with the tassels on the scarf draped loosely around her neck. But beyond that, she was oblivious to the world, and the world was oblivious to her.

Clementine bit her lower lip as two masked men appeared out of a shadowy alley and chased Adriana James—her heroine—through the dark streets of Bangkok. Clem could hear the soft patter of Adriana's feet as her pace quickened; she could feel the warmth of the air as Adriana ran over the bridge toward the safety of the crowded night market. Suddenly, two more masked men appeared before her, blocking her way. Adriana turned to run back, but the two men behind her were already on the bridge, the silver of their gun barrels gleaming in the streetlight. Adriana was trapped. Clutching the backpack containing the ancient jade talisman, she leaped off the bridge and into the murky waters below.

Clem's heart raced. *How was Adriana going to get out of this mess?*

Anxiously flipping the page, Clementine looked up in time to catch a glimpse of a Starbucks advertisement rolling by. *The bus!*

The last passenger was already climbing the stairs. Snapping her book closed, Clem jumped off the bench, grabbed her bag and half-empty cup of tea, and leaped toward the bus.

The doors snapped shut on her nose.

"Wait…" Clem started to protest. As she spoke, the paper cup and book slipped from her hand—landing with a splat at her feet.

The bus driver didn't give the curb a second glance as he jostled back into the early-evening traffic. Sighing, Clementine bent and rescued her now-wet book from the sidewalk. As she stood, the back window of the bus slid open.

"Hey, Lemons, if you ever find your way home, tell Ferg that Coach canceled tomorrow's practice," a cute blond hollered with a laugh.

The window shut, and the bus lumbered down the street, leaving Clementine standing alone in a pool of cold tea.

"Ugh. Might as well change schools now," Clem groaned.

Cheeks burning with embarrassment, she plopped back on the bench of the empty bus stop. With Ferg for a brother, Clem may as well have been invisible. The few times people did notice her, it was only because she'd done something idiotic, like now or like the time she'd tripped in gym class, slid across the floor, and bowled down half the basketball team. Or when the cute new science teacher asked her to name an element from the periodic table, and she thought he'd asked for her name, so she blurted out, "Lementine Clemons." If she were lucky, the school would burn to the ground before morning. *Oh, if only.*

Pulling out her phone, Clementine looked at the clock. Twenty-six minutes until the next bus.

Thursdays were the worst. When they were little, her grandma Eloise watched her and Ferg after school. Things were fun then. But Clem's grandma had passed away when she was ten. Ferg, who was a year older than her, had discovered sports and become a superstar at everything. The next thing Clem knew, he was busy all the time—swim meets, rowing club, basketball, skiing. Ferg was determined to get to the Olympics. The more he achieved, the more Clem's parents insisted she "find her own thing" too. But it turned out, finding your "own thing" was easier said than done.

They hadn't even asked before enrolling her in piano lessons on her twelfth birthday. She'd been taking lessons for over a year and had hated every minute of it.

"You need a productive hobby, Clementine," her mother sighed. "Since sports aren't 'your thing,' and art isn't 'your thing,' you can try music. You can't sit around the house reading all the time. It's not healthy."

But music wasn't "her thing" either. Clem hated playing the piano. Her fingers were too short, and her brain worked too slowly to find the right keys. Her teacher, Mrs. Lee, was strict and boring and rarely spoke unless it was to complain about how poorly Clementine played and how much more she needed to practice. There was only one reason she kept going to lessons. Mrs. Lee's piano school was at the top of a long flight of stairs hidden by a narrow red door at 23 ½ Fan Tan Alley. Anyone who read books knew the best mysteries started at unusual locations. As far as Clementine was concerned, it didn't get any more unusual than 23 ½ Fan Tan Alley. If she kept her eye on the alley long enough, something exciting was bound to happen…eventually.

Wiping the tea from the cover of her book, she dove back in.

"We are not alone! Not alone. *No, no, no!* You aren't even the only one of you! I met myself once. Weird, so weird it was. It wasn't really me, I guess. Sure looked like me, though…" The words met Clementine's ears as unexpectedly as thunder on a cloudless day, echoing in her head and once again ripping her attention from her book.

Working his way toward her, a man strained to push an overstuffed shopping cart up the sidewalk. Clementine had seen him around before. She'd heard people at the bus stop refer to him as "the Professor." With his dingy white lab coat and finger-in-a-light-socket gray hair, he vaguely resembled Albert Einstein. As he shuffled closer, he continued his loud, nonsensical rant about the multiverse and interdimensional travel.

"Have you ever seen a lunar wolf? Magnificent beasts!" He grabbed the arm of the only other person on the street. "Ten to the power of ten, to the power of one hundred and twenty-two distinct possible particle configurations. Infinite repetition over infinite parallel universes. Mind-blowing." The Professor spoke with the conviction of a priest at Sunday mass and the hurried fervor of an auctioneer bent on getting the highest price for an item no one wanted to buy. His sermon was addressed to everyone, yet no one in particular.

Clementine stared at the Professor a moment. She wished she believed in something with such passion she felt the need to shout it from the rooftops. But the reality of life had long replaced the magic and whimsy that had once fueled her soul. What she wouldn't give to believe in unicorns and fairies again…or even lunar wolves, *whatever they were.*

Clem watched a shimmery piece of purple tinsel dislodge itself from the mile-high mosaic of randomness bulging out of the Professor's cart. It slunk down the metal grates and flirted dangerously with a wobbly wheel before a single gust of spring wind sent it sailing freely through the street. The tinsel caught briefly on a timeworn sign before continuing its journey into the unknown. Clementine, however, did not see it disappear. Her attention hadn't left the sign the tinsel had caught on.

It was as weathered as the faded exterior of the brick building upon which it hung. THE COMPENDIUM OF CURIOSITIES, once painted in gold on a navy backdrop, had long since faded to melted butter on drab gray. Peeling paint hung from the front door like strips of bark on a dying tree. Half of the black wrought iron numbers in the address—101016 Pandora Avenue—were missing, their ghostly shadows forever etched into the grime. The glass in the window was too dirty to see through, save for the corner nearest the door, where someone had swirled the dirt just enough to make the Open sign visible. The storefront sagged as if the building were carrying the weight of the city upon its worn-out shoulders.

Clementine wondered how she'd sat across the street from this store every Thursday for over a year and never noticed it until now.

Clem loved antiques. Grandma Eloise often took Ferg and her "treasure hunting." They'd sift through the junk in decrepit barns and at flea markets and auctions all over Vancouver Island. Occasionally they'd even go dumpster diving, though they were careful not to mention the dumpsters to their mom. Together, they'd found all sorts of neat things. Clem's favorite earrings had come out of a trash bin behind a thrift store. Even though her ears weren't pierced then, her grandma had told her, "You found them. You keep them!" Clem loved every second of it. She imagined it was as close as she'd ever get to being Adriana James.

Dog-earing the page of her book, Clementine looked at her phone. There was still a good twenty minutes until the next bus. Besides, if she ducked into the store now, she could avoid the Professor altogether. People said he was harmless, but she was still scared of him. Tossing her book in her bag, Clem made her way across the street.

The shop was much more cavernous inside than its storefront let on. The jingle of the bells hanging above the door frame fell flat as the heavy door shut with resolute certainty. The front counter—nearly invisible under a mountain of mysterious parcels, unopened wooden crates, and a pile of broken clocks—was void of human life. The only movement came from the rusty fan oscillating in the corner. Its sole purpose seemed to be recirculating dust.

"Hello?" Clementine called out, but the word was quickly lost in the jumble of antiques spread out before her. She took the lack of response as an open invitation to explore at her leisure.

Filtered through the dusty air, the shafts of light coming through the windows did little to illuminate the darkness. Clementine wandered away from the front door—the only obvious portal to the outside world—and through the maze-like passages between the tall stacks of furniture and knickknacks. The place felt like an abandoned carnival, but to Clem, this only added to the air of mystery. Occasionally she paused to listen for voices or any sign of life other than her own. The shop was so still she was sure if she listened hard enough, she'd be able to hear the furniture talk. Clem smiled at this thought.

She and Ferg used to make up all sorts of wild stories while their grandma was bargain-hunting. Clem's favorite was a story they'd invented about a grandfather clock that was actually a time machine. You could go back in time as far as you wanted. The only catch was the clock decided where you landed. One time, she'd sent Fergus back to 1852, and the clock had dumped him in the middle of the ocean. He swam to a pirate ship and became their captain, so it all worked out in the end.

Slowly dragging her finger through the heavy dust coating a long table, Clem found herself at a dead end. In front of her was a brick wall.

"You have chosen wrong. Game over, *over, over,*" Clementine whispered to herself.

No wonder she hadn't seen any other customers—they'd probably gotten lost and starved to death trying to escape. The thought of finding mummified remains made her skin crawl. Clementine suddenly felt very alone. Shivering, she turned around, ready to make a quick exit.

A wooden chest sat in the middle of the table she'd just run her finger across. Clem cocked her head to the side and stared at it. She could have sworn it hadn't been there a moment ago. Taking a closer look, she could clearly see the line she'd drawn in the dust wander up to one side of the chest, stop, and pick up again on the other.

"I didn't hear you come in. Can I help you?" A slow, mellow voice came from behind her.

Clementine gasped. She could feel the hairs rising on the back of her neck as she turned to face the wall.

Standing there was a man. Save for deep laugh lines at the edges of his broad smile, his skin was smooth as ivory. Topped with wiry eyebrows, his wide-set obsidian eyes reminded Clementine of a sloth. A thin white beard hung nearly to his waist. He could have been eighty or eight hundred and eighty; it was impossible to tell.

"New?" Pointing at the chest, Clementine did her best to sound like her grandmother.

"Nothing in this store is new," the man answered.

"I suppose not," Clem replied. "What I meant was, did you just put it out?"

"No, that one's been here a while, though it tends to get around on its own. I think it might be magic." His eyes twinkled.

"I'm too old to believe in magic," Clem huffed.

"You young people these days, always so serious. There's magic everywhere—all you have to do is be open to it."

Lightly tugging on one of the four locked drawers lining the bottom of the chest, Clementine raised her eyebrows. Right, be open to magic, and it will be real. Adults were so weird. They were constantly telling you to "grow up" and "act your age," but when you did, they were suddenly upset you didn't believe in magic anymore.

The drawer didn't budge.

"Where are the keys?" Clem flipped open the top lid to see if they were inside, but all she found was a small mound of brown powder in a corner.

"Regretfully, they've been lost to time and space," he replied.

Clem couldn't help but think this man and the Professor would get along great.

"Why do you ask? Do you like it?"

Though crackling and faded in spots, the gold trim made the light grain in the dark wood glow. A deep swirl of green-blue lacquer pooled like water between the raised gold lines of the round crests that adorned the lid and encircled each of the four keyholes. It was in remarkably good condition, considering it was probably hundreds of years old. Clem wondered where it had come from and who it had belonged to.

Grandma Eloise would have loved this place and this shiny wooden box. Clementine wasn't sure what she'd do with a chest with no keys and only one useful drawer, but the longer she stared at it, the more she liked it.

Fondly tracing the golden lines on the lid, Clementine finally responded, "It's beautiful, but I don't have any money."

"That thing's been kicking around here so long I can't even remember how or when I acquired it. I swear I've sold it a half-dozen times in my lifetime, but it always finds its way back. I suppose no one wants a chest with drawers they can't open," he said, smiling sadly. "Not very useful, now I think about it. If you want it, you can have it."

"Really?" Clementine asked. "Oh, I couldn't just take it. I mean, even without keys, it must be worth something?"

Grandma Eloise would have said, *Take it and run, girl!*

"If you want it, it's yours. There's enough junk here, I won't notice it's gone. It's time its story continued beyond the walls of this old shop." The man stroked his beard and shrugged. "Besides, I get the feeling you need it as much as it needs you."

"What's that supposed to mean?" Clem glanced at the chest and furrowed her eyebrows.

The old man didn't reply.

Clem turned to ask again, but he had vanished as quietly and mysteriously as he'd appeared. Clementine shivered. Picking up the surprisingly solid chest, she worked her way through the maze and back to the safety of the now-crowded bus stop.

The bus pulled up, and this time, she got on.

"Why are you so late? And where did that come from?" her mom asked the moment she walked through the front door.

Clem was hoping to make it to her room without being

seen, but her mom was a critical care nurse. Not even the tiniest details escaped her notice.

"I got it from an antiques store…which also explains why I'm late...because I stopped at an antiques store." Clementine sighed.

"That's not what I heard," her brother quipped from the kitchen table. "I heard the bus left you standing on the street because you were so lost in la-la land you forgot to get on.

"You're hopeless, Clem," he added with a laugh.

"Your sarcasm isn't appreciated, Clementine. That box looks expensive for a girl with no job." Their mom shook her head disapprovingly.

Her sarcasm?! What about Fergus?! But Clementine had learned long ago, Fergus could do no wrong.

"She probably stole it to keep her drugs in." Ferg looked up from his phone, a cocky grin spread across his face.

"Shut up, Fergus," Clementine muttered. Sometimes, she couldn't believe they were related, let alone they'd once been best friends.

"Clementine Eloise Lemons, are you on drugs? Do you know how high the odds are for a teenage addict to end up in the system? Or on the streets? Or worse, dead? Do you know how horrible it is to tell someone their child has died of an overdose? If I find drugs in your room…" Fergus looked entirely too pleased with himself as their mom ranted on.

It was always something. If Clem spent too much time alone in her room, she was obviously depressed. If she wasn't hungry at dinner, she must have an eating disorder. Too much time online? Her brain was rotting. Too little time? She must not have enough friends. And now, apparently, coming home from lessons thirty minutes later than usual, carrying an antique wooden chest, was a sure sign she was a drug addict.

There was no winning.

Retreating to the silence of her bedroom, Clementine set the chest on her desk and dusted it off as best she could with the sleeve of her sweater. She had a ton of homework. Finding a permanent home for it would have to wait.

Clem plopped in her chair and opened her book bag to look for a pen. All she found, besides her laptop and textbook, were her favorite earrings, which she'd taken off during gym class.

Clementine opened the top of the box, ready to toss the earrings inside. The mound of brown powder she'd noticed at the antiques store was still in the corner. Clem dipped her finger in it and held it to her nose. It smelled spicy and sweet, like peppercorns and licorice. If her mother saw it, she'd probably lose her mind—insist it was some weird drug—and ground Clementine until her eighteenth birthday. Clem rolled her eyes. Turning the box upside down over the trash, she dumped whatever it was and wiped the remainder out with her sleeve. Satisfied it was gone, she set the earrings in the box, shut the lid, and flipped open her laptop.

CHAPTER 2

Andro dug deep in the woven basket hanging next to his hip and fished for another bundle of tender young rice shoots. As he thrust the green sprouts into the water at his wrinkled feet, he watched a vein of iridescent goo seep out of the nearby mud bank. Hitting the water, it expanded like a rainbow across the surface. His skin burned as the rainbow wrapped itself around his thin ankles. Wincing in pain, he willed himself to stand still and keep working. He dared not say anything. *Head down. Don't cause a scene. Never draw attention to yourself.*

The rice paddies were too close to the garbage heap. But then again, everything was too close to the garbage heap. The factories in the valley sent a constant stream of goods to Nimbina, and in return, they sent back an endless river of garbage. Andro's gaze followed the wave of trash to where it curled into the smog-filled sky. Its poison was seeping, leaching, creeping out in every direction like the tentacles of a giant jellyfish, killing everything it touched. The valley was slowly being consumed by trash and toxic waste.

Andro had a sinking feeling the rice wouldn't survive the season. If the toxic goo didn't kill it first, the mountain of garbage would eventually topple, burying everything—including the field—in its path. It was only a matter of time. But that wasn't Andro's business. His business was to plant the rice, then silently watch it wither until it was as brown and dead as everything else.

Never question the authority of the Black Peacock, at least not out loud. Certainly never in front of them. If he didn't say anything and the crops died, that would be his fault too. He might lose a few Coin or be retasked to a worse job, but at least he wouldn't be labeled a traitor. At least his granny and little sister would be safe. Hungry but safe. There was no winning at this game.

Andro despised the Black Peacock with every fiber of his being. He tried not to. He knew it was wrong; he just couldn't help himself. Beyond power, the Black Peacock didn't care about anyone or anything. Why should he care about them? The more his feet burned, the more the blood boiled in his veins. Sometimes, it felt as if he would explode. If only he were bigger, stronger, smarter, older. If only Granny and Zari didn't depend on him for their survival. Then he'd show them. He'd be like his father, only he wouldn't get caught.

After curfew, when Granny was asleep, he'd sneak out of the house and graffiti the symbol of the New Resistance somewhere the Bird would see it. He'd only snuck out once or twice before, and each time he'd told himself he'd never do it again—it was too risky. But the more his feet burned, the less he cared. It would make the pain worth it. Andro smiled. That would make his fourteenth birthday special, give it meaning. Yes, that is what he would do.

Andro's hand hit the bottom of his basket. Looking down, he was dismayed to find it empty. The burning in his feet had made him concentrate too hard and work too fast. Now he'd be required to take another full basket. He glanced at the smog-filled sky. The faint glow in the west suggested it was late afternoon. Most days, he'd gladly take another basket. Extra work meant extra Coin. Extra Coin meant extra food, and there was never enough food. But today was his birthday. Even though he knew they couldn't afford it, he deserved one early day a year, right?

Andro couldn't be seen with an empty basket. From their elevated perches, the spotters would see he wasn't working. They'd signal the enforcers, who would reluctantly go see what was wrong. The retaliation would be swift and brutal if they had to get up from their shaded post.

Without straightening—a sure sign his basket was empty—Andro scanned the field for someone struggling under their own workload. A few rows ahead, his elderly neighbor, Ablikim, was doubled over under the weight of a nearly full basket. Ablikim was too old to work like this, but he no longer had children to support him. He'd once had a son, but that was long ago. They were tinkerers back then, fixers of all things broken—and everything in the valley was broken.

When Andro was seven, the Black Peacock's agents had dragged his parents and Ablikim's son away in the middle of the night. They called them traitors. Said they were rebels. Andro's granny had lost her job as a seamstress in Nimbina, and the Black Peacock burned the tinker shop to the ground. Nobody wanted to be seen associating with the father of a traitor. Friendless and alone, Ablikim had ended up in the fields, just like Andro. Andro had always wanted to ask the old man about it, but there was no use speaking about what was.

Still bent low, Andro worked toward Ablikim, backing into him with enough force to knock the old man and his basket to the ground.

"Grandfather Ablikim!" Andro cried dramatically. "I'm so sorry. I didn't see you there!"

Andro could feel the spotters' eyes drilling into the back of his head. The enforcers leaned forward in their chairs, watching from the shade. Andro raised his hand and bowed low in apology. Helping Ablikim to his feet, he hurriedly gathered the shoots that had fallen from the old man's basket and placed them in his own. Andro winked, Ablikim nodded in appreciation, and they silently went back to work as if nothing had happened.

Andro waited a few long minutes before daring to glance toward the spotters' watch post or the enforcers' barracks. Thankfully, they were no longer paying attention. He was in the clear.

As Andro stood in line to turn in his basket that evening, he kept his head bent, hoping no one would notice his early departure. Andro was usually one of the last to leave. The people in line shuffled forward. His stomach growled. He excitedly thought about his birthday dinner. It would be rice and beans, as always; his pay didn't stretch far enough to buy much else. But tonight, they'd add a pinch of the secret spice Granny saved for special occasions, and that would make all the difference in the world.

The records keeper, a stern woman with a blunt State-approved haircut, stared at Andro over the rim of her thick glasses, and impatiently cleared her throat.

Andro looked up, startled and embarrassed. He'd been so excited about dinner he hadn't been paying attention.

"May the sun never set on the Empire of the Black Peacock," he mumbled, dutifully raising his left hand in salute.

"Yes"—the woman patriotically saluted back—"may the sun never set on the Empire of the Black Peacock."

Andro glanced at the sky streaked with the black smoke the factories belched out day and night, night and day. The sun could never set on the Empire of the Black Peacock because it never rose.

The woman pursed her pencil-thin lips and began to tally his baskets for the day. Her drab gray suit, the official uniform of the Regime, was perfectly fitted to her squat body—the jet-black emblem of the Black Peacock shining over her heart. Andro wondered if the woman had been tasked as a records keeper or if she'd volunteered to serve. Even though the fields didn't pay well, he was glad he was a field hand. He'd rather starve than voluntarily serve the Bird.

"You're a basket shorter than usual." The woman didn't bother looking up from her clipboard. "Good numbers make good laborers."

She flicked him away with a wave of her hand.

Sitting beside a battered barrel of gray sludge water, Andro rinsed the mud off his wrinkled feet. His ankles were bright red and unbearably itchy, but at least the skin wasn't peeling off yet. Gingerly slipping his toes into his too-small sandals, he rolled down the damp legs of his linen trousers. For a brief while, he was free.

The walk back to the city from the fields was, by far, the best part of his day. Especially now that it was spring and the cherry trees lining the path were in full bloom. The first snow of winter was another favorite time, but lately, it didn't take long for the soot from the factories to turn the snow as steely gray as the sky. As the days shortened and the heavens darkened, it felt as if the world itself were the last embers of a dying flame. During the darkest days, Andro eagerly awaited the first cherry buds for assurance spring would indeed return. When the cherries were ripe, they would leave the muddy rice paddies to pick cherries under the shade of the gnarled trees. With each passing year, the summers shortened, and the winters lengthened. Sometimes, it felt as if the cherry trees would never bloom again. This year, spring had come later than ever. The flowers were thick, but they seemed abnormally anemic. It was as if, little by little, the color was being drained from the entire world. How long would it be until everything went dark?

Even when all hope seems lost, Andro, Granny liked to tell him, *the cherry tree will still find a way to blossom.*

Andro looked at the pale pink flowers hanging overhead, blocking the gloomy sky. If he didn't think too hard about it, he could almost imagine he was elsewhere—Nimbina even. He'd never been to the great city hidden in the hills above the valley, but Granny had told him it was beautiful. In Nimbina, the sky was a brilliant blue. Andro closed his eyes and tried to imagine what it would look like if the sky were blue, purple, or any color other than gray. He wondered why they chose blue and whose job it was to paint it. If he could have chosen any task, that's the one he'd have picked. He would have been in charge of painting the sky blue.

A gentle breeze blew through the orchard. Andro opened his eyes and looked around. When he was certain no one was watching, he stretched out his arms and spun in circles as the petals rained down around him. Near the edge of town, he cut a small branch of blossoms to take home.

Andro found his granny and his little sister, Zari, sitting at the tiny three-person table under the window. Granny was teaching Zari to mend socks. Zari hated sewing, but it made sense she would become a seamstress when she was tasked on her twelfth birthday. The women in the family had always been, and would always be, seamstresses.

Zari was frail and dainty. She looked more like an eight-year-old than the eleven she was. Andro doubted she'd be able to perform any other task. He certainly couldn't see her in the fields, a factory, or a mine. Being a seamstress was, at least, a desirable job. If she worked hard, she might even get invited to sew for the elite in Nimbina, just as Granny had. Andro hated the idea of his sister working for the Bird, but he had to admit the extra Coin (and full cupboards) would be nice.

"Here, Granny, I picked this for you." Andro kissed his granny on the forehead and placed the cherry branch on the table in front of her. He walked to the stove and set to boiling water for rice and beans.

"You're such a thoughtful boy, Andro." The woman's face softened into a warm smile.

As dinner bubbled, Andro walked over to the cupboard. The shelves were bare save for a jar of rice, a nearly empty sack of beans, a shaker of clumpy salt, and the old spice chest. The emptiness made the small cabinet look much larger than it was. He'd have to work a lot longer days if the three of them were going to make it through the next winter. Andro felt a twang of guilt for coming home early. Carefully, he set the heavy spice chest on the table.

Andro smiled fondly at the battered chest and marveled at its beauty. There were four keyed drawers under the top compartment, but the locks had been broken—and the keys lost—long before it came to them. No matter. They'd never owned anything worth locking up anyway. The drawers remained emptier than the cupboards.

Andro ran a calloused finger over the raised golden crest adorning the lid. He loved how the royal blue and green lacquer shone like a deep pool from within the raised gold lines. The colors were so vivid and deep. When he was young, he imagined they were a lake. Andro laughed, remembering how he used to wish he could dive in and swim to the other side. The other side of what—that he never did figure out. But in his young mind, things were better on the other side.

Even with the broken locks, it was the most extravagant thing they owned. It had been in their family for so long that its discovery had become a legend bordering on myth. Granny insisted it belonged to royalty in the time before the Black Peacock. When he was starving and food was scarce, Andro wondered if the chest had any value. But Granny would never allow him to sell it; it was, after all, magic.

For Andro, opening the chest was as much a birthday tradition as spicing the rice. When he was young, Granny would place it in the center of the table and, while the rice boiled, tell them tales of the "magic chest" and the mysterious gifts it had brought their family. Exotic jewelry, funny figurines, odd coins. Even the spice had been a gift from the magic box. After Granny finished telling her story, Andro and Zari would lift the lid, and the three of them would eagerly peek inside, hoping to find treasure.

Finding the box empty had been disappointing when he was a boy. Now Andro was older, he understood the story as more of a fable about the importance of hope and believing in the impossible. Granny was always trying to teach them some sort of lesson.

Or maybe the "magic chest" was Granny's way of explaining how she acquired items that could only have come from Nimbina. Spices hadn't been traded in the valley for eons. Granny certainly never had the money to purchase the jewelry and trinkets she "found" in the chest. He couldn't imagine Granny stealing from the wealthy women she'd worked for—it was far too risky—but there was no other explanation.

Granny must have realized he no longer believed in magic because she hadn't told the story in years. These days, finding there was still something left of the dwindling pile of spice was all the treasure he needed. Andro smiled at the old woman, her arthritic fingers fumbling with the thin needle and sock, and wondered, with a heart full of sorrow, how many birthdays they had left together.

"Granny, will you tell us the story of the magic chest?" Andro lit the lantern above the table and drew the curtains.

Zari's eyes sparkled in the faint light. She was still a child; she loved her granny's stories.

"You haven't asked for my story in so long, I thought maybe you'd outgrown it. I guess I'd better make this time count, in case you never ask again!" The elderly woman cleared her throat.

"Our story," she started dramatically, "begins long after the Empire of the Emerald Peacock had fallen but before the Black Peacock had fully fanned its feathers. Emperor Cetin and his cruel regime terrorized the people of the mountains. Some said he was especially cruel to the mountain people because he believed they were hiding his sister, Princess Cyra. She had murdered their father, and he would leave no stone unturned to find her and bring her to justice. Some believed it was revenge on the monks, who opposed his brutality and use of excessive force. Still, others thought it was his way of strengthening the empire. I think it was because the Black Peacock is, and always has been, evil to its core."

Andro glanced toward the tiny window, trying to pierce the curtain and the darkness beyond to see who might be listening. The streets had eyes and ears. What if a passerby heard Granny's murmured malcontent? Andro shivered at the thought of what might happen.

"Village by village, Prince Cetin rounded up everyone in the Videt Mountains and dragged them into the valley— burning crops and leveling villages as he went. Eventually, the Black Army made it to Cirus. The villagers were not caught off guard, but against the might of the Black Army, they didn't stand a chance. When the battle ended, the few villagers left were taken prisoner. They left with only the clothes on their backs and the few items they could carry. The march out of the mountains took days upon days. The people were given little food or water and were forced to walk long hours without rest. Those who became too weak to walk were beaten and left for dead. The Black Army was as ruthless then as they are now.

"One night, the prisoners made camp in the ruins of a long-abandoned monastery. While everyone slept, a solitary boy snuck into the shadows to look for an escape. Lodged beneath a pile of rubble, he saw something glinting in the moonlight. Digging deep, he pulled out this chest. When he flipped the top lid open, he was amazed to see it was full of sweet treats. He brought the box of treats back to camp and hid it in his sack. The more treats he shared, the more treats appeared. This boy was the first in our family to receive gifts from the magic chest, and those gifts are what allowed our people to survive the long journey out of the mountains.

"Eventually, the sweets dried up, but the chest brought other gifts through the ages. Your great-great-grandfather once found enough gold to buy a cow. Imagine a lowly laborer owning a cow! The Bird didn't like that at all. When I was a little girl, the chest gifted us all sorts of exotic jewels and trinkets. Mother would secretly sell them to the wealthy women she worked for in Nimbina. Those were good times, we ate well back then. Since the chest was left to me, mostly oddities have turned up: strange coins, a ring or two, this—" Granny held up a toy car with plastic wheels.

"I'm not sure what it is, but the chest felt I should have it, so I keep it safe. Before you were born, books with strange markings appeared. Your father was obsessed with those…"

she trailed off.

"The spices appeared after you were born, and then, the gifts stopped again. Enough talk! Open the lid and see if the chest has brought us anything new to mark this special day!"

Even though she tried to hide it, Andro knew Granny faithfully checked the chest every day. She had to know it was empty. Still, he smiled at her enthusiasm. For a brief moment, he stared at the box with the same hope and wonder he'd had as a child.

"Ready, Zari?" Andro tried to sound excited.

Zari grinned from ear to ear.

Closing his eyes, Andro breathed deep in anticipation of the pungent aroma that had faithfully greeted him for as many birthdays as he could remember. Together, he and Zari flipped open the lid.

As he looked inside, Andro's heart stopped.

Though the aroma still lingered fresh in the old chest, every last trace of spice was gone! How had this happened? Andro knew the pile was dwindling, but he could've sworn there was enough to last a few more birthdays. He slammed the lid shut, leaped across the tiny expanse of floor between the table and the cupboard, and ran his hand across the barren shelf. Not a single speck of spice coated his fingers.

Andro walked back to the table. Throwing himself in his chair, he rested his head in his arms. His birthday was ruined.

"Andro, what's wrong?" Granny squinted to see in the dim glow of the lamp.

"It's empty, Granny," Zari replied.

"The spice is gone now. See?" Andro flipped the lid of the chest back open.

Granny leaned across the table and peered into the opened compartment.

"That's because the chest has given you a gift, child," she gasped. "Finally, the magic is working again! Remove it quickly before the chest thinks we're ungrateful and takes it back!"

Andro took another look. Sitting in the center was a set of shiny gold loops with sparkly stones dangling from the bottom.

Mouth open, he stared in disbelief. They had not been there a moment earlier. Of this, he was sure. Andro snatched them up.

"What do you think they are?" Andro didn't dare take his eyes off of them for fear they'd disappear.

"They're earrings, child. The ladies of Nimbina hang them in their ears like this." Granny held one of the loops to her earlobe.

"But what are they for?" Andro asked. "Do they make you hear better or something?"

He held one to his ear as a test and whispered, "Hello." There was no noticeable difference. He frowned. They had to have some kind of practical use, right? Everything had a purpose.

"No," Granny said, chuckling. "They're jewelry. Decoration. Like an ornament for your ears. All the ladies of Nimbina wear them, even the empress."

"I don't get it." Andro gently set the golden loop back on the table.

Zari snatched them up and held them to her ears, tossing her head from side to side.

"Well, I like the idea of something with no purpose beyond beauty." The stones bounced off her cheeks. "Like the branch of cherry blossoms you brought home. They could have been fruit, but instead, they lay on the table, being beautiful. Maybe

Nimbina isn't as bad as you think it is."

Andro rolled his eyes. *Girls.*

He still didn't get it, but they had to be worth something if the empress wore them. Maybe even enough to stock the shelves for the next winter and give a little something to Ablikim. Andro couldn't help but get his hopes up. After all, if the tale of the magic chest was true, maybe anything was possible.

"What do you think they're worth?" He snatched them back from Zari, who whimpered in protest. "How do we sell them?" How could he get rid of these "earrings" without causing suspicion? Who would believe a family like his had come by such lavish things honestly? If the wrong person found out he had them, they'd report him to collect the reward. Who would buy such a thing without asking questions? Andro had done dubious things before, but nothing like this. He didn't even know where to begin.

"Tomorrow," Granny replied in little more than a whisper, "when you go to buy food for the week, wait until just before the store closes. When you're sure you're alone, tell Rozi you have something to trade. He'll offer you far less than they're worth. Tell him your granny will come and beat him with her broom if he isn't fair with you. Take Coin or goods, not credit. Don't get caught. Don't be seen."

When the house was quiet, and he was sure his granny and sister were asleep, Andro opened the door and slipped into the inky-black night. His feet still itched, and he wanted revenge.

CHAPTER 3

Arms folded, Clementine leaned against her brother's doorjamb. She was in no mood for his childish games. It was bad enough that she'd forgotten to set her alarm. But then her earrings had gone missing too. She'd ended up late for class wearing mismatched socks and looking like a swamp monster. She might not have been late at all if she hadn't spent forever looking for the earrings.

"Give them back, Fergus."

"Give what back?" He didn't even look up from his phone.

"You know exactly what, you crayon-munching butt-monkey." Clem's eyes narrowed.

"I honestly have no idea what you're talking about," Fergus mumbled.

"My earrings. The ones I found with Grandma. You stole them from my chest. Give them back right now. I know it was you."

"You can't march into my room and accuse me of stealing something with no proof, loser." Fergus shook his head, obviously amused at her frustration.

Clem closed the gap between them in a single second and plucked the phone out of his hands.

"Give me back my earrings, or I'll drop it." Clem held his phone out the open window.

"I don't have your stupid earrings! Give me back my phone!" She had his attention now.

"Oh, like you didn't have my tablet, or my toothbrush, or my hamster?!" Clementine was livid.

"Okay, yeah, I took your tablet, but you have to admit the clues to where I hid it were pretty clever, and you did eventually find it."

"You buried it in the backyard, Fergus. It doesn't even work anymore." Thanks to Fergus, Clem still didn't have a working tablet because, apparently, she "wasn't mature enough to take care of one."

"And, yes, I did borrow your toothbrush, but I had dog poo on my favorite track shoes, and I had to get it off with something!" Fergus was practically in hysterics. "I was like eleven. I didn't know better. And to be fair, I cleaned it off as best I could. Geez. As for your hamster, are you seriously still mad about that? It was, like, six years ago!"

"Of course, I'm still mad! You kidnapped Mr. Scruffles and tried to collect a ransom for his return! This isn't even about that, this is about my earrings, and I want them back. No games." Clementine let his phone slip between her fingers.

"*STOP!* You're insane! I haven't touched your stuff in years. Unlike you, I have a life now. Why would I waste time on something as dumb as your earrings? I swear to you, they're not in my possession."

Clementine looked for his signature guilty smile, but he looked surprisingly innocent.

"They probably fell through a crack in that ugly old box. Now give me my phone and get out of my room before I push you out the window."

Clementine tossed his phone on the bed next to him.

"If I find out you're lying, you're going to wish you hadn't been born," she muttered on her way out the door.

Clementine flopped on her bed and stared at the fairy lights strung between the rafters. Her room had once been Grandma Eloise's art room. A stack of her paintings still stood in the corner behind the macramé swing chair Clem had begged her mother to buy. Mostly landscapes, the paintings didn't match the "boho" aesthetic Brook and Maddie insisted she create, but she couldn't get rid of them. Clem's plants were mostly dead because she never remembered to water them. She was constantly bringing in weird junk she found on the street. It didn't match anything, but it was *free*. Who could resist that? Her room was a mess, much like her brain.

Clem sighed. Maybe Fergus was right. Her earrings could have slipped into a crack and gotten trapped in one of the keyless drawers. She'd just assumed it was him because it was always him.

Clem marched over to her desk and flipped the lid of the chest. Examining it for cracks, she found none.

She had put her earrings in there, right? She was ninety-nine-percent certain, but the longer she thought about it, the more that one percent ate at her. Maybe she was losing her mind. Could you get dementia or Alzheimer's at thirteen? She made a mental note to look it up. Clem leaned back in her chair. No, she wasn't losing her mind. She had put her earrings in the box, and they had gone missing.

She went over her and Fergus's conversation in her head. He hadn't said he never took them, only that he didn't have them. How did he put it?

I swear they're not in my possession.

That was a weird thing to say. Who says that? He was definitely guilty. Clem couldn't go to her parents and accuse him of stealing her stuff. They'd never believe her. Fergie was their perfect little angel. She'd have to catch him in the act. This gave Clementine an idea.

Clem popped the turquoise-and-silver bracelet off of her wrist. Grandma Eloise had brought it back from a trip to the

Grand Canyon. She'd told Clem this wild story about how she'd found it buried beneath ancient ruins in a box canyon while rafting the Rio Colorado. Clem knew this wasn't true—it had come from the Grand Canyon Gift Shop—but she liked to think it was anyway. It was, by far, her favorite thing. It never left her wrist. Ever. It was as much a part of her as her teeth. Fergus knew this. He would one-hundred-percent notice she wasn't wearing it. It was the perfect bait to catch him at whatever stupid game he was playing.

As much as she hated to admit it, she missed their little cat-and-mouse games. Sometimes it felt like Fergus had grown up while she'd stayed the same.

Clem tossed the bracelet in the top of the chest and shut the lid with a satisfied smile. Fergus was going to be in so much trouble! She propped her laptop on her dresser and pointed the webcam to get a good view of her desk and the chest. Plugging the laptop in so it wouldn't die at the wrong moment, Clem set the webcam to record. She put her screen to sleep, so it looked like it was off, then stood back and admired her work. Except for the white light glowing next to the camera, it was perfect. Fergus was smart; he'd notice that right away. Grabbing a piece of tape and a black felt pen, she covered it.

Her goal was to get Fergus grounded for the rest of the school year. And her mom said she wouldn't learn anything from reading spy novels, *pfft*. Immensely satisfied, she sauntered down the creaky old stairs to put her plan into action.

Ferg had moved from his bedroom to the living room.

"Go away." Busy playing video games, he didn't even glance in her direction.

"You don't own the living room." Clem rolled her eyes and stood between him and the TV. "I need your help."

"With what?" Ferg pushed her aside with his foot.

"I did something to my wrist in gym class today, and it hurts. I think it's twisted or fractured or something. Does this look swollen to you?" Clem thrust her wrist in front of his face.

Ferg glanced at it for a millisecond. "It looks fine. Stop being a baby."

"Are you sure?" Clem rotated her empty wrist in front of his face. "Because it doesn't feel fine."

"Be real, Clem, you don't participate in gym class enough to have injured yourself. So, shut up and play, or go away..." Fergus acted like he didn't care, but Clementine suspected otherwise.

Clem waited patiently until bedtime to go back to her room and check the chest. She didn't want Fergus to think she was acting suspiciously. The moment she closed the door, she made a beeline for her desk. Sure enough, the chest was empty. This was too easy. Poor, naïve Fergus.

Humming happily, Clementine lay down with her laptop to watch her surveillance video. Four hours was a lot of staring at an empty desk, and she only needed to see the five minutes when Fergus was stealing her stuff, so she put it on fast-forward. Clem got all the way to the end before realizing she'd missed him. She played the footage again, only slower. Still, there was no Fergus. Had he been so fast she'd blinked and missed it?

There was only one way to find out. Hidden beneath her blankets, Clementine watched the entire video again, in real time. It was torture, like sitting through four hours of math class. Four hours and nothing! No Fergus, no parents, no random cat burglar, no ghost, not so much as a breeze had rippled the papers on her desk. Clem rubbed her tired eyes. *Unbelievable!*

How had he done that? How could he have possibly known it was a trap? And when had he learned to edit video? Seriously.

Clem thought back to the ransom note Fergus had made when he'd kidnapped Mr. Scruffles. He'd actually taken the time to cut each letter from a different magazine. They'd been glued neatly around a photo of Mr. Scruffles holding a tiny newspaper with the date on it. She had to admit his clues leading to the grave he'd buried her tablet in had been pretty clever too. Maybe editing the video wasn't a far stretch, considering. Thankfully Fergus didn't put this kind of effort into schoolwork, or he'd officially be better than her at everything.

If Clementine was going to catch him, she needed to up her game.

CHAPTER 4

The golden loops burned at the back of Andro's mind all day as he worked the fields. Granny had stitched them into his trouser pocket so he wouldn't lose them. Still, he feared they'd fall out and be lost forever in the muddy water. His hand found its way into his pocket so often he was sure someone would notice.

He regretted sneaking out the previous night. What if he'd been seen? If they came for him while he had this contraband in his pocket, no excuse would save him. He could be dragged out of the fields and searched at any moment. What would become of Granny and Zari if anything happened to him? He needed to be less reckless. Andro ran the back of his hand across his sweaty forehead and pushed the thought as far back in his mind as he could. From now on—well, as soon as he was rid of these earrings—he'd stop doing anything questionable. And this time, he meant it.

It was dusk when Andro finally handed in his last basket. He'd more than made up for the basket he'd been short the day before. The records keeper was pleased.

"Good numbers make good laborers," she reminded him as she finished tallying his weekly count and handed his receipt to the treasurer.

The treasurer, a gruff man with a scowl that could curdle fresh milk, begrudgingly handed Andro an extra Coin with his weekly pay.

"May the sun never set on the Empire of the Black Peacock." He saluted.

"Yes. May the sun never set on the Empire of the Black Peacock," Andro said, his left hand raised in salute.

Determined to be the last person to arrive at the store, Andro waited to walk back to the city with Ablikim. He often walked home with the old man when he had the time. Ablikim had a noticeable limp. His walk could barely be described as a shuffle, which was precisely what Andro needed to slow himself down. Usually, they walked in tired silence. Even when they weren't exhausted, there was rarely anything interesting to say. Today, however, Andro was so excited and nervous that he found it hard not to tell Ablikim about the secret hiding in his pocket. He bit his tongue to remind himself to keep quiet. You didn't go around talking about such things—especially with your elders. The city seemed painfully far away.

At the corner near the store, Andro glanced up a narrow alleyway. Though barely visible in the fading light, his graffiti was still there. If anyone had noticed, they hadn't bothered to report it. Andro's heart raced, thinking there could be others who loathed the Black Peacock as much as he did. He was proud his artwork was still there and even more proud he hadn't been caught. A twinge of sadness tugged at his heart as he reminded himself his days of rebelling were over.

Ahead of them, a lamplighter moved silently up the street, lighting the paper lanterns hanging overhead. Still, it seemed abnormally dark. The old man cursed as he stumbled on the uneven cobblestone. Andro was glad for the long shadows. There was safety in being able to slip into the darkness. Across the street from the small store, a group of men sat hunched over low stools, quietly sipping tea. Andro wished they weren't there—watching, listening. But he couldn't wait for them to leave. It was almost curfew. Soon, the streets would be empty, and the store would close for the evening.

Saying goodbye to Ablikim, he stepped into the cramped shop. The shelves, stacked from floor to ceiling behind a long counter, were half-full at best. A handful of people waited in line in front of him. He recognized most of their faces from work or within his sector, but he couldn't name them if he tried. No one spoke.

If anyone were to line up behind him, what would he do? He couldn't very well move to the back of the line. That would be suspicious. He guessed he'd have to wait and try again when he got paid the following Friday. Andro gulped. He couldn't keep the earrings secret for another seven days. As it was, his tongue still hurt from biting it so hard.

While he waited, he fiddled with the stitching holding the earrings in his pocket, and prayed no one else came in.

His heart raced when the thread gave way, and the earrings fell loosely into his hand. This was the same feeling he got when he snuck out at night. The same feeling he got when he pulled out his paint. He felt alive.

"The usual, Andro?" Rozi, the shopkeeper, asked.

Rozi had been the sector's shopkeeper since long before Andro was born. Andro was never sure if he liked the man or not. He was shifty, but then again, that was the only way to get ahead in Dohi. Besides, if Rozi hadn't been a little dishonest, Andro and his family would've starved to death long ago.

Andro was seven the first time he'd come to the store alone. With his parents gone, and Granny without work, he hadn't waited to be tasked on his twelfth birthday. It was work or starve, so he'd gone to work in the fields. He distinctly remembered his blistered hand trembling as he handed his first-ever Coin to the big, scary man behind the counter. He'd been so proud of that Coin and so sad to give it away after working so hard for it. The big man smiled and, pitying him, had given him far more rice than the small Coin was worth. Rozi often over measured his grain, and for that, Andro was grateful.

The last few years, though, as the fields withered and died, it had gotten tough. The Black Peacock's grip was now so tight even a half cup of missing rice was hard to explain. As the Regime demanded every grain be accounted for, Rozi's measurements had become more and more precise, and Andro left the store with less and less.

"Yes, please," Andro said.

Rozi eyed him keenly as he measured rice and beans and poured them into empty sacks.

"Will that be all today, Andro?" He grabbed Andro's Coins and tucked them safely behind the counter.

"No." Andro spoke so suddenly he startled himself. "I mean, not exactly."

Rozi raised an eyebrow.

Looking around to ensure they were alone, Andro quickly pulled his hand out of his pocket and opened his fist. His hand trembled as much as the day he'd held out that first Coin.

"I wondered," he said through bated breath, "if you could tell me if these are worth anything?"

Rozi glanced at the shiny metal loops and hurriedly closed Andro's fist.

"Oh, I'm sure I have some around here somewhere." Rozi loudly cleared his throat. "Let me close the shop for the evening, and I'll take a look in the back for you."

Waving goodnight to the men on the far side of the street, Rozi slammed the doors shut. He shuttered the windows and blew out the front lamps.

Safely back behind the counter, he asked Andro to once again show him what he had for trade.

"I see your granny still has a few tricks up her sleeve." Rozi pulled out a cracked magnifying glass and examined the pieces closely. "They're not high quality—the gold is thin, and the stones are of little value—but they're pretty enough. Where that woman has gotten her 'trade' items over the years, I'll never know," he muttered in appreciation. "And to be honest, I never dared ask. Some things are best left unknown. If my connections can get them into Nimbina, they'll fetch a reasonable price."

He made Andro an offer.

Andro's eyes nearly shot out of his head. He couldn't make that kind of Coin in a month! Still, he remembered Granny's warning.

"That's too low," he replied flatly. "They're one-of-a-kind. I bet there isn't another pair like them in all of Dohi. They're worth more."

"Your granny's taught you well. I feel for your family, Andro. I really do. Times are tough. But I have to factor the risk I'm taking into the price. Fewer and fewer interesting items pass my way these days. It's not easy getting things like this into the right hands, you know?" Rozi tried again with a slightly higher offer.

Andro was about to say he needed more money just to see what Rozi would do, but the curfew bell startled him. He hadn't realized it was so late. Ten minutes to get home. Breaking curfew wasn't as easy in the early evening as it was late at night when everyone, including the night enforcers, were fast asleep. Just after the last bell rang was when you were most likely to be caught. He agreed to the shopkeeper's price, quickly pointing at items on the shelf he wanted as payment.

Rozi bundled Andro's food together and rushed him out the door.

Andro hurried home as fast as his feet would carry him beneath the weight of the overflowing sacks. Even though there was still time, he was careful to stick to the shadows. He didn't need an enforcer stopping him. Not with a summer's worth of groceries dangling from his arms.

Stepping over the threshold as the last bell chimed, Andro locked the door behind him. He motioned for Zari to drop her mending and pull the curtains shut.

Zari's eyes bulged as Andro stocked the shelves with can after can of fruits and vegetables, fresh flour, dried meats, and all the other goods he'd brought home. Lazy from years of disuse, the shelves groaned and buckled under the weight.

When he'd finished, Andro stood back and stared in awe. The cupboard was fuller than he'd ever seen, fuller than it had been in his lifetime.

"It looks like the store on restock day." Zari admired the shelves from beside him.

"It does, doesn't it?" Andro proudly pulled down the fresh sack of flour. For the first time in longer than he could remember, he cooked something other than rice and beans.

Satisfied in a way he'd forgotten was possible, Andro didn't even care that he still had work to do after dinner. He smiled as he refilled the water cistern for the week and was still smiling when he chopped the firewood. The small garden they were allowed to keep behind their apartment desperately needed weeding. But it would be far too late by the time he'd finished his other chores. It would have to wait until morning.

Careful not to wake his granny or sister, he quietly piled the last of the wood beside the stove. Andro rubbed his eyes.

He was exhausted. On his way to blow out the light, he stopped to admire the full shelf one last time. He ran his hand fondly over the chest.

"Thank you," he whispered. For fun, he flipped the lid open again. Staring back at him was a large silver disk with a stone as blue as he imagined the sky in Nimbina to be.

Andro stared at it a moment, blinking in disbelief. Quickly remembering what Granny said about not being ungrateful, he plucked it out and clutched it to his heart.

Overwhelmed by his good fortune, Andro crawled into bed, covered his head, and wept. He wept because his feet and his back ached beyond his fourteen years. Because no matter how hard he worked, it was never enough. He wept for his parents. He wept with relief their shelves were finally full of food. He wept because he was exhausted. As the tears streamed down his dirty cheeks, he felt something he'd never felt before—hope things could truly be better. For the first time in his life, Andro felt like he wasn't alone. Like someone was watching out for him, helping him. For the first time, he felt like he had a friend.

Andro lay on his bedroll on the earthen floor, clutching the silver bracelet, and wept until exhaustion overcame him, and he fell into a deep, dreamless sleep.

When Andro opened his puffy, sore eyes, the light was already filtering through the small window. Granny was awake, sitting silently at the table.

"Good morning, Granny," he mumbled. "Have you eaten? Where's Zari?"

"Zari's outside, in the garden. I thought you could use the extra sleep. You work too hard," she responded. "Zari can make breakfast too. She needs to learn these things. She can't always expect you to do everything for her. She's not a baby anymore."

Andro sat and stared at the overflowing shelf. For a moment, his tired brain was confused.

"But we have fruit! And oats! And tea!" he chirped as he realized what he was looking at. "And I don't know about you, but I'm hungry now!"

As he hopped out of bed, something metallic hit the floor. The bracelet! He dropped to his knees to grab it before it rolled under the stove.

"I almost forgot, Granny. Look!" Andro excitedly thrust the silver disk in the elderly woman's face. "The chest gave us another gift! Last night, on my way to bed, I stopped to thank the chest for the earrings. Then I flipped the lid open, like this"—he demonstrated—"and there it was!"

Andro's mouth dropped. Again, the box wasn't empty! A thick plate of gold shone brightly from within. Andro picked it up and held it to the light. Etched in the gold was the outline of a man submerged beneath the waves, one arm stretching high overhead. Strange markings ran in a circle around the outside. It was surprisingly heavy and attached to a long blue-and-white ribbon.

"Whoa, what is this?" Andro let the lid of the chest fall shut.

"I don't know." Granny ran her fingers over the etched symbol. "I've never seen anything like it. The chest sends the most peculiar gifts."

"It must be worth a fortune!" Andro tested the weight of it in his open hand. "Feel how heavy it is!"

They'd be set for ten winters now, maybe more! Of course, he would still have to work—everyone had to work—but now he could stop working overtime. With this one precious gift,

Andro would never have to worry about his sister or Granny going hungry again. It was as if the chest had heard his prayers and answered them all at once.

"Slow down, child," Granny responded cautiously. "We'll need to hide the new gifts for now. It'll look bad if we trade too many things all at once. Even Rozi will get suspicious."

"Right." Shaking excitedly, he hid their newfound wealth beneath a loose brick behind the stove.

CHAPTER 5

"Give it back, Clementine!" Fergus practically broke the door off its hinges as he burst into her room.

While Ferg ate breakfast, Clem had helped herself to one of his most prized possessions—the gold medal he'd won at the last Provincial Swimming Championship. Ferg had a million trophies and awards, but he was incredibly proud of this one. It hung above his bed, next to a framed photo of him on the winner's podium. He'd put it there to remind himself if he trained hard enough, that could be him at the Olympics.

Clem felt a little guilty because she knew how much it meant to him, but she also knew it was the only thing he'd realize was missing from his disaster of a room. She just hadn't expected him to notice it was gone so soon.

"Give me back my earrings and bracelet, and you can have it back." Clem had never had the upper hand like this before, and she liked it.

"I already told you I don't have your stupid jewelry. Give me back my medal!" Poor Fergus was practically hysterical.

"Of course, you have them. Who else would take my stuff?" Clem glared at her brother. If he said a ghost, she was going to sprinkle itching powder in his running shoes. When they'd first moved into their grandma's house, Ferg had convinced her it was haunted. A drafty old Victorian, built like a hundred years ago, it wasn't a hard sell. Somehow, he'd figured out that if he jumped on the right floorboard in his room, her door would swing open. That, and a YouTube video of creepy sounds echoing through the vent, had her terrified to be alone upstairs. It had taken Clem longer than she cared to admit to figure all this out. She wasn't falling for it again.

"I don't know who your enemies are, but I don't have them! You have no idea how hard I worked for that. Give it back, or I'll tell Mom and Dad." Fergus glared at her.

"Calm down. It's in the chest." Clem pointed at her desk.

Ferg stormed across her room and flipped the lid of the box open.

"Very funny, Clementine. Where is it, really?" He was madder than she'd ever seen him in her life.

"Don't be like that," Clem said, rolling her eyes. "Just take it and go."

"If it was here, I'd already be gone. Wouldn't I?" Ferg yelled.

"Of course, it's there. I literally put it in there this morning while you were eating breakfast." Clementine peered over Ferg's shoulder. The chest was most definitely empty.

"Um…" Clementine blinked. She couldn't even explain this to herself; there was no way she could explain it to Ferg. She was about to be in so much trouble.

"I, um," she started to explain, "I thought you were stealing my jewelry, like, as a prank because it kept disappearing. So, I took your medal and put it in the chest, thinking the next time you went to take something, you'd find it instead. You know, as an *I'm on to you* kind of thing? I thought it would be funny. I even set up my webcam, so I could film your reaction. See?"

Clem walked over to her dresser and woke her laptop.

"Everything I put in the chest has disappeared—my earrings, the bracelet Grandma gave me, and now your medal. I don't know who's taking it. I assumed it was you. Who else would it be?" Clem eyed the window suspiciously. If someone were to get on the porch roof, could they crawl through her bedroom window? Her room faced the street. Surely a neighbor would have seen it if someone had… The idea of a stranger coming into her bedroom made her skin crawl. Had the eccentric man at the antiques store followed her home?

"Let's check the video then, genius." Fergus was already at her laptop, stopping the recording.

"It's no use. Yesterday, whoever took my bracelet somehow managed to edit themselves out before I had a chance to watch it." Clem sighed as Ferg hit play.

"I didn't know you could edit live video," Fergus mumbled as he watched Clem put his medal in the chest. He hit the fast-forward button and watched the video to the end.

"Wow, whoever it is must super-hate you to go to this much trouble," he said when he'd finished watching the video for the second time.

"Nobody hates me," Clem whined. "Barely anybody even knows I exist."

"Well, maybe some random creep is secretly in love with you, and he's trying to get your attention. Gross." Ferg shuddered. "I tell you what. Because they're obviously smarter than you, I'll give you a whole week to find out who did it and get my medal back. If you don't have it by next Saturday, I'm telling Mom and Dad, and you'll be grounded for the rest of your life."

"How am I supposed to do that?" Clem was at a loss. She could barely get her stuff back from Fergus when he borrowed it, let alone from some invisible thief.

"I don't know, leave them a note! Hide in your closet and watch until they come back! Booby-trap your room! I don't care. Just get it back!" Fergus finished his sentence by slamming her door so hard the wall shook.

Clementine wasn't sure what to do. This was probably one

of those things she should tell her parents about. But then Clem would have to admit she'd stolen (and lost) her brother's gold medal and accepted a gift from a weird man she didn't know.

Clem could already hear her mother freaking out: *How many times have we told you, Clementine? Don't accept gifts from strangers. A six-year-old knows better!* This would almost certainly be followed by *What were you even doing in that store? If we can't trust you to get to and from piano lessons without missing the bus and wandering off, how do we know we can trust you to spend a weekend alone?*

Clem threw herself in the swing chair and wrapped herself in the chunky blanket Maddie had knit her for her last birthday. She'd been begging to stay home alone when Ferg had weekend competitions on the mainland. If Clem told her parents what she'd done, it would ruin any chance she may have had. But she also couldn't watch the chest twenty-four hours a day, and she certainly wasn't going to give the thief anything more to steal. She had no idea how to booby-trap her room. Clem walked over to her desk and glared at the chest.

Ripping a piece of pink paper out of a notebook, she grabbed a pen.

Stop stealing my stuff, she scrawled in giant letters. Between the cotton-candy paper and the heart she'd dotted the *i* with, it wasn't at all menacing. If she couldn't take it seriously, there was no way a thief would.

Clementine grabbed a black felt pen from her drawer and started over.

Who are you? And why are you stealing my stuff? Give it back, and nobody gets hurt.

That sounded serious, intimidating even. The letters were blocky and angry; they looked like they meant business.

Satisfied, Clem smiled. She laid the note deliberately in the center of the box, slammed the lid shut, and threw herself on her bed.

CHAPTER 6

Saturday was Beautification Day, the day anyone old enough to work reported to their sector office for volunteer duty. Andro failed to see how it was considered volunteering since it wasn't like he had a choice, but such was life. Besides, he couldn't complain: his duty was always the same—street sweeping—and he liked that far more than planting rice.

Walking to the closest of his assigned streets, Andro put his broom to the cobblestone and tried to focus on the task at hand. His hands and feet were moving, but his mind was far away, thinking about the chest.

What if something new was in it right now, and he didn't get to it in time, and it disappeared? What if you weren't around to receive a gift, and the chest believed you were ungrateful and stopped giving you gifts forever? Maybe that was why the chest had remained empty for so long; maybe Granny had missed something. Andro resisted the urge to drop his broom and run home to check. He tried not to think about it, but as fast as he pushed one thought away, another popped up in its place.

Where were the gifts even coming from? Andro couldn't be sure, but a sorcerer was the only thing that made sense.

Granny had once told him all about sorcerers and their magic. Some of them were dark, like the sorcerer whose magic kept the Black Peacock in power. Others were good. They were the ones who melted the snow early and sent rain when the crops needed it most. They were also, he supposed, the ones who sent people gifts in enchanted chests.

Pondering the mysteries of the magic box, Andro wasn't aware of where he was until he bumped into something solid.

"Watch it!" Someone grabbed him firmly by the arm.

Startled, Andro looked to see who he'd bumped into and came face-to-face with an enforcer. The man's muscles bulged beneath his drab gray uniform. His deep-set eyes glared, cold and harsh, from his weathered face.

"Name and sector?" the enforcer demanded.

Andro obediently stuttered a response.

"You know who did this?" The man jerked his thumb behind him.

Andro's gaze drifted down the alley and came to rest on the back wall of Rozi's store. It took him a moment to realize it was the symbol of the New Resistance he'd painted the night of his birthday. Andro gulped.

The enforcer's fingers dug deep into the flesh of his arm. "I said, do you know who's responsible for this?"

Hatred seethed in his veins. Andro wanted to scream, *It was me! May the sun finally set on the terror of the Black Peacock!* But he couldn't. He dared not. His lips trembled and the words caught in his throat as he slowly shook his head.

Behind them, an insane cackle burst out of the mouse-quiet audience that had gathered on the far sidewalk.

"Who was that? Who dared laugh at this treachery?" The enforcer dropped Andro's arm and lunged in the crowd's direction.

Andro spun around and watched the crowd part. As people scattered, he spied Ablikim shuffling down the street and darting into the safety of a nearby doorway.

A frail woman, her brown hair as matted as a stray dog's, sat against the wall where the onlookers had stood. Despite the whispered pleas from the parting crowd, she would not stop laughing. Her gaping, toothless grin accentuated the insanity of the deep guttural sounds pouring into the street.

"You did this, didn't you?" The enforcer kicked her in the ribs.

The woman only laughed harder.

When her rabid, desperate gaze met Andro's, he held his fingers to his lips, silently begging her to stop laughing. The woman slowly shook her head. Andro couldn't shake the feeling she knew it was him. That she was protecting him. Or maybe, like so many others, she'd simply lost her will to continue.

"Crazy old bat," a female enforcer muttered, joining in the attack. "Think you can disrespect the Black Peacock like this? Everything you have, everything you are, is thanks to the Black Peacock. How dare you! You'll get yours. We'll see to that."

As the female enforcer tackled the woman, the man strode back across the street and kicked a bucket of water toward Andro.

"Take care of this. The next time I look at this wall, it had better be completely gone. Or I'll find you and deal with you myself." He jabbed his finger into Andro's shoulder.

Together, the enforcers dragged the woman away. Her maniacal laughter hung in the air long after she'd disappeared from view, haunting Andro's thoughts. He knew he would never see her again.

As he scrubbed, he cursed the Black Peacock, the enforcers for their brutality, and himself for not standing up to them. He should have said something. He should have spoken for the woman who couldn't speak for herself. But instead, he'd cowered in fear like everyone else.

This wasn't living. This couldn't be it. There had to be

something better than this. Anything would be better than this. Andro fought back angry tears as he watched the red paint run like blood down the clay wall.

There had to be someone who could help them. But who was powerful enough to stand up to the Black Peacock? For hundreds of years, men had tried and failed. The Black Peacock was far too cunning and powerful.

It was late by the time Andro finished scrubbing the wall and sweeping his assigned sector.

Tired and miserable, he stumbled home and leaned his broom against the cupboard. His hands were filthy. Andro knew he should wash them first, but he couldn't resist the urge to flip the lid on the spice chest as he walked by.

Inside, a piece of pink parchment with bold black markings stared back at him. Andro carefully plucked it out of the chest, leaving dirty finger smudges on the corners.

As he stared at the thick black squiggles, a strange feeling came over him. He couldn't read or write—besides the record keeper's ledger, he'd never even seen a book—yet somehow, he knew these symbols meant something. The sorcerer was sending him a message, and if a sorcerer sent you a message, it had to be important.

If only he knew what it meant.

Andro flipped the piece of parchment upside down, then on its side. He held it horizontally, then vertically, but no matter how he looked at it, it made no sense. What could a powerful sorcerer possibly want to tell him?

A thought crept up behind him and smacked him over the head. If their spice had gone missing, the chest must work both ways! If he could find out what the sorcerer was saying, he could send a message back. He could ask the sorcerer for help! If, as Granny had said, the Black Peacock only remained in power because of the work of an evil sorcerer, maybe a good sorcerer would be able to defeat them! Andro stood there, mouth open. He dared not dream of the possibilities.

"What is it this time?" Zari asked excitedly as she came in from the garden. Granny was behind her, a small basket of spring greens at her hip.

"I don't know, but I think it's very, very important." Andro watched the piece of paper wave in the breeze of the open door.

"Hogwash." Granny snatched the parchment from Andro's fingers. She was such a quiet woman, her response caught Andro off guard. "Trust me, Andro, no good will come of this. The chest gave us these symbols before—book after book of them. Your father thought they were important too. He refused to burn them, even though owning books is forbidden and could've cost us our lives. He wanted to learn what they meant. He and Ablikim's son, Olli, wasted every spare minute for years trying to make sense of them. Then he, your mom, and Olli started painting that weird symbol all over the city and talking about ending the Black Peacock's reign. And look what happened to them…"

Tears ran down Granny's cheeks. "…dragged away, leaving a helpless old lady to raise two babies, alone…no job…couldn't even find work because my son was a traitor…'an enemy of the Empire,' they called him. The chest was angry too…no more gifts. No help at all. Curse Ablikim for teaching your father to read, curse those wretched symbols, and curse the chest for sending more of them!"

Andro had never seen Granny upset like this. She opened the stove and tossed in the piece of paper.

"Promise me you'll let this be," she pleaded. "My heart cannot take losing you too."

"Yes, Granny, as you wish." He kissed Granny tenderly on the forehead.

Andro had never disobeyed Granny before, but when she wasn't looking, he pulled the paper out of the cold ash and tucked it away in his pocket. He couldn't throw away their only chance at getting help.

If his son had been involved, maybe Ablikim knew the meaning of the dark squiggly lines. Perhaps he, Olli, or Andro's father had been in contact with the sorcerer before. Risky or not, Andro had every intention of finding out.

CHAPTER 7

By Sunday, Andro was back at work. *It was a shame Beautification Day wasn't two days long*, he thought, trying to distract himself from the parchment hidden within his pocket.

Every time Andro reached into his basket, he was tempted to stick his hand in his pocket to ensure the piece of pink paper was still where he'd put it. But his hands were damp, and he wasn't sure if the symbols would fall off if they got wet.

Even though his hidden treasures meant he no longer needed to, Andro decided to work late, so he could speak to Ablikim. There was a huge difference between taking extra work because you wanted to versus doing it because you had to. He couldn't describe it, but it made him feel powerful.

As he emptied his last basket, Andro looked around for Ablikim. He spotted the old man at the front of the line, speaking with the records keeper. He couldn't leave yet!

"Grandfather Ablikim, wait!" Andro yelled, forgetting himself.

Ablikim stopped in his tracks. A hush fell over the field.

Enforcers moved toward Andro, raising their hands for him to stop. The smaller of the two rested his hand on the leather whip curled at his hip. The few workers standing in line between Andro and Ablikim cowered.

Andro gulped. What had he been thinking? The enforcers were trained to react to anything out of the ordinary.

Don't search me, don't search me. Not today. The enforcers moved closer.

Writings? Paper? There was nothing worse he could be

caught with. It would be better to be found with the emperor's sword in your pocket than a piece of paper. This was how you disappeared. *Permanently.*

Thinking quickly, Andro lowered his head, pointed at his ears, and then over to Ablikim, insinuating the old man was hard of hearing.

"Allow me to walk you home, grandfather," he continued loudly.

The enforcers looked at them suspiciously. They'd caught Andro sneaking the old man food before, but they usually let him get away with it because he was a good worker.

Looking like a frightened rabbit about to become dinner, Andro's eyes darted between the enforcers.

"It's late. You're not worth the hassle, you filthy little rat. Move. Quietly," the bigger man grumbled, letting Andro pass.

"Dock him a Coin for causing a scene," the smaller man called to the record keeper as they sauntered away.

A whole Coin? If not for his newfound wealth, Andro would have been devastated.

Andro and Ablikim walked in silence until they were safely hidden by the cherry trees. The ground was pink with fallen petals. Pale green leaves rustled gently in the breeze.

"Grandfather Ablikim," Andro finally asked when he knew they were out of earshot, "do you know what this is?"

Quickly looking around to ensure no watchful eyes were hidden among the branches, Andro pulled the parchment from his pocket. Reluctantly, he handed it over.

Ablikim gingerly held the piece of paper and stared at it for a moment. Eyebrows furrowed, he handed it back to Andro. "Have you gone mad, child?! Put that away and never pull it out in public again," he muttered harshly.

Andro obediently tucked the paper back into his pocket.

"Do you know what it says, though?" he pressed.

"How would I know that?" Ablikim barked. "You know as well as I do reading is forbidden."

"I know, but Granny said you taught Father to…" Andro stopped. It was best not to accuse the old man of such things if he wanted help.

They walked for an eternity in silence before he dared to speak again. "It does mean something, though, right?"

Ablikim sighed. "Maybe," he answered slowly. "Come."

Nodding, Andro followed the old man through the narrow, maze-like streets of the city. Ablikim stopped in front of a crooked door at the end of a cramped alley. A tower of jumbled apartments teetered overhead like a house of cards on the brink of collapse. Following the old man inside, Andro blinked in the darkness.

He could hear Ablikim shuffling around, a familiar pop, and the faint sulfur whiff of a freshly lit match. Instantly, the room was aglow with the soft light of an oil lamp.

Andro had distant memories of playing in the tinker shop before the Bird burned it to the ground, but he'd never been to the old man's house. It wasn't much to look at. Ablikim's place was even smaller than his own. A thin wooden counter hung limply from the far wall; save for a well-worn washbasin, it was bare. A single shelf clung to a few nails. Not that it needed more nails—it held a bowl, a rusted tin of tea leaves, and a jar of rice with barely enough in it for dinner.

Ablikim sat on a rickety stool at the far end of the counter. Behind him, a well-loved pot and a fire-blackened tea kettle stood on a lonely mantelpiece over a cold, empty fireplace. Next to the fireplace, a sagging cot drooped against the clay wall. The wood floor was covered by a rug so threadbare it was nearly transparent.

Often Andro wondered how other people lived. Knowing they lived much like he did was depressing. He made a mental note to bring the old man more rice, a can or two of vegetables, and as much firewood as he could spare.

"Now, let's take a closer look at your writings." Ablikim put on a pair of spectacles held together at the nose with thickly wrapped twine. Andro handed him the paper and eagerly awaited his response.

Ablikim cleared his throat. Stroking his chin, he stared thoughtfully over the top of his glasses. "Where have I seen this text before?" he muttered. "It's foreign, and yet somehow, it feels familiar. But not a good familiar."

"Can you tell what it says?" Andro prodded.

"This isn't Dohiani," Ablikim answered, "but I've seen it before. I simply can't recall where. Who gave this to you?"

Andro stared at the old man. Granny had told him never, under any circumstances, was he to mention the magic chest to anyone. Andro had always found this silly, but it made sense now he knew it was actually magic. A chest like that had to be extremely valuable. Everyone, including the Black Peacock, would be after it if word got out.

Andro shifted uncomfortably as he debated how much he should say. He needed Ablikim's help, but at what cost?

"I found it." Andro shrugged casually. "And I thought it might be important."

It wasn't a lie, though it wasn't the entire truth. Andro could tell from Ablikim's face he wasn't buying it.

"Found it lying in the street, did you?" Ablikim shook his head. "Who put you up to this? The Bird? That explains how suspiciously you've been acting all week. Was it your granny who ratted me out? What did they offer her? Well, you can tell them the old woman was wrong. I can't read. They can drag me off in the dead of night if they don't believe it. I don't care. I won't help them. Not now, not ever."

The first curfew bell rang.

"I can't help you." Ablikim removed his spectacles and handed the piece of paper back to Andro. "You should go."

Andro turned to leave. At the door, he paused and stared at the thick black lines. This was worth fighting for. He couldn't go without knowing what it meant. Closing his eyes, he took a deep breath.

"It appeared in an old spice chest," he said, looking Ablikim in the eyes. "Granny has this chest, and…well, sometimes things appear in it, like magic. This was one of those things."

Ablikim stared at Andro in disbelief. "I've been around a long time, Andro, and I've heard a lot of crazy excuses, but this has to be the worst. Please leave. *Now*."

Andro reached for the latch on the door but couldn't bring himself to open it. If he wanted the old man to trust him, he would need to trust the old man.

"Look. I didn't believe it either until recently. It doesn't sound real, but it's true…" Andro hesitated. Granny was going to be livid.

Slowly, he told Ablikim everything—how the chest came to be in his family, the gifts they'd received through the ages, and how it had sat empty for many long years. When he'd caught Ablikim up on the past, he told him about the recently missing spice, the appearance of the earrings, and how he had traded them to Rozi for food. The bracelet. The weird metal disk on the long blue ribbon. He held nothing back. He needed Ablikim to believe him.

They stared at each other in an uncomfortable silence far too big for such a tiny room.

"Please," Andro pleaded, "I don't know why or how, but I know whatever this says is important. If you tell me what it says, I'll go, and I'll never ask you for another thing again, I swear. Granny mentioned you taught my father to read. I thought maybe you could help."

Ablikim said nothing.

"Granny was right: no good would come of this. Forget I asked. It doesn't matter."

The last curfew bell rattled down the empty alley and banged against the door. Defeated, Andro went to leave.

"They were such smart boys, my Olli and your father, Idris," Ablikim whispered. "Always taking everything and anything apart to see how it worked. Your granny's right: I taught them to read. After they found out I could, they wouldn't leave me alone. It was impossible to get anything done, the two of them begging me incessantly to teach them. Together I think they read nearly every book I ever managed to salvage. The more they read, the more they saw, and the more they saw, the more they wanted to change what they saw. That's the danger of knowledge—once your eyes are open, it's impossible to close them again. That's why the Black Peacock burned the books and banned reading and writing. The Bird fears knowledge above all else."

Andro gently pushed the door closed. He dared not move for fear Ablikim would stop talking.

"I was busy tinkering back then and didn't pay as much attention as I should have." A tear slid down his wrinkled cheek. "More than once, I heard their fanciful whispers and what-ifs. What if everyone could read? What if someone cut the head off the Black Peacock and they fell from power? What if we were free? I should have stopped it then and there, but they were just young men—boys with big imaginations. I didn't think… Who could have known… Your granny has never forgiven me.

"Still, I don't regret it," Ablikim said, his gaze meeting Andro's. "I don't regret teaching them to read or to think for themselves."

"Then teach me," Andro begged. "So I can read this. *Please*." He held the thin piece of paper out to the old man.

"I cannot read that, Andro. I honestly don't know what it says. Somewhere in the dusty corners of this ageing mind, it feels familiar. Yet, all that's left is the realization of how much I've forgotten." Ablikim shook his head. "You'd best toss it in the fireplace and go. It's not something you want to be caught out with."

Andro nodded solemnly and stepped toward the fireplace. Hopelessness was a feeling he knew all too well, yet somehow, it felt worse now than before.

"Granny said my father once found books with the same symbols in the chest. Those texts were why he and Olli started the rebellion. The books went missing just before Father did. Maybe you saw those writings. I guess we'll never know." Andro took one last look at the pink paper.

As it fell from Andro's fingers, Ablikim held out his hand and caught it.

"I know where I've seen this!" A look of stunned recollection flashed across his wrinkled face. "Quick, roll back the rug!"

Confused but excited Ablikim remembered something, Andro dropped to his knees and obediently rolled up the rug.

"I recalled a memory I hadn't thought of in a long time." Ablikim dropped to the hearth and thrust his head deep into the fireplace. "I saw the boys, as plain as day, standing in front of me in the tinker shop, the same look of determination on their faces as you had now. In their hands was a handful of small books. Idris told me he'd found them in an old cupboard, or was it a chest? No matter, I didn't believe him one way or another. I assumed your granny had stolen them from a wealthy woman in Nimbina. The boys tried to convince me they were important. Classified information, they claimed! A secret code! I glanced briefly at the books. The language was odd, yes, but they were merely picture books meant for children."

Ablikim fiddled with something in the chimney high above his head. Andro watched as the floorboards began to quiver and move. A small hole, a few feet wide, appeared at his feet.

"I brought the boys down here"—Ablikim pulled his head out of the fireplace—"and quickly showed them how to translate the simple words, then I left them to their fanciful game of make-believe.

"I never thought much about it until now. Certainly never thought they discovered anything of… Hand me that lamp, will you, Andro?" Ablikim stood.

Andro watched him disappear with the lamp beneath the floor. Blinking, he shook his head in the sudden darkness. His life had been exceptionally dull for fourteen years. Besides his parents' disappearance and the few times he'd snuck out after curfew, nothing exciting ever happened. Now his whole world had gone mad. Granny's "magic box" turned out to be real, a fact he could barely wrap his head around. He'd traded prohibited goods for food, and he owned writings. Now Ablikim, possibly the oldest, dullest man he had ever known, was disappearing into secret holes beneath the floorboards. Things like this didn't happen, not in Dohi. Not to people like him. He had to be dreaming. But if this was a dream, Andro never wanted to wake up.

Ablikim's head popped back out of the hole.

"Well, are you coming or not?" he asked briskly before disappearing once again.

Andro peered into the hole. In the dim lamplight, he could make out the top rungs of a ladder. Without hesitation, he followed it down.

Ablikim busied himself lighting the handful of torches hanging on the smooth clay walls. The room was four times bigger than the house above, the walls twice the height.

Shelves ran the length of the room, every one of them crammed with ancient leather-bound books, stacks of tightly rolled scrolls, and reams of loose parchment. Some shelves were so stuffed they'd burst under the weight, spewing books and papers into the aisles. Mountainous stacks of books teetered high above Andro's head. There was barely room to walk.

Following Ablikim's muttering, Andro gently picked his way through the mess. He found the old man in the center of the room, hovering over a wooden desk so heavily laden with books it sagged under their weight.

"What is this place?" Andro whispered.

"A library of sorts." A sad smile played at the edges of Ablikim's lips.

"A what?" Andro ran his hand across the top of a dusty shelf.

"A library. Books! Piles and piles of them! A curated collection of knowledge, albeit not a complete collection by any means," Ablikim explained excitedly.

Andro stared at him blank-faced. *Reading*, *books*, and *library* were all just words. Spread at his feet was a world of history, knowledge, and stories, yet it all meant nothing. The

Black Peacock had seen to that. Teach the people to question what they know, and they might get smart enough to question your authority.

"Each of these books is filled with symbols, much like the ones on your parchment." Ablikim lovingly patted the leather binding of a book. "Each of those symbols is a letter. Letters form words, and words form sentences. Those sentences teach us things, important things."

Andro wasn't entirely sure how squiggles on paper could tell you anything meaningful. Still, he was anxious to know what his symbols meant, so he kept nodding.

"Before the Great Unification, different groups of people spoke different languages. Basically, they used different words to describe the same thing. Your words are not written in Dohiani—our language—so I cannot read them. But I knew I had seen them somewhere before, and it wasn't until you mentioned your father's books that I remembered where. Come, sit."

Ablikim patted the stool next to him. Walking around the desk, Andro joined him. A handful of smaller books and a large stack of loose paper coated in thick dust sat on the table. They did not look like the other books in this strange library.

Andro wiped the dust off the cover and flipped through one of the more colorful ones. It was full of pictures. People with funny hair who dressed in strange clothes stared back at him.

When he got to the third book, he stopped cold. On the flimsy paper cover were the letters P-E-A-C-E O-U-T beneath a white hand with a thick red outline. The hand was closed, save for the middle and index fingers, which formed a V. The symbol of the New Resistance! So that's where his father and Olli had gotten the idea! Andro excitedly thumbed through it. Within its pages were people holding giant signs. Screaming, they fought with men in matching uniforms. The symbols marched across the pages like the soldiers of the Black Army. Andro didn't understand, and yet somehow, he did.

"Look, grandfather!" Flipping back to the cover, Andro pointed to the hand folded in the V-shape.

"What were Olli and Idris up to down here?" Ablikim muttered under his breath.

There were other books, too—books with more rigid covers. Andro picked up the one closest to him. The outside was full of colorful drawings. Across the top were the letters *My First Dictionary*. Andro flipped it open. Some of the pictures he recognized; some of them he didn't. Setting down that book, he picked up another. It was thicker and more worn. The cover was boring. The letters on the front spelled *Dictionary for Students*. Andro opened it, but there were no pictures, only symbols. He didn't like this book; it was too boring. Putting it down, he reopened the first. Looking at the cover, he compared it to the pink slip of parchment.

"Look, grandfather, these symbols look like my symbols." He pointed at the *M* and the *y*.

"Yes, Andro," Ablikim said, smiling. "You're quick, like your father. Those two letters form the same word on your parchment as on that book. Now, we need to know the translation."

Andro blinked. Ablikim picked up the picture book and flipped it open. "What is this?" He pointed at a pig.

"Porcuz," Andro answered.

"Right, but in this language—whatever it is—they call it a p-i-g. Now, we know *pig* and *porcuz* mean the same thing. If we talked to the people who speak this language, we would say *pig*, and they would know we were talking about porcuz. That is a translation, matching the words from one language to another. It's like deciphering a secret code.

"This book," Ablikim continued, "was made for children to learn words in this language. It allowed your father and Olli to learn enough about this language they could then begin translating other writings, like this one with the symbol of the New Resistance on it. They never mentioned these other books to me. Maybe they thought if they could read them, it would give them answers." Ablikim tossed the magazine back on the desk with a frown. "As you know, it did not."

Ablikim looked lost and sad. "Why do you want to know what your piece of paper says so badly, Andro? I would hate for you to start down the same path as your father and Olli."

Andro dared not tell Ablikim his real intentions—that he planned to ask the sorcerer for help. Not yet. He wasn't even sure the old man fully believed his story. "I'm curious, I guess," Andro replied. "I've never seen writing before, so it feels important."

Though Ablikim was hesitant, Andro could tell he, too, was curious. It had been a long time since he'd seen new writings.

Ablikim pulled a stack of loose paper closer to them. Each piece was divided into two columns. "This must have been the translation your father and Olli were working on. They learned well. These are remarkable." Ablikim proudly ran his fingers down the neat columns in front of him. After a long pause, he continued.

"On this side"—he pointed to the left column—"are words from these books. On the other side are what those words mean in Dohiani. So, if we find the words on your parchment over here, we can learn what they mean over there."

Ablikim stopped talking and closed his eyes.

"Andro," he said gravely, "if I help you with this, you must tell no one. You must never speak of this in public. In fact, it's best not to speak of this at all. If your parchment… if this room… if I were to be discovered, it would not only end poorly for you and me. In this room is some of the last of the ancient knowledge of Dohi. It is one of the few places books exist outside of Nimbina. These books are priceless. If they are lost, the knowledge they contain can never be replaced. Do you understand?"

Andro didn't understand the importance of the knowledge the room contained. He had a hard enough time wrapping his head around the fact six squiggly lines could represent a pig. Yet somehow, he understood, like the lines of text on his parchment, this was more important than himself. And because he understood that, he solemnly nodded in agreement.

"Go now," Ablikim said, "and leave an old man to his work."

CHAPTER 8

Something didn't feel right. The air was unbearably heavy. Andro tried to convince himself it was the mounting suspense. All week Ablikim had been ignoring him as if nothing out of the ordinary had happened. Over and over, the same questions plagued Andro until he thought for sure he would go insane. Could Ablikim not translate it? Was it taking so long the sorcerer would give up on him? What did it say?

Andro's skin felt electric, too tight, and too small for his body. He tried to tell himself it was the approaching storm. But in the pit of his stomach, he knew it wasn't that either. In the towers, the spotters were on high alert. The enforcers, usually lounging in the shade, were actively patrolling the fields. Something was up. Andro instinctively moved to the back corner of the paddy. He wanted to be as far away as possible from whatever was about to go down.

By noon, a low mist had settled between the smog and the valley floor. The skies opened with a single crack of thunder, and a torrent of rain plummeted to the earth. Still, they kept working. Still, the enforcers patrolled, unblinking, up and down the earthen bunds between the flooded paddies.

Drenched, Andro used his wet shirt to wipe the water from his eyes. Through the fog, he watched as a squad of enforcers marched, four by four, up the road. When they reached the end of the farthest paddy, they stopped and stood at attention. A second squad followed, coming to a halt in front of the field he was working in. Andro put his head down and continued planting. When he dared lift his head again, it was only to see a third squad blocking the road to town. A group of official-looking men stood talking to the field supervisor and the records keeper.

"Out of the fields! Inspection!" the supervisor yelled.

"Out of the fields! Inspection!" the enforcers parroted.

Andro reluctantly set down his basket and made his way to the road.

Lining up on the side of the muddy path with the rest of the workers, Andro sniffled and stood at attention. Slowly but surely, the fields emptied—small groups of field hands standing miserably in front of whichever paddy they had been summoned from. This wasn't a routine inspection. Andro shivered. Had the old man turned him in?

Ablikim stared at him from across the road, the rain following the wrinkles down his worried face.

A solitary official broke away from the group of agents and strode up the middle of the road. The breast pocket of his black leather coat was highly decorated with medals. The rain ran down the visor of his black peaked cap. Black Army commander? Lead agent? Andro wasn't sure. All he knew was the man wasn't there to inspect the rice.

Unclasping his gloved hands from behind his back, the official motioned for the nearest squad of enforcers to follow. They obediently fell into position.

"Who among you are traitors to the Regime?" His accusation pierced the misty fields, reverberating off the mountain of garbage. "I will find you!"

Traitors? More than one. Andro and Ablikim caught each other's fearful gaze. Had someone seen him leave the old man's house? Heard them speaking at the door?

Slowly the official led the enforcers down the road, halting to inspect every field hand individually as he passed. He stopped in front of Andro for an eternity, his warm breath crawling up Andro's cold, wet face. Sneering, the man studied him. The rain drummed against the tin roofs of the enforcers' barracks, echoing in the stillness. Andro clenched and unclenched his fists, resisting the urge to run. He wouldn't make it fifty feet. He knew this.

When the man finally moved on, Andro felt as if he would faint. He bowed his head, focusing on the drops of rain collecting in the fresh boot prints at his bare feet.

At the end of the fields, the official stopped.

"Who among you are responsible for poisoning this crop?" He thrust a gloved finger in the direction of the nearest paddy. "Who dared to kill the crops of the Black Peacock? Do you not know you eat by the Black Peacock's grace alone? Ungrateful traitors!" He spat at the feet of the nearest field hand.

A large chunk broke loose from the mountain of garbage and tumbled into the far edge of the dead field. Wave after wave of iridescent water washed over the withered brown stalks.

Andro stared at the official, dumbfounded. Surely he wasn't serious?

The official signaled for the far squad of enforcers to fall in line behind the first, and together, they began the slow march back. Only this time, they were out for blood.

"Him." The official thrust his finger into the chest of the nearest worker. An enforcer dragged the man into their ranks.

"And her." He stopped at a woman a few steps down.

Back they marched, dragging half the field hands with them. The closer they got, the more Andro wished the mud around his bare feet would swallow him whole.

The official pointed at two men near the end of Andro's

line. Then he turned his attention to the far side of the road. Andro's heart drummed in time with the rain. The man came to a grinding halt in front of Ablikim and slowly raised a gloved finger.

No, not grandfather. Please, not grandfather. Andro's legs shook like the leaves in the nearby trees.

The woman next to Ablikim sneezed. The official turned his head.

"Her!" he barked. Without a second glance in the old man's direction, he moved on. Andro and Ablikim stared at each other in terror. Andro stood stone-still, afraid to move. His lower lip quivered as the water slowly dripped off his chin and splattered at his feet.

"I said, get back to work!"

It took a minute for the field supervisors' words to register. The official and the squad of enforcers were long gone, and with them, nearly half the laborers. Those left behind stumbled back to the fields in a stupor.

All afternoon Andro worked his way across the empty field toward Ablikim. The spotters and enforcers, huddling beneath the tin-roofed barracks, halfheartedly stood watch. It was as if they, too, were shocked by what had just occurred.

"You almost… they almost…" Now Andro was next to the old man, the words wouldn't come.

"I thought maybe they knew." Ablikim fumbled for his water canteen and uncorked it. He pulled a sliver of pink parchment from under the lid and held it between his trembling fingers. Under the original writing, he had scribbled new words.

"If they'd have..." Andro's heart stopped. He didn't want to think about what would have happened. "Does this mean you…?"

Tucking the note back in the lid, Ablikim nodded.

"And?" Andro gasped.

"It says"—Ablikim's whispered words swirled in the mist—"*Who you? Why to take items? Return now, and people no more suffering.*" I checked it over and over to make sure it was correct. I'm reasonably confident it is. Olli and Idris got further than I could've ever imagined."

"No more suffering," Andro repeated. No more suffering? Only a mighty sorcerer would be capable of that. "I knew it!" he breathed. "We need to write the sorcerer back right now! We'll return the things and ask him for help!"

"Sorcerer?" Ablikim looked confused. "Andro, there's no such thing as—"

"Of course, there is," Andro reasoned. "Who else could make things magically appear in a spice chest? I know you still don't believe it, but it's true. I've seen it with my own eyes. I've given it a lot of thought. It has to be a sorcerer. Who else could it be? And if it's a sorcerer, and they can make no more suffering, we have to ask for help!"

"There's no such thing as magic or sorcerers," Ablikim said gently. "That's nonsense—things people say to explain what they don't know. This is some sort of science. I've also given it much thought. I've asked myself a hundred times, how? What could explain the appearance and disappearance of items such as you've mentioned? The only thing I recall that even comes close is the ancient theory of teleportation.

"Before the Black Peacock," Ablikim said and then paused to look around, "education—philosophy, mathematics, science—was valued above all else. The Monks of Videt Mountain spent millennia gathering knowledge. They used what they learned to accomplish incredible things. So much wisdom has been lost; it makes my heart ache to think of it. I can't fathom all that was once known; I've had the opportunity to see so little. A few of the manuscripts I've managed to hide away mention teleportation, but only as a theory. There are so many gaps in history now. Could teleportation have been real? I don't know. But if so, how is your granny's chest still functioning all these years later? Could it operate autonomously? I don't believe so. The only logical conclusion is a scientist or group of scientists is behind the teleportations. But who? And why are they only offering their assistance now?"

"What's science?" It was Andro's turn to look confused. The old man had lost him at "there's no such thing as magic or Sorcerers."

"Verifiable magic," Ablikim sighed before launching into a detailed explanation.

"We need to write back," Andro said, stopping him. Andro had no idea what the old man was going on about. He could call it what he wanted, but magic was magic. And the only people capable of magic were sorcerers.

"It's too risky," Ablikim responded. "We don't know who's behind the message. It could be anyone. We could end up making things far worse."

"Too risky?" Andro fought to keep his voice to a whisper. "Too risky?! Are you insane? Dozens of people we know won't be returning home tonight. You were almost one of them. And for what? A few sacks of rice? What could possibly be worse than this? What could possibly be riskier than trying to survive in Dohi?"

"You're right." The old man closed his tired eyes. "No point being safe if you're dead. Your 'magic' box may be our last hope."

"How long do you think it will take to write a response?" Andro looked at the sludge beneath his feet. "It won't be long before the rest of the rice dies. When it does, we might not be so lucky."

"I'll be at your door as soon as we're done volunteering tomorrow. Two o'clock. Collect the items and be ready."

"I sold the earrings," Andro said, his smile turned to a frown. "What happens if we don't return everything?" Andro wasn't sure what was worse—that he wouldn't be able to return everything or that he was about to lose all of his treasures. What if the sorcerer, or the science people, refused to help because he'd sold the earrings? What if they never sent another gift again? It was, he supposed, a chance they'd have to take.

"I'll find a suitable replacement in the junk I have lying around from my tinkering days," Ablikim assured him. "We'll apologize and tell them you traded the others for food. Hopefully, they'll understand and are still willing to assist."

Please be willing, Andro silently begged as he handed in his basket and put his wrinkly feet back in his too-small shoes. *Please.*

"Grandfather," he asked as they ambled home from work, "do you think Father and Olli knew? Do you think they were trying to get help too?"

"I don't know, Andro, I really don't know..." The old man said nothing more.

True to his word, Ablikim showed up at precisely two o'clock the following day.

Glancing up and down the street, Andro let him in and swiftly closed the door behind them.

"I can't stay long," Ablikim said. "Let's get to it. Where is this magic box of yours, Andro?"

Andro pulled the chest off the shelf and placed it on the rickety table.

"No need for formalities, Ablikim," Granny said, scowling.

"Kiraz," Ablikim responded nervously, not meeting the old woman's stony glare, "I didn't see you there. I trust you've been well?"

"As well as could be imagined, given the circumstances," she replied coldly. "And you?"

"Surviving, barely." Ablikim pulled out his spectacles.

"Yes, news of what happened in the fields leaped like wildfire through the streets yesterday. The Bird won't be happy until we're all dead. All afternoon, I sat here, terrified my Andro wouldn't be coming home. My joy at seeing him softened the blow of his confession that he'd spilled our greatest family secret. And worse, that he'd directly disobeyed my order to leave the strange writings alone." Granny stared pointedly at Ablikim. "My only son wasn't enough for you? You want to get my grandson killed too?"

"Granny," Andro sighed. He'd been arguing with her all morning. "I told you, this wasn't his idea. It was mine! We need help. You're right: more than anything, the Bird would rather see us all dead, or disappeared, or starved. What kind of life is this? Waiting, silently dreading tomorrow. I'm so tired. What does it matter if I'm dragged off for treason from the fields or from the house? At least if they take me, I'll know I died trying to make a difference. I don't know why. I can't explain it. But I know in my heart this is our only hope."

The old woman closed her eyes and took a long, unsteady breath. "I don't like it," she said, tears filling her eyes. "It's risky. I hope you two know what you're doing."

Pulling the wooden chest toward himself, Ablikim

inspected it. It was a thing of beauty, the craftsmanship apparent. Despite its age, what was left of the gold gilding shone brightly. Ablikim traced his fingers over the circular crest on the lid. While many had long forgotten this crest and what it stood for, he had not. "This is the mark of the Emerald Peacock. I've seen it in books from the times before everything went black. To bear this crest could only mean this chest came from the Royal House."

"I knew it!" Granny cried. "I've always said it belonged to royalty."

Ablikim flipped the lid open, then tried one of the four drawers. It fell out of its cubby and into his hand with the gentlest tug.

"It's never had keys, and the locks have always been broken," Andro told him. "Not like we've ever owned anything worth locking up anyway."

Ablikim held the drawer to his nose and examined it closely. The locking mechanism had been destroyed. A faint outline of a gold circle and a splinter of lacquer was all that remained of the ornate keyhole. He flipped the drawer over. Along the bottom was a symbol with which he was familiar. One he'd very much hoped to find. One that confirmed his suspicions.

"This"—Ablikim pointed to the small mark on the bottom of the drawer—"is the maker's mark. It's the symbol of the Order of the Monks of Videt Mountain."

"What does it mean?"

"It means your chest is most definitely not magic. It's science. Though what kind of science, we can only speculate."

"What's science?" Zari asked from where she stood behind Granny.

"Verifiable magic," Andro answered with a knowing nod.

"I wonder who does the vera-fly-able magic," Zari responded. "Whoever it is, I hope they send more jewelry."

"Who, indeed." Ablikim exhaled deeply. "I suppose we're about to find out. Speaking of gifts, where are the gifts you received, Andro?"

Andro ducked behind the stove and returned with the silver bracelet and the gold disk. "Did you bring the replacement earrings?"

Ablikim pulled two pieces of twisted metal out of his pocket and added them to the pile.

"*Pfft.*" Granny shook her head. "Those aren't earrings. Men." She shuffled over to her sleeping mat and opened the small wooden box where she kept her clothing and personal items. Digging deep, she pulled out a red velvet satchel. After struggling to open it with her knobby fingers, she dumped the contents in her palm and threw the empty pouch on the mat.

"These were a gift from the chest many years ago," she said. "I was saving them for Zari, but such is life. As much as I hate to admit it, Andro is right. If we don't get help, there won't be a future for any of us."

Zari gasped. Granny shushed her with a single glance and sat back down. Stretching out her hand, they watched as two gold moons dropped into the open chest. With a twinge of sadness, Andro piled his treasures on top. He turned and looked expectantly at Ablikim.

"Oh, right! The most important part." Ablikim produced Andro's original note—now heavily smudged with dirt and ink—along with a new message he'd written on a thick piece of yellowed parchment.

"What does it say?" Andro took the new note and studied it.

"Well, if my translation is correct, it says, *We are Andro and Ablikim from the Empire of Dohi. Who is this? Where are you? Sorry, we sold your earrings for food; please accept these new ones. We need help! Will you help us?"* Ablikim took the note from Andro and placed it in the chest.

"What now?" Ablikim stared at the chest, waiting for the magic to happen.

Flipping the lid closed, Andro took a deep breath. "Now," he said, "we wait."

CHAPTER 9

Clem couldn't believe the entire week had come and gone without a response. No one had admitted to stealing her stuff, bothered to return it, or left it in an anonymous package on her doorstep. Not so much as a clue. She sat at her desk, head resting on her arm, and idly flipped the lid of the old chest up and down. Clem wished she could say she was enjoying her last few hours of freedom, but she wasn't. Luckily, Fergus had gone to a swim meet and wouldn't be back for a few more hours. A few more hours before she was grounded for life.

Lid up. Lid down. Lid up. Lid down.

It wasn't like she had much of a social life anyway. She could read books alone in her room as well as she could anywhere, she guessed.

Lid down. Lid up. Lid down. Lid u…

Clem shrieked and yanked her hand back from the chest so fast she fell off her chair.

What kind of voodoo magic was this?

Scrambling to her knees, she peered over her desk. Quickly reaching out her hand, she flipped the lid open again. She hadn't imagined it! Her brother's medal, her bracelet, and a large piece of yellowed paper stared back at her from within. The hair shot up on the back of her neck. Clem's heart thundered in her chest. For the first time in a long time, she wished she wasn't home alone.

Clem desperately wanted to remove everything from the box before it disappeared again. At the same time, she was afraid to touch it. Touch the creepy voodoo box, or be grounded for life? Tough call.

Her hand darted out. She snatched everything up, then dropped it in a pile on her desk as if it were hot coals she'd pulled from a fire. Clementine stared at the chest. It still wasn't empty.

Two tiny moon-shaped earrings glistened in the light of her desk lamp. She'd never seen them before. Was this some sort of trick? She couldn't be sure.

Clenching her hands open and closed, Clementine took a deep breath. In one fell swoop, she grabbed the tiny moons with one hand and slammed the chest closed with the other.

Hands trembling, she covered her mouth. Should she cry? Should she run screaming out the front door? What was the proper response in a situation like this? Clem closed her eyes and took a deep breath.

No, that didn't happen. Nope. No way.

Slowly, she forced one eye open and then the other. Everything was still there, right where she'd dropped it. She took another deep breath and slowly exhaled.

Her brother's award was back, and her bracelet. That's what mattered. Her note, crumpled and dirty, jutted out from beneath the edge of the medal. What else was she missing?

Remembering her earrings, she scanned the desk. They were nowhere to be found. Clem picked up one of the tiny moons. Well, those weren't right, but what was she going to do, complain to the manager? Return them?

Dropping the earrings back on her desk, Clementine turned her attention to the piece of yellowed paper. She gulped. It felt thick and rough beneath her fingers as if it were handmade. The yellow tinge suggested it was old. Clem flipped it over— there was writing! The lettering was wobbly but legible.

We Andro Ablikim from Empire Dohi. Who you? Where

you? Sorry, we sell earrings for eat, please to accept new.

Beneath that, in larger, darker letters, it read: *We need help! Will you to help us?*

Clem dropped the note on the floor. Not taking her eyes off the chest, she scrambled backward toward the door. Safely in the hallway, she turned and ran down the stairs, out the front door, and into the rainy street.

Was it haunted? Black magic? Clem wished she'd grabbed her phone. She'd call Maddie or Brook and ask them. Brook was super into magic. She had a Harry Potter wand, tarot cards, and a shelf full of books on Wicca and spells. Not that any of her spells had ever worked. Well, one had kinda worked. When Brook moved to Victoria in the second grade, she ended up at the desk behind Maddie (which had been Clementine's desk before Mrs. Thom moved her for talking too much). Brook had told Maddie she was a witch, so Maddie asked if she knew a spell to get Clem moved back. Brook had brewed a potion and stuck it in Mrs. Thom's coffee. Halfway through class, Mrs. Thom was called to the office and never returned. Brook said it was because she'd vanished, but Clementine heard her mom say it was because of a family emergency. Either way, the substitute teacher had no idea there was a seating plan, so Clementine switched seats with Kenny. From then on, it was Clem, Brook, and Maddie. Well, lately, it was Brook and Maddie and sometimes Clem. In fact, Brook and Maddie were probably doing something fun together right now. Maybe it was better she didn't have her phone with her. There was nothing Brook could possibly know about black magic that Clem couldn't learn on the internet anyway.

Hours passed before their car pulled up in front of the house. In her daze, Clem hardly noticed.

"What are you doing outside, Clemmie?" her dad asked as he and Ferg sauntered up the steps. "Trying to get a suntan?"

He laughed at his own joke. He always laughed at his own cheesy dad jokes. Clem smiled and rolled her eyes.

"Needed some fresh air." She rubbed her cold arms. It had stopped raining, but the air was still chilly. She would've grabbed a jacket hours ago if she hadn't been too afraid to go into the empty house alone.

"Probably came out here to vape." Fergus stuck out his tongue.

"Clementine Eloise Lemons," her mother started, "really?"

"I swear—on the life of the kitten you won't let me have— I don't vape." Clementine glared at the back of Ferg's head as she stormed into the house behind him.

"Tone, Clementine!" her dad said from the kitchen.

"Augh," Clem yelled dramatically as she climbed the stairs. She'd rather take her chances with whatever voodoo magic was happening in her room than suffer even two minutes with her family. Maybe she'd get lucky, and the chest would swallow her whole.

Fergus was waiting on the landing.

"Where is it?" he demanded.

"It's on my desk," she sighed.

"You're such a loser." Ferg stormed into her room, grabbed his medal, and stormed back out. "'My magic box ate your medal. I swear it, Fergus'," he whined, waving his hands in the air mockingly. "Now I wish I would've stolen your stupid jewelry, so I could show you how to do a prank that didn't suck."

He slammed the door in her face and was gone.

Clem didn't wait a single second. She knew what she had to do. Before the door finished vibrating, she marched to her desk, grabbed the chest, and crammed it into her backpack.

"I'll be back before dinner!" She ducked out the front door and took off, at a full sprint, toward the bus stop.

On the bus ride, Clementine couldn't stop thinking about her stuff just appearing out of thin air. It wasn't there, and then it was. How? Magic? Maybe the weird old shopkeeper dabbled in the dark arts. He had said magic was everywhere. Clem shivered. Was it haunted? Was it possible Andro Ablikim was a ghost? Perhaps they didn't know they were dead. She hoped they hadn't escaped into the house.

As the bus turned down Pandora, Clem half expected the antiques store to have vanished—*poof*—in a cloud of smoke. But no, the building was still there, as decrepit and forlorn as before. Long after the bus pulled away, Clementine stood on the sidewalk, eyeing the storefront. Maybe it was the low-hanging clouds, but it looked particularly ominous.

Slinging her bulging backpack farther up her shoulder, Clem took a deep breath, clenched her jaw, and pushed on the door.

The front counter was still piled high with junk, only now someone was there. A college-aged woman with pixie-pink hair and oversized glasses sat behind the desk, idly chewing gum and staring at her phone.

"Excuse me," Clementine said timidly. Ugh, she hated talking to people she didn't know. "I'd, um, I'd like to return something."

The woman looked up, annoyed. Without a word, she pointed at the faded sign next to the register. NO REFUNDS. NO RETURNS. NO EXCHANGES. Staring at Clementine, she blew a single bubble, waited until it popped, then went back to looking at her phone.

"No, you don't understand. I don't want a refund. I want to

give it back. I'll leave it right here." Clem pointed at the cluttered counter and started to unzip her pack. "I just don't want it anymore."

The clerk set her phone down and let out a long huff. "No refunds. No returns. No exchanges." She tapped the sign with each word as if Clem couldn't read.

"But…" Clem might as well have been speaking to an empty desk. Frustrated, she picked up her pack and left.

Clementine wandered the downtown streets, debating what to do. She couldn't return the chest, but she certainly didn't want to keep it either. As she walked past a deserted alley, she stopped. A dumpster! That would end this.

Ducking into the alley, she unzipped her pack. Clem stood in front of the dumpster for an eternity, clutching the chest with both hands.

Toss it in and go, she told herself. But no matter how badly she wanted to, she couldn't bring herself to do it.

Sighing, she stuffed the chest back in her pack and went home. As she walked up the steps, Clem had an idea. She'd bury the stupid thing in the basement with all the other unwanted and forgotten things her family owned. Out of sight, out of mind.

Once she'd propped the door wide open and turned on the single light, Clementine made her way down the uneven stairs. She hated the basement. It was dark and creepy and smelled like damp earth and mold. Plus, there were spiders everywhere. The chest would be right at home.

Clem found a box of baby clothes her mother refused to give away and dumped it out. She shoved the chest into the bottom of the box, then piled the clothes back on top.

"There," she whispered. "Try doing your weird voodoo magic in there."

If Adriana James had taught her anything, it was that mysterious artifacts always ended up buried in government-run storage facilities or museum vaults. It was the adult thing to do with anything you weren't sure what to do with.

Stopping on the first stair, Clem turned and looked in the direction of the chest. "If you show up in my bedroom by yourself tonight, I'm going to light you on fire," she threatened. Then she raced up the stairs as fast as she could and slammed the door behind her.

CHAPTER 10

As hard as she tried to forget about it, the chest was never far from Clementine's thoughts. The childlike words hastily scrawled on the yellowed paper echoed in her head.

We need help. Will you help us?

Help how? Like *We've been kidnapped* help? Or like *We're lost in the forest, and there's no cell reception. Call 911!* help? Or *What's the answer to question thirty-nine? I can't afford to fail this exam* help?

Clem briefly debated going to the police, but no one was going to believe she'd found an SOS note in a voodoo box. Especially when the message looked and read like it was written by a six-year-old. That would be ridiculous. Even if, by some miracle, they took her seriously, the note wasn't much to go on.

Tuesday night, when she should've been doing her homework, Clem found herself absentmindedly googling the Empire of Dohi. Unless it was in North Korea or China, no such place existed. There was a town called Dohi in the state of Madhya Pradesh, India. She'd also found a hamlet called Dohi Gbadji in Benin. But that was it. Dohi was a dead end.

By Thursday, Clem had set her sights on Andro Ablikim. Was it first name *Andro*, last name *Ablikim*? Or were they two people? It was hard to tell; the message did say *we*. Not that it mattered. Regardless of how she searched, nothing relevant came up. There were billions of people on the planet. What had she expected? And why did she care so much?

She'd spent the weekend combing through obituaries in

case Andro Ablikim was a ghost. But if he was, he wasn't a local ghost. At least not one who had died anytime in the last hundred years.

Clem tried to convince herself it was nothing. A hoax. But no matter how hard she tried to forget about it, she couldn't.

Help how? Help who? played on repeat in her head.

"Earth to Ms. Lemons… Do you have somewhere better to be today? Or will you be returning to Earth to join us?" Her history teacher, Mr. Waxley, sounded annoyed.

Clementine looked up, startled. Two dozen sets of eyes stared in her direction. It took her a full minute to realize where she was. *Wednesday. History. Right.*

Clementine's end-of-year report card flashed into her mind: *Clementine is bright and could be a straight-A student if she'd stop daydreaming in class and apply herself.*

"I was paying attention, but I didn't understand the question." It was the line Clem often used when she hadn't been listening. Somehow, it always worked.

The class laughed. Mr. Waxley pursed his lips and ran his tongue back and forth over his teeth. His thick brown mustache wriggled like a caterpillar trying to crawl off his upper lip.

"I asked, 'What would have happened if we hadn't helped?'"

"Uuugghh!! Help who? Help how?" Clem cried, exasperated.

The class erupted in laughter.

"I don't know what drama is happening on Planet Clementine," Mr. Waxley responded. The caterpillar above his lip twitched uncontrollably in frustration. "But on this planet, we've been discussing Canada's involvement in World War II. So, do you feel the war—again, that's World War II for those of you just joining us—would have had a different outcome had we—Canada, location planet Earth—chosen not to aid our allies?"

The bell rang.

"Alright, class, you can thank Clementine for this one. This week's assignment is a thousand words on how you feel World War II's outcome would have been different had we not joined the war effort. Keep in mind removing even one soldier from the equation could've caused a ripple effect altering the entire course of history as we know it. Feel free to get creative. Extra marks if your story can keep me entertained through dinner. Pete's a great cat, but he's not exactly an exciting dinner companion."

The class collectively groaned.

"Next week, please try to focus, Ms. Lemons." Mr. Waxley sighed as Clem walked out of class.

"Are you okay?" Maddie asked once they were in the hall, away from the disapproving wriggle of the Caterpillar.

Clem wished she could tell Maddie about the note, the chest. What she needed was advice from someone on what to do next. She wanted someone to reassure her it was a hoax, to tell her it wasn't her problem. But the story sounded absolutely insane. Not even Mad would believe this one.

"Yeah, totally. Why?" Clem lied through a forced smile.

"Well, not to be rude, but you've been more, um, distant than you usually are. If you get what I'm saying." Maddie seemed genuinely concerned.

Brook came up behind them and wrapped Maddie in a giant hug. "Are you talking about our favorite space cadet?" She laughed, looking over at Clem. "I know you don't have to pay attention to get decent grades, but Mad's right. You've been totally zoned out for the last few weeks, amnesiac even. Better be careful, or you might get so lost in la-la land you can't find your way home."

"You guys suck." Clem stuck out her tongue and smiled. "Now, if you'll excuse me, I need to see how many people I can injure in gym class."

Mr. Waxley's innocent homework assignment had more of an effect on Clem than he probably could have imagined. That night, she sat at her desk and tried to envision World War II without Canada. Would they have lost the Battles of Normandy or Dunkirk without the thousands of Canadian soldiers who fought? The idea that the absence of one single soldier could have changed the entire course of the war was mind-blowing. She should have been writing, but instead, Clem found herself googling the "ripple effect." She couldn't help but wonder what effect her not answering the note would have on Andro Ablikim. What could she do, though? She wasn't a soldier. She was just Clementine. Most days, she couldn't even make it out the front door with matching socks on her feet.

Clem needed a distraction before she drove herself insane. Closing her laptop, she decided to head downstairs.

"What are we watching?" she mumbled, plopping down in front of the TV. "Better be something good."

"Tail end of the news." Her mom shushed her.

Clem watched in horror as a camo-painted army tank shelled a desert city.

"Since December," the newscaster reported in a British accent, "nearly three hundred thousand have been displaced. With the regime rapidly closing in, these refugees need the international community now more than ever. For ways you can help, visit—"

"God, does everyone need help these days? Seriously!" Clem cried. "Help? What's the damn point! You can't fix that. No one can."

"Clementine!" her mother gasped.

"Entitled much…" Ferg rolled his eyes in disgust.

Jaw clenched in frustration, Clem returned to her room and buried her head in her pillow. Some days the world was just too much.

All day Thursday, Clem pushed the magic box and Andro's childlike request for help to the back of her mind.

There's nothing you can do to help, she told herself, *so why waste any more time thinking about it?* The more often she repeated it, the easier it was to believe.

When Mrs. Lee told her to play "Let It Go" during her piano lesson, Clementine took it as a sign. That was precisely what she needed to do, let it go. As soon as she got home, she'd do what she should've done days ago—burn the piece of paper and toss the chest in the trash where it belonged.

After weeks of mental torment, she was ready to let it go. As she left Mrs. Lee's studio, Clementine felt so light her feet barely touched the stairs. Popping out the bright red door, she closed her eyes and took a deep breath. The air smelled of rain and freedom.

"Why don't you go home? You don't belong here!" someone yelled. Clem's shoulders dropped. The heaviness flooded back in. "We don't want you here! Nobody does!"

Reluctantly opening her eyes, Clem looked down the alley in the direction the voice had come from.

Backed against the brick wall was a kid she vaguely recognized from school. He was in a few of her classes. His family had recently immigrated, but Clem couldn't remember where from. He never said much in class, and regretfully, she'd never spoken to him. He was surrounded by a half-dozen guys. She didn't recognize any of them.

Eyes wide, Clem froze in the doorway. She should say something. She knew she should say something. But what? There were so many of them. What if they had weapons? And they were all guys. What if they came after her too? There was no way she could defend herself. She pulled out her phone and fumbled to turn it on.

"He doesn't even understand what you're saying," one of the guys said, sneering. "You don't even speak English, do you?" He punched the kid in the shoulder.

Head hung low, the boy said nothing and tried his best to duck around them.

"Airport's that way." They pushed the kid back into the semicircle they'd formed around him.

Hate filled the narrow alley, sucking out the air and blocking the sky. Clem felt like she was suffocating in it. She stood there, furious. Terrified. Miserable. Powerless. She wanted to scream, *Stop! Shut up and leave him alone!* But the words caught in her throat. She was vastly outnumbered, and they were so much bigger than she was. Clem scanned the alley for someone, anyone, who could help.

She stood unmoving and watched as first one punch and then another landed squarely across the kid's cheek. He stumbled backward and fell to the sidewalk with the first drops of rain.

"You leave him alone! I've called the police. They're coming!" Mrs. Lee wielded a broom as she barreled through the alley. Clem hadn't even noticed the tiny woman thunder down the stairs behind her. "Go on, you go home! That attitude isn't welcomed here!"

How a five-foot-tall woman could be so intimidating was beyond comprehension. Clem watched as the bullies cowered, then turned and ran, calling the elderly woman names as they fled.

As the last of them disappeared, Mrs. Lee reached out her hand and helped the kid off the ground. She brushed the dirt off of his face and gently patted his cheek, whispering something in his ear Clem couldn't quite hear. Head bent, the boy walked by, trying to avoid eye contact. Even through the drizzling rain, Clementine could see the tears in his eyes.

"You make me sad, Clementine Lemons. You see this, and you know it's wrong. But, still, you don't say anything. You don't do anything. I'm disappointed in you. You know better. Next time someone needs your help, you help them." Mrs. Lee shook her head and slowly climbed back up the stairs.

Rain ran in long thin streaks down the dirty glass walls of the bus stop. Clementine sunk into the booth and buried her head in her knees.

Closing her eyes, she found herself staring right back into the disappointed face of Mrs. Lee. She didn't need Mrs. Lee staring at her from her memories; she was disappointed enough in herself for both of them. Why hadn't she said something? Anything. She could've screamed. Someone would have come. Clem wasn't like the heroines in her books. She wasn't Fergus. She wasn't born ready to take on the world. Who was she kidding? She wasn't even brave enough to be alone in her house, knowing the chest was buried in the basement. Tears streamed down her cheeks like rain on the gritty glass.

A rock splashed in the puddle in front of her. Then another. Clementine pulled her head off her knees and looked around.

The Professor stood on the far side of the bus stop, leaning against the glass. His mile-high shopping cart sat wrapped in a tattered blue tarp beside him. Though damp, his hair still jutted out of his scalp in every direction. His lab coat poked out from under a rain jacket that was more silver duct tape than fabric. He stared in her direction.

Clementine's eyes darted around, but there was nowhere to escape. This wasn't what she needed. *Not now.*

The Professor tossed another rock into the puddle at her feet.

She watched it splash, ripples expanding out in all directions from where it landed. The waves picked up a green leaf and pushed it gently to the water's edge, to safety. A moment of chaos and calm returned to the puddle as if nothing had happened.

"The only real question is, are you the rock, or are you the leaf?" the Professor mumbled loudly.

Clementine stared at him, puzzled. She knew she shouldn't engage, but she couldn't help herself.

"What?" she asked with a sniffle.

The man took a long sip of coffee from a red paper cup and wiped his mouth on the back of his duct-taped sleeve.

"Are you the rock, or are you the leaf?" he asked again. "There are only two types of people in this world. Either you drift along, waiting for someone else to push you to shore, or you dare to make waves. Do you choose to make an impact or drift aimlessly through this life? The answer is that simple."

"What if you're too scared to be a rock?" Clem's honesty shocked even herself.

The Professor raised his eyebrows and tossed another rock into the puddle. "A rock is a rock whether it believes it's a rock or not. It cannot change the nature of what it is," he answered. "Besides, the rock's job is easy. All it does is make the ripples.

The magic is in the ripples."

Clementine stared at the crazy-haired Professor. He stared back, although Clem wasn't sure if he was staring at her or at something beyond her head only he could see.

The bus slowly came to a halt in front of them. Clem hopped over the puddle, tossed a half wave in the direction of the Professor, and climbed aboard. As the bus pulled away, she saw him throw another rock in the puddle and mutter something to himself.

Clementine rested her puffy red cheek against the cold window of the bus, the Professor's words spinning around inside her head. The traffic lights distorted and flipped upside down in the fat raindrops clinging to the window. Clem felt dizzy and nauseous.

Stepping off the bus, her foot landed squarely in a puddle. Looking at her soaking-wet foot, she watched the ripples dance in the light of the streetlamp. The world stopped spinning. Clementine saw things more clearly than she ever had before. She was a rock—a reluctant and timid rock, but a rock, nonetheless. Well, maybe she was more like a pebble. But, still, a pebble was a type of rock. For the first time in her entire life, Clem knew what she needed to do.

The house was silent. Good, she was the first one home. Fewer questions. Taking a deep breath, Clementine flipped on the basement light.

"I am a rock," she whispered as she descended the creepy old staircase. "I am a rock. All I need to do is make the waves, and they'll do the rest. I. Am. A. Rock."

To her relief, the chest was precisely where she'd left it. Before she had a chance to change her mind, she plucked it out of the cardboard box and raced back up the stairs.

Clementine set the chest on her desk, then sat on the end of her bed and stared at it. She told herself she could still change her mind if she wanted to. But she knew she wouldn't; she couldn't. After all, a rock was a rock.

Clem moved to her desk chair, where she stared at the chest some more. Her gaze landed on the pad of pink paper.

"Okay, fine! I'll do it!!" she yelled to no one in particular. Or maybe it was to herself. She couldn't be sure.

Hand trembling, Clementine picked up her pen and wrote a response.

CHAPTER 11

Andro banged on the old man's door with such force the apartments overhead shuddered and creaked. A neighbor glared down disapprovingly.

"You're early, boy." Ablikim cracked open the door. "I appreciate your enthusiasm, but I haven't had a chance to eat yet."

Ever since they'd sent the message, Ablikim had been teaching Andro to read during the hours between dinner and curfew. Andro was exhausted, and Zari was unhappy to pick up his slack at home, but he was determined to learn all he could. Besides, it took his mind off the relentless worry of why the sorcerer was taking so long to respond. The treasure, and their message, had disappeared so quickly that Ablikim had almost had a heart attack. But then, nothing. It had been nearly two weeks without a response.

"I know, grandfather." Andro breathed heavily from his sprint through the streets. He nodded toward the neighbor, still glaring from the balcony overhead. "But I picked some fresh vegetables from the garden, and I thought you may want to have them with dinner."

It's important, he mouthed.

"How kind of you." Ablikim followed Andro's glance toward his nosy neighbor. "Well, I suppose you might as well come in and help prepare them."

Andro ducked inside Ablikim's windowless apartment. After tossing the vegetables on the counter with a thump, he waved a fresh piece of pink parchment in one hand and a floppy rectangle of folded paper in the other.

"We got a response! We actually got a response! Can you believe it? They answered! I'm sorry I'm early, but I couldn't wait!"

"Well, I never..." Ablikim snatched the papers from Andro's hand and disappeared through the hole in the floor.

Andro leaped down the ladder behind him, barely stepping on a single rung.

Ablikim unfolded the thick rectangle of paper and furrowed his eyebrows.

"What is it?" Andro stared at the large patches of color on the pale blue background.

"It's a map," Ablikim muttered. He turned his attention to the piece of pink parchment.

"Well, what does it say?" It had only been a few minutes, but the silence felt so long Andro was sure an entire day must have come and gone around them. It was far fewer words than the last message, and the old man had been poring over Olli and Andro's father's translations every night for weeks. Surely he knew all of the words by now! Andro had already learned more words than were written on the pink scrap of paper. How long could it possibly take?

"Do you want to do this?" Ablikim asked.

"But I can't..."

"Exactly. Be patient. Go practice your letters and leave me be. If you can't manage that, go home for the evening and come back tomorrow. Either way, be quiet while I work."

Leave? No way! Andro wanted to be right there when the old man figured it out. Reluctantly sitting at the table across from Ablikim, he pulled out his lessons.

Time ticked slowly as Andro mouthed out the words and letters in his book. Every so often, Ablikim would clear his throat. Andro would look up expectantly. But Ablikim would reach out a hand and tap Andro's papers as if to say, *Get back to work and mind your own business.*

As the evening faded to night, Ablikim leaned back in his chair and scratched his leathery cheeks.

"Well…?" Andro leaned forward.

"It says, *I am Clementine Lemons from Victoria, Canada. I will help you…but how?*" Ablikim answered.

"*Clementine Lemons*, that's a weird name for a sorcerer, or a scientist, or whatever you call them." Andro frowned. "It doesn't sound like a powerful sorcerer's name at all. Where's Canada?"

"This doesn't make any sense at all." Ablikim turned his attention back to the map.

"What doesn't make any sense?" Andro followed the old man's finger as it moved across the large patch of blue.

"Nothing on this map makes sense," Ablikim responded.

"This is Canada." He pointed to a large patch of green. "I assume this big star is Victoria, where we would find one Clementine Lemons. But where's Dohi? It's as if Dohi has disappeared entirely. It's…it's as if we don't even exist."

"We need answers." Ablikim disappeared down one of the cluttered aisles of books. "Our search for any record of the chest, why it was created and how it functions, has become more urgent."

"But does it really matter if we aren't on the map drawing?" Andro didn't understand what the big deal was. "They said they would help, and we have the chest. So, they can send us anything! What should we ask for, grandfather?" Andro's mind raced. "Food," he continued quickly, "we should ask for food. Enough for the whole city. No, a sword. Yes, weapons! We could use weapons. Or an army! Maybe Clementine Lemons can send us a whole army. No, I couldn't even fit in the chest—that's ridiculous. Wait, a sword won't even fit in the chest. Maybe we should ask for Coin! Yeah, we could use it to buy food and weapons, and then we could build an army of our own! Let's ask for Coin! Oh, and more books with pictures! And some jewelry for Zari. She said to ask for more of those dangly ear things."

Ablikim wasn't listening to Andro babble.

"I think"—Ablikim carted a pile of books back to the table—"we need to learn more about your magic chest and this Clementine Lemons before we ask for anything."

Ablikim scribbled a few words on a piece of paper, then plopped a giant book in front of Andro. "These are the words for *chest* and *wooden box*. I want you to scan this book and look for either of these words. If you see one of them, call me."

"What if I don't see them?" Andro flipped open the dauntingly large book in front of him.

"Then move on to the next book, and the next, and then the book after that."

Page after page, and night after night, they worked.

"How about this one, grandfather?" Andro asked for the thousandth time.

Ablikim peered over his shoulder and yawned. "No, that's not it. Keep looking."

From dawn to dusk, they labored in the fields. From darkness, until their eyes refused to stay open, they scanned through book after book and scroll after scroll. In the brief moments between, Andro cared for Granny and Zari. A week passed. And then another. Andro wasn't sure how much longer he could keep it up.

When his head nodded and hit the book in front of him, he

would move to the floor or perch awkwardly on a stack of books. The goal was to stay uncomfortable enough to continue reading without falling asleep.

"I think I need to call it a night," he said, yawning. "I can't see straight anymore."

Andro looked down from his perch on top of one of the high shelves. Ablikim was fast asleep at the desk.

Andro flipped through what was left of the book he was working on—a dark green leather-bound volume with 1662 written in gold across the front. Full of beautiful handwriting and intricate drawings, it was slow going. There was no way he would finish it tonight. As the pages gently fluttered by, something caught his eye.

Andro slowly flipped back and forth until he found the exact page he was looking for.

"Grandfather!" Andro nearly fell off the shelf as he scrambled to the floor with the heavy book. "Wake up! You're not going to believe this, but I found it!"

Poor Ablikim's head jumped off his chest as Andro slammed the book down on the table with a thud.

"Andro? What are you still doing here?" he grumbled, rubbing his eyes.

"Look!" Andro jabbed his finger into the page.

Ablikim fumbled to pull his glasses off his head and over the bridge of his nose. He squinted at the page where Andro's finger pointed.

"I found it," Andro said triumphantly.

Ablikim pulled the book closer to the light. Sure enough, staring back at him was a drawing of not one but two chests that looked identical to Andro's.

"Well, what does it say?" Andro had never been more annoyed that he couldn't read.

The old man ignored him as he flipped from one page to the next. He'd flipped through a half-dozen pages before coming to a set of notes scrawled in the margins. With a magnifying glass, he inspected the hastily scribbled words.

Sitting back in his chair, Ablikim placed his hand over his mouth. He was so deep in thought Andro didn't dare breathe, let alone speak.

"Come!" The old man jumped up with such speed he knocked over a stack of books and the wooden chair he'd been sitting on. Andro bent to pick the books off of the floor.

"Leave them, Andro!" Ablikim said from halfway up the ladder. "We must go *now*!"

"Go where?" Andro hurried up the rungs behind him. "What did it say?"

Poking his head out of the hole, Andro watched as Ablikim crammed clothing and a few random items into a small sack.

"Go to your house. Get a few hours of sleep. In the morning, pack some clothes and enough food for a good day's walk. Tell your granny my friend Daro Jira is gravely ill, and I need you to accompany me into the hills to pay him a visit. If she asks about permits, tell her she needn't worry, everything will be in order. Meet me at the Outer East Gate on the eighth bell. Don't be late."

"What? Where are we going? I don't understand." Andro had never been beyond the Outer Wall. You needed travel permits, a valid reason to travel, and Coin—lots of Coin. Even if you had Coin, the paperwork took time. Not just anyone could get beyond the wall.

"There's so much to do. I'll explain on the way, Andro! Go quickly and rest. We have a long journey ahead of us."

Andro knew he would get no more answers, so he asked no more questions.

CHAPTER 12

"I forbid it." Granny stared at him from across the table.

Andro was in no mood to argue. He'd been too excited and worried to sleep, and now he was exhausted. Staring at the cupboards, he wondered what *pack enough food for a good day's walk* meant.

"Grandfather Ablikim is an old man." Andro sighed as he pulled down one can after another. "He can hardly be expected to make this kind of a journey by himself, and he has no family of his own to help him."

"The fact Ablikim doesn't have any family is his own doing," Granny said with a snort. "You do! And who's going to care for your family while you're away? Who's going to volunteer today? Who will do your work and bring home Coin?"

"Zari's old enough to care for things for a few days, and she can take my place volunteering today. You've said it yourself: she needs to learn these things." Andro picked up a shirt and sniffed it. Clean enough. He crammed it and his least dirty trousers on top of the food. "I can't imagine Ablikim will manage to secure more than a three-day pass, which means I'll only miss two day's work. We still have full shelves. We'll get by."

"I don't trust Ablikim. I don't buy for one moment he has an ill friend in the mountains. That man has never had a friend as long as I've known him. This has to do with that message, doesn't it? What are you two up to? What if you get caught?" the old woman retorted.

"We aren't 'up to' anything...*yet*," Andro said with a cocky grin. "But you'll be the first to know when we are."

Granny shook her head, but Andro could see the faintest hint of a smile playing at the edges of her lips.

"Ablikim asked me to travel with him. I've never been outside the Outer Wall. How could I say no? Please, Granny, just this once? We'll have all the correct paperwork in order, so there won't be anything to get 'caught' for. We'll be safe. I promise!"

"Fine! Go! Get yourself disappeared in the hills with that old fool. Who am I to stop you?" Granny threw her hands in the air.

"Thank you, Granny! I'll be back Monday night, I swear it!" Andro slung his pack over his shoulder. He kissed the old woman on the forehead and darted out the door.

Andro knew his sector like the back of his hand. A few quick turns and he was ducking through the open gates of his own sector and into the next. Sector gates were only closed between curfew and sunrise, and during the odd lockdown and mandatory drills. Or if they were looking for someone.

The farther from his sector Andro got, the less familiar the city became. The narrow streets made it hard to make good time. He cut through alleys and back lanes where he could, but since he rarely ever left his own sector except to get to work (which was in the complete opposite direction), he was afraid of getting lost. He should've left earlier.

The inner-city gates surrounding the old city were easy enough to get through. Although manned by watchers, they barely gave him a second glance when he flashed his volunteer pass in their direction. It wasn't valid, but they didn't know that.

Andro made it to the Outer East Gate as the first of the eight bells started to chime. Jumping to get a better view, he spotted Ablikim talking to an enforcer. He pushed his way through the crowd. As the last bell chimed, Andro sidled up to the old man.

"Grandfather," he said breathlessly, head bowed.

"Ah, here he is now," Ablikim said to the enforcer. "This is Andro, my neighbor's boy. He'll accompany me to ensure we make the journey safely and efficiently so we can get back to the work of the Black Peacock as quickly as possible."

The enforcer studied Andro. To Andro, all enforcers looked the same. Same dull gray uniform, same hardened expression. The same cold, dead eyes. If you'd seen one, you'd seen them all.

Without a word, the enforcer moved to the side and motioned Ablikim and Andro into the narrow backstreet behind him. Andro wasn't sure what was happening.

As Andro passed the enforcer, the man seized him by the shoulder. Andro and Ablikim stopped cold in their tracks.

"Good job with the graffiti the other day, kid. You can't even tell it was there." He nodded.

"Thank you, sir," Andro muttered. Oh, so this was *that* enforcer.

In the alley stood an agent, a folder tucked under his arm.

"Did you bring it?" the agent asked Ablikim.

Pulling a weird-looking contraption out of his sack, Ablikim nodded. Andro couldn't tell what it was, but the agent seemed pleased.

"You always were the best tinkerer in the valley." He took the folder from under his arm and opened it. With a pen, he checked a handful of boxes and scribbled something across the bottom of a stack of pages.

Andro finally understood what was happening. Ablikim was making a trade for the documents they needed. This had to be highly illegal. And to make such a deal with an agent, nonetheless! Ablikim had some nerve! Andro was impressed, though part of him wondered if Granny was right. Maybe Ablikim was an old fool.

"I know I don't need to remind you this transaction never happened, but what about the boy?" The agent handed Ablikim the official-looking documents.

"I saw nothing, sir," Andro answered quickly. "If anyone asks, I wasn't here."

"Good answer." The agent silently flicked his hand toward the gate.

The line moved tediously slow as the wall agents methodically inspected everyone's documents and rummaged through their meager belongings. No one spoke unless spoken to. Every now and then, the agents motioned to an enforcer, who dragged someone out of the line.

As they inched closer to the front, Andro's hands trembled. He was ten feet from the gate. Ten feet from being farther away from his granny and sister than he'd ever been before. Ten feet from escaping the valley, something he never imagined possible. And yet, ten feet was still so far. What if the documents the agent had given them were fake? What if the wall agent didn't let them through? *Deep breath.*

"May the sun never set on the Empire of the Black Peacock." Andro and Ablikim saluted in unison when they finally made it to the front of the line.

"May the sun never set on our glorious Empire, indeed," the agent responded, fondly touching the onyx pin over his heart. "Name and sector?" The man scrutinized their documentation.

"Ablikim Amosi, Sector Six."

"And where are you headed?"

"Madea."

"And the reason for this journey?"

"My friend Daro Jira is old and quite ill. I should like to see him one last time," Ablikim replied gravely.

"Seems like a waste of a good travel permit," the agent responded emotionlessly. "And the boy?"

"This is Andro Ilham, my neighbor's boy. He has offered to accompany me. I am old. My feet and eyes are not what they once were."

"You will be back within these walls before the sun sets on Monday, and you and the boy will be back in the fields the following morning."

Ablikim nodded. "Yes, of course. The work of the Black Peacock is of the utmost importance."

"For the good of the Empire," Andro added as patriotically as he could muster. The gate was so close he'd have said anything to get through.

"For the good of the Empire," the agent repeated. His stamp landed on their documents with a resounding *thump*.

"Don't lose these. Be sure they're stamped upon entry and exit from Madea." Handing the documents back to Ablikim, he waved the next person forward.

Andro and Ablikim were herded through a heavy door, and just like that, they were on the far side of the Outer Wall. Andro paused and stared at the impenetrable gray stones towering into the smog-filled sky. The Black Peacock insisted the wall was for the people's protection—to keep out invaders and those who would threaten the Empire. It ran like a fortress around the entire valley, save for where the mountain of trash had completely buried it. An invader would have to be insane to enter the valley through the dump; that would be a death sentence.

Andro was officially as far from home as he'd ever been, and already he knew he never wanted to return.

Waiting until the foot traffic around them had fallen away, Andro asked the two questions he'd been dying to know the answer to.

"Where are we going, grandfather?! What did the book say that was so important?!"

Ablikim tossed a nervous glance over his shoulder. "We're going somewhere top secret. Somewhere almost no one knows exists. Like my little library, it is a place you must never speak of."

"Did my father ever go there?" Andro asked.

"No. Idris and Olli did not know of this place. It's far too secret. Few outsiders, other than myself, have been there. As much as it pained me, I stopped going many years ago. Daro Jira and I realized it was too dangerous. Had my movement been detected, it would have jeopardized everything. But this trip is of the utmost importance. It's worth the risk."

Andro nodded. "Who's Daro Jira?"

"Daro Jira is a dear friend and a protector of knowledge. With his help, I hope to find the record mentioned in the notes scribbled in our book, so we can learn more."

"More about what?" Andro pressed. "You still haven't told me what it said!"

"Right," Ablikim answered. "It won't be word for word, as it was a long and incomplete read. But I'll do my best.

"As you saw in the picture you discovered, your granny's magic chest is not one-of-a-kind. It has a twin. The two chests were crafted hundreds of years ago. In the year 1662, if we're being exact. The chests were created by the Monks of Videt Mountain for Prince Cetin and Princess Cyra's seventh birthday.

"Prince Cetin and Princess Cyra were the twin children of Emperor Aarav, the last emperor of the dynasty of the Emerald Peacock," the old man explained. "Before the reign of the Black Peacock began."

Andro nodded. As excited as he was to learn more, it was hard to pay attention. The thick green forests hugging the shoulders of the road were unlike anything he'd ever seen before. Who knew trees grew so tall?

"As I mentioned before, the Monks of Videt Mountain were brilliant scientists, philosophers, inventors, creators, and teachers. They were well respected by all, including the emperor. Their motto was 'perfellik inde statengeli'—perfection in balance. It is said they traveled to many lands and many worlds in search of the secret to balance. They were versed in all the ancient studies—alchemy, medicine, astronomy, botany, philosophy, ecology, mathematics, qi, numerology. They loved music and art. They also had a passion for new studies—divination, teleportation, levitation, flight, frequency. Perhaps even time travel. As I've said, much of what was known has been lost. I myself thought many of these subjects to be theory at best. But now, after what I've read, I'm not so sure.

"When the emperor's twins were born, the monks came to congratulate the emperor and bless the newborn children. However, they immediately recognized something was amiss. The balancing force which governs our existence, the very thing they'd worked so diligently to maintain, had shifted. The kingdom was off balance. The monks theorized the twins' qi—the balance of yin and yang—had been separated during their birth. They didn't know what to do; this had never happened before. They didn't think it was even possible."

Andro stared blank-faced at the old man.

"We are all born with a qi, a life force. An energy that's invisible, like the wind." Ablikim paused briefly to rest. "That energy is known as yin and yang. Yin energy wells up from within the earth, while the yang energy comes from the sun and the sky. Yin energy is dark—negative. It is the voice that whispers in your ear to do things you know you ought not to. Yang energy is light—positive. It's what makes you share your rice and vegetables with an old man. When yin and yang are perfectly mixed, there is balance. When there is too much of one or the other, there is only chaos."

Chaos Andro understood. Life was chaos.

"The Black Peacock is governed by yin, then?" Andro asked.

Ablikim nodded before continuing. "The monks feared as the prince and princess grew, one would become progressively darker, crueler, while the other would become lighter, kinder. The monks were anxious. Until they figured out a solution, the Empire and possibly the world would only be safe if the children stuck together to balance each other out.

"The monks told Emperor Aarav of their suspicions. They warned him under no circumstances should he separate the children from each other. But the emperor was blinded by his love. He couldn't see what the monks saw.

"Back in the monastery, the monks searched high and low for a way to rejoin the twins' qi, all the while keeping a close eye on the children as they grew. As their seventh birthday neared, it was decreed Prince Cetin would follow in the steps of his father and begin his studies in Mariz, near the sea. Princess Cyra would stay and study in Nimbina. The monks begged the emperor not to send the young prince away for fear of what would become of light without dark, dark without light. But the emperor would not listen.

"For their birthday, the monks crafted a set of chests for the children to take with them wherever life might lead them. According to the specifications listed, the top compartments of both chests opened without a lock and key. They were linked via teleportation so the children could share things regardless of distance. The monks hoped this ability for the children to stay connected would be enough. The bottom four drawers had locks that could only be opened with specific keys. This way, the children could hide away secrets, even from each other, should the need arise."

"Clementine Lemons must have the other chest!" Andro said excitedly. "Is that what the note scrawled in the margin was about? How to find Clementine Lemons in Victoria?"

"No child, don't be ridiculous," Ablikim answered. "It was far more important."

Andro tried to think of something more important than finding the scientist-sorcerer Clementine Lemons, but he couldn't.

"The note," Ablikim continued, after waiting for a handful of weary travelers to pass by, "it said, *Princess Cyra has hidden the Stones where the Mad Prince can never get them. We sent the princess and the chest through safely before he came, though we're unsure where she landed in the chaos. The portal was destroyed in battle; we cannot bring her home that way. Those left have been searching for the Mad Prince's chest, so we might send word to the princess. To restore balance, we must find Princess Cyra and bring the Stones back to Dohi. The Mad Prince cannot find her before us. He must not get the Stones, or all will be lost, and his terror and chaos will be unstoppable for all eternity. If you are reading this and the Black Peacock still reigns, join us in our cause. We must not fail. Record book 1681 explains more, as we have neither the time nor the space to do so here. May balance be restored before all hope is lost.* It was signed with the mark of the monks."

"What Stones?" Andro asked.

"I'm not sure. But obviously, they were of the utmost importance. That's what we're going to find out. With any luck, record book 1681 still exists. And if anyone can find it, it will be Daro."

Andro and the old man walked in silence, each lost in thought. Every now and then, Andro would ask a question like, "What's a portal?" But Ablikim had no answers, and the silence quickly resumed.

All day, they walked. First on a wide and crumbling road, then on a narrower cart path, and finally on a single-file trail that wound into a deep valley wedged between two towering mountains. They stopped only once to eat lunch on a large flat rock. As they stood to leave, Andro's stomach growled. He wished he'd packed more food. He hadn't realized adventuring would make him so hungry.

Though the path looked rarely traveled, signs of the Black Peacock were everywhere. Most of the trees had been slashed, leaving ugly scars on the surrounding mountains. Having just seen a forest for the first time, Andro was saddened by these large barren swaths. What if the Black Peacock cut all the trees until nothing was left? Giant pits had been gouged deep into the earth. Abandoned buildings stood dilapidated along the banks of a muddied river. The Black Peacock had come, they had taken, and when the earth had nothing left to give, they had moved on, leaving a swath of destruction in their wake. That was what the Black Peacock did. What they had always done. How there was any beauty left in the world was beyond comprehension.

The going was tough as they clambered over the fallen trees and around the giant boulders littering the trail. At times, Andro couldn't see a path, yet Ablikim continued on. Even though he'd said he hadn't been this way in decades, he seemed to know exactly where they were going.

Night had nearly fallen by the time they stumbled to the gates of Madea. The town was hidden behind a rusty tin wall topped with barbed wire and sharp nails. Andro noted bleakly the points were facing inward and not out. The wall wasn't meant to keep intruders out; it was meant to keep the townspeople in. It dawned on him that was also the purpose of the wall around the valley. He would have been angry if he had not been so exhausted and hungry.

Ablikim knocked loudly on the closed gate.

The door swung open. Out stepped a man who looked as if someone had carved him out of the mountain itself. The buttons and seams on his uniform were about to explode. If he'd ever had a State-approved haircut, it had long since grown out. His hair and beard flowed down his shoulders in long dark waves. A scar ran from his forehead through his right eye and ended in a sneer at his upper lip.

"We're here to visit Seda Dojara," Ablikim said, pulling out their papers. "I'm Ablikim Amosi. This is my helper, Andro Ilham."

"It's after dark." The giant of a man grunted as he held a lamp to their faces. "I don't have to let you in."

"Forgive our late arrival." Ablikim bowed. "I am old and slow."

The agent grunted again and snatched the documents out of Ablikim's hand. He held them against the rusty tin wall and banged a stamp on them. The sound echoed like a gong through the quiet streets, announcing their arrival.

"My town, my rules. Understand?" As Ablikim tucked the freshly stamped documents away, the enforcer jabbed him on the shoulder with an oversized finger, nearly sending him to the ground. Andro reached out and caught him as he stumbled backward.

"Yes, of course. May the sun never set on the Empire of the Black Peacock."

"*Pfft*…sunset…Black Peacock…" Ducking back into the guardhouse, the agent slammed the door.

"Pleasant man," Ablikim muttered under his breath as they walked away. "Lucky we shan't be in his town for long."

CHAPTER 13

Madea sat precariously on a long narrow ledge, caught between a cliff plunging hundreds of feet into the river below and a cliff jutting straight into the sky. A set of rusty rails ran through the town's center and disappeared into a gaping hole in the mountain. Ore carts sat empty, waiting for a new day to dawn.

Ablikim led Andro up the tracks and onto a side street where a row of houses leaned lazily against the cliff. Near the end of the row, he stopped at a two-story shanty. Ablikim ran his fingers over a nearly invisible symbol carved in the doorjamb. The same symbol from the drawer of his chest and the margin of the old man's book—Andro now recognized it as the symbol of the Monks of Videt Mountain.

"This is it." Ablikim quietly knocked three times.

A tall, thin woman with waist-long hair and piercing gray eyes opened the door. This must be Seda because it certainly was not the "sick friend" Andro was expecting.

"Ablikim Amosi..." The woman stared at the old man, recognition slowly dawning on her face. "It's been such a long time."

"Yes, I'm afraid it's been a while, and I would not be here now if it weren't urgent," Ablikim said, smiling. "You were a young girl the last I saw you, Seda."

Noticing Andro for the first time, Seda stopped talking and stepped back.

"It's alright," Ablikim said. "Andro can be trusted. He understands the need for secrecy. It is his discovery, persistence, and research that has brought us here tonight."

Andro beamed. This was the first time Ablikim had referred to him as anything other than his assistant.

The woman side-eyed him. Apparently deciding he must be okay, she asked, "Will you be spending the night or—"

Ablikim didn't let her finish. "I'm afraid not. As I mentioned, our mission is urgent, and I could only secure a three-day pass. We mustn't waste any time getting to the Last Library. I need to speak with Daro."

Andro looked at the old man. It was dark. His feet hurt, and they'd already come so far.

"Our final destination is on the far side of the mountain. We have a ways to go yet," Ablikim said, answering the question Andro hadn't asked.

Andro couldn't imagine the hulking agent at the gate was about to let them back out into the night. This was as far as their documents allowed them to go.

Nodding, Seda led them to the kitchen at the back of the house. She pulled a lantern off the wall, lit it, and handed it to Andro. Then she walked over to a tall cabinet.

Andro prayed it was full of food, but Seda did not open it. Instead, she pulled on the handle of a broom, leaning against the wall. The cabinet swung sideways like a large door, revealing the entrance to a tunnel.

Ablikim took the lantern from Andro and disappeared into the mountain. No matter how many he came across, Andro would never stop being surprised by secret doors.

Smiling knowingly, Seda gestured for Andro to follow. As soon as he was inside, she swung the cabinet shut behind them.

"Well, the only way out is through." Ablikim and the faint patch of lantern light were swallowed by the darkness.

The blackness felt claustrophobic, hopeless, and empty, like his nightmares where he stood staring into a silent, dark void. Andro was suddenly grateful he hadn't been tasked as a miner. Shivering, he raced to catch up to the old man.

"Drag your hand along the right wall," Ablikim instructed. "I want you to remember the way in case you ever need to come here without me."

Andro obeyed, though he wouldn't be caught dead in these tunnels alone. Every now and then, his hand would drag into the nothingness of a side passage. Each time, the skin crawled up his spine, and he'd yank his hand back, terrified some unseen monster was about to reach out and grab him.

"The fifth one, Andro. Remember that," Ablikim said, counting the opening as they walked.

"Fifth right," Andro repeated with a yawn.

Another turn. A ladder. A rickety bridge over a bottomless gap. Andro's brain was far too tired to remember. The passage led steadily up, the air getting warmer and drier as it rose.

"What is this place?" Andro's words, though spoken softly, bounced and echoed in the silence.

"Abandoned mine shafts," Ablikim replied. "The Bird has taken so much of this mountain it's practically hollow. These shafts have been long forgotten, making them the perfect place to hide our biggest secret."

They walked for hours, maybe more. In the nothingness, Andro lost all sense of time and space. His feet hurt, and his legs ached. He fell farther and farther behind the light.

"Andro, keep up!" Ablikim barked. "If I lose you in here, I'll never find you again."

Just when Andro felt he couldn't possibly take another step, Ablikim stopped. They'd reached a dead end. In front of them, a wall of rock, four men wide and twenty feet high, blocked the way.

"We must have taken a wrong turn," Andro said with a groan as Ablikim fumbled in the dim light ahead of him.

"Don't be ridiculous," he muttered. "I may be old, crippled, and half-blind, but I'm not senile. Not yet, at least. Now, where is it? Ah, yes."

Ablikim stuck his hand in a square hole half-hidden behind a large rock. The wall groaned, shuddered, and turned sideways. Light poured out from the other side.

Andro blinked. After so much darkness, it took his eyes a moment to adjust to the brilliant light. Rows of stone-carved shelves stretched into the distance.

When his eyes had fully adjusted, he realized the light wasn't as bright as he'd first thought. Instead, it came from dim torches lining the long rock walls and the soft glow of candelabras hanging overhead. Long narrow shafts of moonlight hit the floor at regular intervals.

Andro half expected it to be morning; it had taken them so long to get there.

"Welcome to the Last Library, Andro," Ablikim murmured.

A thin man with a long white beard drifted up one of the aisles. His blue robes kissed the polished stone floor. When he saw Ablikim and Andro, he stopped dead in his tracks. He was easily as old as Ablikim, though time had been kinder to him.

Ablikim? The man mouthed the word as if looking at a ghost.

"Ablikim, old friend!" he continued heartily, finding his voice. "It's been so many long years. What brings you to the Last Library at this late hour? I thought we agreed…"

"Daro," Ablikim said, embracing his friend, "I've come on urgent business, or I wouldn't have come at all. The boy has discovered something that may be a game-changer. I need to find a specific record book, though not at this hour. We've walked all day and most of the night, and I'm afraid I couldn't see straight now, even if I wanted to."

Daro looked at Andro as if noticing him for the first time.

"Andro, this is Daro Jira, keeper of the Last Library and one of the last monks of the ancient Order of Videt Mountain," Ablikim said. "Daro, this is Andro Ilham. He has proven himself trustworthy. I would not have brought him otherwise."

"Very well." Daro eyed Andro as suspiciously as Seda had. "Perhaps you'll share your urgent business over dinner, then we'll find a place for you to lay your weary heads."

Daro led Ablikim and Andro to the outer wall of the cavernous room and down a long hallway. Taking the third door on the right, Andro found himself in a grand but sparse dining room lit by a roaring fire burning from within a massive stone fireplace. Along either side of the fireplace, moonlight drifted in through long open slats. *Fresh air!* Without thinking, Andro walked around the wooden table, stuck his head through one, and breathed deep.

The stuffy mine shafts had led them to the top of the mountain, the cliff beneath the long narrow windows dropping thousands of feet to the valley floor. Andro pulled his head in enough to feel safe but not so far as to block his view of the moon.

Andro had only ever seen the glow of the moon through the smog over the city. He hadn't realized it was so solid, round, or bright. It was the most beautiful thing he'd ever seen. A handful of lights sparkled like candles across the night sky. Turning to ask what they were, he found Ablikim and Daro Jira deep in conversation.

While he'd been gawking at the moon, bowls of rice and

vegetables had appeared at the table. He ravenously wolfed his down. Every now and then, Andro would hear Ablikim say things like "magic chest" or "Clementine Lemons" and knew the old man must be filling the monk in on their story, but his brain was too tired to follow the conversation.

Stomach full, Andro lay on the floor next to the fireplace and was asleep before his eyes had fully closed.

When he awoke, large drops of rain were falling outside the window. Although someone had placed a bowl of rice and a cup of tea on the table next to where he'd fallen asleep, Andro found himself alone.

"Hello?" he called, but there was no answer.

Andro gulped down his breakfast. He wasn't sure what time it was or how long he'd been asleep. He figured Ablikim was already up, combing the library for the record book they'd come to find. He was annoyed the old man hadn't woken him so he could help. They had so little time!

After licking his bowl clean, Andro hopped out of his chair and headed to the library.

In the daylight, he could see the nearest wall had tall narrow slats that ran from floor to ceiling and opened to the outside world, much like the dining room had. Looking out, Andro hoped to see the mysterious twinkling lights he'd seen the night before, but a white mist hung like curtains, obscuring the sky.

The library was not a part of the tunnel system but a natural cave. Stalactites hung like icicles from the ceiling. Andro watched, spellbound, as a single droplet of water landed with a splat on one of the jagged stalagmites jutting up from the floor. Giant candelabras hung from the invisible ceiling on chains as thick as an enforcer's arm. The light flickered between the rock icicles, casting ghostly shadows across the room.

Leaving the safety of the outer wall, Andro picked a row of books at random and wandered down the long aisle in search of Ablikim.

The patter of his feet echoed in the empty space. It seemed strange and wrong for all this knowledge to be secreted away where no one could use it. When he was done learning to read, Andro vowed to return to this place and read every single one.

Halfway down the seemingly endless aisle, he found a young woman standing at the top of a tall ladder, filing away a handful of books.

"Excuse me, have you seen Grandfather Ablikim this morning?" Andro asked cheerily.

The young librarian glanced down in surprise. In answer, she put her finger to her lips and pointed toward the end of the aisle. Andro bowed his head and walked on.

Where the long stone shelf ended, Andro had expected to find a wall. Instead, the cavern continued. Rows of half-carved shelves sat unfinished. The floor had not yet been polished smooth. A small spring dribbled through a crack in the ceiling, ran across the uneven floor, and disappeared out the last window.

Teetering stacks of books stood like mountain peaks beneath ratty canvas tarps. Other stacks stood uncovered. A half-dozen blue-robed librarians silently moved between the great mounds, documenting the titles. Hard at work, they did not acknowledge him as he silently passed by.

In daily life, Andro didn't speak much. He rarely had anything to say, and there was never anyone to listen anyway. Usually, he was not bothered by the silence, but in this cavern, he found he missed the chatter of birds and the sound of leaves rustling in the breeze.

Andro was starting to feel quite hopeless when he caught a glint of light shining like a beacon. Closing his eyes, he listened. But all he heard was the steady drip of water hitting cold stone. Still, where there was light, there was bound to be people!

Wading through the folds of a moldy tarp, he halted at the base of a monstrous stack of books. Daro Jiro stood atop the heap, silhouetted in the light of the oil lamp in his hand.

"Andro, my boy, so happy you could join us," he called. "Ablikim has filled me in on your story and persistence in finding answers. You'd make a good monk! I trust you found breakfast?"

"Yes, thank you." Voices had never sounded so sweet.

Ablikim's muffled voice drifted out through the cracks in the pile. "Good, you'll need that energy to help us search."

Trying not to cause an avalanche, Andro clambered to the top. Standing next to Daro, he looked down. This wasn't a mountain of books; it was a volcano. Ablikim stood at the bottom of the crater four feet below them. One by one, the old man inspected titles and, not finding what he was looking for, handed the unwanted books to Daro, who would stack them elsewhere.

"As you can see"—Daro gestured at the vast range of unshelved books—"my library is a work in progress."

"Andro, come!" Ablikim barked.

Andro scrambled into the pit. It wasn't wide, but there was enough room for them to stand comfortably. It reeked of mold and damp earth.

"You take that side"—Ablikim pointed behind them—"I'll take this side. That will speed this search up considerably."

"We are looking for this—" The old man held a piece of

parchment with the markings 1681 on it. "It will be here or here," he added, pointing to the spine and front cover of the book he held in his hand.

Afraid he'd forget what he was looking for and accidentally miss it, Andro kept one eye firmly on the parchment. Book after book flew up to Daro, but all they accomplished was digging a deeper crater.

"Are we sure it would be in this batch?" Ablikim asked when they'd handed up more than half the mountain.

"It could be in no other," Daro Jira responded. "If it's not here, it has been lost."

"Where did all these books even come from?" Andro picked up one that was damp to the touch.

"When the Mad Prince began his reign of terror, and the dynasty of the Black Peacock began," Daro answered after instructing a librarian to dry and preserve the damp book, "the monks were his greatest opposition. He relentlessly attacked the monasteries, burning them to the ground. For over a hundred years, the monks fought for their freedom and the freedom of the people. But eventually, they were too few in number to continue fighting. Those left were forced into hiding in caves and secret sanctuaries in the remotest parts of the mountains—anywhere they could find where they'd be safe from the Black Peacock. They took their books, as many as they could save, with them. I'm not sure how, but the books made their way here—first a few dozen, then a few dozen more. For many years, the monks sent out librarians to collect all the books they could find. As time passed, they found fewer and fewer. Now we mostly focus on preserving the ones we've got. Ablikim and I saved hundreds of books when we were wee boys. Ah, if only you had stayed, Ablikim."

"You two were friends when you were young?" Andro

stared at the back of the old man's head. It was hard to imagine he was ever young.

"Yes," Daro answered. "Ablikim and I grew up in one of the last hidden sanctuaries."

"Wait…so you're a monk too?" Andro asked Ablikim.

"Not exactly," Ablikim muttered. "When we were ten or so, the Black Army attacked the sanctuary in the dead of night. The monks were caught off guard. They thought the sanctuary was remote enough that the Bird would never find it. In the panic, the monks rounded up the youngest of us and locked us in the library. Daro and I were small for our age. We hid between the base of a statue and one of the thick stone walls. The memories after that come in flashes—people screaming, running, the clash of swords, flames leaping up the curtains. It got dreadfully hot. The next thing we knew, it was morning, and all that was left among the ashes, besides Daro and I, were a handful of books that hadn't been burned in the fire. We knew it was our duty to save them. Braving the hot coals still smoldering on the floor, we salvaged all we could. My feet haven't been the same since.

"When Daro and I learned of this place, we started bringing the books here. The librarians would feed us, so when we brought in the last of our own stash, we headed out in search of more. Eventually, we were asked to stay. It wasn't long before I got restless. I missed the open sky, green grass, and sounds above a murmured whisper. I left. Daro became a monk, I became a tinkerer, and that was that. Time is short, Andro. Keep searching."

Andro highly doubted "that was that." The more he learned about Ablikim, the more he wanted to know. But there wasn't time. Andro turned and got back to work.

Morning faded to afternoon. The hole grew, and the

unsearched stack dwindled.

"Aha!" Ablikim yelped triumphantly. "I've found it!"

He bent over and picked up the last book from the second to last stack. Its dark leather cover was ancient and fragile, the edges damp and black with mold. A thin layer of moss grew in the dip of the binding. The once-silver letters were so faint they were nearly illegible. Ablikim gently handed it to Daro.

"Looks like we found it just in time. Another year, and there would've been nothing left," Daro said as Ablikim and Andro squeezed back into the aisle.

They followed the monk to a long, hand-hewn table. With a feathery finger, he lifted the cover. The pages were moist, but they appeared legible. The three of them sighed in relief.

"We can't save them fast enough," Daro lamented. "We'll have to be as gentle as we can."

Ablikim sat in front of record book 1681. Pulling his spectacles out of his pocket, he peeled back the pages. Occasionally—as he searched for any mention of Princess Cyra, Prince Cetin, or the wooden chest—he would pause and grunt.

With each pause, Andro and Daro leaned forward in anticipation. But Ablikim only muttered a few words under his breath and continued on.

Andro sprawled on the table and stared into the darkness. The minutes ticked away in time with the hollow echo of dripping water. Stalactites were forming faster than time was moving. A bat fluttered out the open window and into the night. At this rate, he'd be as old as Ablikim before they found what they were looking for. Daro's eyes drooped, and he began to softly snore. Ablikim flipped on.

Andro was beyond bored and hungry. It had to be dinnertime, maybe later. He'd just gotten up to stretch his legs and see if he could find something to eat when Ablikim gasped and stopped turning pages altogether.

Andro anxiously peered over the old man's shoulder, but there was nothing to see besides text he could not read. Near the edges of the page, the words melted into damp swirls of dark ink; he hoped it still made sense.

His hunger forgotten, Andro plunked himself down and watched intently as the old man dragged his finger across the parchment below his bespectacled nose. Time stood still as he slowly flipped from one page to the next. Ablikim read until the text ran out. The rest of the book was blank.

Ablikim's hand reached from the empty pages to cover his open mouth. He looked at Andro, blinked, and then slowly looked at Daro.

"Daro…" he whispered.

Daro snored on.

"Daro, wake up!" Ablikim cried.

"Wha…?" Daro mumbled.

Ablikim shoved the record book under the monk's nose and pointed. Daro silently flipped the pages. The suspense was absolutely killing Andro! He needed to finish learning how to read. The monk looked up, his eyes wide in shock.

"The Stones…the Sword…" he muttered in a barely audible whisper. "I thought that was a myth but that would change…"

"Everything," Ablikim finished.

"What stones? What sword?" Andro yelped, tired of being ignored.

"Shhh, Andro." The monk put his fingers to his lips.

Ablikim gestured for Andro to move closer.

"This," he said in a voice barely above a whisper, "is the Order's record of the last days of the Emerald Empire. It recounts the story of the downfall of Emperor Aarav. The monks were, of course, correct in their suspicions about Cetin and Cyra. When the emperor sent the children to school, the monks continued to watch them. The older Princess Cyra got, the more her light shone. She was goodness personified. But light cannot exist without darkness. The people of Dohi began taking advantage of her kindness. They would not pay their taxes, stopped growing crops, and no one wanted to work. Chaos.

"Prince Cetin, on the other hand, had become increasingly dark and brooding. He loved to fight. He tortured small animals and worse. His teachers and fellow students feared him. Prince Cetin was sent home the summer of their sixteenth year, his teachers deeming him 'unteachable.' He begged his father for a position in the army. Proud his son was choosing to serve the Empire—and hopeful the discipline of a soldier would keep him in check—Emperor Aarav readily agreed. But Cetin wasn't concerned with serving the Empire. He had other aspirations—war, blood, terror. Darkness cannot exist without light. Chaos.

"Cetin was power-hungry. He poisoned the soldiers' minds, slowly turning them against the Emperor. He began treating his father's army as his own, leading unsanctioned raids against the unsuspecting townspeople of the more remote villages. When word got back to the emperor of his vial deeds, Prince Cetin would lie and say they were righting wrongs, restoring balance. The emperor was so preoccupied with keeping Princess Cyra from bankrupting Dohi with her kindness that he didn't argue. But deep in his heart, he feared the monks had been right all along. Perhaps his son was all yin. He began to listen to the whispers floating through his halls. Cetin had his sights set on the throne."

"Rule of the Emerald Empire was not passed from father to firstborn as it is now," Daro quietly cut in. "When the rule of one emperor ended, the monks were called upon to select the next. They scoured the Empire, testing likely prospects until they found someone with a perfect balance of qi. Cetin would never have been chosen to rule after his father."

Ablikim nodded. "Prince Cetin knew this, but it did not stop him from lusting after the emperor's position or the emperor's sword. Emperor Aarav knew if Cetin got his hands on the sword, he'd be unstoppable."

"Why? What was so special about the sword?" Andro asked.

"Beyond myth, nothing much is known about it," Daro Jiro answered. "According to legend, it was known as Zossimo, the Great Balancer. Within its hilt were four Stones handpicked by the monks to harness the power of the elements. It is said the might of the universe radiated from its steel. When wielded by an emperor of perfect qi, it restored peace and balance to the land."

Andro looked from Daro to Ablikim.

"Emperor Aarav's job was to keep the balance, to protect the people," Ablikim continued. "The emperor was getting old. His army was no longer under his command. He doubted he could defeat his young son in battle, even with the sword. The emperor sent word to the monks asking them to seek out his successor. The monks set to work immediately, scouring the land for someone capable of wielding the sword against the now-mad prince. This was a difficult task as everything had been thrown into chaos. Fearing they were out of time, the emperor called a secret meeting with Princess Cyra. Her unfaltering goodness was their only hope. Knowing she would stop at nothing to protect the people of Dohi, the emperor instructed her to hide the sword where Cetin would never be able to find it.

"When Cetin learned of what the emperor had done, he flew into a blind rage, killing his father on the throne. He spread lies across the kingdom that Cyra had murdered their father and stolen the sword for herself. Cetin poisoned the people's minds against her, and without her light to protect them, they were consumed by his darkness. The monks hid Cyra for as long as possible, but Cetin was out for blood. Towns and villages burned as he hunted Cyra and the sword. Cyra's heart broke as the people of Dohi cried for help, and the lands were laid to waste. She longed to run to them, to protect them. But she had promised her father she would keep the sword out of Cetin's reach, and she knew she must not break that promise.

"As long as the sword existed, Dohi would never be safe. But without the sword, Dohi stood no chance. With the Mad Prince on their doorstep, the princess instructed the monks to separate the Stones from the sword. It was agreed the monks would hide the sword—which was powerless without the Stones—somewhere safe. Meanwhile, Cyra would hide the Stones. They would reunite the sword and the Stones only when they'd found the emperor's successor. As Cetin and his army breached the monastery's gates, the monks pushed Princess Cyra and her wooden chest through a... I don't know exactly. The records say a 'portal,' but the only legible text after that is 'she is lost in time and space,' whatever that means.

"The rest did not go well, as we know from the scribbled notes in the earlier record book. The monastery was burned, and all the monk's technology was destroyed. Thus dawned the age of the Black Peacock under Emperor Cetin. The few monks who were left began searching for Cetin's chest so they could use it to contact Princess Cyra. Obviously, they were unsuccessful, and here we are, all these many years later."

The old man, the monk, and the boy sat in silence.

"Wait," Andro said, slowly piecing together what he'd just heard. "If Granny's magic chest was Prince Cetin's, that would mean the sor...scientist Clementine Lemons has Princess Cyra's chest."

The two men nodded.

"And if the monks built the chests with drawers that could hide away secrets, even from each other—" Daro continued.

"—then Clementine Lemons may very well have the lost Stones of Dohi," Ablikim finished.

"And if we had the lost Stones and the sword, we could..." Andro's jaw hit the floor.

CHAPTER 14

Clementine's map came back almost immediately, accompanied by a small, hand-drawn map showing the location of Dohi. Clem tried to match it to her map, like a puzzle piece, but it didn't fit anywhere. Dohi was a complete mystery.

A week passed with no new messages. Clem worried. Had she taken too long to answer? Was she too late? Had something terrible happened to Andro Ablikim? But then final exams started, and most of Clem's brainpower had been diverted from worrying about Andro to trying to remember everything she'd learned over the last year. How was she supposed to remember what she'd learned about plant biology in October? Why couldn't they ask what she'd worn for Halloween? That was easy; she'd gone as Adriana James. The only good thing about exams was they were followed by summer vacation. For two short months, Clem would be free to lie around and read as much as her mother would let her. Maybe she'd even figure out how the chest worked.

Clementine had no logical explanation for any of it, but she feared the strange chest a little less with each passing day. Like with a good book, she'd become addicted to the mystery of it.

Throwing a stack of textbooks and review materials on the desk, Clementine sat down to study. But first, she flipped open the lid, just in case.

Finally! She held the yellowed paper and read: *We need the Stones.*

Clem furrowed her eyebrows. *What Stones?* she wrote

back.

The lost Stones for making the sword powerful. In drawers? came an almost immediate reply.

Clem stared at the chest. She'd never considered the drawers might have something in them. With no keys, she'd assumed they were empty.

Picking the chest up with both hands, Clementine held it next to her ear and shook it. Was that…? She shook it harder. Yes, she could definitely hear something rattling around inside.

Drawers locked. Keys lost, she answered back.

Find the keys. Get the Stones.

Find the keys? The chest was at least a hundred years old, maybe older. The keys could be anywhere—a garbage dump, buried in the dirt, hidden in some elderly lady's closet. They might not be in Canada, maybe not even in North America. She didn't even know what they looked like. How was she supposed to find them?

Clementine pursed her lips and strummed her fingers on the top of her desk. She might not be the most intelligent person on the planet, but she could figure this out. Deep in thought, she pulled on one of the small drawer handles. It didn't budge. Laying her head on the desk, she examined the chest more closely. The seams were so perfect she couldn't even slip a piece of paper in the crack between the drawer and the chest. She stuck the tip of her pen in the keyhole and tried to turn it. It didn't budge. What she needed was to befriend a thief or… *A locksmith!* She needed a locksmith! Clementine grabbed the chest and headed for the door.

"I'm going to the library to study for finals," she yelled as the door slammed behind her. She couldn't exactly tell her dad she was off to find a locksmith. He'd have said no for sure.

But the library? The library was a free pass.

Clem rode the bus downtown and got off at the corner of Government and Fort.

Crossing the street, Clem headed in the direction of the wharf. It wasn't the closest locksmith to her house, but it had the best reviews. Halfway down the block, she spotted it: SMITH & COMPANY LOCK AND SAFE, SINCE 1916.

A bright neon sign in the window read, NO LOCK ON EARTH WE CAN'T OPEN. A flashing arrow underlining the letters pointed to the door. Clem smiled at the sign. *Keys? Who needs keys!* Impressed with herself, Clementine opened the door and stepped inside.

An antique safe sat unlocked in the corner, a boxy black-and-white TV on top of it. A retro, red plastic chair was wedged between the safe and the counter. The place had 1970s vibes, right down to the wood-paneled walls. The entire store could have fit in her bedroom. But then again, how much space did a locksmith need? Behind the counter, the back wall was covered with rows of uncut keys neatly hanging on pegboard. In the center of the wall, a partially closed door led into another room.

"Be right there," a friendly voice called from beyond.

Clementine set the chest on the counter next to the key cutter and absentmindedly perused the keys while she waited. There were a lot of different kinds. Which would be the magic key that opened her drawers?

"Well, hello there, little lady! What can I do for you today?" A cheerful locksmith with curly red hair beamed as she maneuvered her wheelchair out of the back room.

Clementine smiled back. "I need to get into these," she said, pointing to the drawers.

"Ah, lost the keys, did ya?" The locksmith chuckled.

Clementine shrugged. "Didn't come with any."

"Might be treasure in there!" The woman winked. "Well, you've come to the right place. No lock on Earth I can't get into! You want me to make some keys or just get 'em opened?"

"Opened is fine, thanks." Clementine doubted she had enough money for one key, let alone four.

"Well, give me a few days, and I'll crack 'em wide open for you!" The locksmith handed Clem a business card and a collection tag.

Being a rock and not a leaf was a lot easier than she'd thought. Now all she had to do was wait.

On Friday, Clem found herself back at Smith & Company, eagerly standing at the counter. She was already having a great day. The fuzzy caterpillar on Waxley's lip had actually curled into a smile when he marked her exam, so she knew she'd passed. The message from the locksmith, telling her to come and pick up the chest, was the icing on the cake.

"I've never seen anything like it." The woman set the chest on the counter. "It…it's incredibly well made. I don't know what mechanisms they used, but… I mean, I tried… Good lord, how I tried… Haven't done much else this week."

"So did you…" Clementine wasn't sure what the locksmith was getting at.

"Nope." The woman sighed in frustration. "I'm sorry, but nothing I've got will get in there, hun."

"But I thought there was no lock on Earth you couldn't…" Clem couldn't hide the disappointment in her voice.

"I'm so sorry. It was a first for me too, kid." The locksmith wrinkled her nose and shrugged. "I tried every trick in the book. That thing's sealed tighter than King Tut's crypt. Seem to have misplaced a set of lock-picking tools in the process."

Clem raised her eyebrows and tried not to laugh. She had a feeling she knew where the tools went.

"Well, thanks for trying," Clem sighed. "What do I owe you?"

"Nothing," the locksmith said, patting the top of the chest. "Couldn't get into it, so I don't feel right charging you."

Clem thanked the woman again. She heaved the chest off the counter and started heading for the door. Hand on the handle, she stopped and turned back toward the counter. "Can you at least tell me what you think the keys might look like?"

"I dunno. It's a pretty fancy box. I bet it has some pretty fancy keys," the locksmith answered. "If you ever get in there, stop by and let me know how you did it and if you found any treasure!"

"Guess I'm going to need a new sign," she added with a chuckle.

In between exams, Clementine did everything she could to open the chest. She pulled the keys out of every padlock she found in the garage, but none of them fit. She bought a bag of old keys from the antiques store and another from a thrift store. No luck.

Clem googled—and tried—every crazy suggestion for opening a lock without keys on the internet. If she heard "like and subscribe" one more time, she was going to lose her mind. Exhausted, she let her family take a whack at it.

Her dad took a pair of pliers and a screwdriver to it—then a saw. When the saw didn't make a dint, he threw his hands in the air and cried, "What kind of voodoo magic is this?"

Oh, if only he knew!

Her mom sprayed it with WD-40 and every other

"loosening" oil she could find beneath the sink. Coated in every weird-smelling, clothes-staining lubricant they owned, she shrugged and said, "Well, I'm out of ideas."

Desperate, Clem had even let Fergus drop it out of his bedroom window. "Weird. That usually works on anything" was his only response when they retrieved the chest from the backyard, only to discover it didn't have so much as a scratch on it.

And the notes kept coming.

You to find keys?

No. Still looking.

She wished Andro understood how hard she was trying. She'd been so preoccupied with finding the keys she'd woken up on Monday morning and made it halfway down the block before remembering school had ended the previous Friday. That was huge because, besides Halloween, the first day of summer break was Clementine's favorite day of the year. She'd had it all planned out. She was going to sleep in, start a new book, and eat breakfast for lunch. But then, she'd stayed up so late Sunday trying to pry one of the drawers open that she'd forgotten to turn off her alarm. On Monday morning, she'd hit snooze twice, freaked out because she'd slept in, then ran out the front door with her empty backpack screaming about how she was going to be late for her English final. Clem was halfway to the bus stop before her dad caught her and asked where she was going.

Did you to find them?

No.

Did you to find them?

Still no. I promise I'll tell you as soon as I do.

It to be okay. We still must to find the sword. Also is lost.

What sword? Clem wondered. How could stones possibly

make a sword powerful? It didn't seem logical, but then again, she had a magic box that randomly received messages from a stranger who lived in a country that didn't exist. So, what did she know?

Please to keep looking urgently.

Clementine turned the last note into a paper airplane and sent it sailing out the window. She gave up. This was why people chose to be leaves and not stones because even when you tried to make waves, life had a way of saying no anyway. Why did she bother listening to the crazy Professor in the first place? It was pretty obvious he didn't have his life together. What kind of waves did he think he was making out on the streets yelling nonsense to random strangers? Sighing, Clem slammed the lid of the chest shut and marched downstairs.

"Why so sour, Lemons?" her dad asked as she moped around the kitchen. "You still trying to get into that voodoo box to find some treasure?"

"Nope," Clem said, pouting. "I've given up."

"Figures," Fergus muttered under his breath. "Clementine Lemons, the great giver-upper. If giving up was a sport, you'd be a world-class athlete."

"When I'm stuck on a problem, you know what I find helps?" Her dad swatted Fergus on the head. "Giving my mind a break. It's a beautiful day. Why not go outside and play with your friends?"

"Yeah, Clem… Go outside…and play…with your friends." Fergus snorted.

Clementine narrowed her eyes, but she had to admit, it was pretty funny how out of touch her dad could be. She hadn't "played outside with her friends" since she was nine. He was, however, right. She needed a distraction.

Clem met Maddie and Brook downtown. If anyone could

lift her spirits, it was them.

"How about that couple?" Brook asked.

They were sitting by the harbor, inventing backstories for tourists. It was one of their favorite summer games.

"American. Definitely American. I want to say, Californian? He's one hundred percent a lawyer for the mafia. At least he was," Maddie answered. "She started out as an undercover agent for the CIA, but then she fell in love with him. You don't just leave the mob. Or the CIA. So, they skipped the border, and now they're in hiding. Mexico was closer, but they didn't speak Spanish. That complicated things. They're on a watch list. They couldn't fly. So, they stole a sailboat and came here. They don't know it yet, but their dog's an informant. I mean, look how shifty he is. No, actually, he's a hitman for the mob. He wants out too, but he's addicted to Milk-Bones, so the mob has him right where they want him. If he wants to keep getting the treats, he has to do the job. He's going to eat them in their sleep when they least expect it. It'll be a total bloodbath."

Clem looked at the little mop wriggling around the woman's four-inch heels and burst out laughing.

"We need to stop." Clem rubbed her cheeks. "My face hurts from laughing so hard."

"Yeah, mine too," Brook said. "And I'm hungry. Let's go find some food."

"Wait. Didn't we used to come here, like, every year for your birthday?" Maddie pointed to a busy-looking restaurant as they wandered through Chinatown.

"Bǎoshí!" Clem cried. "I totally forgot about this place! They have the best Donut Chicken!"

For years, Bǎoshí had been her favorite place to eat. Every

year for her birthday, this was where Grandma Eloise would bring her, Maddie, and Brook for lunch. Clem always ordered Donut Chicken, which is what she'd called orange chicken when she was little.

"I miss your grandma," Maddie said.

"Me too." Clem frowned.

"Me three," said Brook. "Should we?"

As the three of them squeezed into a cramped booth near the back of the restaurant, Clementine remembered why she loved Bǎoshí so much. Ornate paper lanterns with long red tassels hung low from the ceilings. The dark wood booths were carved with lions, tigers, and dragons. The walls were covered in murals depicting life in ancient China and ancient Chinese legends. It was like visiting a foreign country without ever leaving the city.

While they waited for lunch, Clementine examined the section of the mural behind their table. She hadn't been here for so long; it was like seeing it again for the first time. On the far end was a jade-green forest surrounded by tiny gold hummingbirds. Fierce jaguar-like creatures with crimson red eyes lurked behind the trees. The forest melded into a great sea, its surf lapping against the ceiling. All sorts of ships—Clementine imagined they were pirate ships—climbed the steep blue waves. At the other end, a vast desert dotted with oases and canyons melted into a snowy arctic scene that ended at the foot of a volcano. The volcano jutted fiercely into a jet-black sky. Wrapped around the volcano, a fire-breathing dragon spewed flames across the ceiling.

Above their table was a village. The village was Clementine's favorite part. She looked at the men pulling carts down narrow streets lined with tile-roofed houses. Children played with dogs in the streets. In the center of the town was a well. Next to the well stood a girl with long black hair. Clementine hadn't noticed it before, but the girl's clothes were much fancier than anyone else's. In her hands, she held a chest. The chest seemed oddly familiar.

Clementine jumped on the booth and looked closer. *It couldn't be.* In her hands, she wasn't holding *any* chest—she was holding *her* chest! It was unmistakably her chest! At the girl's feet was a set of keys.

"Clementine!" Brook yelped. "What are you doing? Oh my god, sit down!"

Clementine turned around. Everyone in the restaurant was staring at her. The manager, a dad-aged man in a black dress shirt, worked his way toward their table. Clementine froze.

"There's a lot of detail in that mural. Glad to see you're enjoying it," he said, smirking.

"Do you know who this is?" Clementine pointed at the girl with the chest.

"I don't," the man admitted, "but that particular mural happens to be my grandmother's favorite. She is well-versed in the legend it depicts. She's here this afternoon. I bet she'd happily come and talk your ear off about it if you'd like."

Clem nodded enthusiastically.

"It's a long story, though, so you may want to sit for it," he said, chuckling.

Clementine sunk back into her seat.

"You're unbelievably weird." Maddie laughed. "But at least you're never boring."

The manager's grandmother hobbled out at the same time lunch arrived.

"I hear you girls are interested in my mural." The woman gracefully swept her hands toward the wall. "At home, I have this exact scene in a woven tapestry my mother brought with her when she came here from China. My grandson says it's far too old and valuable to be hanging in the restaurant, so I had a replica of it painted on the wall. It's one of my favorite stories. Seeing it here makes my heart happy. It is The Story of the Lost Princess.

"A long time ago, the people of the river village of Shendu were going about their day when a young woman appeared—*as if by magic*—next to the village well. At first, the villagers were scared of this mysterious stranger, but the girl radiated love and light, so they did not fear her for long. A brilliant storyteller, she would often sit beneath the cherry trees and regale the people with stories of exotic lands and the bizarre and wondrous things she'd seen there.

"It was said that before she appeared at the well, she was a princess, the daughter of a fair and beloved emperor. The emperor was murdered by the princess's evil twin brother, but not before their father entrusted the princess with the most important of tasks. She was to hide the Empire's most sacred possession—four Stones of unimaginable power—from her brother so the people might be saved from his darkness. Knowing her brother would leave no rock unturned in his quest to find the Stones, the princess traveled to the farthest reaches of the farthest lands. Enlisting the help of friends she met along her journey, she hid the Stones where her brother would never be able to find them."

The woman gestured toward the forest. "To the feathered of the great forests, she entrusted the Earth Stone. They, more than any, valued the earth, for it was their sanctuary. First and foremost, a place to roost and rest."

Pointing toward the sea, she continued. "To the seafarers, she entrusted the Wind Stone, for, without the winds that carried them along, they were nothing."

She pointed at the desert. "To the nomads of the desert, she entrusted the Water Stone, for only those who had truly thirsted understood the importance of a single drop of water."

She pointed at the volcano and the night sky. "And to those cast into eternal darkness, she entrusted the Fire Stone that it may serve as a symbol of hope in their darkest hours.

"From each place, she took a special token as a guide—a clue—to the location of each Stone and locked it away in her royal chest so that, one day, she might reclaim the Stones and return home.

"Many long days and nights, the princess waited for her people to come for her. Days turned to months and months to years. But no one came for the lost princess. The princess kept to herself, tucked away in a hut on the outskirts of the village. It was, she told the villagers, for their own good. This, they did not understand, for they considered her to be good luck. In her presence, the crops grew better than ever, brilliant new things were invented, and trade improved. Shendu prospered all the years of her life, and there was great peace. As much as she loved the villagers, to her final breath, the princess never stopped hoping to return to her people. When she died, a great sorrow came over the land. It is said even the heavens wept on that sad day."

"What kind of tokens? Are the Stones still hidden out there, waiting to be found?" Clementine wondered aloud. If she could find the keys and get the clues to Andro, would he be able to find the Stones all these centuries later?

"It's a story, Clem," Maddie said, shaking her head.

"But it isn't the whole story." Clementine's mind was racing.

"Yes," the woman said, nodding in Clem's direction, "I thought that too. It needs an ending. Personally, I think it's the greatest unfinished story ever told."

As the woman shuffled back into the kitchen, Clementine stood back up in the booth and snapped a photo of the Lost Princess. Then she snapped another of the keys, lying in the dirt at the princess's feet.

"Apparently, Clem, *You will soon be embarking on a grand adventure.*" Brook tossed a broken fortune cookie on Clementine's empty plate.

"That's nice…" Clem muttered absentmindedly. She wasn't listening. She was staring at the photo of the keys on her phone.

She needed to finish this story. She needed to find the keys. And now, finally, she had an idea of what she was looking for.

CHAPTER 15

Clementine reread the long letter she'd written. She needed Andro to know what she knew. She needed him to understand finding the keys and the Stones wouldn't be as easy as simply opening drawers. What kind of tokens, she wondered, were in there? She hoped, together, they'd be able to decipher whatever the clues meant. Clem worried about what the "farthest reaches of the farthest lands" meant. It wasn't like she could jet off to Antarctica or Africa. Maybe Andro could, though.

Focus. One thing at a time.

Clem glanced back at the paper in her hands and hoped Andro could understand it. English was clearly not his first language. She wished she knew what language they spoke in Dohi, so she could try to translate it. All his responses had been short and to the point, like they'd been translated by hand, so she was pretty sure they didn't have internet in Dohi. Clem printed off some photos she'd taken of the mural and set them in the box with the note. Maybe they'd help him understand.

Satisfied she'd explained things the best she could, Clementine got to work joining vintage-key collector forums and scouring the internet for her keys. If they were out there, she would find them.

Clem scrolled back to the images she'd taken at the restaurant. If the actual keys looked anything like these, they'd be unmistakable. The head of the keys fanned out in what looked like green and blue peacock feathers. The rest of the key was gold, though she hoped it wasn't real gold because she wouldn't be able to afford them if they were. The part that slipped into the locks, which she'd learned was called a bit, looked weird too. There was no way to know for sure, but based on the size of the chest, Clem figured the keys were about the length of her pinky.

In the mural, all four keys hung together on a gold loop. Could they still be together after all these years? Somehow, she doubted it.

Clem enlarged the image and posted "in search of" ads in every key forum she found. It was strange how many people were into collecting antique keys.

The sun was already coming up when Clementine fell into bed, exhausted. She was determined to do this every night for as long as it might take.

It was noon when Clem rolled over and, bleary-eyed, grabbed her phone off the nightstand. She had almost a hundred notifications. Clem scrolled.

Wow, that's a beautiful key.

I hope you find it.

That looks fake. No key looks like that. Troll.

Clem rolled her eyes.

Wow, cool key.

Can I buy that from you?

Clem rolled her eyes again.

Hope you find it.

I think I have one of the keys you're searching for. I messaged you.

Clem's heart skipped a beat. Could it be? Had she already found one?

Opening her messages, she discovered a photo of a real-life version of her key. She gulped, her fingers trembling as she typed. *Would you be willing to sell it? If so, how much?*

It's my favorite key. Why do you want it?

Clem snapped a photo of the chest and sent it back. *Because I think I have the chest it belongs to, and I'm dying to see what, if anything, is in the drawers.*

No way, mate! Cool bananas. Yeah, I'd be willing to part with it for the right price.

In an instant, Clementine transferred all the money she'd ever saved—along with her allowance for the foreseeable future—to a woman in New Zealand. Now all she had to do was wait.

Thus began the longest ten days of her life. Clem obsessively tracked the package from Kerikeri to Auckland (where, in her opinion, it stopped for entirely too long).

Andro wasn't helping. Every day since she'd sent him a postcard of New Zealand saying she'd found the first key and it was coming by airmail, Andro would ask, *You have?* She was tired of having to tell him no.

After a week, it popped up in Vancouver. Three days later, and the tracking location hadn't budged.

"Why is Customs taking so long to inspect my package? It's a key!" Clem groaned. "I could have swum to Vancouver and back already!"

She needed to get outside. She needed fresh air. Texting Maddie and Brook to meet her at the beach, she headed out the front door.

Clementine wandered back around dinnertime, her pockets full of beach glass and bits of broken shell. Her mom stood in the kitchen, stirring a pan of sauce. When she saw Clem, she set the ladle on the counter and picked up a small yellow envelope.

"Look what came in the mail for you this afternoon." She waved the package in the air.

Clem had been annoying her family with package updates every five minutes since she'd asked for the advance on her allowance. She was sure her mom's joy had nothing to do with the package and everything to do with not having to listen to Clem whine "Why isn't it here yet?" twenty-nine times a day.

Snatching the envelope from her mom's hand with an excited "thanks" and a quick kiss, Clementine turned and ran up the stairs.

"Dinner's in ten minutes!" her mom called behind her. "So, see if it fits your box *quickly*."

Clem hadn't told her parents the real reason she needed the key. She used the same "maybe there's treasure" reason the locksmith had used. They were just happy she'd found a hobby to spend her summer obsessing over. Her mother had even complimented her "dedication and diligence," which was a first.

Ah, my baby's growing up, she'd said, which had made Clem want to barf.

Shutting her bedroom door behind her, Clementine tore into the envelope, which fell to the floor, forgotten.

"I am a rock!" she squealed triumphantly, holding the key in the air.

It was lovely. When she held the lacquered head and turned the stem, the bit fanned out in an arc, like a peacock's tail. She turned it back, and all the pieces lined up again like a regular old key. No wonder the locksmith hadn't been able to open the chest.

"She took a special token as a guide—a clue—to the location of each Stone and locked it away in her royal chest," Clementine sang to herself. She stared at the chest of drawers, then at the key in her hand. *What did that even mean?*

Clem gingerly inserted the key into the first lock. Taking a deep breath, she cautiously gave it a turn. Nothing.

She slid the key into the second lock; it turned with surprising ease. Clem hesitated.

What would she find in there? And would she be smart enough to figure out what it meant? She'd never been good at puzzles or brainteasers.

"Be the rock, not the leaf. Be the rock, not the leaf. All you have to do is make the waves. You are a rock," Clem whispered to herself.

Exhaling, she gave the key grip a firm tug. The drawer was open; there was no going back.

Peering inside, Clementine could see a small figurine in the shape of a bird.

Lifting the little green bird out of its nest in the drawer, she turned it around in the palm of her hand. She was probably the first person to have held it in hundreds of years, maybe even since the princess had locked it away.

It was unmistakably a hummingbird and, on closer inspection, appeared to be a flute. The tail feathers folded in on each other, forming a mouthpiece. Three small holes ran straight down its tiny body toward a long, thin beak, at the end of which was another hole. The wings, outstretched in flight, curved slightly upward at the tips. It hadn't always been green but had been tarnished with age. Here and there, a fiery glint of orange copper still shone brightly.

It reminded Clem of the hummingbird that occasionally hovered outside her bedroom window. She could never figure out why he visited—there were no flowers in their front yard—but it made her happy every time he showed up. The fact this token was a hummingbird had to be a good omen!

Flipping the figurine on its back, Clementine ran her fingertip across the bumpy underside of the wings. If it held a clue, it wasn't obvious. Holding the bird by the tail, she bent her head for a closer look.

Had Clementine not been so focused on the little flute in her hand, perhaps she'd have noticed the clatter of her mother making dinner in the kitchen fade away—replaced first by silence and then by the sweet whistle of a distant songbird. Had she not been so mesmerized by the sudden bursts of copper shining brightly in the light as she twirled the tiny bird in the air, perhaps she'd have noticed, where her bed once stood, a spring now bubbled, deep and black, from beneath the gnarled roots of an ancient tree. Or that under her feet, a lush carpet of brilliant green moss had replaced her shaggy rug. Maybe she'd have seen the pair of piercing green eyes watching silently from a nearby branch.

Had she not bent her head for a closer look, maybe, just maybe, she'd have seen the large shadow circling overhead. Or heard the sudden whoosh of outstretched wings.

Perhaps, had she not been so focused on unlocking the secrets of her newfound trinket, she'd have had time to run…

PART TWO

CHAPTER 16

Clementine shrieked, a bloodcurdling cry she was sure the entire city heard. From behind, a vicious laugh crawled up her neck and echoed in her ears.

"Oh my god, I'm going to kill you, Fergus!" She tried to shrug him off. "Not cool!"

Clem hadn't even heard him come in. She hated it when he didn't knock. When he let go, she was going to punch him in the face. Well, maybe not the face, but she was definitely going to punch him. *What a jerk.*

Clementine slapped at her shoulder, trying to make him loosen his grip, but what she felt was cold and scaly and definitely not her brother's hand. Clem's hair stood on end. Her gaze crept toward her shoulder. Long black talons attached to brown claw-like feet—half-human, half-bird— dug deep into her skin. Clem's eyes inched their way up… Tufts of short black feathers protruded from a thick leg. Beyond that, trees, limbs, green. Hands trembling, she grasped the flute as tightly as she could.

What was this thing? Her breathing came fast and shallow. Where was she? She felt weak at the knees. How did she get here? Frantically, she looked for an escape, for something to grab on to. But everything was swirling and floating. She felt nauseous. In a rush of air, they broke through the forest canopy. Clementine's feet dangled into nothing.

"Oh god, I'm about to be dinner," Clem said, panicking. It figured. This was her kind of luck.

What had she been thinking? She wasn't a rock. She wasn't meant to make waves. She was just Clementine…a leaf adrift in an ocean far too big to navigate.

Clem screamed and wriggled and swung at her captor. If she was about to be dinner, she was at least going to put up a fight.

"You want down, Wingless? Alright, if you insist…" a voice taunted from above. The talons unclenched.

Clementine shrieked as she plummeted back to the earth.

A blur of feathers and another creature swooped in and grabbed her.

"What are you doing in our forest, Wingless?" this one snarled, flinging Clem high in the air.

"Yeah, Wingless, you get lost? What's wrong, couldn't see the forest for all those trees?" Another set of talons wrapped tightly around her waist. "Here, let's get you a better view."

Circling higher and higher, Clementine watched as the forest became nothing more than a distant sea of emerald. She blinked, willing herself not to pass out.

The sky erupted in cackling laughter, like hungry seagulls mocking a child for dropping its ice cream in the sand—only worse.

"What's the matter, Wingless? Can't you fly?" the voice overhead taunted. Clementine tried to wriggle around to get a better view of her attacker.

"Let it go, Falk!" a female voice cried out. *Boom!* Something collided with them, an explosion of black and red feathers spreading like fireworks over Clem's head. They drifted back toward the earth, something, someone, hot on their heels.

"'Leave the Wingless alone, Falk. Don't hurt it.' Ugh, you're no fun, Ravi. I guess I should go ahead and put it back where I found it, then?" Her captor released their grip. "Don't worry, Wingless, you'll find the ground eventually. Your kind is good at that."

Clem screamed.

"Have a nice flight…"

Clementine was in free fall. In ultra-slow motion, individual treetops appeared below. Branches. Moss. Ground.

This was going to hurt.

Clem did the only thing she could think of. She closed her eyes and quoted *The Wizard of Oz*: "There's no place like home. There's no place like home. There's no place like…"

Landing with a soft thud in a pile of down, she laughed. Had that actually worked? No way! Was it possible Dorothy really had gone to the Land of Oz? No, that was ridiculous. She had to be dreaming.

"Are you alright, Wingless?" a voice cooed from above.

Winded, Clem lay there with her eyes closed, thinking about how to answer. She wiggled her toes and fingers. They all seemed to work. Her back and shoulders ached like a cougar had clawed her skin off, but at least she wasn't splattered all over the ground.

"Yeah, I think so." Groaning, she opened her eyes and rolled into a seated position. "Thanks, I—"

Clementine stopped midsentence. Two human-sized feet stood planted on the ground before her, only they weren't feet. They were talons, like the ones that had dug into her shoulders. The weird, scaly, half-human, half-bird feet ended in a puff of black feathers where a human ankle should be. Terrified, Clementine crept backward until she bumped into a tree trunk. Feeling braver with her back protected, she raised her eyes, petrified at what she might find attached to the feet.

Halfway up the creature's calf, the feathers ended as

abruptly as winter boots. Wait, were those human legs? Clementine felt a wave of relief wash over her at the sight of something familiar. She looked up. Half-hidden behind a poof of curly gold and black hair, brilliant green eyes watched her. She was staring into the face of a girl not much older than herself. Her high cheekbones, long curved nose, and the way her head sat alert, yet graceful, on her slender neck reminded Clementine of a bird. Across her cheekbones and in the center of her forehead, patches of tiny black feathers glistened in the light.

Forgetting the girl's talons, Clem smiled. Hopping up, she stretched out her hand in greeting. As if frightened by Clem's sudden movement, the girl stretched a set of giant wings and fluttered out of reach.

She knew it wasn't nice to stare, but Clem was spellbound by the iridescent blue, purple, and green shimmering through the long jet-black feathers. What was she? Some sort of forest fairy? No, fairies didn't have feathers.

"Whoa, are you an angel?" Clementine stammered. As it dawned on her what that meant, she squealed in horror, "Oh my god, did I die?!"

There was no way, right? There was no such thing as angels or fairies or…or… Where was she? How had she even gotten here? This had to be a dream. Yes. She must've fallen asleep waiting for the key and dreamed of unlocking the drawer and finding the hummingbird flute. But it all felt so real.

Clem looked at her hand. Her fist was clenched so tightly that her knuckles had turned white. Her nails dug bloody holes in her palms. Unclenching her fist, Clem stared at the tiny hummingbird and gasped. This wasn't a dream.

Had the token the princess hidden away been more of a portal than a clue? No. That was ridiculous. But then again, the princess had appeared at the well "as if by magic" from…from where? Dohi? Where was Dohi anyway? Was it on a different planet? Impossible. This had to be a dream. But what if it wasn't? How was she supposed to get home? She couldn't die here, could she?

"Oh…no, no, no, no… What have I done? I don't know enough about any of this to be here."

She felt sick. Why had she opened the drawer? Her head spun. She was as lightheaded as when she'd been falling through the air. The trees closed in. The giant forest felt too small, too tight. The air felt thick. Breathing was like sucking ice cream through a straw.

Clementine sunk into the soft green moss. Dropping her head on her knees, she tried to catch her breath. Wave after wave of overwhelming panic washed over her. She breathed deeply and stared at the copper flute in her hand, wishing it would disappear, and she'd wake up in her bed.

"Are you alright, Wingless?" the girl asked again. "Sorry about Falk. He can be…well, Falk. I'm Raveen, by the way."

"Um, I'm Clementine. Clementine Lemons." Clem looked up. "Excuse me, but where are we?"

"Aww, are you lost, Wingless?" Raveen asked playfully as if this were somehow funny.

"You have no idea…" Clem exhaled. "Do you know how to get to Dohi?"

"Dohi?" Raveen was smiling, but there was a coolness in her piercing gaze. "Never heard of it. Is that one of your river villages or mountain villages?"

"It's a…" Clementine was about to say *country*, but something stopped her. "River village," she finished, though she wasn't sure why.

Raveen cocked her head to the side and stared at her for an

uncomfortably long time. It was hard to guess exactly what this winged girl was thinking, but Clementine got the distinct feeling she knew more than she was letting on.

"Well, the river is pretty far from here." She pointed downhill behind Clem's head and added, "That way."

Clementine looked for a landmark, but all she could see were the enormous trunks of trees the size of skyscrapers.

Raveen reached out and helped Clem to her feet. As she shakily returned to standing, the hummingbird slipped from her grasp and landed on the moss between them.

"Augh, could I be any worse at this?" Clementine muttered.

Before she could retrieve it, Raveen scooped up the flute. Holding it by its long narrow beak, she twirled it in front of her face.

"Give it back!" Clem demanded. Her words echoed off the trees and bounced high into the canopy. The birds stopped chirping. The forest fell silent. Clem didn't mean to sound so harsh or demanding, but this little flute was her only tie to home. She couldn't lose it.

"Kei'hea mana ko'e whi'a tenia…" Raveen sang, bird-like.

Clementine's eyes widened. *What was that?* Raveen continued as if this were completely normal. As if she had always spoken like this.

Clementine reached out her hand, palm upward, silently demanding the hummingbird back. Their eyes locked. For a brief moment, she didn't think Raveen was going to return it. But then, to her relief, Raveen cocked her head to the side and handed it back with a smile.

"Where did you get that, Wingless?" Raveen asked. "I only ask because…"

Clementine let the hummingbird slip through her fingers.

"…i…whakao i'kwha'a…"

She picked the hummingbird back up.

"…seen one like it before. They're extremely old—ancient even—and very rare."

Clementine looked at the hummingbird. Oh great, not only was it her only connection to home, but somehow it seemed to act as a translator. Any hope of figuring out where she was or how to get home would be gone if she lost it.

"You say you've seen one of these before?" Clutching the flute as tightly as she could, Clem thrust her hand into her pocket.

"I have," Raveen said, smiling. "It's getting dark, and you're obviously lost. Why don't you follow me home and you can ask my father to tell you all about them? He knows a lot more about these things than I do."

"That would be great!" Clementine smiled, adding, "Oof, this is all too much," under her breath.

"Too much what?"

"It's nothing." Clem stopped. She hadn't thought she'd said it loud enough to be heard. "It's been a weird day."

"That's an understatement," Raveen called back as she turned and flitted deeper into the forest.

Clementine followed behind, contemplating the enormity of her situation.

CHAPTER 17

The trees towered overhead, snagging the clouds and dragging them toward the earth in long, misty tendrils. Even the giant cedars of Vancouver Island seemed small in comparison. Peeking through the dense canopy, the late-afternoon sun cast a magical glow on the mutant ferns and mushrooms growing beneath the ancient giants. Clementine ran a finger along the curved spine of a mighty fern frond and watched with delight as it curled shut at her touch. With each step, the moss sunk, pillowy soft beneath her feet.

Monster butterflies fluttered in and out of the thin rays of light, the patterns of their wings an ever-changing kaleidoscope of color. The chorus of a million birds wafted from high in the canopy, filling the empty spaces between the trees with song.

Clementine wondered if it was birdsong or if, hidden in the leaves and branches, more people like Raveen were watching, whispering about her in their singsong language. Or maybe, they were preparing to swoop down and eat her for dinner.

"You Wingless are impossibly slow," Raveen complained. "It's a wonder you get anything done in a day."

"You could try walking, so I could keep up," Clementine said, trying not to sound annoyed as she struggled to climb over a massive root.

"Walking is for Wingless." Raveen perched on a mossy rock and stroked her feathers. "If the gods wanted me to walk, they wouldn't have blessed me with wings."

Sliding down the rough bark, Clementine face-planted in

the dirt. This sent Raveen into a fit of laughter.

The more Raveen talked about how great she was for "being blessed" with wings, the more Clementine wanted to slap the perpetual smirk off her face. With each step forward, Clem questioned whether she should keep following this girl. There was something about Raveen that seemed off. But then again, Clem had no idea where she was, and the only other "people" she'd met had sent her skydiving without a parachute. It wasn't like she had options.

The forest shadows deepened. The birdsong faded to deathly silence with the last rays of light. In the day, the forest had seemed so magical. In the darkness, it seemed nightmarish. Clementine shivered.

Clem wished she had a light source, her phone, a backpack, or anything really. As she stumbled along in the twilight, she was grateful she hadn't taken her shoes off at the door like she was supposed to. She may be horribly unprepared, but at least she wasn't barefoot.

"Hurry up, Wingless," Raveen whined from ahead. "It's almost dark. You don't want to be eaten, do you?"

Eaten?! Tossing a terrified glance over her shoulder, Clem hurried toward Raveen's voice.

In the distance, orbs of faint light twinkled like fireflies in the treetops. If the butterflies were the size of dinner plates in this strange land, how big were the fireflies? Were they carnivorous? Clem prayed there weren't spiders lurking about.

When she dared look up, Clementine was relieved to see the faint outline of brightly lit houses, not the giant flesh-eating bugs she'd imagined. Blue, green, and yellow light illuminated the still forest for as far as she could see.

"Welcome to Ra'ani Oh'nana." Raveen smiled proudly. "I'm sure you've heard of it. Even Wingless know it's the greatest city in Pangier."

Pangier, so that's where she was. Not that knowing this made her any less lost. Clem raised her eyebrows. From below, Ra'ani Oh'nana didn't seem that great. The forest floor was piled high with trash, the smell of rot and decay making her nauseous. Her feet sank into something squishy. Covering her mouth with the back of her hand, she tried not to vomit.

"Of course, it's much more impressive from above," Raveen added. "We don't usually have a need to come down here."

Clem hopped between things that looked firm as they traveled beneath the city.

"This is us." Raveen alit on the gnarled root of a particularly tall tree.

Clem looked up. Hundreds of feet overhead, a series of woven egg-shaped domes with gleaming glass fronts hung suspended between enormous branches. Warm light pooled out from all but a few windows. Sprawling wooden decks and rope walkways connected the domes.

"Cool," Clem whispered, circling the tree trunk.

"Uh, where are the stairs?" She'd made an entire loop but hadn't found a way up.

"If there were stairs, anyone could get up and down, silly," Raveen said with a snort. "The only way into Ra'ani Oh'nana is with a pair of these."

Spreading her wings, Raveen flew halfway to the nearest dome. Turning abruptly, she dove down and scooped Clementine off the ground.

"Next time, warn me first!" Clem half yelled in fear as Raveen plopped her on the deck of the largest dome.

"Wait here," Raveen responded. "I need to warn...tell...my dad I've brought home a new...friend."

Clementine wandered to the edge of the deck and peered into the twilight. Ra'ani Oh'nana spread out below, above, and around her. Nest-shaped buildings circled entire trees. Much too big to be homes, Clem guessed they were apartments, or shopping malls, or something. Mysterious round doors with glowing fungus decks led directly into the trunks of trees. A lot of the houses were domes like Raveen's. Others hung like teardrops from the branches. They all had similar woven wood exteriors and large glass-like panels which opened to the fresh air.

"This place is like the world's coolest treehouse city," Clementine whispered to herself. "And they have lights? This is so wild."

"Of course, we have lights. Did you think your kind discovered fire and bioluminescence? Don't be stupid, Wingless."

A shiver ran up her spine. Clem spun around so fast she nearly lost her balance.

"Don't fall. Raveen will never forgive me if anything happens to her new little pet. I do wonder what my sister sees in you," Falk said, glaring at her.

"Pet? I'm not a—" Clem huffed. She was starting to feel like she wasn't as welcome here as she'd hoped.

"Clementine, come meet my father!" Raveen interrupted.

Walking a wide circle around Falk, Clem followed Raveen inside. She wasn't sure what she'd expected, but this wasn't it. Inside, Raveen's house looked like any modern house back on Earth. Back on Earth? That sounded so weird. Where was Pangier? Clem wished she at least knew that. Maybe if she could figure out where Pangier was, she could figure out how to get home.

Raveen's dad stood next to a crackling fireplace in the

living room. His piercing yellow eyes judged Clementine's every move. Rows of brilliant white feathers ran from the top of his hooked nose across his forehead. They disappeared into perfectly coiffed, snow-white hair. Folded at his side, his broad, dark wings were much larger than Raveen's. Proud and fierce, he made Falk look like a child.

"Father, this is Clementine, a Wingless I met in the forest today." Raveen slowly looked between her father and Clem and back again. "Wingless, this is my father, Akylas."

Clementine thrust out her hand. If she was ever going to get out of this mess, she needed this man to like her, and she had a feeling that wasn't going to be an easy task.

Akylas leered down his beak-like nose, not moving a muscle. As Clementine quickly pulled her hand back, the corners of his lips turned up in the faintest of smiles.

"Clementine, is it? That's an unusual name, even for a Wingless. But then again, Raveen tells me you aren't like other Wingless." The man's smile widened as he raised a snowy eyebrow. "Where are you from, little pet?"

"Victoria." Clementine squinted her eyes and curled up her nose. That was a stupid thing to say. "I meant the river. I call my street Victoria. It's-it's the street name. Victoria Street, in Dohi."

Akylas nodded slowly, his eyes never leaving hers. Clem was used to feeling small and foolish, but not like this. This was even worse than when Mr. Waxley put her on the spot by asking her the hard questions in class when he knew perfectly well she hadn't been listening. Everyone staring, waiting for her to say something stupid. Clem swallowed hard and glanced nervously at the door.

"I imagine Falk scooping you up and dropping you in the woods was quite unsettling," Akylas said, his smile softening.

"You'll have to excuse him. He meant no harm. He was just having a little fun. You know how boys can be."

A little fun? He tried to kill me. How boys can be? What kind of excuse was that? Clementine wanted to scream, but she didn't dare. Despite his smile, Akylas was the most intimidating person she'd ever met. Instead, she nodded silently.

"Are you hungry? Of course, you are. Let's get you some dinner, little pet." The man gestured to the long wooden dining table separating the living room from the kitchen.

Clementine hadn't even thought about food since her mom had told her dinner would be ready in ten minutes. Now that Akylas mentioned it, she was starving! Maybe these people weren't so bad. Well, except Falk. He was the devil. Clem followed Raveen and her father to a seat at the end of the table.

Akylas raised a muscular arm in the air and snapped his fingers. A door opened, and a string of people filed into the kitchen and began preparing food. They kept their heads down, saying nothing. Every now and then, she'd catch one of them staring at her, but they'd lower their heads and turn away whenever she met their gaze. Clem couldn't help but notice none of them had wings.

Her first dinner in this foreign and exotic land was surprisingly not horrible. There were vegetables she'd never seen before, nuts, and some sort of meat she prayed hadn't once been something cute and fluffy. Whatever it was, it tasted delicious. With every bite, Clem felt more at ease.

"Raveen tells me you have a rather interesting artifact in your possession you'd like to know more about?" Akylas pushed his chair away from the table and dabbed at the corners of his mouth with a napkin. "Did she tell you I'm the head of archeology at the Museum of Natural History here in Ra'ani?"

"She didn't, though she did mention you'd be able to help me." Clementine couldn't believe her luck. What were the odds she'd meet someone who could help her—and an archeologist nonetheless—so quickly? Unzipping her jacket pocket, she held out the hummingbird flute.

When Akylas reached for it, Clementine instinctively snapped her hand shut. She couldn't very well let him take it, or she wouldn't be able to understand what he said about it. The man smiled, but his piercing eyes flashed a look of annoyance.

"I-I-I'm sorry," Clem stuttered, "I can't... I'd rather not let go of it. It's-it means a lot to me."

Akylas stared at her, unblinking, ever watchful.

"I can see that." His smile looked like he'd licked a lemon. "But I can't tell you much about it if you're going to keep it clenched in your fist."

Clem opened her hand so Akylas could examine it.

"It is quite old, indeed. Ancient even." He flipped the hummingbird over in her hand. "Likely created before the first Wingless children were born.

"Legend tells us upon creating the first bird, the gods were so pleased with the perfection of what they'd made they stopped creating all other creatures. They fashioned more and more birds until the mountains and the waters burst with color, and birdsong could be heard from the very heavens themselves. The hummingbird was the last and most perfect of their creation. The gods sat back and marveled at all they had made. They were so enamored with Pangier that they made themselves wings and gave up their immortal position in the heavens to live among their creation. We, the Winged, are the children of those gods. In need of an earthly home befitting a divine being, the gods planted the First Tree—a place off the ground, away from the creatures that slither and crawl in the filth and mud. A place they could safely roost, feast, and sing with their feathered friends. In the sprawling canopy of the First Tree, they carved flutes and added their voice to the dawn chorus all their long days. Since the days of the gods, the Winged have always lived in the treetops among the birds."

Akylas looked wistfully toward the window and into the night sky. Clementine could have sworn she saw him wink at his own reflection.

"Of course, as beautiful as it is, that's simply legend. The modern theory is that the first flutes crafted by Winged may have been used for hunting—to call in prey. Flutes are also thought to have been the first musical instruments of our ancestors. As the Winged culture advanced, flutes became more ornate and complex, as did our music. Due to their rarity, it is theorized hummingbird flutes, like this one, were used by shamans—or to'huna—as talismans and good luck charms during rituals. Among our people, hummingbirds are admired for their speed and agility. They are known as bringers of good fortune.

"Many ancient cities my team and I have discovered deep within the forests have yielded incredible artifacts, including flutes. Though I've never seen anything quite like this…"

Akylas ran his finger across the long thin beak, then brought his hand to his chin as if in thought. "I personally curated an exhibit dedicated to the ancient cities and the artifacts we've unearthed. It's quite spectacular, if I do say so myself. Perhaps tomorrow, Raveen can take you to see it, little pet." He smirked at his daughter.

"Oh, that would be great!" Clem said excitedly. Maybe there would be clues at the museum as to the whereabouts of the Stone!

"Do you mind if I ask where you found it?" Akylas's mind-drilling stare bored into Clementine's head.

"I found it locked in the drawer of a wooden chest," Clementine answered honestly.

"Hmm, how curious." Akylas's tone was steadily becoming more loathsome. "It's not something I'd think a Wingless would lock away in a drawer. I didn't think the average Wingless was cultured enough to care about our past. I'd have thought you were all too busy chopping trees and slashing and burning the forests to plant your little crops and build your pathetic villages and sail-rails. Or otherwise destroying Pangier as you do. Meanwhile, we're up here tending the canopy and reseeding the forest. I didn't realize you all had time to devote to things like history. You haven't any respect for nature, the canopy, or anything in it. So why should I believe you'd respect an artifact belonging to the Winged?"

"What?" The conversation had taken a turn Clementine wasn't expecting. She didn't know what to say. "I, um…"

"I'll ask you again, Wingless, where did you get it?" Akylas had gone from smiling to furious in a matter of seconds.

"I-I-" Clementine stammered. "I found it in a drawer, honestly."

"Honestly?" Akylas laughed. "What would a Wingless know about honesty? Jealous, horrible little creatures that you are. No respect for anything. I've seen what you do to our people."

"I'm not like that," Clementine pleaded in self-defense. "Trust me, I'm not one of them—"

But Akylas kept on ranting. "You expect me to trust you?

You found it in your grandma's old jewelry box, did you? No. I'll tell you what happened. You stole it. You know it. And I know it. Rotten thief." Akylas's fists hit the table with a thud. "Who did you take it from? Where. Did. You. Find. It?"

Clem's fingers closed protectively around the flute in her hand, but beyond that, she was too frightened to move.

"How does it work, Wingless?" Arms folded, Raveen leaned forward in her chair. "I saw you. I saw you appear out of thin air in the forest. Only the Winged gods could have created something that powerful."

"Yes, and thank the gods, Raveen caught you in the act of stealing it. It needs to be properly studied. It belongs with the Winged. Now, hand it over, you filthy little Wingless thief!" Akylas jumped off his chair, his wings spread terrifyingly wide.

Trembling, Clementine prized herself from her chair. Her legs wobbled like a baby taking their first steps. Ever so slowly, she backed toward the door.

Arms grabbed her from behind, squeezing her tight. Too tight to breathe.

"Good boy, Falk," Akylas said with a sneer. Turning his attention to Clementine, he grabbed at her flailing wrist.

Clem looked to Raveen for help, but the girl sat at the table, an ugly smirk smeared across her otherwise beautiful face. Everyone in the kitchen had scattered at the first sign of trouble.

"But I can't. You don't understand, I'm not from… I need it to get…" Clementine faltered as Akylas wrenched the tiny hummingbird from between her fingers.

Akylas said something, but without the flute, she could no longer understand. He nodded to Falk.

Falk dragged her toward the door. Clem was positive he

was about to toss her off the deck. She imagined herself lying, broken, in the putrid rotting garbage beneath the city, Akylas calling the birds to come pluck at her eyeballs and tear off her flesh. Terrified, Clementine kicked and twisted, trying again to release herself from Falk's iron grip.

In her desperate attempt to wriggle free and get the hummingbird back, Clementine smacked her head hard on the door. She heard the tinkle of glass falling like rain. Felt the weightlessness of her body as it crumpled to the floor. Through stars, she saw Akylas walk back to the fireplace and set his newly acquired prize on the mantle, and then, as her head hit the floor, darkness.

CHAPTER 18

Rubbing the massive bump on the side of her head, Clem groaned. The orange glow of a new day filtered through her closed eyelids, but she had no desire to open her eyes.

Why had she opened the drawer? Why had she touched the cursed hummingbird? There had to be something seriously wrong with her.

Think before you act, Clementine. Isn't that what every adult had told her at one point? But nope. And now, because she never learned, here she was. Did she even want to know where she was? Probably not.

Sighing, Clem peeled the hair away from her puffy, sore cheeks. Maybe if she fell back to sleep, she'd wake up from this nightmare. Rolling onto her side, she felt whatever she was lying on sway beneath her. Ugh, that couldn't be good.

Find the Stones. Be a rock, not a leaf. Clem laughed. *What a joke.*

Well, she may as well open her eyes and see how horrible her situation was.

Clementine found herself sitting on a soft, round bed with tightly woven wicker walls, which got narrower and narrower until they met, like a teardrop, a few feet above her head. It wasn't big enough to stand in, but almost.

On either side, daylight shone in through round openings. A folded blanket and a large bucket lay against one wall. Clem didn't want to think about what the bucket was for.

Crawling to one of the round holes, she poked her head out. The tree city was more impressive in the daylight. Craning her neck upward, she could barely see the bottom of one of the domed rooms through the thick branches. She looked down. Her teardrop prison was hanging a few hundred feet off the forest floor. Clementine pulled her head back in.

That's what it was—a prison. There were no bars, but unless she grew wings, Clem wasn't going anywhere. How could she be so bad at this? In less than a day, she'd been nearly killed, trusted all the wrong people, lost her only clue to finding the Stone and getting back home, and been imprisoned. Or was this kidnapping? She wasn't even sure. Adriana James would not be impressed.

A shadow passed beneath her jail cell. Then another. Other Winged creatures! Maybe they weren't all bad.

"Hey, help!" Clem called as a flurry of brown, purple, and white passed beneath her. Fluttering to a stop, three Winged hovered out of reach.

"Help me, please!" Clementine begged.

The Winged stared at her, confused. They couldn't understand her, and she couldn't understand them. If only she hadn't lost the flute.

Firmly grabbing the opening with one hand, Clem stretched her free hand as far as she dared, hoping one of them would take hold and pull her to safety.

They pointed and laughed. The closest Winged flapped his brilliant purple wings and flew to a nearby branch. He picked up a softball-sized pinecone and threw it, nailing Clem squarely in the head.

"Ouch, that hurt! *Jerk.*" Clementine retreated back into the hole. The flock of Winged flew away, cackling with laughter. Curling in a ball, Clem cried herself back to sleep.

For three days, she lay alone in her bar-free cell. It took

nearly a whole day to stop crying. When she finally stopped feeling sorry for herself, she got angry and tried kicking a hole in the roof. The plan was to climb the rope and escape, but it hadn't worked. Now she was bored.

She wished she had a book. How could she not have a book with her? She always had a book. To pass the time, Clem made a list of all the things she wished she'd done and said differently. It started with never having walked into the antiques store and ended with kicking Falk's butt. If she ever found her way home, Clem vowed to learn self-defense.

Twice a day, someone lowered food and water down on a rope. It wasn't much, but it was better than nothing. It was also the highlight of her days, as sad as that was.

Chowing down on brunch, or what she liked to call mid-morning-nut-crusted-cracker-bread-with-weird-purple-gunk, Clem wondered if her parents had reported her missing. The thought of Ferg being all sad, wishing he'd been nicer to her, made her smile. More likely, though, he was reveling in the idea of being an only child.

Clem's mind wandered to Andro. She wished she'd brought the chest with her, so she could tell him the key had arrived. She imagined there was a *You have?* note in the chest at that very moment. How disappointed would he be that she'd found the first clue and then immediately gotten lost? Or maybe he knew where Pangier was and how to get out of this mess. If only she could ask him.

Tossing the leaf her lunch had been wrapped in out of the hole, Clem lay down and closed her eyes. Nap. Eat. Nap. Stretch. Nap. She sighed. Was Akylas planning on leaving her hanging forever, or just until he needed another house servant? Well, she wouldn't do it. She needed to get out of there. But how?

Clem drifted off to sleep.

A low buzz filled the cocoon, working its way into her dreams. Something swooped by her head. Clem didn't dare open her eyes. She imagined all the bugs in Pangier were the size of birds back home. With any luck, it would fly back out. But it didn't. It got louder and louder until whatever it was, was right above her nose. If a giant bee or a wasp landed on her face, she would absolutely jump out of the hole. Clem swatted it away, but a second later, it was back.

Clem half opened one eye. The tiniest emerald-green hummingbird hovered above her head, its bright red throat glistening like rubies. It reminded her of the hummingbird that visited her windowsill back home.

"Well, hello there, little hummer." Clem hoped the hummingbirds of Pangier didn't hate Wingless as much as the Winged did. Akylas did say the Winged and hummingbirds had once been so close they could talk to each other or something like that. Maybe it wanted her to open her eyes so it could spear her with its long, needle-like beak.

Raising her hand, Clementine stretched out a pinky as if sipping tea with a queen. The bird perched on her finger.

Never in her life had she been so excited to see another living, breathing thing.

"I don't suppose you know how to get out of here, do you?" Ever so carefully, she sat upright.

The hummingbird flew toward one of the round holes.

"No, don't go!" Clem begged, following it. As soon as she reached the hole, the tiny bird zipped to the other side of the cocoon. Clem turned and followed. When she caught up, the hummingbird turned and flew back. Back and forth they went, playing the world's shortest game of cat and mouse.

"What are you—" Clem stopped midsentence. Their

motion had caused the cocoon to swing.

The hummingbird flew out the door and hovered halfway between her hanging prison and the tree trunk.

Looking around to ensure no one was watching, Clem tossed her feet out the hole and pumped her legs as if she were on a giant swing. With every pump, she swung a little closer to the tree. As she got nearer, the hummingbird moved to a branch. If she pumped hard enough, Clem knew she could reach it.

"Why, you clever little devil, you," she said, smiling. As she spoke, the hummingbird turned and disappeared in a brilliant flash of emerald and ruby.

Long after it flew away, Clem sat there, her feet dangling in the air, an escape plan forming in her head.

Maybe hummingbirds were good luck after all.

CHAPTER 19

The lights of Ra'ani Oh'nana slowly flickered out like the last embers in a campfire.

Clem had spent all afternoon scouting the branches, watching, and formulating Operation Flight of the Wingless. Since sunset, she'd gone over the plan about a thousand times. In her head, it sounded simple: Swing to the branch. Scale the tree. Cross the deck. Break into Raveen's house. Steal back the flute. Climb down the tree. Get out of Ra'ani Oh'nana. And then, well, that part she'd figure out after she was back on solid ground. Anywhere had to be better than here.

Clem was afraid of what lurked in the long shadows of the forest. But she knew for her plan to work, she needed to wait until the city was asleep. She didn't want to get eaten, but darkness was her best chance of not getting caught. If she were seen, she had a feeling Falk would send her free-falling again. Only this time, no one would be there to save her.

Poking her head out one side of the cocoon and then the other, Clem scanned the canopy for any sign of life. Satisfied everyone was asleep, she swung her legs over the edge. It was now or never.

Clem inhaled sharply, the cool night air rushing past her teeth, pricking her lungs. Exhaling deeply, she pumped her legs.

The cocoon slid silently between the trees, gliding ever closer to the branch. It was farther away than it looked. Her legs ached with the effort.

One more pump. Just one more, she kept telling herself. On the upswing of her next pump, the toe of her shoe kissed the thick bark. This was it. *Now!*

Without thinking, Clementine let go of the cocoon and leaped out of the hole. Flying through the air, she landed with a shaky thud on the branch. Stumbling forward, she barely managed to catch herself before tottering over the far end.

Phase one complete.

Pacing the branch, Clem searched for a way onto the next limb. No matter where she stood, she couldn't quite reach. She ran her hand across the gnarled, chunky bark of the colossal trunk. There were plenty of hand and footholds. She didn't like it, but it would have to do.

The only experience she had climbing anything was a kiddie wall at the play place she and Ferg used to go to. Clem had always been scared, but Ferg would stand below her, telling her where to put her hands and feet, promising he wouldn't let her fall. What she wouldn't give to have Ferg here now. Clem wedged her foot deep in a crack and reached for a handhold.

"It's easy, Clem. You've got this. Don't look down." She wedged her foot into one foothold and then the next.

Inch by inch, she crawled up the tree.

Hefting herself onto a branch that hung over the deck, Clementine stopped. Squinting in the moonlight, she willed her eyes to pierce the darkness. If only she had the night vision of an owl or a hawk. She sincerely hoped the Winged didn't have extra good night vision. The deck seemed longer and more exposed than ever. Clem heard nothing and saw no one. But once she was down there, she'd need to move quickly.

What if she tripped? Or fell?

She wasn't particularly coordinated. Definitely not the person you invited to be on your relay team (or any team, for that matter). At least not if you wanted to win.

"Focus, Clementine," she whispered under her breath. "We're trying to escape here."

She'd come this far. Besides, what was she going to do? Put herself back in that tiny jail cell? Never. Clementine was no one's pet.

Fueled by anger at the memory of Akylas calling her a pet, Clem darted to the edge of the limb and lowered herself onto the deck. Sprinting across the open space, she ducked beneath the overhang of the dome. Now all she needed to do was get the flute and get out. Easy.

Catching her breath, Clem peered through the glass. Everything was as dark and still inside as it was out. Her heart leaped—the flute was on the mantle, exactly where Akylas set it. There'd been so many other artifacts in the house Clementine doubted Akylas had any intention of taking it to the museum to study it. She was right.

Clem nearly laughed out loud, wondering how much time Akylas and Raveen had spent trying to make themselves disappear. The fact they thought it was magic was kind of funny. Although it had brought her here, so maybe it wasn't that funny.

Clem tiptoed to the door, her warm breath spreading like fog across the cool glass. Stretching out her shaking fingers, she quietly slid it open. She paused. Was this breaking and entering? No, this was escaping with a minor detour. Quickly, before she chickened out, she ducked into the house and made a beeline to the fireplace.

Clem plucked the flute off the mantel with a smug smile, shoved it in her pocket, and zipped it shut. She would not risk losing it again. Ever. Proud of herself, she spun around and darted toward the door.

In a move only Clementine could perform, her foot caught on the side of something solid. Arms outstretched, she slid across the coffee table and did a swan dive into the couch. Clem winced. She knew this was going too well. Had she made too much noise? Lying there, her face buried in the soft cushions, she listened.

Hearing nothing, Clem stood and scanned the room. From the kitchen, a Wingless stared at her, open-mouthed. Clementine held her finger to her lips. The Wingless nodded. Clem winked.

Silently, she slipped out the door, across the deck, and beneath the cover of the branches. *Phew*, that was close.

Climbing down the tree took a lot longer than Clementine anticipated. Before she reached the ground, the edges of the dark night had begun to soften. Here and there, a solitary bird began to sing. A single light flicked on above her head, and then another. When her feet finally hit one of the gnarled tree roots, Clem could have kissed the ground, but there was no time.

Wading through the trash, Clementine headed in the direction she thought she and Raveen had come. Sticking to the shadows was becoming more challenging by the minute. At the edge of the city, she stopped. This was as far as she'd thought her plan through, and if she was being perfectly honest, she was surprised she'd made it this far. Where was she supposed to go from here? It wasn't like the Winged had highways or paths to follow.

As Clem tried to make up her mind, an arrow whistled by her head and lodged itself in the garbage at her feet.

"Hey! Where you going, Wingless?!" The words thundered across the silent forest. More and more lights came on. A door opened. Heads popped out of windows.

Clementine turned to see Falk sling a bow over his shoulder and swoop off a nearby branch. Was he trying to kill her?

She wasn't going back. No way. She thought fast. Down! Raveen had pointed downhill and said there were Wingless communities on the river. Maybe she could hide there.

As Falk swooped overhead, talons out, Clementine turned and ran. Despite what books had her believe, running through the forest wasn't easy or fast. She finally understood why Adriana James carried a machete.

Clem tripped over a fallen branch. No time to see if she was injured—she was back on her feet running. Batting and swatting a tangle of low-hanging vines out of the way, she ducked under one root and scrambled over the next. High in the treetops, she could hear Falk, Raveen, and their posse taunting her.

Her only advantage was they, too, were having trouble flying through the messy tangle of branches and vines. Clementine purposely stuck to the thickest, most jumbled bits of forest. It was slower but safer.

Little by little, the voices became more distant. She was doing it: Clem was escaping! But, as tired as she was, she couldn't slow down, not yet.

Seeing a patch of light and no trees ahead, Clementine thought quickly. An open spot in the forest. She'd have to make a mad dash through it. It would expose her but hopefully only briefly. Picking up speed, she realized her mistake a millisecond too late.

The patch of light wasn't open forest at all! Like in a bad cartoon, Clem was running on air. Grabbing a vine, she swung back around, hitting the rocky cliff face with a thud. Clementine groaned. Falk and his friends could fly over at any second. She couldn't stay here. Clem scrambled up the vine and ducked back into the cover of the forest.

The drop-off wasn't huge, maybe a hundred feet, but it went on in both directions as far as she could see. She couldn't walk around it. Walking along the edge, she spotted a fallen log dangling off the cliff and into the treetops below. Clem couldn't be sure it stretched to the forest floor, but it was her only hope.

Clem fought her way through the dense vegetation, arriving at the log at the same time Falk got to the cliff. She couldn't climb on top and walk down like she'd hoped. They'd see her for sure.

Clem searched for a place to hide. Beneath the tangle of roots, the log was hollow. Clem climbed inside just as someone landed with a thud above.

"Do you see her?" It was muffled, but Clem could tell it was Falk. He sounded angry.

Another thump.

"No, but she couldn't have gotten far. She's here somewhere," Raveen answered.

Something big, with many hairy legs, crawled over Clementine's leg. Throwing both hands over her mouth, she tried not to scream.

"There's no way she made it down this cliff. Tui and Corvus, check the bush to the left. Raveen and Robyn, check the bush to the right. I'll search this area." Falk was obviously in charge. "You should've let us deal with her when we had a chance instead of bringing her home to Daddy," he added. "She was on our land."

"Well, you didn't see her appear out of thin air, you big brute. That artifact she stole has some sort of magical power. It has to be from Tua'mua Taup'aku. If Dad can find the

Forgotten City, he'll be famous. We'll be rich. He wants the flute back. After that, you can drop her off this cliff for all I care." Raveen's voice grew fainter as she flew off.

Eyes adjusting to the darkness inside the hollow log, Clementine looked around. She could easily stand with room to spare. Was it hollow all the way? Did the bugs get bigger, deeper in?

"Here, little Wingless, Wingless, Wingless… Where are you? I know you're here somewhere." Clementine couldn't see Falk, but his voice was less muffled. He had to be outside the root wad somewhere. "Come out, come out wherever you are…"

"You wish," Clementine muttered. She'd take her chances with whatever creepy crawlies lived in the tree.

Down she crawled. Occasionally something would brush up against her hand or slide across her foot. Clem was glad she had no light source, so she couldn't see what horrors lurked in the darkness.

A thin patch of light shone ahead. At first, Clementine thought her eyes were playing tricks on her, but the closer she got, the brighter it became. She must be nearing the bottom!

Please don't let this log be hanging in thin air. She'd had enough falling to last a lifetime.

The light shone up from a thin crack beneath her feet. Getting on her hands and knees, Clem pressed her face against it. The ground was only a few feet below, but the gap was too small to squeeze her body through. As she pressed firmly, the spongy wood gave way beneath her dirty fingers. Clem stood and jumped, the rotten wood beneath her feet crumbling. Clem landed on the ground with a thud, a tangle of slimy worms and beetles wriggling around her ankles. Ugh! She danced around, trying to shake off any hitchhikers.

Overhead, Falk, Raveen, and their gang combed the high forest. She doubted it would take them long to figure out she wasn't up there or how she'd managed to escape. Not wanting to lose her head start, Clem slipped under a fern and disappeared.

The vegetation in the lower forest was sparser as if it had been manicured. It was far easier to travel through, but Clem knew it also meant she'd be easier to spot.

Her legs and arms ached. Clem almost wished she were back in her hanging prison so she could lie down and rest. She'd done more exercise since she appeared here than she had in an entire year's worth of gym classes.

As the sun crept across the sky, her tired feet caught every rock and root in her path. Clem wasn't sure where she was going, only that she shouldn't stop. Couldn't stop.

Tired and hungry for lunch, Clementine leaned her sweaty face against the cool moss on a boulder and closed her eyes. She was so exhausted she could've fallen asleep standing. As her breathing slowed, a low steady static filled her ears. Peeling her face off the boulder, Clem listened.

Water! It was unmistakably the distant roar of rushing water! Clem wasn't sure where the energy came from, but her feet flew down the hill. If she could make it to the river, she'd… Well, she wasn't sure what she'd do. All she knew was she needed to get to the river.

Breaking out of the forest, Clementine came to a screeching halt on a large slab of slate. Below her feet, jade green water coursed through the valley. She'd made it. She'd actually made it!

Akylas had made the Wingless sound like monsters, but Clem doubted they could be worse than Falk. Since they'd mistaken her for a Wingless, she might blend in, find somewhere safe enough she could think for a minute, and figure out how to get home. The hummingbird was supposed to be a clue. If only she could find a quiet, safe place to pull it out and examine it.

Upstream, steep rock walls jutted formidably from the forest floor, forcing the water through an impossibly small gap. Impassable. Downstream, the river widened, the swift water disappearing around the bend. Hopefully, the villages were downstream because that's where she was headed.

"Going somewhere, Wingless?" Clementine spun around. Raveen hovered off the ground behind her.

Clem's shoulders dropped. Instinctively, she took one step back. And then another. Her hand covered her pocket, protecting the flute.

"Give it to me, and I'll leave. You'll be free to go home." Raveen held out her hand, eyeing Clementine's pocket. Falk and his friends landed silently beside her, Falk's hand resting on the knife sheathed at his hip.

"No." Clementine took another step back.

"It doesn't belong to you, Wingless. Give it to me!" Raveen flew at her, grabbing at her pocket.

"Get her, Ravi," Falk said, laughing.

Clementine wrestled her arm away. There was no way Raveen was getting the flute.

Taking another step back, Clem was overcome by the all-too-familiar feeling of nothingness. She grabbed for Raveen, who stared back at her in shock and horror. Clementine landed with a splash in the deep green water.

Icicle fingers jabbed at her from all directions. How could water be this cold and not be frozen? *Air!* She needed air. Clem gulped, choking on water and spray as her head broke the surface. Icy hands pulled her back under. Everything spun, tumbling in and out of view, like being in a washing machine—treetops, sky, water, rocks, treetops, sky, water. It all swam in and out of focus. Clem reached for something—anything—to grab onto. A fistful of gravel. Her hands slid across the smooth rock. Sky, trees, water. Her lungs burned. She felt dizzy. Cold. Numb.

CHAPTER 20

Clementine lay facedown on a pebble beach, her legs floating in the shallow waters of an eddy. Flopping over like a fish, she choked up water. The fun didn't stop.

"Whoa, are you alright?" a timid voice asked.

Clementine's eyes flew open. Curious, wide-set yellow eyes stared at her from within a round, freckled face. Long, wispy silver curls mixed with fine little feathers shot out in every direction.

"What are you doing in the river, silly?" A finger reached out and booped Clem on the nose.

Clementine swatted the hand away and rubbed her face. Pebbles dislodged themselves from her cheeks and fell like rain around her.

"The river's part of the adventure, I guess." Clem pushed herself up. "Where are we?"

"Oh, an adventure! I love adventures! What part are you at? Can I come? If not, it's okay, my dad's taking me on an adventure this summer, and I'm so excited! If you're done with your adventure by then, maybe you can come with us. What do you mean, where are we? Did you hit your head? We're on the Kako'Mao Kohaku River, duh. I'm Kiwi, by the way!" Kiwi thrust her hand in Clem's direction.

She had a splitting headache and struggled to follow what Kiwi was saying. "The Kako'Mao Kohaku, of course. How stupid of me." Clementine cautiously shook Kiwi's hand. "I'm Clementine. Clementine Lemons." She frowned. "Hey, you don't happen to have a map on you, do you?"

"Not on me, but my dad has maps…so many maps. He's always planning and scheming and dreaming. He's going to be the person who discovers Kot'ani. That's where we're going on our adventure. Can you imagine? The Winged are going to go absolutely mental when we find Kot'ani! They're like, 'It's ours! We were here first!' Yeah right. So dumb. Everyone knows Kot'ani was built by the Wingless, but like whatever. They're all crazy. What are you looking for, Clem? Do you mind if I call you Clem? Clementine Lemons is so long. Your parents must be really weird, no offense."

Clementine looked at Kiwi and blinked. How could so many words tumble out of one mouth so quickly? "Who says I'm looking for something?" Clem answered defensively, her hand gravitating protectively to her pocket.

"You said you were on an adventure. Everyone on an adventure is looking for something. Otherwise, there wouldn't be much point in going on an adventure, would there?"

Clementine couldn't argue with that logic.

"I'm looking for a Stone," she answered. She wasn't sure she should say anything, but there was something so familiar about Kiwi she couldn't help herself.

"Oh, you're in luck! There's, like, a million stones around here. I can help you find the perfect one. Does it have to be a particular size or shape?" Kiwi ran her hand over the pebbles on the beach.

Clementine's eyes narrowed. "I'm not looking for any stone. I'm looking for one of the Lost Stones of Dohi."

"I don't know what a Dohi is," Kiwi said at half the speed of anything else that had tumbled out of her mouth. "What do the 'Lost Stones' look like?"

"I don't know what the Stones look like," Clementine sighed. In retrospect, that would have been an excellent question to have asked Andro.

"Then how do you know it isn't that stone? Or that one? Or this one even?" Kiwi picked up a stone and eyed it suspiciously.

"Are you the Lost Stone of Dohi, little rock?" she asked seriously.

Clementine's eyes narrowed. She liked Kiwi, but she seemed to be at least two eggs short of a full carton, maybe three.

"It's an ancient stone. An important stone. The people of Dohi left it here for safekeeping a long time ago. I imagine it looks…I dunno…special? I think I'll know it when I see it," Clementine said, trying to reassure herself. "By the way, where are we going?"

While she'd been talking, Kiwi had turned and walked into the forest, and Clementine had instinctively started following her.

"Home, for a map," Kiwi called over her shoulder.

"Right…"

The Wingless had paths. Clementine's sore feet and bruised and battered legs were happy for this. While they walked, Kiwi's mouth ran nonstop. Clem half listened, not wanting to be rude.

Every now and then, they'd come to a signed intersection. Whatever translation capacity was built into the flute in her pocket obviously didn't work for written text because Clem couldn't understand a single symbol.

"Shhh!" Clementine stuck her finger to her lips and pulled Kiwi under a nearby mushroom cap. "Did you hear that?"

Kiwi stopped and listened. "You mean that bird?"

"Are you sure it wasn't a Winged?" Clem whispered.

"Winged don't come this far down the Kako'Mao Kohaku

unless they have a reason to…" Kiwi cast a sideways glance in Clem's direction. "What did you do? Are you in trouble?"

"No…I'm… Maybe? I dunno," Clem sputtered. She didn't want to tell Kiwi about the flute in her pocket and risk losing it again. "I accidentally ended up in Winged territory, somehow, I guess. I don't really know how things work here. Anyway, I ran into this Winged named Raveen and her brother Falk. Falk tried to murder me, but then Raveen saved me, sort of. She invited me back to her house in a city called Rani Banana or something like that. And her dad was super intense, and he kept calling me 'little pet' like I was a dog. Then, after dinner, he got super angry and started yelling about how horrible Wingless people are. Then they hung me in this cocoon-jail-thingy. But I escaped, and they were chasing me, and I almost ran off a cliff, and worms were crawling on me, and then I fell in the river."

Kiwi opened her mouth to speak, but no words came out.

"Is that bad?" Clem winced.

"Whoa… You were in Ra'ani Oh'nana? For real? Did you see other Wingless there? Because everyone says if a Winged catches you, they'll take you into the trees and force you to work for them because you don't have wings, so you can't escape. They say we deserve it for being in their territory, but according to them, everywhere is their territory. They make our lives a living nightmare every chance they get, burn our crops, attack us from the sky, and kidnap us while we're foraging. They love sticking Wingless in trees, like, as a joke. The harvesters carry ladders whenever they leave the city, just in case. The Winged are horrible."

Clem nodded.

"They'll forget about you soon enough." Kiwi patted Clementine's cheek. "We're only birdbrained little Wingless, after all.”

Clem stuck her hand over the hummingbird in her pocket. “I hope so…”

“Whaka’wai is well protected anyway, and we’re close,” Kiwi comforted her. “How is it you don’t know about the Winged? You must have hit your head so hard.”

“Where I’m from, only birds have wings.” Clementine suddenly missed home. It had been what, four days? Five? It felt like a whole other lifetime.

“‘Only birds have wings’… You’re hilarious. Super weird but hilarious,” Kiwi said, giggling. “We’re going to be great friends.”

They continued on, Kiwi talking a mile a minute.

“Ta-da!!” Kiwi stopped so abruptly that Clementine walked right into her. Laughing, Kiwi spread her arms wide and shook her hands. “Welcome to Whaka’wai! It’s not much, but it is home!”

Behind Kiwi, a wall towered above the trees. Every few feet, a perfect circle opened to the outside, letting the sun and the forest through. Like lattice fencing, the wall was far too holey to serve any purpose.

“Why the wall?” Clementine asked as they walked through one of the larger circular openings.

“Protection. Well, the holes are to let in light and nature because who wants to live in a cave? But they have a built-in defense system to keep out all the things that want to eat or attack us. Unfortunately, the Winged have figured out a way around the defense part, but they don’t come here as often as they used to. At night, it glows and lights up the whole city!”

Clem was confused by the lack of buildings within the city walls, but the longer she stared, the more she saw. The structures blended into the forest so well that she barely noticed them. Everything dripped in vegetation. Skyscrapers of glass with basket-woven walls towered overhead like vases bursting with flowers. The roofs were covered in grass.

People walked and rode sail-powered scooters through the mossy streets. There were no cars. No noise. No pollution.

Clementine stared in awe at a ten-story building draped in purple and blue orchids. Next to it, an entire apartment was carved into the trunk of a single old-growth tree.

Surrounded on two sides by the crystal-clear river, the whole city was one giant, perfect park. If she couldn't find her way home, she could live in Whaka'wai.

"This place is incredible." Clem was stunned. "The Winged said you lived in 'miserable, dirty villages,' and all you were good at was 'chopping trees and burning down the forest.' I wasn't expecting this."

"Augh, they should talk. The Winged litter the forest floor with garbage until everything dies. They harvest until nothing's left, always having to fly farther and farther to find resources, forcing us off our land. It isn't sustainable. We're constantly cleaning up after them. Our job is to protect the forest, to keep it clean and healthy for future generations… They don't care," Kiwi said with a sigh.

Kiwi's house sat on the far edge of the city. It looked like a smushed picnic basket on stilts. The wall, just beginning to glow in the fading twilight, cast an otherworldly hue on the river beyond. How was it possible any one place could be so beautiful?

"You're home late! I was beginning to think you'd gotten eaten or snatched!" Kiwi's dad said from the kitchen as they walked in the front door.

Kiwi's dad was tall, very tall. Like Kiwi's, his head was covered in a thick shock of fine silver feathers and hair, only his hair was much shorter. His yellow-green eyes were wide set to accommodate an abnormally broad nose.

"And who do we have here?" he asked, a friendly grin spreading from ear to ear.

Clementine wondered if he noticed she had no feathers. She seemed to be the only person in Pangier who didn't.

"Oh, this is Clementine, Clementine Lemons." Kiwi ran her hands up and down the length of Clementine like a game show host presenting a new prize. "You can call her Clem, though, because seriously…Clementine Lemons? What were her parents thinking, right? Anyway, I found her floating in an eddy on the Kako'Mao. I think she was almost dead, but it's hard to say, really. She's on an adventure. Looking for a lost stone, but not any stone, like, a specific stone. She doesn't know what it looks like, but it's old, so that should narrow it down to only, like, a billion possibilities. I'm pretty sure she bumped her head on a rock, though, because she says where she comes from, only birds have wings, and there are no Winged. Too funny. Anyway, she ended up in Winged territory, and she didn't know they're, well…you know. They tried to murder her, kidnapped her, took her to Ra'ani Oh'nana, and put her in jail. But then she escaped and ran away, and they chased her, and she fell into the Kako'Mao. Which was just before I found her." Kiwi took a deep breath before finishing. "She needs to borrow a map."

"Huh, is that so?" The man raised his eyebrows in amusement and disbelief.

"More or less." Clementine shrugged.

"Oh, by the way, Clem, this is my dad, Emos, but you can call him Dad. I do." Kiwi gestured grandly toward her father.

Clementine bit her lip and gave an awkward half wave.

"Well, our door is always opened to fellow adventurers,"

Emos said with a smile. "Kiwi gave us the overview, but maybe you can fill in the details of your adventure over dinner. Then we can find you a map."

All through dinner, Kiwi and Emos joked back and forth. Emos was a history teacher at the university. Most of the jokes were Pangier-related and went right over her head, but Clem laughed anyway.

"What about your family, Clem? What do your parents do? Brothers? Sisters?" Emos asked, more seriously.

"Um, my mom's a critical care nurse, and my dad's an artist. He does sculptures and carvings, mostly. He has a gallery in Victoria, where we live. My brother's good at everything…especially sports, though." Clementine loosened her grip on the hummingbird in her now-unzipped pocket.

"How did they feel about you going off on this adventure?" Emos pressed.

"They don't, um… I didn't exactly get the chance to tell them I was leaving. It kind of happened suddenly. I didn't even know I was… It's hard to explain."

Emos seemed worried. For the first time, Clem felt guilty. Were her parents freaking out?

"Must have been pretty important business to just up and leave." Emos looked like a parent about to give a lecture, but he didn't. "So, what kind of adventure is this? What type of Stone are you looking for? Maybe we can help you find it, so you can get back to your family. They must be worried sick."

After her experience with Akylas, Clem wasn't sure how much of her story she should give up. She looked at Emos and Kiwi, their faces full of concern. If she ever wanted to get home, if that was even a possibility, she needed help.

Pulling the flute out of her pocket, Clementine began to talk. For the first time in possibly her entire life, she held nothing back.

When she finished, no one spoke.

Emos ran his fingers through the coarse gray feathers hanging off his chin. Kiwi, whose mouth never seemed to stop, sat there, silently staring at the hummingbird in Clementine's hand.

They didn't believe her. She knew it. Why did she tell them everything? She should have made something up. No one in their right mind would believe this story. It was her story, and even she barely believed it.

Emos finally spoke. "Well, if the purpose of the flute was to bring someone back to collect the Stone, it seems probable the Stone would have the power to return that person to wherever they came from. Or finding the Stone would trigger a return of some sort.

"I mean, whoever created that"—Emos pointed at the hummingbird—"must have considered the need for a return trip."

"Wait, what? *You believe me?* Oh, thank God." Clementine sighed in relief. "I'd kinda hoped that was the case too, that the Stone would return me to the chest, or at least there'd be instructions of some sort. How else would the princess have gotten the Stones back to Dohi? But I'm not good at science, so…" Clem prayed they were right.

"This makes so much sense," Kiwi said, nodding solemnly, "because I wondered why you didn't have feathers. I didn't want to be rude and say anything, but you look like a plucked hen. Kinda naked, you know? Like, you're seriously the weirdest-looking person I've ever seen. No offense."

"That obvious, hey?" Clementine and Emos burst out laughing.

"Well, I wasn't going to say anything, but now it's out

there." Emos grinned. "When did the princess come here? A timeline might help us pin down a location."

"I have no idea," Clem said with a shrug. "Andro and Ablikim's messages were short and missing a lot of details. The woman at the Chinese restaurant said the story was old, like a myth even. When Akylas saw this hummingbird, he told me it was an ancient artifact, probably a talisman used by a shaman for rituals or good luck. And it was created before the first Wingless children were born, or something like that."

"Lies!" Kiwi looked disgusted. "You can't print something in a history book and call it a fact. Everyone knows Wingless were here first."

"Before the first Wingless children were born, hey?" Emos shook his head. "The Winged do live in their own reality, don't they? Akylas is the worst."

"You know Akylas?" Clementine's fingers closed protectively around the hummingbird.

"Unfortunately, I do," Emos admitted. "For many summers, I've led amateur exploration teams into the forest in search of ancient ruins and lost cities. History is a bit of a hobby of mine. It is for Akylas, too, although for entirely different reasons. We don't see eye to eye on plenty of subjects."

"Akylas is a tomb raider who likes to take credit for Dad's work," Kiwi blurted out. Emos cleared his throat.

"Well, it's true…" Kiwi pouted.

"We have different methods, and we arrive at different conclusions," Emos said diplomatically. "May I examine it?"

Trust was a tricky thing, but Emos was trusting her crazy story.

"I can't understand a word you say without it," Clementine reminded him, reluctantly turning it over.

Emos gently twirled the flute around in his fingers and handed it back.

"Akylas is correct. I'd guess by the style, it's thousands of years old. Though I wouldn't necessarily factor the date of this artifact into our timeline. If the princess left something of great importance, she might have been given something of great importance in return. Time may have worked differently for her, or she may have found it somewhere—it's hard to say."

"It's supposed to be a clue, or have a clue. I don't know," Clementine said. "I kinda feel like I jumped into the adventure story on page one-fifty-five, you know? Like I'm missing some valuable information."

"Well, maybe it isn't an obvious clue. Clear the table so we can get to work, you two." Emos disappeared into a back room.

Clementine had just grabbed the last plate when he returned.

"Might as well start big and narrow it down from there." He spread a huge map across the table.

A massive green-and-brown island surrounded by a blue sea lay in front of her. Clem couldn't read any of the words. Still, it looked vaguely familiar, like she'd seen a version of it somewhere before. Where had she seen it? Science class? No. Wait. Yes!

Clementine's head nearly exploded.

"This…is…Earth! This is the supercontinent of Pangaea! I'm on Earth!" she yelled gleefully. "I'm on Earth!"

Clementine's mind was blown. She wasn't on some alien planet—she was on Earth! Back in time? No, there were never winged people on Earth. Another dimension, maybe? A reality where the supercontinent of Pangaea never broke apart? Things were starting to make sense. Well, not really, but sort of. She couldn't find Dohi on a map because Dohi didn't exist in her reality either. Andro lived on Earth. In a whole other dimension. Did this mean the Professor was sane or had she totally lost her mind?

"Of course, this is Earth. Only this isn't Pangaea. It's Pangier. Where did you think you were?" Kiwi poked her head over Clementine's shoulder.

"I dunno, a different planet, I guess. But this is just a different dimension, maybe? I live on Earth. Only on my Earth, the supercontinent broke apart, like, a billion years ago or something, and now it's a bunch of smaller continents. I live in North America. Roughly"—Clem examined the map, trying to remember where North America was—"here!"

"Well, this day keeps getting stranger and stranger, doesn't it?" Emos rubbed his eyes and pointed at a spot on the far side of the map. "Physics has never been my strong point, but I know my geography, and in this version of Earth, you are here."

"I don't know how it works, but the token, the flute, wouldn't have put me a long way away from the location of the Stone, would it?" Clementine leaned over the map and stared at the place Emos had pointed.

"A decent theory." Emos smiled at the girls leaning over the map, trying to figure it all out. "Maybe the flute brought you to the exact place the princess left from to go back to her version of Earth. It's tough to say. Where were you when you arrived?"

Clementine stared blankly at the map.

"Never mind. That was a dumb question," Emos muttered. "How about this—what did you first see?"

"Well, I didn't really arrive. It was more like I wasn't here, and then I was. There were trees. A lot of trees. Enormous trees. And then Falk attacked me, and we were flying for a while. He and his friends were tossing me back and forth, so everything was swirly. Then Raveen made them drop me. We were only walking for a few hours before we got to Ra'ani Oh'nana, and it was uphill most of the way. Falk did ask me what I was doing in their territory." Clementine wasn't sure that was helpful, but it was all she had.

"Well, that's a start. The Winged consider everything their territory, but they're very territorial with other Winged. So, we can probably assume you were in Ra'ani Oh'nana territory."

He pulled out another map.

"The Winged of Ra'ani consider this to be their land."

"That's huge, though." Clem bit her lower lip and furrowed her eyebrows in frustration.

"Okay, tell me again what the woman at the restaurant told you about the Earth Stone," Emos said.

"'To the feathered of the great forests, she entrusted the Earth Stone. They, more than any, valued the earth, for it was their sanctuary. First and foremost, a place to roost and rest,'" Clementine repeated.

"'They valued the earth, for it was their sanctuary. First and foremost, a place to roost'—to congregate—'and rest'…" Emos paced the floor, deep in thought.

"'First and foremost'…" Kiwi whispered. "The Earth Stone was super important to Dohi. The flute was probably important to us. So, we must have hidden the Stone somewhere equally important… 'First and foremost'…first…the First Tree!"

Emos stopped pacing. "The First Tree! Brilliant, Kiwi!"

"Great!" Clementine's eyes lit up. They were so close to figuring this out! She leaned over the map, searching. "Where's the First Tree?"

Kiwi looked at Emos. Emos looked at Kiwi.

"Well, no one knows. No one remembers."

Clementine's heart sank. Of course, no one knew. Why would they?

"When Pangier was young and new, the Wingless wandered the vast nothing in search of food and shelter. They didn't have much, but they happily shared what they found with all the other creatures. Seeing the Wingless were good of heart, the gods sent their messenger, the hummingbird, with a gift from heaven. The hummingbird opened its beak and placed the smallest seed beneath the fresh soil. 'From this seed, a mighty tree will grow,' the hummingbird told the people. 'So long as you care for it and all its offspring, it will provide you, and all the creatures of the land, with everything you need to thrive.' The Wingless did as they were told, and from that seed, the First Tree grew. All the creatures were drawn to the tree—worm and beetle to its deep roots, the four-legged creatures to the hollows of its massive trunk, and the birds to its sprawling canopy. The Wingless cared for all the animals who gathered at the First Tree, but they were especially fond of the birds. We could once talk to the birds. The birds carried the seeds of the First Tree far and wide. From them, the mighty forest of Pangier sprang forth. We have always been stewards of the forest, and the forest has always provided for us.

"It is said the First Tree grows in the forest garden of the Forgotten City of Kot'ani. It has also been known throughout history as Mother and the Origin Tree. No one knows if it really was the first tree, but it was called that due to its sheer size and age.

"The first Wingless supposedly used flutes to talk with the birds. More likely, they were trained to plant trees, and the flutes were used to call them back. I've seen other flutes like yours. They're often found in archeological digs or lying here and there on the forest floor. I've never seen one shaped like a hummingbird, though. Despite the story, hummingbirds would have been too small to carry most seeds. It would have made more sense to train bigger birds, like ravens and crows."

"Akylas told me a similar story about the Winged," Clementine said thoughtfully. "Well, his story was more about how the Winged are the perfect children of the gods, but it had the First Tree and people who could talk to the birds too. He said the Winged admired the hummingbird for its speed and agility. And they were lucky charms. I kind of have to agree with that part because a hummingbird helped me escape Ra'ani. Akylas believed my flute was from a place Raveen called TwoeyMooey. He wants it because he thinks it's magic and will lead him there."

Emos shook his head and grinned.

"My exploration team and I have been searching for Kot'ani for years. The Winged call it Tua'mua Taup'aku. Akylas has teams constantly searching as well. It's become a race to see who can get there first. Akylas thinks it will prove Winged superiority once and for all. Also, he wants to loot its contents for his museum. We'd like to find it before they do to prove Wingless were the first to inhabit this side of the Central Pangian Range. Evidence does show ground dwellings existed here long before treed structures. Not that it matters beyond clearing up a little misremembered history."

"Where did the Winged come from then?" Clem wasn't sure she wanted to hear the answer.

"Many people believe it's a genetic mutation. Wingless, who were born with wings. They felt superior because of their heightened abilities. They were lazy and didn't want to work on the ground, so they took to the trees. Some people believe we've always been two distinct races. The Winged migrated over the Central Pangier Range into our lands, searching for more resources. It's hard to say for certain. You may have noticed there is no love lost between us. They think we're ruining the forest by thinning trees and growing crops, meadows, and gardens. We know caretaking the Earth is the only thing keeping the forest healthy. We think they're lazy and arrogant. They overharvest, leaving no seeds for the trees to regenerate. They aren't interested in helping manage the forest, only in reaping the benefits of our hard work."

Maybe you're both crucial to the ecosystem, Clem thought. But she dared not say it. This wasn't her fight.

"Anyway, enough of that!" Emos said. "Back to the maps! Based on the little we know, I've always thought Kot'ani was over here. In this general area."

He pointed to a place on the map where he'd marked a small red *X*.

Clementine studied the map intently. The *X* was a long way away, and no roads or paths led there. All she saw were trees and swamps, rivers and valleys, and more trees.

"What are the black *X*s?" Clementine asked, noticing the two-dozen other *X*s for the first time.

"Those are places we, or others, have already searched. We have an expedition heading out next week once school ends for the summer. Kiwi's coming. You're welcome to join us. With any luck, we'll find it this time. I have a good feeling about this expedition. Then you can find your Stone, save Andro, and get home to your parents."

"Really?!" Clementine jumped off her chair and hugged him.

"Don't get too excited yet," Emos said with a laugh. "It

will be dangerous, definitely not an easy journey. We're weeks away from getting close, and that's if the Mutina'kol'e Swamp is navigable right now.

"You and Kiwi both need to be prepared for an arduous journey. This isn't going to be a holiday. Efficiency will be key if we're going to find the Forgotten City and return before the fall semester. Kiwi's been training for months, and I'm not sure she's ready for what we'll be facing. I hesitate to take you because of the danger involved, but if Kiwi were lost in a strange land, I'd hope someone there would help her find her way home too. No complaints. No giving up. No turning back. Understood?"

Kiwi's and Clementine's heads bobbed in agreement.

"It's late," Emos sighed. "You girls get to bed. We have a lot to do between now and next week."

CHAPTER 21

While Emos finished his last week of work, Kiwi and Clementine packed and repacked gear and food into their backpacks. It didn't look like much, but Emos said they'd resupply along the way.

When they weren't packing, they were exploring Whaka'wai. Clementine tried to keep notes, so she could tell Andro all about Pangier…if she got home, that was. After school hours, Emos would teach them things like how to set up their tent, use the camp stove, and read a map.

Often Clem found herself absentmindedly twirling the hummingbird in her fingers, willing it to give up its secrets. Even though she was homesick, she had to admit life in Whaka'wai with Kiwi and Emos was pretty awesome. If she didn't think too hard about it, she could almost convince herself she was at summer camp and home was just a ferry ride away.

Clem leaned over the map on the table and traced the long route with her finger. They'd be taking the s-rail from Whaka'wai, over the Kako'Mao Kohaku River Gorge, to Kakarula. That was a two-day journey. From there, they'd travel on foot, past a half-dozen smaller villages, to Wheku Whak'ani on the edge of the Mutina'kol'e Swamp. It would take a whole week to cross the swamp to Mau'una Kupuka. After hearing what lived in the murky waters, Clem had asked if they could go around, but Emos insisted it would take half a year or more. After Mau'una Kupuka, they'd fall off the map. No more towns or villages, only uncharted rivers, unexplored ridges, and, with any luck, lost civilizations. Best-case scenario? She'd be home by the end of summer. Worst-case? Well…

"It looks so far, and exciting, and scary," Kiwi chirped from over her shoulder. "A whole summer of adventure. *Eeek!* I can't wait! And now you're coming, which makes it a million times better. I'm so happy!"

Clem had always wanted to go backpacking, but her parents weren't outdoorsy. This was like thirteen years' worth in one trip. Tiny blue butterflies fluttered inside her stomach. She'd told Kiwi a hundred times she'd never been backpacking, but Kiwi refused to believe that was possible. Clem had never even slept in a tent before. She hoped she didn't hold up Emos and his team. She felt like an accidental tourist who somehow ended up on a hard-core adventure. A scaly monster slithered up her intestines, ate the tiny blue butterflies, and curled in a knot in the pit of her stomach. She was a fraud, and everyone was about to find out.

"You are a rock…" Clem whispered for the nine-thousandth time.

"What's that?" Kiwi pulled her head out of her pack.

"Nothing," Clem sighed.

"Are you worried we won't find it?" Kiwi asked. "Because you shouldn't be. Dad and his team have put so much research into this. It's got to be there. Then you can go home. And if we don't find it, you can live here. I always wanted a sister. But we will find it. Don't worry. It's going to be awesome. Dad will be super impressed because our packs are absolutely perfect this time. Hey, you wanna go explore? There's so much of Whaka'wai you haven't seen yet!"

"Oh, good. You're home." Emos burst through the front door, his usually smiley face entirely too serious.

"You're home early," Kiwi said, smiling. "We were about to head out so I could show Clem more of the city."

"There's been a change of plans." Emos was agitated. "Get your packs. We've got seats on the next s-rail. It leaves in thirty minutes."

"But I thought we weren't leaving until—" Kiwi started, but Emos cut her off.

"There's a rumor the Winged are planning an attack on Whaka'wai. All morning, we've been watching them fly over, doing recon. First one, then a few dozen. Right now, there's a group of them perched by the university. They haven't outright attacked the village in years. The only reason I can think of that they would now is that they either know or suspect Clementine is here. We need to leave. *Now.*"

Clem gulped and obediently picked up her pack.

"Where's the flute, by the way?" Emos scooped the half-dozen maps off the table and crammed them into his pack.

Clementine patted her pocket.

"That won't do." Emos disappeared into his office, then reappeared with a long piece of leather. "If you lose your jacket, or worse, it falls into the wrong hands, it's gone. Then we aren't going to have a clue what you're saying. Let me see it a moment."

Clem handed him the hummingbird. He fashioned a harness securely around its wings, tied the loose ends together in a tight knot, and handed it back to her.

"Hang it around your neck and tuck it under your jacket. That way, you'll lose your head before you lose it." He added with a wide dad-joke grin on his face.

Were all dads this way? Shaking her head, Clem hung the little bird around her neck and tucked it out of sight.

"Maybe put your hood up too." Kiwi slid the front door

open. "So no one spots that weird featherless head of yours."

The rest of the team was already waiting when Clem, Kiwi, and Emos arrived at the station.

"Made it," Emos said breathlessly as they sidled up to three others.

"None too soon, from the looks of it," the stout man beside Emos replied. His beady eyes looked perpetually surprised beneath bushy yellow eyebrows. His lime-green and yellow feathers were slicked back into his jet-black hair. He gestured toward the top of the wall where four Winged sat, scanning the city.

Clem could see more Winged a short distance down the wall.

"I think that's Akylas's son, Falk, over there." Clementine pointed.

"Best stay out of sight." Emos pulled Kiwi back from the platform's edge and under one of the large triangular sunshades. Clem followed, tugging her hood lower. Now she was wearing Kiwi's clothes she fit in better. But like Kiwi said, her lack of feathers was a dead giveaway.

Clem's hood hung so low she barely saw the train sail up the monorail and into the station. She peeked out in surprise. The cars—Kiwi called them gliders—traveled together, but they weren't connected. They looked like a cross between a reed boat she'd once seen in a museum and a mini-submarine. Tall, leaf-shaped sails jutted out of their roofs. She'd been expecting a train, though now she thought about it, she wasn't sure why. Clem watched as, one by one, the gliders came to a halt at the end of the platform. This was going to be fun!

"We should sit in separate gliders, Emos," the beady-eyed man suggested. "There's no way Akylas knows the girl is with us. If he thinks there's even a remote chance she's leading you to Kot'ani, who knows what he'll do. He's insane. As far as Akylas knows, our group isn't headed out for a few more days. We should keep it that way. It will look far less suspicious if we travel separately."

"Good thinking, Strigops," Emos said. "Casso and Auk, you two go together in one of the front gliders. Strigops and I will try to get something in the middle. Kiwi, you take Clementine and head to one of the back gliders. The back is always full of kids, so you'll blend in."

Clem and Kiwi shot each other an excited glance.

"Keep your heads in the glider. If, for any reason, you have to get off at a stop, stick with a group. We'll be overnighting in Ra'ern. We'll wait on the platform for you there, so don't head into town without us. Clem, keep that hood up. Got it?" Emos handed them their tickets.

Clem and Kiwi nodded.

He pulled Kiwi into a tight hug.

"Augh, Dad!" Kiwi pulled away in protest. "We're only going to be like six gliders behind you. We'll be in Ra'ern before dinner. You worry too much."

"Go then, be independent. See if I care." Emos shook his head as Clem and Kiwi tucked in behind a group of college-aged students and followed them toward the end of the train.

"Do you think we should be worried they'll follow us? Your dad seems worried." Clem bit her lower lip and stared out the round window. Their glider was half-full at best, and they'd managed to find seats away from everyone else. Still, Clem kept her hood up like Emos told her to.

"No," Kiwi said. "No way. The Winged can't know for sure you're in town. They can't know you're with us. They definitely don't know you're on the s-rail. How could they?

We're fine, trust me. He's being paranoid and worried. He's never let me take the s-rail by myself before. He seriously thinks I'll fall out the window and be lost forever. He's just being a dad, you know?"

"Oh yeah," Clem said, snickering. "You should have seen the first time my dad let me take the bus by myself. I swear he followed the bus so close in the car he almost rear-ended us."

As the glider slid forward and sailed through a hole in the wall, the Winged took flight.

CHAPTER 22

BOOM!

"What...?" Clem's heavy eyelids struggled to open. "Sorry, what did you say, Kiwi? I must have..."

They couldn't have been on the s-rail for more than a few hours, but they were moving at the perfect speed to lull you to sleep.

Clem shook her groggy head and tried to focus. What was that sound? In front of her, Kiwi's shocked face was—ever so slowly—rotating upside down. Clem felt her butt lift off the seat. She felt light and floaty. Why was she floating? Time stopped. Clem's eyes moved around the glider. Bags and luggage, arms and legs, her long dark hair—all hung suspended in the space between the floor and the roof.

"So weird..." she mumbled.

As if someone pushed the play button, time started moving again, and everything came crashing to the floor with a thud.

A pile of limbs and debris lay strewn around Clem's feet. She was hanging from her chair, which was somehow above her head and not below her butt where it belonged. Her legs dangled precariously above a large gash in the ceiling.

"Kiwi! Kiwi!" Clementine yelled frantically. Kiwi and her seat were missing entirely.

"Kiwi?" Her voice sounded foreign in her own ears.

"Clem?" a muffled voice called back. "Clem! Down here!"

"Down where?" Clem couldn't focus through the panic.

"Look straight down," Kiwi called back.

Clementine looked through the gaping hole beneath her

feet. Kiwi stood on the ground, blood trickling down her dirty face.

"Are you okay?" Clem whimpered.

"Yeah, I think so. Can you get down here?"

"I'm hung up on something. I think my jacket is caught between the seats." Clem unbuttoned her jacket and wriggled onto the ceiling. She tossed their packs to Kiwi, then crawled through the hole.

"Whoa, what happened?" Clem surveyed the damage. What was left of their glider hung from the rail. It had speared through the glider ahead of it, nearly splitting it in half. A dozen crumpled gliders were strewn across the forest floor. Two of the cargo carriers were in flames.

Hundreds of Wingless staggered about, calling names, screaming, crying.

"I dunno," Kiwi mumbled, bewildered. "I think we derailed."

A shadow flashed across the ground, followed closely by another. Clem knew the shape all too well. Grabbing Kiwi by the arm, she pulled her under the wreckage.

"Did you see that?"

Kiwi nodded. "Winged. What do we do?"

"We need to find your dad." Clem pulled a knit cap from her pack and crammed her featherless head into it. "Come on."

Slipping on their packs, they crept up the rail, careful to stay hidden beneath the overturned gliders. Near the front of the disaster, the first glider dangled precariously over the edge of the gorge. The bridge was gone.

"There he is!" Kiwi stepped into the open.

Emos caught Clementine's eye and shook his head. Nodding, Clem pulled Kiwi back under the debris.

"Oh, Clementine. Where are you?" howled a voice from

somewhere overhead. Clementine's skin crawled.

Falk, she mouthed to Kiwi.

Akylas alit on the ground in front of Emos.

"Where is she?" he screeched, the feathers on his neck standing on end. Wings flared, he knocked Emos to the ground with a single punch.

"Dad…" Kiwi simpered.

"Where's who?" Emos picked himself up.

"My daughter saw your kid with her at the river. I know she's here. I know you're hiding her!" Akylas kicked Emos in the stomach.

"I don't know what you're talking about." Whenever Emos tried to get on his feet, Akylas sent him back to the ground.

"Where is she? Where is it? It's mine, and that little thief stole it from me!" Akylas raged on.

"Psst…Kiwi, Clementine," a voice whispered in Clem's ear.

"Strigops!" Clem squeaked, relieved to see a friendly face. "You scared me—"

"They blew the bridge. We couldn't stop in time," Strigops whispered in a hurry. "They say Whaka'wai is burning."

Clem and Kiwi gasped.

"I said, where is she, Emos? Did you honestly think I would let her lead you and your pathetic team to Tua'mua?" Akylas ranted.

"I don't know how many times I'll have to tell you before it sinks into your feather brain, Akylas: I don't know what you're talking about." Emos was angry now. "Does it look like I have children, or an expedition team, with me?"

"You two aren't safe here. And as long as you're here, your dad's not safe either." Strigops thrust a map at Kiwi. "You need to go now! There's a bridge downriver. No one's used it in decades. Casso, Auk, and I will get your dad out of this mess, and then we'll be right behind you. Don't stay in any one place too long. Avoid being out in the open. Keep heading for the swamp. I marked the way on the map."

Kiwi protested, but Strigops turned and disappeared.

"I'm not leaving without my dad…" Kiwi shook her head. "Never…"

Getting up on his hands and knees, Emos looked in their direction. Seeing the pain on his face, Kiwi jumped forward to help him. Clem held her back.

"Let me go," Kiwi said with a sob.

Run! Emos mouthed as Akylas picked him off the ground by the throat. Casso and Auk full–body tackled Akylas. Clementine grabbed Kiwi by the hand, and together they ran as fast as their legs would carry them.

"We need…to…stop. It's getting dark, and I can't…I can't run anymore." Kiwi stumbled to a halt and threw herself on the ground.

"Yeah," Clem agreed, breathing heavily. "I'm exhausted."

She wasn't sure how long they'd run, but it felt like hours. She'd run more since she'd been in Pangier than she'd run in her whole life. Adventures were the worst, just running and narrowly avoiding death. When she got home, she was going to write the author of the Adriana James series and let her know she needed to add a lot more running and almost dying to her stories.

"It's getting too dark to see anything," Kiwi panted. "I could sleep for a hundred years."

They set up the tent in silence, hiding it beneath the fronds of a fern. Clementine was sure Kiwi hated her. But what could she say to make this better? *Sorry, I'm the reason the Winged derailed your cool train thingy, burned your beautiful town to the ground, and beat up your dad?* That somehow didn't cut it.

When the tent was set up, Kiwi ducked out from behind their cover and rearranged the long green tendrils until the tent was completely hidden. Back under the fern, she pulled four wooden dice, the size of the palm of her hand, out of her pack and set them on the ground at equal points around the tent.

"What are those?" Clem didn't recall seeing them when they were packing.

"They're oro'nalu alarms. They emit high-pitched sounds to scare away anything that may want to eat us." Kiwi sighed heavily. "If anything gets by them, they make a ton of noise. Same technology as the wall around Whaka'wai. Don't set them off if you need to get out of the tent for any reason."

Clem had forgotten there were things in the forest that wanted to eat them. This was too much. Fergus, Fergus should have been the one to open the drawer. He'd have found the Stone and been home by now. He may even have won some awards and had a statue built in his honor while he was here. He certainly wouldn't have left a trail of terror and destruction wherever he went. Clementine had been here less than two weeks, and all she'd done was screw everything up. Like normal.

"I'm really sorry, Kiwi." Clem's lower lip trembled. "About all of this. I don't know what I'm doing. I didn't want anyone to get hurt. I should never have opened the drawer. I shouldn't have tried to help Andro… I didn't know— I'm not good at this. I'm just— I'm only…me."

"It's okay, Clem. I know you didn't mean for this to happen," Kiwi whispered, her own voice trembling. "It was bound to happen eventually. As long as the Winged dominate the skies, Wingless will never be safe. Especially us. Akylas absolutely hates my dad. But my dad will be okay. Akylas needs him. Akylas couldn't find a feather on top of his own head if he was staring in a mirror. Every major archeological discovery made in the last decade has been thanks to my dad. Akylas swoops in, takes all the credit, and steals everything of value. If it helps, I'm only me too. Dad's never taken me exploring before because I'm always getting lost and screwing things up. Everyone says I'm a walking disaster."

"That makes two of us," Clem sighed as they crawled into their sleeping quilts.

"I wish my dad was here," Kiwi mumbled as she drifted off.

Sleep did not come easy for Clementine. This wasn't how she'd imagined her first night in a tent. The forest was too big, whispering and murmuring in haunting creaks and groans. Shadows silently crept up one side of the tent and slunk down the other. A twig snapped. Soft footsteps surrounded them. A sniff. Clem held her breath and hoped whatever things stalked the night weren't as hungry as she was.

When she finally did drift off, her sleep was plagued by nightmares. In her dreams, Andro cried for help, but no matter how hard she tried, she couldn't find him. Nameless shadows hunted her, attacking her from above. Then she was falling, falling forever through an endless blue sky.

CHAPTER 23

Clementine awoke with a start, Andro's cries for help echoing in her head. His daily notes asking about the key had annoyed her, but now she'd give anything to know he was okay.

Through the tent door, she watched the light dance playfully in the leaves. It had to be early.

"Where do you think we are?" She crammed her sleeping quilt in its sack.

"I have no idea," Kiwi said with a yawn and rubbed her eyes. "I kinda forgot to pay attention while we were running for our lives. I was hoping you knew."

Clem shook her head. "I was too busy trying not to trip and fall on my face. Maybe if we look at the map, we can figure it out."

Clem racked her brain, trying to remember anything Emos had taught them about reading maps.

"Yeah…maybe." Kiwi pulled out the stove.

While their breakfast boiled, the girls spread the map atop a lilac-colored mushroom cap and examined it.

"This must be where the s-rail derailed," Kiwi said. "As it was crossing the Kapu'le'loa River Gorge. When we ran off, the river was on our right. So, I guess we're over here somewhere?"

"That sounds logical," Clem said with a nod. "How long do you think we were running?"

"I dunno, but it felt like forever. My legs feel like we ran fifty kiro'mika."

"Is that far?" Clementine had no idea.

"So far," Kiwi said with a nod. "So, so far."

"Well, Strigops marked the old bridge here. So, I guess we must be close?"

"Probably."

"Then the river should be over there." Clem pointed left. Kiwi pointed right.

"Um…which way do you think we came from?" Kiwi pointed left. Clem pointed right.

"I don't think so." Kiwi shook her head. "I remember passing that tree."

"You remember *that* specific tree? *How?* They all look the same," Clem countered. "Are you sure?"

"I think so." Kiwi shrugged.

Together, they searched the ground for any sign of footprints, but they'd all but vanished overnight.

"How did you find the river when you ran away from Ra'ani?" Kiwi asked.

"I just ran downhill," Clem admitted. "It was a total fluke."

"Well, that's no help." Kiwi clenched her jaw and huffed.

"Maybe we should stay put and let your dad find us." Clem's voice wobbled. She'd never felt this lost before. "In school, they always told us, 'If you get lost in the forest, stay put.'"

"*Stay put? Stay put?!* What kind of advice is that? What kind of school do you go to? How are they going to find us?" Kiwi's panicked voice made the leaves quiver.

"We could be anywhere over here—" She pointed at a vast swath of the map. "What are the odds Dad's going to stumble across us? We have, like, five days of food, maybe. We'll starve to death before anyone finds us. If we can't even find the bridge by ourselves, there is no way my dad's going to take us on the rest of the expedition.”

“But we don’t know…” Clementine protested.

“Strigops said not to stay in any one spot too long.” Kiwi defiantly picked up her pack and tossed it over her shoulders. “It’s too dangerous.”

“Yeah, b-but…” Clem stammered.

“You showed up and were invited, Clementine Lemons.” Kiwi’s cheeks were bright red beneath her tiny gray feathers. “You have no idea how hard I worked to be able to come on this trip. I’m going that way whether you want to come or not.”

Kiwi marched off.

“Wait!” Against her better judgment, Clem snatched her backpack off the ground and ran after her. “I’d rather be more lost with you than only kinda lost by myself!”

“I don’t think you have to worry about that,” Kiwi answered. “I’m pretty sure we can’t get any more lost than we already are.”

They only spoke once all morning—when they decided against eating lunch in case it took them longer than five days to find the bridge and for Emos to catch up with them. Clem’s stomach growled. Guzzling the last of her water, she tried to ignore it.

“How is anyone supposed to know where they are in here?” she moaned, karate-chopping a giant leaf.

“Most Wingless are excellent wayfinders. It’s an instinct. Not me, but like ninety-nine percent of us. You need instincts when you can’t see the forest for the trees,” Kiwi said, frowning. “Everyone says it’s a feeling. Like, they just know. The only feeling I ever get is *hopelessly lost*. Can we not talk right now? I’m trying to concentrate.”

With a long sigh, they returned to silence. Hours passed

before Clem dared to say anything again.

"Um, Kiwi. I know you don't want to talk right now, but, um, we've been here before."

"Impossible," Kiwi snapped.

"Then why are my shoeprints in front of us?" Clem pointed at a set of tracks in the mud. They were unmistakably hers.

"Augh!! Why am I so bad at this?" Kiwi tilted her head back and screamed at the trees. "Why?! I swear I fell out of the nest and hit my head as a child or something." She dramatically flopped to the ground.

"Well, on a scale of one to ten, how screwed are we?" Clem asked.

"Oh, I'd say we're pretty screwed. Like maybe an eleven. Or a hundred, even." Kiwi put her head on her knees. "I'm the world's worst Wingless. It's one of the reasons I don't have friends. Well, that and everyone says I talk too much. You would've been better off with literally anyone else in Pangier."

"Are you joking?" Clementine sighed. "There's no one on this Earth I'd rather be lost in the forest with."

"This Earth…" Kiwi snorted, a hint of a smile playing at her downturned lips.

"Well, maybe my Earth too… But I can't say for sure about any of the others. Might be someone with mad skills out there somewhere." Clem couldn't help but giggle.

"Hey, you alright down there?" a voice echoed from the treetops. "Second time we've seen you today."

Clem's heart skipped a beat. She looked up, half expecting to see Falk and his gang. High overhead, a dozen baskets dangled like Christmas ornaments from the upper canopy. One of the baskets was rapidly descending on a long rope.

"Oh great," Kiwi moaned. "Harvesters."

"What do you mean, *oh great*?" Clem whispered. "Isn't

that good? They can tell us where we are. I thought it was the Winged."

"I almost wish it was," Kiwi muttered as a handsome Wingless jumped out of the basket and headed in their direction. "These guys are so full of themselves. Not just anyone can become a harvester. You have to have top marks in forestry stewardship and botany. And you have to be super fit. And have zero fear of heights, wild animals, bugs, or anything. These guys are out here for, like, weeks at a time. Oh, and did I mention they're excellent navigators? They're super talented, and they know it, and they want you to know it. This guy will die laughing when he finds out we're lost. Harvesters don't get lost."

"Hey! What are you two doing all the way out here? Lost?" The harvester ran his fingers through his shaggy green-and-brown feathered hair.

"Totally!" Clementine said.

"Momentarily misplaced," Kiwi said at the same time. "I know where we are, just not exactly."

"No, we're lost." Clementine elbowed Kiwi. "Completely lost. Like, very, very lost."

Kiwi's eyes narrowed.

"Well, where are you trying to get to?" The harvester sat on a boulder next to them. "I'm Po, by the way."

"Clem and Kiwi," Clem responded. "We were headed for Wheku on the swamp, but the bridge is out on the s-rail, so we thought we'd cross the old bridge and go that way."

"That's a big trip." Po studied their packs. "Are you sure you have enough gear and food for an expedition like that?"

"We're meeting my dad and his team at the bridge," Kiwi mumbled, her cheeks flushed. "We're just having a little trouble finding it."

"You have a map?" Po raised his eyebrows.

Kiwi halfheartedly handed it to him.

"You are right here." He barely glanced at it. "If you head northwest, you should hit Op'ala Creek before nightfall. Then tomorrow, follow Op'ala to the river. You'll be less than a day from the bridge at that point.

"The bridge will be downstream," he clarified. "The direction the water is flowing."

Clem looked at the place on the map he was pointing to. It was a teeny sliver away from the s-rail. They'd only gone that far?

"Northwest to Op'ala, Op'ala to the river," Kiwi repeated, not looking Po in the eye.

"And northwest would be?" Clem pointed in the direction they'd been going.

"Not very good with wayfinding, are we?" Po pointed in the complete opposite direction. "No worries, I'm a horrible wayfinder myself."

"Right," Kiwi said sarcastically. "I'm sure that's how you became a harvester, with your horrible wayfinding skills."

"It's a true story. I cheat, and I learned how to cheat from a prof at university who wasn't a great wayfinder either. Half the harvesters up there have no natural wayfinding talent. I think 'all Wingless have wayfinding instincts' is a horrible generalization."

"What?" Kiwi stared at Po. "I've spent my entire life thinking something was wrong with me."

"I know, right?" Po smiled. "I did too. I almost didn't try out for harvesting because I thought there was no way I'd pass trials, and I didn't want anyone to know I couldn't wayfind. My prof wouldn't let up about it, though. It took a lot for me to admit to him why I wasn't trying out. I expected him to laugh. But when I finally told him, I learned there are lots of us with zero instincts. Want to know some cheats?"

"Yes!" Clem glanced at Kiwi, who looked like she was about to jump up and kiss Po on the lips.

"Alright, Cheat One is figuring out directions. Grab a stick, and find a spot where the sun reaches the forest floor." He hopped up and did just that. "Stick it upright in the ground, then place a rock at the tip of the shadow it casts, like so. Now we wait. Thirty minutes should do the trick."

While they waited, Po grabbed fresh kaw'a berries and panai'a nuts out of his basket—or *hikipai* as Clem learned it was called—for them to snack on. Clem unapologetically stuffed nuts and berries in her face like she hadn't eaten in days.

"Now the shadow has moved," Po said, returning to his lesson. "We place a rock at the end of the new shadow. If we draw a line between the two, the first rock is west, and the second is east, more or less. Now, we draw a perpendicular line through the first, forming a cross, and the second line becomes north and south. So if you want to go northwest, you need to be heading that way. Eventually, you'll be able to track the shadow movement of the trees, and you won't need a stick."

"Cool!" Kiwi said. "But even if we head northwest, we'll probably see you again before morning because we seem to be walking in circles."

"That's Cheat Two." Po winked. "Once you have a direction, you want to pick a feature, like a tree or a boulder, in line with the direction you want to go. Walk to it and then pick another feature a ways ahead and walk to that. Make sure your features line up behind you and ahead of you as far as you can see. If you get disoriented or think you're veering off course, go back to Cheat One and reorient yourself. It's that easy.

"There are a few other cheats I could show you, but I've got to get back to work. Besides, if I teach you too many, you'll forget these two, and they're the ones that will get you to the bridge.

"If I can do it, you can do it." Po stood and dusted himself off. "You think you've got it?"

Kiwi and Clem nodded.

"Best of luck! Hope I don't see you again!" Po yelled as he zipped back into the canopy in his hikipai. "By the way, the Winged are out in full force, so be careful you don't get hung in a tree!"

"That guy was so nice," Kiwi said as they walked away. "I actually feel bad for assuming he'd be a jerk. I can't believe…" Her mouth was back to moving as fast as an s-rail glider going downhill.

The afternoon faded to evening as they made their way from one tree to the next, carefully lining up where they'd come from with where they were going, like Po had taught them. Twice they stopped to make sure they were going the right way. Both times, they were happy to discover they were mostly still on track. The ground turned to pudding beneath their feet.

"Well, at least it's not the same mud we saw earlier. That's a good sign." Clem looked at her muddy legs.

"It *is* a good sign," Kiwi agreed. "Where there's this much mud, there's bound to be water."

Near dusk, they stumbled upon the creek gently twisting its way through the trees.

"Holy Ti'kea, I can't believe it worked—we made it!"

Kiwi dropped her pack and crouched for a drink of water. Catching her reflection, she squeaked, "I looked like this when we were talking to Po?! Augh, why didn't you say anything?"

"Why, were you planning on marrying him?" Clem laughed. "Dinner? Camp?"

Ignoring her first comment, Kiwi answered, "Absolutely. I'm dying right now. I've never been so sore or hungry in my life. My legs feel like they're going to fall off."

"I wish mine would fall off," Clem agreed. "If you set up the tent, I'll cook dinner. That way, we can get to bed faster."

Clem never slept better. Her head hit the pillow, and she remembered nothing until morning.

"I think being lost yesterday will work out in our favor," Kiwi told Clem as they ate breakfast.

"How's that?" Clem peeled the skin off one of the panai'a nuts Po insisted they take with them.

"Well," Kiwi explained, "after they fought with Akylas, Dad and the guys would've headed back to town for more supplies. I figure they're probably two days behind us. We wasted a day being lost, so I bet we see them at the bridge."

"How long do you think it will take us to get to the swamp on the trail Strigops marked?" Clem asked as they broke camp and headed downstream.

"A few weeks, maybe? Not sure. Dad will know. We'll ask him."

"Well, I hope the trail's better than this," Clem complained, fighting her way through a curtain of vines that hung like ropes between the canopy and the forest floor. "We should've brought a machete. All good adventurers pack machetes. Ugh, this forest reminds me of a game we play back home called Twister."

Clem carefully planted one foot on the soft edge of the stream, grabbed a nearby vine, and swung herself in a large arch to the far side.

"Or maybe more like Mission Impossible—this game where gym teachers set up an obstacle course, and you have to try and make it through alive." Grabbing a branch, Clem tried hard to control her rapid descent down the clay-slick bank before she ended up in the creek.

"We could call it Twister Impossible?" Kiwi giggled, sliding into a nearby tree.

Twister Impossible didn't even begin to describe the mud-filled adventure they found themselves in from the moment they'd started hiking. When they weren't ducking beneath the umbrella leaves of a hamalu plant or navigating around the razor-sharp spines of the hoar'kaua tree, they were scrambling over roots and crawling beneath logs. Trying not to get hopelessly tangled in vines or knock themselves out on anything overhead was a job in itself. Despite the obstacles, they clung to the creek as if their lives depended on it.

"Hey, you guys ever ride those things?" Clem panted as two dragonflies flew over their heads. Their crimson-and-black-striped bodies were as long as she was tall. "If we could saddle one up, think about the time we'd save."

"What?! Could you imagine? How hilarious would that be? The Winged would lose their minds if we started flying! Seriously, though, dragonflies have poisonous dust on their wings. It's a defense mechanism. Frogs are immune to it, but it's deadly to people."

"Of course they do." Clem shook her head. "What else is poisonous around here? You know, so I can avoid it?" Clem wasn't sure why she asked. She didn't want to know.

"For bugs? Mostly you want to avoid dragonflies. The

green popo'nahe bite feels like your skin's melting off. Oh, and butterflies are super venomous. I hate butterflies. They're vicious when they bite too. I got bitten once and was in the hospital for a week. Other stuff bites, but nothing's as bad as those three."

"You're joking, right?" Clem burst out laughing, but Kiwi didn't even crack a smile. "Butterflies? You can't be serious. What about spiders? Or those bugs that crawl in your ear and tunnel through your brain? Or mosquitos? Or wasps?"

"Spiders? Venomous? Not to people…that's crazy. We keep them as pets around the city, so they'll eat other bugs and rodents. You're nuts." Kiwi laughed. "Bugs that burrow into your brain? What kind of horror show is your Earth, and why would you want to go back there?"

Their laughter drifted in the breeze with a rainbow of mushroom spores. The silence opened its gaping mouth and ate what little hope Clem had awoken with. Her legs ached. The raw skin on her blistered heels sent jabbing pains up her ankles. She was hungry. Butterflies, her favorite insect ever, were deadly. Her head throbbed behind her eyes. What was she doing out here? She couldn't do this. What if Po was wrong? Even if they made it to the bridge, it was still so far. And there was no guarantee they'd find Kot'ani or the Stone. Hopelessness crept through the silence and attached itself to her like a shadow.

"I'm not taking another step!" Clementine's shriek of protest shattered the stillness, sending startled birds screeching into the late-afternoon sky. "My ankles are dripping blood and sore. My legs are numb. My head is throbbing, and this weird hum in my eardrums is driving me absolutely mad!"

"Wait"—Kiwi tilted her head and squinted—"You hear

that too?"

"Yeah," Clem moaned. "It's been getting louder and louder. I've never been so tired in my life. I wish butterflies would come and eat me and put me out of my misery."

"Clem," Kiwi said slowly, "I think that sound is a waterfall. I think we're almost there. Let's try and make it to the river, okay?"

Clementine nodded. She didn't want to continue. She wanted to face-plant in the dirt and stay there until the moss crept over her body and she melted into the forest floor. Willing her feet to move, she stumbled forward.

A blue smear between her drooping eyelids was all she saw of the river. Her hand moved between the dinner pot and her mouth, but the food tasted like nothing. She and Kiwi fumbled with the tent, then gave up halfway through. It sagged in odd places, but Clem didn't care. She fell asleep, not even bothering to crawl beneath her quilt.

"With any luck, we'll see Dad tomorrow," Kiwi said, stirring the mush in her bowl, "because we only have two momo breakfast left."

Clem stared at the spicy, grainy mush, saying nothing. Her hair was a tangled mess atop her dirt-streaked face. Everything hurt. *Everything.* She was sure her brain was still asleep because finding her mouth with the spoon took tremendous concentration. Was this why adults drank coffee?

"Do you think we'll make the bridge today?" She yawned.

"I hope so. It would suck if Po was wrong and we're supposed to head upstream and not down."

"That's the worst joke I've ever heard," Clem said, blinking. "Not even remotely funny."

Unsure of how many creeks they'd cross, they scooped

water from the stream and filled their bottles. Clem dipped her head in the cold water, forcing her brain to wake up.

As they walked, she prayed they hadn't passed the bridge. She knew Kiwi meant it as a joke, but what if? Or worse, what if the bridge was no longer there, or they were attacked by butterflies? She tried not to laugh since, apparently, the threat was real. What would Adriana James do? Clem drifted off into la-la land, *Adriana James and the Attack of the Killer Butterflies*, writing itself in her head.

"We made it!" Kiwi's gleeful cry snapped Clementine back to reality.

"Um, yeah. That's not a bridge." Clem wasn't complaining. She was stating a fact. They'd been stumbling along the canyon's edge, or as close as they'd dared get to it, all day, only to find this…this…

"Sure it is." Kiwi furrowed her eyebrows in confusion. "It's an old bridge, but it's a bridge."

"No. That is a tightrope with handles." Clementine looked at the three ropes spanning the gaping hole in the earth, the river raging far below. The "bridge" had one thick rope for your feet and two thinner ropes to hold onto. At random, a wooden V held the ropes in place.

Kiwi shrugged. "Well, it's all we've got. We can hole up and cross in the morning or do it now and try to get a few kiro'mika on the far side before nightfall. I think it would be safer to cross now while it's clear. Plus, Dad will be way more impressed if he finds us on the far side!"

"You're right. Let's do it now. If I have to think about it all night, I won't be able to." Clem's knees felt weak just looking at it.

"I'm not excited about this either," Kiwi said, wincing. "These are my second-least favorite kind of bridges. The two-rope bridges are worse."

Surveying the canyon, they watched and waited. Nothing moved in the forest. They could hear no sound over the roar of the Kapu'le'loa.

"You want to go first or second?" Kiwi asked.

"Second, I guess? Unless we can go together." Clem wanted to see how Kiwi did it.

"It will tip over if we go together," Kiwi said matter-of-factly.

"It can do that?" Clem whimpered, but Kiwi kept on talking.

"Wait till I'm on the far side before you cross. Don't go too fast or too slow. Don't stop. And whatever you do, don't look down!"

Clem nodded and watched Kiwi bravely step onto the rope. She slowly but steadily made her way to the far side. Clementine was beyond grateful for Kiwi; she'd never be able to do this without her. Even scared, Kiwi made it look as easy as Ferg would have, only unlike Ferg, she wasn't a jerk about it.

When Kiwi was safely on the far side, Clem walked to the bridge. She clenched her fists into tight balls to try to stop her fingers from shaking. Everything trembled, even her breath. Clem closed her eyes. Andro had better be in serious trouble.

In one fluid movement, Clementine unballed her firsts, grabbed the support ropes firmly in each hand, and took five steps onto the bridge before she could change her mind.

The ropes swayed unsteadily in her hands. She needed to keep moving. Not too slow. Not too fast. Timid step after timid step, Clem shakily balanced across the chasm.

Halfway across, Kiwi started waving her arms and frantically pointing upstream. Clem didn't dare turn her head to see what she was freaking out about, but she knew she had to move. The ropes bucked wildly as her pace quickened. Two feet from the end of the bridge, Clem let go of the ropes and took a flying leap. As she crashed to the ground, Kiwi grabbed her and dove behind a snag.

"What's the—"

Kiwi clasped her hand over Clementine's mouth and shook her head.

Clem could see the bridge still bucking wildly from where they were hidden. A flash of red skimmed past, turned, and circled back.

Clem didn't dare breathe.

A Winged hovered and stopped next to the bridge. He touched the still-swaying rope. Taking two steps in their direction, he scanned the forest. Clem could've reached out and grabbed his feathered ankle if she hadn't been too terrified to move.

Behind them, an ear-splitting screeching and howling drowned out the drumming of her heart. A flash of brown fur and pink skin streaked overhead. The Winged flared his flame-red wings, stumbled backward, and tripped over a branch. Whatever it was that had passed by–Clem hadn't seen what–ran onto the bridge.

The Winged stood and dusted himself off. "Stupid maki'pua!"

Striding over to the bridge, he pulled a blade from its sheath and sliced through the ropes. Clem and Kiwi watched, horrified, as the bridge tumbled into the gorge. The Winged laughed as the maki'pua scampered up the dangling ropes on the far side. Satisfied, he spread his wings and soared downriver.

Clem and Kiwi waited five whole minutes before they dared speak or move.

"What's a maki'pua?" Clem whispered.

Kiwi pointed. On the far side of the gorge, four of five baboon-ish creatures beat their chests in anger. Or maybe they were monkeys? Pigs? Like monkeys, they had long fluffy tails and limbs far too big for their bodies. Their faces resembled furry pigs, with smooshed-up noses, lower teeth-like tusks, and large fuzzy ears, but their hands, feet, and backsides were bright pink and furless, like a baboon's.

"They're so ugly they're actually cute." Clem smiled. "Are they dangerous?"

"Not usually. Unless they're defending their young," Kiwi answered. "Mostly, they stick to the high branches. They don't like the Winged because the Winged hunt them."

"Well, we're lucky they were here." Putting two fingers to her neck, Clementine checked her pulse. "That guy was one step away from finding us. I think I almost had a heart attack."

"I don't know if *lucky* is the right word." Kiwi raked her fingers through the frayed rope. "Dad's not going to be able to get to us now, and we can't get back. There aren't any villages on this route, and we have two and a half days' worth of food at best."

"Well, this sucks." Clem lobbed a rock into the gorge. "What are we going to do?"

"I dunno…" Kiwi raised her shoulders in a half shrug. "It's getting late. I guess we should get away from the river before we set up camp, though. In case that guy comes back."

"Yeah, that would be smart," Clem said. "I think I saw a stream marked on the map not too far ahead. Maybe we can camp there."

Turning, they headed away from the gorge. The trail was overgrown from disuse, but it still made for easier walking than the forest. Clem's exhausted body was glad for the path, but her mind felt more hopeless than ever.

They set up their tent beneath the jumbled roots of a tree and ate half a dinner. Their meager rations didn't make a dent in Clem's hunger. How were they going to make it to the swamp? It had to be weeks away. Clem didn't want to think about it.

"You know what I don't get?" she wondered aloud. "Why do they want me so bad? I mean, it's a flute. Akylas said he had tons more at the museum. And they seem pretty smart, well, you know…like, they can't seriously believe it's got magical powers."

"If you were a Winged, they wouldn't care that you have it." Kiwi's shoulders slumped. "In fact, they'd probably congratulate you. They only care because you're Wingless. Understand?"

"Yeah, I do." Clem frowned. "But I wish I didn't."

CHAPTER 24

"Wai'pea jerky, natikui bars, dried fruit mix, one and a half momo breakfasts, and two dinners." Kiwi dumped the contents of their food bag on the ground in front of her. "Oh, and half a sack of the nuts Po gave us. Three days, if we ration."

"Okay, so where can we get in two or three days?" Clem snapped as she stared intently at the map. She hadn't meant to sound so snarky, but they'd had a lousy night's sleep and barely any breakfast.

"Nowhere." Kiwi was in a mood.

"Well, there's got to be somewhere we can get to." Clem refused to believe they were in as bad a situation as Kiwi thought.

"There isn't." Kiwi didn't even look at the map.

"We know where we are, and there's a trail," Clem offered. "Two days ago, we were completely lost in the middle of nowhere. So we've got to be in a better situation than we were then. Maybe we can work our way back toward the s-rail on this side of the river and meet up with your dad there?"

Kiwi pursed her lips.

"We can't"—she jabbed her finger at the map—"because of this. So, unless you know how to scale a five-hundred-foot cliff, swim up a raging river, or build a bridge, the only way out of here is Strigops's path. Which, at best, will take us weeks. And that would have been fine if Dad were coming with more food, but now he can't."

"Well, can't we eat things from the forest? You must know

what we can eat out here, right?" Clem asked.

"Are you for real?" Kiwi's eyes narrowed. "How would I know that? What do you think harvesters are for? I get my food from the market, like everyone else. Do you know how to collect food from your forest?"

"Well, I know what raspberries and huckleberries look like. I think," Clementine mumbled. "Everyone here seems so earthy. I thought…"

"Well, there are no raspberries or knuckleberries in Pangier. I know how to find mokipo nuts—but they don't grow here—and kaw'a berries. But those grow in the canopy, and we don't happen to have a hikipai or a ladder. And, in case you forgot, the Winged hang out in the canopy. We can eat blue tarantulas and pirali beetles…but, eww, gross. We don't have nets, bows, or spears. And even if we did, I'm not killing anything! Would you?! Because you don't look like a butcher! So, my best guess is we'll starve to death right about here." Kiwi angrily stabbed at a place right next to where they were camped.

"What's…this?" Clem pointed to a mark on the map an inch from Kiwi's finger. It looked like an egg on stilts with an *X* through it. Next to it was some text.

"No way." Kiwi leaned in for a closer look. She stared at Clem wide-eyed. "That's a rakia! It's like an emergency hut for hunters, loggers, harvesters, and explorers. They're usually stocked with medical gear, a signal system, blankets…and rations. Lots of rations."

"Can we take them?" Clem asked.

"This is totally an emergency, so yeah." Kiwi nodded.

"So, what are we thinking…" Clem spread her fingers, measuring the space between them and the rakia. "It's longer than the distance from the s-rail to the bridge, but this time, we won't get lost. Four days? Five?"

"If we hike fast, I bet we could do it in four." A glimmer of hope returned to Kiwi's face. "We'll be starving by the time we get there though."

"I'm already starving." Clem threw on her pack. "Let's go!"

"Yeah. Let's do this."

Despite being overgrown, the trail was easy to follow as it wound its way into the hills.

"Who made this trail, anyway?" Clem asked, more out of boredom than curiosity.

"Loggers. But all the log camps around here were abandoned a long time ago. There are three marked on the map, but they all say 'uninhabited.'" Kiwi answered.

"Maybe there's food in one of them too." Even though they'd just eaten breakfast, Clem was still hungry.

She tried to focus on anything else. The soft, velvety moss beneath her feet. The scenery. How could one place be so green? She missed the never-ending blue of the ocean, the steel-gray sky, Victoria's vibrant colors, the ruby-red lanterns at Băoshí, and Orange Chicken. God, how she missed Orange Chicken! And bubble tea. Every thought circled back to food.

"This is it." Kiwi broke a natikui bar and handed half of it to Clem. "The last of the food."

They'd hiked all day, and this was it. This was dinner. They managed to stretch their rations to three whole days. The less they'd eaten, the slower they walked. They'd optimistically thought they could make it to the rakia in four days, but they were moving at a snail's pace. Clem doubted they made it more than halfway.

"I'm so hungry." Clem's mouth watered. "But I don't want

to eat this because then it will be gone."

"We could save it for breakfast?" Kiwi eyed her piece with the same mix of longing and sorrow.

"But I'm so hungry," Clem repeated. "I don't know how we'll make it two or three more days without food."

Hunger winning out, they greedily wolfed down the last few morsels, careful not to drop a single crumb. Still starving, they crawled into bed.

Their first day without food was horrible. There was nothing Clem could think about but food. The bark of the trees curled like fruit leather. Giant mushrooms became freshly baked buns. Her mouth watered at the chocolate-pudding mud jiggling beneath her feet. And the flowers? The flowers smelled like a candy shop. How had she not noticed that before?

Kiwi managed to find a handful of nuts she thought were edible. They tasted bitter and sucked the moisture from their mouths, but they ate them anyway.

"Two more days," Kiwi groaned as she pulled off her boots and climbed into bed. "And then we feast at the rakia."

"You know what's sad?" Clem pulled her quilt over her dirty body. "When my stuff went missing from the chest, I wrote a note to get it back. Andro sent back everything but a pair of my earrings. His note said, *Sorry, we sell earrings for eat*. They weren't expensive, so I assumed he used the money to buy snacks after school, you know? But Dohi sounds bleak, really bleak. I've been thinking about it all day, and I think he sold them to eat. Like, because he was hungry. I didn't think…I didn't know hunger like this was real. Had I known, I would've never demanded my stuff back. I feel terrible."

A shame so deep washed over Clementine that she thought

she might drown in it. She turned toward the tent wall, so Kiwi wouldn't see her wet cheeks. Kiwi tried comforting her, but Clem was inconsolable.

The second day was worse than the first. Clem wondered if the gnawing hunger ever went away. She drank water until she felt like she'd burst, but the hunger persisted, eating her from within.

The hungrier they got, the slower they walked. They barely spoke; talking took too much energy. The less they said, the slower time moved.

Without food and conversation, their lives were reduced to trudging along. The trail had long since ceased to be fun. The incessant green annoyed her. Clem would have climbed a tree just to see the blue sky if she had the energy. All that was left to look forward to was the next sleep, when she could dream she was back home for a few short hours.

Clementine woke in the dead of night, desperately needing to pee. That's what she got for trying to drown her hunger. Outside the tent, things were slithering, creeping, waiting. She wasn't going out there. No way. Pulling the leather necklace from around her neck, she tried to distract herself with the flute. There had to be a clue somewhere.

It had been two days since she'd eaten, six since they'd had their last full trail meal, and nine days since they'd left Whaka'wai. Why was she even looking for clues? There was no way they'd make it to the rakia, let alone Kot'ani.

She really had to pee. Sighing, Clem made a move for the tent door.

A twig snapped.

"Oh, heck no," she whispered under her breath and went

back to thinking about how long she'd been in Pangier. She'd been in Whaka'wai for nearly five days. That took her back to when she'd fallen in the river. The icy-cold river. Water. Flowing water. She couldn't wait until morning. She had to pee now.

Unclipping the door, Clem blinked. The forest wasn't nearly as dark as she'd expected. Everything glowed green, blue, and purple. Not a bright glow like the wall around Whaka, just enough to outline things.

"Don't look around," Clem whispered to herself. "Just go and come back."

Careful not to breach the perimeter of the oro'nalu alarms, Clem darted out of the tent. As her eyes adjusted to the green-tinged gray, she saw two glowing orbs staring at her from behind the nearest tree. Eyes! Clem blinked. One pair became two and then a hundred. Big eyes, small eyes, glowing red eyes. The forest was alive, and it was watching her.

Clem swallowed hard. She shouldn't have opened the tent. Why did she drink so much water before bed? Even with the perimeter alarms, she was never going to sleep again. Not now that she knew hundreds of creatures were out here.

As Clem stood, ready to dart back to the safety of the tent, something large and furry dropped off an overhanging branch and landed on her head.

Clementine shrieked. Arms flailing, she stumbled backward as a blue puff landed at her feet. Grabbing a stick, she clubbed wildly at the ground.

The oro'nalu alarm began beeping and screeching. The eyes of the forest, once still and silent, thundered off in every direction. Someone screamed.

"What the—" Kiwi frantically poked her head out of the tent.

"I had to pee," Clem panted, staring at the ground where eight hairy legs lay in a twisted pile. "It fell…it fell on my head! Oh my god, what is it?"

Kiwi scrambled out of the tent, silenced the alarm, and nudged the fuzzy blue heap at Clementine's feet.

"Well, it was a blue tarantula," she answered. "They're harmless."

"It didn't feel harmless when it dropped out of the tree and attacked me," Clem said, defending herself. "Hey, didn't you say blue tarantulas were edible?"

"Yeah, but they're, like, pets…" Kiwi scrunched her face in disgust.

"Tasty pets?" Clem asked. "I mean, it is dead…"

"Yeah, it would be a shame to waste it, right?" Kiwi shrugged.

Once they'd collected a handful of sticks, they roasted the tarantula over a small fire.

"This is delicious." Clem broke off another leg. "It tastes like crab. I wish we had butter."

"It's so good. I can't believe I'm saying that… I'm so sorry, tasty little friend." Kiwi swallowed. "I promise I wouldn't eat you if I wasn't starving. I honestly don't think I could make it another day without food, though."

The new day dawned as they sucked the last morsels of meat from the charred legs.

"Guess we should pack up and get going," Kiwi said, deflating like a puffer fish. "We'd better make it there today."

"Just keep thinking about all the food." Clem said, encouragingly.

Crawling up the hillside, Clem's stomach growled as if she hadn't eaten at all. Too bad a maki'pua hadn't landed on her head. She could have eaten the whole thing and finished it with a milkshake.

Near the top of the hill, the trail forked. A mossy old sign, draped in flowering vines, pointed right. Clem didn't need Kiwi to translate; the rakia was marked with the same egg-shaped symbol as on their map.

"First one there gets all the rations!" Clem ran up the trail using the last ounce of energy she had.

Popping out in a small clearing in the forest, Clem scanned the sky. Blue, it was so beautifully blue. How could anyone live without open sky? She could have stood there, staring at it forever. But they couldn't risk the exposure. It was the first time they'd been in the open since they'd crossed the bridge, and that had nearly been their demise.

The shelter sat at the far edge of the clearing. Behind it, the hill dropped steeply into a long horseshoe-shaped valley. Clem laughed. The rakia looked exactly like the mark on the map—a giant woven egg on stilts with two large red *X*s painted on it. Slits of glass ran down the sides, letting in the light. A long set of wooden steps and a small deck hung off the side facing the valley.

"We should get inside quick," Clem said, scanning the sky. "The Winged have an uncanny ability to find us whenever we're in the open too long."

"Probably because they have excellent long-distance vision," Kiwi explained as they darted across the clearing and up the steps.

"I wondered about that." Clem furrowed her eyebrows. "I bet they have good night vision too. Hey, is the door supposed to be open like this?"

Kiwi shook her head. There was no use being quiet now. If anyone was in there, they'd already heard them coming.

"Hello?" Clem bravely poked her head inside.

The rakia was a disaster. Chairs and a table lay overturned on the floor. The blankets and sleeping cushions from the two bunk beds near the back looked like they'd been put through a wood chipper. The logs in the fireplace had been thrown everywhere; one of them was lodged in the wall where the signal system had been. Every cupboard and drawer was open, half their doors hanging from a single hinge. Medical supplies and the tattered remains of ration pouches lay scattered across the floor.

Clem and Kiwi darted from cupboard to drawer.

"No, no, no…" Kiwi moaned. "No, please, no."

Empty. They were all empty.

"Winged?" Clem picked a shredded ration pouch off the floor and checked to see if there was anything edible inside.

"No. Probably that troop of stupid maki'pua." Kiwi examined the long claw marks across one of the blankets. "Or a puhi mang'oa. They're cute but super destructive, like a fuzzy, slow-moving hurricane. Someone must have forgotten to latch the door."

"Well, there has to be something left." Clem scoured every square inch of the shelter.

"We're going to die here. And I'm too hungry to even care." Kiwi dropped the blanket on the floor and wandered outside.

Clem followed her.

"Well, at least we picked an incredible place to die. This place is…" Clem plopped on the steps and set her head on Kiwi's shoulder.

"Magic, right?" Kiwi's head rested against Clementine's. "The map says it's called Rao'āwa o Mansani Anue'anue, the Valley of a Thousand Rainbows."

Poking out of the greenery, a steep cliff encircled the

valley. Hundreds of gleaming white ribbons of water cascaded over the cliffs, racing toward the broad river far below. Rainbows. Clem had never seen so many rainbows. They ricocheted off the waterfalls, arching one after another across the valley. She wasn't about to count them, but a thousand seemed right.

"Well, we made it nine days on our own without dying," Clem said after a long while. "That's eight days longer than I thought we'd make it."

"You thought we were going to die on our first day?" Kiwi snorted.

"Oh, absolutely. I thought I'd die in the first five minutes after I appeared here." Clem wasn't sure why, but she found this exceptionally funny. "And then again when Raveen took me to Ra'ani. When I tripped and landed on the couch in Raveen's house. When I was climbing down the tree. Then, like, a dozen times when I was running for my life."

She and Kiwi were in hysterics.

"Again, when I fell in the river. When you found me, I thought you were going to kill me. When the s-rail derailed. Just before we met Po. Crossing that ridiculous bridge. When the tarantula landed on my head last night. Every time I see a butterfly. Basically, all the time. Except maybe when we were in Whaka'wai. I felt safe there."

"I miss home." Kiwi stopped laughing and wiped her eyes on her sleeve. "And my dad."

"I miss home too," Clem sighed. "And my family. I even miss my brother. And I didn't think that was possible."

A cloud blocked the sun. One by one, the rainbows disappeared. When the sun poked back out, they flickered back to life, dancing across the valley. How was it possible to be surrounded by so much beauty yet feel this miserable and hopeless?

Clem's eyes closed, the bright sun warming her eyelids. She wished she'd sent Andro a note telling him the key had arrived. Now he was going to think she'd abandoned him. She imagined the chest, sitting on her desk, crammed full of urgent messages.

If only she'd known how the flute worked, she'd have hugged her family goodbye and told her parents she loved them. She couldn't say why, but even if she'd known then what she knew now, she still would've picked it up. She still would've chosen to come to this place. She still would've tried. Maybe she was a rock, after all.

"Clementine?"

"Mmhmm," Clem mumbled.

"Do you see that?"

"See what?" Clem's eyes fluttered open. Two hummingbirds chased each other into the valley.

"That—" Kiwi pointed in the direction the birds had flown. "See the pond down there? Look to the right."

"What is that?" Clem furrowed her eyebrows and squinted. "Smoke?"

"That's what I thought," Kiwi responded.

A long wisp of white curled out of the canopy and drifted off in a thin line.

"People?" Clem asked. "Or a forest fire?"

"It wasn't there, and then it was," Kiwi answered. "Has to be people."

"I thought you said no one lived in this valley? That the logging camps were abandoned."

"Well, that's what the map says." Kiwi tilted her head. "But the map only lists Wingless settlements."

"Winged? Harvesters?" Clem thought aloud.

"Maybe. You think whoever it is, has food?"

"I was wondering the same thing. They're out here in the middle of nowhere. They'd have to, right? Besides us, who would come to a place like this without food?"

Kiwi jumped up. "What if it's my dad? What if, because we got lost, they passed us and crossed the bridge before we did? What if they've been ahead of us the whole time?"

"Maybe!" Clem answered. It would be good to have someone who knew what they were doing in charge again. "But why would they be there? Doesn't the trail stay high?"

"Shortcut? Maybe they thought they could cut us off up ahead?" Kiwi offered.

"We should go down there. Oh, I really hope it's your dad. What if it's not, though? What if it's Winged, and they catch us and take us back to Akylas. I don't want to go back there. Falk will kill me. I know it."

"We'll be careful," Kiwi assured her. "We'll scout it first. We can wait for them to fall asleep, climb the tree, and steal their food! Even if it is Winged and they catch us, at least they'll feed us. And we can always escape. You've done it before."

"Okay," Clem said, trying to convince herself.

"How exactly are we getting down there?" She pointed at the steep drop-off in front of them.

"Strigops's path stays high to the west of here." Kiwi pulled out the map and double-checked. "We're supposed to return to the fork and take the other trail. But if we go east instead, the trail crosses a creek and turns into the valley."

"It's going to take forever to get there." Clem's eyes wandered from the late-afternoon sky to the valley far below. "We should go, so we can make it before nightfall."

They grabbed their packs and headed back to the trail. They

hadn't walked long when they came to a deep, broad creek. The dark water moved fast over the slick rocks. If there had ever been a bridge, it was long gone.

"What is it with us and bridges?" Clem moaned. "Seriously!"

"Maybe there's a shallower place to cross downstream." Kiwi turned and followed the creek.

"Is that a boat?" Clem pointed at a mossy bow-shaped log leaning against a tree.

"Yeah, looks like an old dugout." Kiwi ran her hand over the hull. "Weird place for a boat."

"Could we use it to row across?" Clem eyed the swift-moving water.

"Are you serious? There's a cliff ahead. Maybe if it had wings and could fly. Could you imagine? A flying boat?"

Clementine was about to explain airplanes to Kiwi when they stumbled to the cliff's edge. The creek should've leaped over, but it didn't. The water had been funneled into a wooden chute that swooped over the ledge like a giant waterslide and disappeared into the valley.

"Cool!" Kiwi smiled excitedly. "A flume! When the loggers harvest the forest, sometimes they'll move logs like this! They must have built this one back in the day to send logs to the Anue'anue River. That explains those ponds we saw by the smoke. They're probably holding ponds!"

Clementine stared at the thick pieces of rotting lumber nailed together in a giant U shape. Sagging wooden pillars held the weight of the entire creek high in the air. Water seeped through the cracks, streaming from the thick moss underbelly.

Clem's gaze followed the flume. At the bottom of the first sharp dip, it curved into the forest. Wave after wave of water sloshed over the side of the bend. Farther down the mountainside, it peeked out between the trees again. As far as she could tell, it was intact all the way to the pond. How it was still standing was a mystery.

"Are you thinking what I'm thinking?" Clementine raised her eyebrows mischievously.

"Well, there is a boat," Kiwi said, nodding slowly. "So obviously you can. I mean, people have."

"The flume kinda looks like if we kicked it, it would fall apart, though," Clem countered.

"Then we won't kick it. It would be way faster than walking. We might even be able to catch up with Dad tonight."

"We can't even get to the trail." Clem exhaled deeply. "Besides, I have blisters under my blisters."

"And we're starving, don't forget that. We need to conserve our energy by any means possible," Kiwi added. "We'd be stupid not to. You think it's safe?"

"Well"—Clem wandered back to the dugout—"I mean, there wouldn't be a boat if it wasn't, right?"

"True," Kiwi agreed.

They prized the heavy boat away from the tree, stumbling backward as it broke free of the roots and vines.

"It's carved out of a single log," Kiwi said, inspecting it. "So, it probably doesn't leak."

Together they pushed the small craft over the bank and into the water.

"Have you ever done this before?" Kiwi bit her lip.

"Kinda." Clem tossed her pack in the back of the boat. "I went on a log flume ride at an amusement park once. But there was a seatbelt and minimal risk of injury or death."

"A what?" Kiwi had one foot in the front of the boat.

Clementine explained what an amusement park was while searching for something they could use as an oar.

"Your Earth sounds so wild." Kiwi breathed deeply. "Maybe one day I can visit you there."

"Are we really doing this?" Clem hopped into the back of the boat.

Before either of them had a chance to change their minds, the current caught them and sent them rocketing downstream.

CHAPTER 25

The dugout plummeted downhill like a bobsled. The wind rushed through Clem's long dark hair, blood surged through her veins, her heart leaped into her throat. She felt weightless in the best way possible. Clem threw her hands in the air and screamed.

At the bottom of the first drop, the tiny boat smashed against the wood railing, nearly overturning as the flume curved into the forest. Water sprayed over the hull.

A flash of green. Another bend. The boat slowed. Clem could have sworn she saw the face of a monstrous sloth poking out from behind the foliage. Before she got a second look, the flume dipped, the dugout picked up speed, and the forest became nothing more than a blur.

Clementine was just hoping the ride would never end when they splashed to a halt in a small pond. She was drenched, half a foot of water sloshed at her feet.

"Oh my god, that was so much fun!" Her heart pounded beneath her rib cage.

"I wanna go again!" Kiwi squealed from the front of the boat.

"Fun ride?" an unfamiliar voice chimed in.

Clem cringed. In all the excitement, she'd let her guard down. She could hear her mother in her head: *Clementine! You have to pay more attention!*

She and Kiwi nervously scanned the shore.

"Up here, girls," said a brawny woman waving at them from atop a pile of abandoned logs. Everything about her said *don't mess with me*, except for her welcoming smile and soft brown eyes.

Grabbing their packs from the bottom of the waterlogged boat, they clambered onto the rickety dock. The woman was off the woodpile in three giant steps.

Her two-toned brown hair, flecked with gold plumage, was slicked back in a mullet. Streaks of tiny cream-colored feathers ran from the bridge of her nose, across the top of her brown eyes and tanned forehead, and into her hairline.

Clem loved that no one in Pangier looked the same, and they didn't try to. Like snowflakes, no two people were alike. They all had their own feathers, patterns, markings, and colors. Even though she was more or less accustomed to the feathers, she still found it hard not to stare. Everyone was so unique. Clem assumed her own "uniqueness" hadn't gone unnoticed by the strange glances she was getting.

For the first time ever, Clem wondered what Andro looked like. Did he have wings or a forked tongue? It hadn't crossed her mind to ask. Not that it mattered, but she was suddenly dying to know.

"Hullo! I'm Wek, forest steward of the Anue'anue. What brings you girls this far out in the middle of nowhere?" Wek thrust a muscular arm toward them, firmly gripping their hands in greeting.

"Funny you should ask," Kiwi said, inhaling. Before Clementine could stop her, she went off. "We were headed off in search of Kot'ani with my dad and his team, but then the Winged blew the bridge, and the s-rail derailed, and Strigops gave us this map and told us they'd catch up with us. We ran for, like, ever, but then we got lost. So lost. But a harvester told us how to get to the creek, and thank the many gods, it led us to the river. Then, as we crossed the bridge, this Winged flew up. Anyhow, he cut the ropes, and the maki'pua were howling like crazy. We ran out of food days ago, but Clementine clubbed a tarantula to death, and we ate it, poor thing. The stupid maki'pua have destroyed the rakia, and all the rations are gone. Then as we were getting ready to literally die on the front steps, we saw smoke down here. We were hoping it was my dad with food. There's no bridge over the creek anymore because I seriously think bridges hate us or something. Which is fine, whatever. We were too hungry to walk anyway. Then we found the flume and a boat. We need to get to Wheku, on the swamp, because Strigops said they'd meet us there if they couldn't catch up to us. But we'll probably die out here because we are so bad at this. I'm Kiwi, and this is Clementine, by the way. But you can call her Clem because *Clementine* is so long. Hey, you don't have any food, do you, Wek? 'Cause I think I'm about to pass out."

"Is that so?" Wek raised an eyebrow and surveyed Kiwi and Clementine with the same look of incredulity Emos had the day Kiwi brought Clem home.

Clem shrugged and nodded. Kiwi's thirty-second recap was more information than she would've shared with a complete stranger, but it was what it was.

"Well, we'd better head to Base and get you girls some dinner then. Come on." Wek turned and strode up the dock. "You can set up camp in the yard for the night. Maybe take a bath and wash those clothes because you look and smell like you've been out here for a year. Then we'll figure out how to get you to Wheku in the morning."

The Forest Steward Base—a cozy round hut on stilts—sat beside a meandering creek on the edge of a clearing. They found Wek's partner, Rea, in the garden, furiously scribbling notes in a logbook.

"There's some sort of foreign invader I've not seen before in the roo'bis. And I saw no less than three Winged while I was inspecting the North Forest today." Rea continued scribbling. "I wonder what they're up to…"

"I found some foreign invaders myself while I was out by the abandoned log ponds," Wek replied. "And they're hungry. They'd probably eat the whole forest if we let them."

"Oh, no. Really?" Rea looked up in alarm, ready to grab her gear and go save the trees.

Wek pointed at Clem and Kiwi, still dripping from their ride down the flume.

"Foreign invaders." Rea smiled and laughed, but she seemed confused. Clem couldn't imagine they got many visitors. "They look more like guests to me. To what do we owe the pleasure?"

While Wek and Rea cooked dinner over an open fire, Clem and Kiwi used their last bit of strength to wash off the dirt and set up their tent. Clem wasn't sure what was cooking, but it smelled like the best summer BBQ ever. Clem wiped the drool off the tent. She was so hungry she could rip the meat off the fire and eat it raw. Would it be rude to tell Wek and Rea there was no need to waste time cooking it?

"There's been a lot of Winged activity over the valley the last few days." Rea set a bowl of greens on the outdoor table. "Like I was telling you earlier, Wek, I saw three today. They're probably looking for new territory. We should send them a message. Let them know we won't be giving up the Anue'anue without a fight."

"I don't think so. Their flight patterns and high perches suggest they're looking for something." Wek slapped piles of charred meat on a plate and side-eyed Kiwi and Clem. "You girls wouldn't know anything about that, would you?"

"Oh, don't be ridiculous, Wek. They're just girls…"

"Just girls?" Wek responded. "When I was their age, I ran away from home, attached bedsheet sails to a dugout, and tried running the Kako'Mao River to the ocean. If I recall, you were scaling trees and placing booby traps to mess with the Winged. Not to mention sneaking into Winged villages and stealing stuff."

"Well, you did eventually make it to the Pantha. And in my defense, it's not stealing if it didn't belong to them in the first place. I like to think I was liberating Wingless property."

Wek laughed. "That's not the point. The point is, these two are plenty old enough to wreak havoc, and judging from their guilty faces, they are. So, what kind of mischief have you two been in that's gone and got the Winged's feathers all ruffled?"

"Well," Kiwi started. Cringing, Clem put her hand over the flute beneath her shirt and shook her head. "Clementine, as you may have noticed, is not from around here. In her, uh, travels, she has found some…clues…that might help the Wingless discover the location of the Forgotten City of Kot'ani. She's partnered with my dad, Emos, and his team to find it this summer. The Winged are aware of this because Clem had an unfortunate run-in with them while crossing their territory on her way to meet with the expedition. And now, they're kinda, um, after her…us…because they want the…clues…so they can discover 'Tua'mua' first."

Clem nodded, impressed. She hadn't known Kiwi could control what tumbled out of her mouth.

"Ah, the Kot'ani/Tua'mua issue rages on, I see," Rea said with a sigh. "We've been out here so long, I forgot that was a thing."

"I didn't want to say anything because it's rude and irrelevant"—Wek smiled—"but I wondered why you looked like a plucked hen. You certainly don't look Amphi. Where exactly are you from, Clem?"

"A long way away..." Clem drifted off, staring at the mounds of food on the table. "God, I'm so hungry..."

"She's from the other side of the Central Pangian Range." Kiwi licked her lips.

"Pretty obvious we aren't going to get the rest of the story now there's food on the table." Wek chuckled. "Let's eat."

While Clem and Kiwi ravenously crammed food in their mouths, Wek and Rea regaled them with tales of their adventures. They'd met in college, where they'd realized Wek's dream of becoming the first person to raft the Kako'Mao River from its source to the Pantha Ocean. They'd been arrested for protesting logging in Winged territory.

"People were living in those trees! Winged and Wingless might not be friends, but that's crossing a line." Wek shook her head in disgust.

They'd climbed a handful of mountains, one of which they'd named Kew'a'aer, which spelled Wek and Rea backward. When they finally decided to get serious about life, they became harvesters.

"We were harvesting when we first saw the Anue'anue Valley. Even in the state it was in, having been heavily logged, we fell in love with it! Went home, applied for the forest steward position, and haven't looked back since!" Rea smiled out at the meadow.

"Wouldn't want to be anywhere else!" Wek added.

"Where do you get your food and supplies, though?" Clem wiped her mouth with the back of her hand and leaned back in her chair. Her stomach was about to explode, and it felt oh-so-good. "This was delicious, by the way. Thank you."

"Well, the few things we can't harvest, grow, hunt, or make

ourselves, we carry in from town. Every few months, we'll hike to the s-rail and head to Whaka'wai for a weekend. Sounds like we're going to need to do some bridgework before we go again, though. In the spring, we head to Wheku and spend time on the swamp with some Amphi friends, where we stock up on the basics. Mostly we live off the land. And you are very welcome. It's nice to have guests who enjoy our cooking."

"How far is it to the swamp from here?" Kiwi rubbed her belly.

"Two weeks, if you know what you're doing," Rea answered. "Three weeks if you stick to the main path."

"Three weeks?!" Kiwi groaned. "Are there any villages along the way?"

Rea shook her head.

"It took us nine days to get this far. It's going to take us a month to make it to the swamp," Clem grumbled. "We can't carry that much food."

"Dad might still be ahead of us," Kiwi reminded her. "With supplies."

Rea broke it to them gently: "We haven't seen anyone pass by in months. We'd have noticed even if your dad and his crew had stuck to the high trail. We make it our job to know who's in the area." She paused. "I know you girls are anxious to catch your father, but I think there's a real chance he's on the far side of the bridge, and you won't see him until you reach Wheku."

"Ugh, we're gonna die," Clem moaned, looking at Kiwi's disappointed face.

Wek and Rea glanced at each other.

"We think it would be best if you girls stayed here a few days," Rea continued. "Wek and I can teach you some basic harvesting. How to hunt and trap a few of the smaller, easier targets. Enough skills to get you to Wheku."

"The rest would do you good too. Give you time for your blisters and bruises to heal, and we can fatten you up a bit," Wek said, smiling. "I wouldn't feel right sending you off as you are."

Clem and Kiwi looked at each other.

"We appreciate the offer, and I know we need all the help we can get," Clem responded. "But Strigops said not to stay in any one place too long. With what the Winged did to the s-rail and Whaka'wai, we don't feel right putting you in that kind of danger."

"Don't you worry about the Winged," Rea said with a snort. "They don't come within two kiro'mika of the Base because they're scared of us. They know they'll get a sleeper arrow in the butt and wake up wingless if they mess with Wek and Rea."

"Do you think Rea was kidding about Winged waking up wingless?" Clementine asked as she and Kiwi walked back to their tent.

"I dunno." Kiwi yawned. "Probably not. Except for food, Wingless avoid killing all living things if it can be helped. When the Winged attack us, if any prisoners are taken, or if anyone is left behind because they're injured and can't fly, we don't kill them. They're just de-winged, so they're no longer a threat. Wek and Rea seem decent, so I could see them doing that."

"That seems like a fate worse than death," Clem said, cringing. "Being so free, then suddenly you can't fly, ever again. Even though I hate Raveen and Falk, I'd still never wish for someone to chop off their wings. That's cruel."

"Well, what are we supposed to do?" Kiwi was on the defensive. "Let them go home and bring their friends back to attack us again? They have no problem killing us and taking us hostage. It's not like we enslaved them unprovoked like they do to us. De-winged can get jobs and go to school. They live among us freely. They just don't have wings anymore, like the rest of us."

"And Wingless accept them?" Clementine asked.

"Well, yeah. I mean, mostly. They're still Winged. It's complicated. You can't really understand if you don't have Winged where you live," Kiwi said with a huff.

Clementine understood, and it made her heart hurt.

"We should just be happy we're somewhere safe with lots of food and good people who want to help us," Kiwi mumbled. "I'm going to sleep so well tonight."

"Yeah," Clem sighed. "Let's sleep until noon."

CHAPTER 26

"You girls up?" Any dream Clem had of their stay at Wek and Rea's being a restful vacation was shattered in the wee hours of the morning.

"No," Clem moaned, forcing her eyes open. It was pitch-black outside.

"What time is it?" Kiwi protested.

"Time to learn how to survive in the bush." Wek sounded entirely too happy. "Different things are best harvested at different times of the day, and dawn is one of the best times. Thought we'd start early and collect some breakfast!"

Clem and Kiwi unenthusiastically rolled out of bed and followed Wek and Rea around the meadow. Wek held a plant while Rea explained what it was. Afterward, they'd grill Clem or Kiwi on what they'd learned. It was like being in school.

"What is this called?" Wek picked up a long yellow fruit with fluffy red orbs jutting out of its skin.

"Pan'a kamo'uka?" Clem wasn't sure. She'd learned like a dozen new words in a row.

"Somebody's paying attention!" Wek smiled.

"And how do we tell a pan'a kamo'uka from the deadly kamo'a pan'uka?"

"The pan'a has fuzzy red orbs, and the kamo'a has rough red spots?" Kiwi answered.

"And?" Rea prodded.

"And pan'a only grows on the ground, but kamo'a vines climb trees?"

"Opposite, but close." Rea nodded. "You will never find a

pan'a on the ground."

They were back in the garden by sunrise, washing and cleaning their finds and learning what parts of each plant they'd collected were edible and what wasn't; what was best eaten raw and what was best cooked; what could be carried all day and eaten later, and what needed to be eaten immediately.

"Food really does taste better when you gather it yourself." Kiwi smiled as she went for a second bowl. "And here I thought that was something harvesters said to be smug."

Wek and Rea laughed.

"Do you even remember what half of this stuff is called or how to find it?" Clem stared at her bowl. "Because I don't."

"Hang out for a few days. You'll get there," Rea assured her.

After breakfast, Wek and Rea put them to work in the garden. After lunch, they got a crash course in building tarantula and beetle traps.

"You can try spearing them, which we'll cover later, but at the end of the day, a trap's less messy and more efficient." Wek examined the point Clementine had carved on the end of a long stick. Finding a hamalu plant, its large umbrella leaf nearly touching the ground, she hammered the half-dozen pointed sticks through the stalk, so the sharp bits stuck out the bottom of the leaf. Then Wek pulled the stem back until the leaf lay upside down in the opposite direction. She propped the stalk back with a stick tied to a trip cord, and sprinkled bits of leftover breakfast on the ground.

"Ants will be attracted to the fruit," she explained. "The tarantula will come for the ants. The spider moves across the ground, tripping the cord with its many legs and—" Wek pulled the cord. The stick fell, causing the umbrella leaf to snap forward like a giant fly swatter. It hit the ground with a thud, driving the spikes deep into the dirt. "With any luck, one of the spikes has hit the tarantula, and you wake up to breakfast!"

"If you're not in an area with hamula plants, or if you want to catch small game, you can also set a deadfall trap or a hanging snare."

Wek demonstrated both techniques, then left Kiwi and Clementine to set their own traps.

"I know we need to know this," Kiwi said. "But what are we going to do if we actually catch something? I can't imagine cooking something cute and furry."

"Me neither," Clem agreed. "But then again, I never thought I'd get hungry enough to eat a spider."

In the morning, Clem and Kiwi checked their traps.

"Empty, empty, and we got something?" Clem wasn't sure what it was, but it was something!

"A pirali beetle!" Rea sounded impressed. "Well done!"

"Four traps and only one catch, though," Clem said with a frown. "I thought we'd made pretty decent traps, but two didn't even work."

"You'll get it." Wek tossed the beetle on the grill. "Takes a lot of practice to get good at this. I'm impressed you got anything on your first try."

Clem and Kiwi beamed at each other.

Pirali beetle wasn't tarantula, but it wasn't the worst thing Clem had ever eaten. Plus, it was easy to cook, and they'd caught it themselves.

They learned to fish over the next few days, though they weren't great at it. Wek tried to teach them to spear things, but all they'd managed to do was punch a hole through the roof.

"Maybe you should stick to traps." Wek laughed heartily

as a spear narrowly missed her foot. "Might be more your thing. Rea and I need to check the North Forest and see how the roo'bis is doing. Plus, we want to do a little recon and see if the Winged are still hanging around the valley. While we're gone, maybe the two of you should read up on plants you'll find closer to the swamp. We don't have many swamp species around these parts, but you'll need to know about them in a few weeks. That'll keep you indoors and out of sight while we're gone, too…in case any Winged decide to get brave."

Wek led the girls inside to a long, low shelf half-hidden behind pots of hanging vines. Though there were nearly as many plants inside as out, the Base was cozy and homelike.

"Hey, Rea? Where are those books on edible and useful plants of the Mutina'kol'e Swamp Basin? I thought the girls could look them over while we're out."

Rea popped out of a back room, a backpack full of potions and powders slung over her shoulder. "Wasn't sure what would work best on the pests attacking the roo'bis"—she patted the backpack—"so I'm bringing the entire arsenal." She pulled two books off the shelf and handed one to Clementine and one to Kiwi. "You'll want to look these ones over. That ought to keep you busy for a while."

Clem opened her book and pretended to read until Wek and Rea left.

"You have no idea what that says, do you?" Kiwi said, snickering.

"Not a word." Clem slammed it shut and leaned over the table to get a better look at what Kiwi was reading. "Hey, no fair, yours is all pictures!"

"The important parts are text," Kiwi countered. "There's actually some pretty useful stuff in here. Listen to this…"

Clem and Kiwi were still deeply engrossed in the book when Rea and Wek returned around nightfall.

"Well, the roo'bis will live another day, but there are still two Winged out there, watching the north end of the valley." Rea sat at the table. "Why are they after you again? What could you possibly know about Tua'mua?"

"Oh, that's pretty." Wek pointed at the hummingbird Clementine had been absentmindedly fiddling with while Kiwi read passages from the book.

"This is what they're after," Clem said, holding up the flute.

"Why that?" Rea asked.

"My friend Andro asked me to help him find some sort of sacred stone that was left here long ago for safekeeping. I told him I'd help him, but I'm doing a terrible job so far.

"This"—Clem took the hummingbird from around her neck and held it in the air—"is supposed to be a clue to the Stone's location, but I can't figure it out. No matter how much I look at it, it's just a hummingbird flute.

"Emos and Kiwi believe the Stone may be hidden in Kot'ani. When I came here, I was unaware of the Winged-versus-Wingless issue. The Winged know Emos is trying to help me, but Akylas wants to discover Tua'mua first. I think he thinks this will somehow magically lead him there."

"Not much of a clue, is it?" Rea spun the hummingbird dangling from Clementine's hand.

Clem shook her head.

"It's a flute, right? Have you tried playing it?" Wek asked.

"Yeah, but it doesn't sound like anything," Clem answered. "You can barely hear it."

"Well, I'm sure you'll figure it out when you need to." Wek smiled. "For now, tuck it away safe, and come help me make dinner."

By the end of the week, Wek and Rea were sending Clem and Kiwi out on their own to collect food for breakfast, lunch, and dinner. Clem was trapping something almost every night, and Kiwi had even caught a fish.

"Not that one!" Rea took a long green stalk with a gray root from Clem's hands. "That one will have us sweating bullets and seeing imaginary monsters for days. The root of the noo'anga has to be bluish-gray. If it's all gray, it's too ripe."

"Oops," Clem said, cringing. "I forgot."

Harvesting was hard; so much to remember.

"It's all good"—Rea patted her shoulder—"You girls are doing great. Ninety-nine percent of what you're bringing back is edible, and that's impressive considering you've only been here a week."

"Amazing teachers!" Clem went back to chopping the tough blue-gray roots. Mr. Waxley could learn a thing or two from Wek and Rea.

After lunch, which thankfully left no one seeing imaginary monsters, Wek and Rea ran their daily recon mission to the North Forest to check for real monsters.

"Well, I'm sad to report the Winged appear to have left the valley," Wek said upon their return. "As much as we've loved having you here, I guess it's time for you to go."

"Noo," Kiwi and Clem moaned in unison. They'd been so busy learning to fend for themselves and helping out around Base they'd almost forgotten about their mission.

"I know." Wek smiled sadly. "But the Stone isn't going to find itself. And I'm sure Emos is worried sick in Wheku, wondering what's taking you so long."

Kiwi perked up at the mention of her dad. Clem let out a

long slow sigh.

"It's alright," Rea whispered. "You girls are ready. I have faith in you. Just stay away from the gray roots."

Gray roots were the furthest thing from Clem's mind. Wek and Rea were like the world's coolest hippie aunts; they reminded Clem of Grandma Eloise. Leaving the comfort and safety of this place would be like losing her all over again.

"Rea and I will go to the top of the valley with you," Wek continued. "That's a good two-day trek. I'll feel better knowing we've gotten you to the edge of our territory, and we can double-check the Winged are really gone."

"And make sure you're finding enough food on the trail," Rea added.

Clementine didn't trust herself to speak without crying. She knew she couldn't stay here forever, as lovely a thought as it was.

"I am the rock that makes the waves," Clem whispered to herself. Her adventure wasn't over, and as much as she wanted to sometimes, she couldn't give up. Not if she ever wanted to get home.

Squeezing her grandma's bracelet for comfort, Clem nodded. It was time to go.

"Well, it's settled then," Wek said. "We'll leave first thing in the morning."

CHAPTER 27

"When Wek said, 'first thing in the morning,' I didn't think she meant before sunrise," Kiwi groaned as they took down the tent. "How are we even supposed to see where we're going?"

Clem shrugged. She wasn't in the mood to talk. Her stomach was twisted in knots, her mind a jumble of thoughts. She was sad to leave this place, these people. Anxious to find the Stone. Worried Andro was in danger and she was taking too long. Hopeful of finding Kiwi's dad and getting home. She missed her family. Her room. Her life. Yet somehow, she didn't want this adventure to end. Mostly though, she was terrified of having to survive three weeks on their own, knowing there would be no one to help.

Over breakfast, Wek pulled out Strigops's map and reviewed every last line and note she'd made the night before.

"Even though the main trail is fairly well marked, it can be tough to follow. It gets muddy here, so watch your step. This section is not fun to get down. Eventually, we'll hang a rope. About halfway, the trail wraps around a monstrous tree. You can't miss it: there's a huge white tohu'ala symbol on it. Pan'a kamo'uka vines grow thick around there, so stock up. Our shortcut leaves from there."

"Don't even go there!" Rea shook her head at Wek.

"Why not?" Clem asked. "We like shortcuts!"

"It's only a shortcut because Wek and I know it like the back of our hands. It's poorly marked, and it's dangerous."

"It's nothing the sure-footed can't handle," Wek disagreed.

"It's marked well enough."

"No." Rea folded her arms across her chest. "Absolutely not. It's a sure way for these two to break their necks, get hopelessly lost, or both. I don't even know why you'd mention it. Absolutely not, Wek."

"Fine." Wek scribbled over a few lines on the map and made new notes beneath them. "There's a washout and a huge stretch of blowdown over there. Are you sure you can read this bit?"

"Stay to the left of the creek." They'd gone over it so many times Kiwi didn't need to look. "I got it."

"I'm just making sure," Wek said, fussing. "Once we turn around at the end of the valley, you girls are on your own. For peace of mind, I need to know you understand my directions."

"If you keep interrogating her, she'll be able to get to Wheku without a map." Rea crammed more food into Clementine's pack. Nodding at Clem, she added, "In case your traps don't work, or you can't find any of the food we've shown you when you get to the swamp. It's different over there. It's going to be wet. Not as many animals and insects come out in the rain. Most of this food will last weeks, so fend for yourselves when you can and save this for when you absolutely need it."

"Are we ready?" Wek folded the map and handed it back to Kiwi. "You girls sure you have everything?"

"I hope so," Clem groaned as she hefted her overstuffed pack onto her back. "If you put anything else in our packs, Rea, we're not going to be able to move."

"I want you to be prepared for whatever the trail throws at you." Rea snuck an edible-plant book into the top of Kiwi's pack. "Can't be too safe."

At the edge of the clearing, Clem turned and took one final

look at the Forest Steward Base.

"Goodbye, sweet Base. I'll miss you." She'd learned so much in this sunny clearing.

"No need to be sad, mate." Wek took the lead. "You can stop back on your way home from finding your Stone and tell us all about your adventure. You girls will always be welcome here. Next time, we might even put you to work."

"We should totally do that!" Kiwi's smile faded. "I mean..."

"Yeah, it's weird, right?" Clem responded as they fell in line behind Wek and Rea. "I want to find the Stone and go home. But if I do..."

"Yeah, let's not talk about that. I don't want to be sadder than I already am." Kiwi sniffled.

The well-worn path meandered gently through the giant trees, loosely following the right bank of the Anue'anue River. Wek and Rea had built wood and rope bridges over every creek crossing and perfectly placed stepping stones across all the muddy bits. Even with heavy packs, the going was easy.

Where the path led through long sprawling meadows, Wek and Rea would leave Clem in Kiwi in the safety of the forest. Bows raised, they'd march like soldiers into the clearing, scanning the sky and canopy. When they were happy the clearing was safe, they'd motion for the girls to follow.

Finding food was strictly up to Clementine and Kiwi.

"Can we eat this?" Clem held a thick-skinned yellow pod. It looked familiar, but they'd been hiking through the valley since before sunrise. Her brain was too tired to be sure.

"I don't know. Can you?" Rea responded. "You tell me. If you don't know, don't eat it. After tomorrow, Wek and I won't be here to give you the answers."

"Please don't remind me." Clem closed her eyes.

"You can do this," Rea said.

Clem drew a blank. This was like taking an exam. She'd studied and knew the answer, but her brain was like *Error: File not found.*

"Yellow pods that shine like the sun…" Wek hinted.

"…are tasty treats for everyone!" Kiwi popped out of the forest with two fish on her line. "Oh, you found a pana'nati! Good job, Clem!"

"Right, I knew that," Clem exhaled. She sure hoped her brain wouldn't fail her like this when they were on their own.

A good-night's sleep made finding breakfast easier. Clem's traps had worked flawlessly. By the time they hit the trail, she was feeling more confident.

"I think we've got this," Kiwi said, smiling as they climbed out of the valley.

"Oh, absolutely," Clem agreed. "All we need to do now is run up this little hill and down the far side, swim across the swamp, run over a few mountains, cross a handful of canyons, and walk right into the Forgotten City. Easy."

Wek and Rea burst out laughing.

"I meant at least now we don't need to worry about starving to death." Kiwi stuck out her tongue.

"I think Rea crammed enough food into our packs that we probably wouldn't starve even if we couldn't find food." Clem shifted her pack. It hadn't been so noticeable on the flat valley floor, but now they were going uphill, her backpack felt like it weighed a hundred pounds.

"Break?" Kiwi panted.

"Up ahead, there's a perfect place for a break," Wek answered. "You'll love it. Trust me."

Groaning, Kiwi let her head fall against the top of her pack.

"Does this hill ever end, or does it keep going up forever?" Clem wiped the sweat from her forehead. They'd been climbing for over an hour since Wek had said their break spot was "up ahead." Her legs and back ached. If only log flumes went uphill. Why couldn't she have landed in a dimension with reverse gravity?

"Whoa!" Kiwi came to a halt.

"Not bad, right?" Wek and Rea smiled.

"What is it?" Clem moaned from behind. "Are we there?"

"You have to see this!" Kiwi slipped in front of Wek and Rea.

Clem poked her head over Wek's shoulder. The trail popped out of the forest and ran across a wide ledge directly beneath a thundering waterfall. Prisms of light danced off the sparkling water, sending rainbows across the valley like fireworks.

"Unbelievable," Clem muttered. "Is this where we're taking a break?"

"Yup. You two can rest here while we scout around the bend."

Clementine watched Wek and Rea disappear behind the waterfall and re-emerge on the far side. As they worked their way around the cliff, Clem flopped on the ground next to Kiwi and stared at the tiny patches of blue sky hidden behind the green.

"I wish we were like camels," she thought aloud as she pulled a small woven bag of nuts from her pack, took a handful, and passed it to Kiwi.

"What?" Kiwi asked.

"You know how camels can store fat in their humps and then not eat for weeks and still be fine? I wish we could do that—eat all our food right now and not have to eat again until Wheku. Then we wouldn't have to carry as much."

"What are you talking about? What's a camel, a walking cupboard?" Kiwi's look of total confusion cracked Clem up. Sometimes, she forgot how far from home she was.

"It's this animal that lives in the desert back on my Earth. It has a long neck, gangly legs, and humps on its back. Like this"—Clem picked up a stick and drew a camel in the dirt—"They're like twelve feet tall, and they spit on people. I saw one in a zoo once. It tried to eat Fergus's hair. He freaked out, ran into a pole, and knocked himself out."

"That can't be real," Kiwi said, looking at Clem's childish drawing. "You're joking, right?"

"You think camels sound crazy? Wait until you hear about trash pandas and…"

Kiwi's mouth dropped. Her head tilted to one side. She blinked.

"Clem, a Winged just landed behind you, and she looks exactly like me," Kiwi whispered. "Like, we could be twins."

Did she see you? Clem mouthed back.

Kiwi nodded. Clementine whipped her head around. Fifteen feet behind her stood Kiwi's twin. If it weren't for the fluffy gray wings folded neatly behind her, Clem would have sworn she was looking at a reflection.

"This is so weird," said the Winged, who couldn't take her eyes off Kiwi.

"So weird," Kiwi replied.

"Totally," Clem agreed.

"Hey, you're that Wingless everyone's looking for, aren't you?" The Winged looked at Clementine as if noticing her for the first time. "The featherless one?"

"No." Clem shook her head. "I don't know what you're

talking about.”

“You are!” the Winged gasped. “This is so great! They dared me to fly over here and check out the falls. Everyone says how amazing they are (if you don’t get caught by those crazy stewards). I finally got the courage to do it, and here you are. This is so awesome! Raveen’s always blabbing about how she’s not afraid of anything, and she’s such a great tracker. She’ll die when she finds out it was me who found you…and on steward land too. This is the best day ever!”

Clementine was at a loss for words. This girl was so much like Kiwi it was impossible to be angry with her.

“You can’t tell Raveen you saw us,” Kiwi said.

“Are you serious? Like I’m going to pass this up.” Spreading her wings, she leaped in the air. She didn’t make it twenty feet before she fell back to the earth in a crumpled heap, a long thin arrow protruding from her side.

Clem stared at the lifeless face lying in the dirt. She tried to see the enemy, but all she could see was Kiwi.

“Are you girls okay?” Wek ran toward them, bow in hand.

“We were near the far forest when we saw her,” Rea gasped. “We thought we could beat her back, but they’re so fast.”

“She came to…” Kiwi trailed off.

“…look at the waterfall,” Clementine finished. “Is she dead?”

“No.” Wek gently pulled out the arrow and examined the point. “Rea and I aren’t killers. They’re sleeper arrows. She’ll wake up in a few hours, and then—”

“Whoa,” Rea said as she rolled the Winged over, looked at her face, then up at Kiwi. “That’s trippy.”

Clem and Kiwi nodded.

“The resemblance is uncanny.” Wek shook her head.

"You're not going to de-wing her, are you?" Clem dreaded hearing the answer.

"Did she recognize you?"

Clementine hesitated.

"*Did she recognize you?*"

She reluctantly nodded.

"Did she mention if she was with others?"

"I dunno. Maybe? I guess so. She said 'they' dared her to fly over and check out the falls. I don't know what that means, though."

"You girls need to go." Wek rubbed her face and sighed. "Rea and I cleared the trail as far as the forest. We didn't see anyone. They probably don't know you're here if she wasn't looking for you. We need to keep it that way. Rea and I will stay and make sure she keeps quiet. If her friends come looking, they won't be surprised to find us."

"But you're not going to…?" As Clementine spoke, Wek turned her face away.

"You've got to get your pack on." Rea stuck out her hand and pulled Clementine to her feet. "If we let her go, she will tell her friends she saw you, and the forest will be swarming with Winged by nightfall. Wek and I won't be able to protect you. You need to go now, while you can. Let Wek and I handle this."

"But she only wanted to see the waterfall." Clem stared at the pile of soft gray plumage beneath Wek's hand. "You can't… She won't be able to… Her family… Wek, please…"

Wek didn't answer.

"She won't feel a thing." Rea gave Clem a tight hug. "She'll be fine. We'll make sure of it. Go, now."

"Come on, Clem." Kiwi grabbed Clementine's hand and pulled her toward the waterfall. "We need to go."

"But y-you look identical," Clem stammered. "How are you okay with this?"

If Kiwi responded, the roar of the waterfall drowned it out. As they dipped behind the falls, Clementine wished a cloud would cover the sun and turn off all the happy little rainbows dancing across the valley.

CHAPTER 28

They hiked until dark in silence. Set up the tent in silence. Woke in silence. Walked all morning without so much as a word.

The trail was beyond difficult to follow. Sweat dripped down Clementine's face. The forest on the far side of the Anue'anue Valley was uncomfortably hot and muggy. She felt like a tea kettle simmering on the stove. And then she stubbed her toe.

"I don't understand how you're okay with it," Clem exploded. "It's wrong!"

Kiwi stopped dead in her tracks. Hands on her hips, she turned around. "What do you think would have happened if Wek and Rea hadn't shown up when they did?" Kiwi asked, fuming. "I'll tell you what would have happened. That Winged would have flown off to her friends and told them she saw us. And they'd have come back. Then what? Do you think they'd have taken your stupid flute, said 'thank you,' and flown off home? No. They'd have thrown you, me, Wek, and Rea off that cliff, and they wouldn't have thought twice about it. At least this way, everyone gets to live. She's not going to die without wings."

"What if the Winged chopped your legs off so you couldn't walk?" Clementine screamed.

"They wouldn't do that because they'd rather kill me!" Kiwi roared. "It's not something we do for fun."

"It's still wrong!" Clem shouted.

"What were Wek and Rea supposed to do?" Kiwi clenched

her fists. "Put a leash on her and fly her home like a kite? Keep her as a pet? Winged are ten times stronger than us. She'd have escaped, and then we'd all be dead!"

"Maybe we could have tried talking to her when she woke up." Clem's cheeks hurt from clenching her jaw so tight. "Did you think of that?"

"Are you delusional?" Kiwi said with a snort. "Do you honestly think a Winged would have listened to you? They hate us. I don't know why. We didn't do anything to them. They hate us for existing. We're Wingless, Clementine. We're barely people as far as they're concerned. And you're barely even Wingless. You don't even have feathers!"

"What's that supposed to mean?" Clementine's eyes narrowed.

"Nothing." Kiwi pursed her lips. "Can we just keep walking so we can get to Wheku and meet up with my dad? Then you can get your stupid Stone and go back to your stupid world where everyone's featherless, and you all get along because you're so perfect."

"People hate each other where I'm from too." Clementine closed her eyes, Fan Tan Alley and the disappointed face of Mrs. Lee flashing in her mind. "For equally stupid, terrible reasons. People fight about everything and nothing all the time. It's worse than here even. Maybe people everywhere are horrible."

"We're kids. What are we supposed to do if adults can't even figure it out?" Kiwi frowned and continued up the trail.

"I don't know." Clementine trudged along behind her. "The Professor, this crazy dude who hangs out on Pandora Avenue, says we're supposed to be the rock that makes the waves."

"What does that even mean?" Kiwi asked.

"I dunno."

They walked a while in silence before Kiwi finally asked, "Is that why you keep whispering 'I am a rock' to yourself?"

"Yeah," Clem said, rolling her eyes. "So far, all it's done is get me in a lot of trouble. I guess that's why my mom's always going on about not talking to strangers. God, I miss my family."

"Do you actually believe the Stone will take you home?" Kiwi asked.

"I dunno," Clem said. "I really don't know."

The farther they walked from the Anue'anue Valley, the less Clementine thought about Wek, Rea, and the winged Kiwi. It wasn't that she'd forgotten. Her mind was occupied by other things, like finding food and navigating the ever-worsening trail. It was obvious no one came this way.

Uphill was nearly impossible. Grabbing vines or roots as far in front of her as she could reach without ripping her arms off, Clem lifted her leg as high as it would go. Hooking her foot on anything solid—a rock, a root, a vine—anything that wasn't slick clay and mud, she'd hoist the rest of her body and her overstuffed pack up behind her. Her legs ached from doing so many lunges. Lift one foot up, slide halfway back, and repeat. If only her gym teacher could see her now.

Clementine called the downhill stretches Human Pachinko. So as not to pick up too much speed, they'd slide into a tree. Stop. Turn. Slide into the next tree. The spiny ones were the worst. Clem's arms felt like pincushions. When the hills were too steep, they sat on their filthy butts and tobogganed to the bottom. Wek didn't need to install one rope; she needed a whole series of them.

The flat stretches were where things got interesting. The chocolate-pudding ground jiggled and bubbled beneath their feet. Clem poked a stick as tall as she was into the trail ahead of them. The mud swallowed it whole.

"Yikes, better not step there," Kiwi said with a grimace. "When we were young, we used to play this game called The Floor Is Mud at school. We'd pretend the floor was mud and have to get from one place to another without stepping on it."

"We used to play that! Only we called it The Floor Is Lava."

"Dangerous," Kiwi responded. "Mud's bad enough. I seriously hope we don't find any lava out here."

They fought for every step forward they made. Progress was painfully slow.

Whoever made it through first would turn around and instruct the other: "Okay, put your stick at the base of that fern, then grab a vine and swing around. Put your left foot on that root right there. If you can get your stick back out of the mud, jam it in by those rocks and put your right leg on that root. Once your right leg is there, you can grab this palm frond and swing over."

The mud, when they couldn't avoid it, sucked at their shoes.

"This is like 4x4ing without a truck." Curling her toes in a tight ball, Clem prayed her shoe came back out with her foot.

"I don't know what any of those words mean." Kiwi hopped from one root to another, trying to avoid the ground altogether. "Sometimes you say the weirdest things."

"Right,"—Clem balanced on top of a small rock—"I forgot, no trucks in Pangier."

Coming upon a particularly nasty section of trail, Clementine searched for a way around. There was nothing solid to stand on for hundreds of feet in any direction. Mud oozed halfway up her ground-testing stick before it hit anything firm.

"We're gonna have to swing," Clem said, grabbing a vine. As she lifted off the ground, her foot caught on a root. Her body shuddered, and she came to an abrupt halt. Suspended above the mud, her grip loosened. Her hands slipped down the vine.

"No! Don't overturn turtle!" Kiwi grabbed Clem's arm.

"Overturn turtle?"

"Yeah, don't go shell down in the mud. You'll never get back out." Kiwi said, pulling her back to solid ground.

Don't overturn turtle was her new favorite expression. She added it to the long list of things she wanted to tell Andro, not that he was likely to understand the joke.

"I am Clementine Lemons, master of the mud!" Making it to the far side, Clem picked up a fistful of grime and smeared it across her cheeks like war paint.

The mud on her face dried, caked, and eventually cracked, but Clem didn't try to remove it. There wasn't a point. Mud was matted in her hair; it coated her clothes and oozed between her toes. There was no escaping it.

"This place is like a fairy tale and a nightmare." Clem ran a dirty hand over the smooth bark of the fallen log they were camped on. If she forgot about the mud, the Winged, and her scraped and bruised body, she could almost believe she'd wandered into a dream. It was the magical time of night when the forest began to glow. High above the branches, wispy little clouds wrapped themselves around the twinkling stars. The birds sang their never-ending lullaby. Clem's eyes fluttered closed.

"If you don't open your eyes soon, you'll fall asleep out here." Kiwi yawned as she crawled toward the tent. "Fair warning, I'm exhausted. If something comes to eat you, I'm not getting up to save you."

"Fair enough." Clem rolled over and dragged herself off to bed.

While they slept, the wispy little clouds knit themselves together, blotting out every last star. A single drop of water hit the tent, then another.

The skies opened up, and down came the rain. Not a drizzle or a shower; for days, it rained as if someone had turned on a firehose and forgotten to shut it off.

"I'm so done with mud and water and falling and being scraped, and cut, and bruised. I haven't been able to feel my toes for two days." Clem's toe poked out a hole in her shoe.

"At least we're cleaner, and our packs are getting lighter." Kiwi's usually bouncy feathers hung limp, plastered to the sides of her head.

"I don't know if our packs getting lighter is a good thing." Since it had started raining, Clem hadn't caught anything in her traps. They foraged what they could, but now that the mud was hidden beneath ankle-deep water, just staying above ground took all their attention. They were burning through the extra food Rea had packed faster than they'd hoped.

"Hey, Clem," Kiwi called from ahead. "You're not going to believe this, but I think we made it to the halfway point!"

"How can you be…holy ti'kea!" Clem still wasn't sure exactly what it meant, but Kiwi said it often enough she could make an educated guess. "Wek wasn't kidding when she said it was impossible to miss."

All the trees in Pangier were enormous, but even the biggest looked like toothpicks compared to the monster blocking their path. The white tohu'ala symbol painted on its side glared down like an interstate billboard advertising fast food at the next exit.

"I'm proud of us. Rea said she and Wek do this in eight days, but it might take us eleven. I thought it would take a month, but according to my calculations, it only took us ten! And that's with the rain and finding our own food." Clem set her pack in a hollow between the thick chunks of bark and gave Kiwi a hug.

"That means we're probably only ten or eleven days from Wheku, right?" Kiwi smiled.

"Yeah. I hope your dad has a feast waiting for us. And a hotel room. It feels like five hundred years since I've slept in a real bed. Speaking of feasts, didn't Wek say pan'a kamo'uka vines grow thick here? I'm hungry."

"You're always hungry." Kiwi set her pack beside Clem's and stretched. "But yeah, she did say that. She even marked it on the map so we wouldn't forget. We should probably harvest as many as we can…not that I want to carry them."

The farther they wandered from the trail, the thicker the pan'a grew. Heavy with yellow-and-red fruit, the vines hung like beaded curtains from the branches. Snaking their way down the tree trunks, they draped over all the low bushes.

"Woah, Wek wasn't kidding," Clem said. "We've hit the pan'a jackpot."

"Yeah, who needs a feast in Wheku? We've got an all-you-can-eat buffet right here!" Kiwi grabbed the first pan'a she saw. "If it weren't raining, I would sit here and eat all afternoon."

"How many do you think we can fit in our packs?" Clem broke one open and crammed the mushy red fruit in her mouth. Pan'a was one of her favorite Pangian fruits. It tasted like banana and coconut dipped in strawberry jam.

"I dunno. They're long but thin… A dozen each?"

Swallowing hard, Kiwi immediately crammed another bite in her mouth.

"I could pick a dozen in five minutes flat." Clem discarded an empty peel on the ground and tore open a second. "This is my kind of harvesting."

A dozen pan'a stacked like firewood in their arms, Clem and Kiwi headed back to their packs. Clem parted a curtain of vines and was about to splash onto the trail when movement caught her attention. Clem pulled her foot back and let the vines fall silently into place.

"Winged," she whispered to Kiwi.

Hidden in the vines, they watched as three Winged rummaged through their packs. They appeared to be in a heated debate.

"What are they doing?" Clem whispered.

"Looking for the flute?" Kiwi watched one flip through the pages of the book Rea had stuffed in her pack. "Can you hear what they're saying?"

Clem shook her head. "Too much rain. I'm going to try and get closer."

Stacking the pan'a on a mossy rock, Clem and Kiwi crept through the forest to the far edge of the enormous tree. They darted across the trail and hid among the jumbled roots.

"I'm telling you, it's not them. Hand-foraged food? Rope? *Edible Plants of the Mutina'kol'e Swamp Basin*?" The guy holding the book tossed it to the ground. "There isn't even a map here. These are harvesters or those crazy old bats from the Anue'anue Valley."

"Well, I think we should look around, just in case. Akylas's Wingless informant told him they'd be coming this way. It's the only path between the bridge and the swamp," a guy with green wings responded.

Clem and Kiwi looked at each other.

"Wingless informant?" Kiwi whispered. Clem shrugged.

"I don't even know why we're still looking for them. They're Wingless. They've probably starved to death by now," the book-tosser continued.

"No way. I heard the featherless one comes from the other side of the range. She escaped from right under Akylas's nose…twice! She's got mad skills. Falk said someone cleaned out the rakia on the far side of the Anue'anue, then trashed the place to make it look like wild animals did it. It had to be them. They've got a month's worth of food, at least." Clem couldn't see the third guy, but he was her favorite.

"Exactly. Do you see any rations in this pack? No. Now can we please go home? It's wet and miserable out here. My wings are never going to dry," Book-tosser whined.

"But Falk said—" Green Wings tried, but the other two weren't having any of it.

"Who cares what Falk said. He's not the boss. I hate that guy. Besides, if we're looking for anyone, it should be Hoku. Nobody's seen her in over a week." The third guy was definitely her favorite.

"True that. Let's just toss this stuff in the tree and get out of here. I really don't want to run into those stewards today." The book guy apparently liked tossing things.

The three of them spread their wings and disappeared into the sky, throwing Clem and Kiwi's packs in the high branches as they left. Clementine watched as her only other shirt drifted back to the earth.

"Well, this is just great!" Kiwi kicked at the water.

"*Ssh!*" Clem said.

"It's fine. They're gone." Kiwi plucked the waterlogged book from a puddle. "Trust me, Winged are babies. They've flown home to dry off their precious baby wings. Do you think we can get up there?"

Clem looked up. The first limb was hundreds of feet in the air; her pack dangled from one of its many branches. She shook her head.

"What are we going to do?" Kiwi bit her lower lip. "Go back to Wek and Rea's and see if they can lend us gear?"

"I vote we keep moving forward." Clem ran a hand through her wet hair.

"But we have nothing! No tent, no food, no knife, no oro'nalu alarms, nothing to start a fire with, nothing warm and dry," Kiwi argued.

"I know, but that symbol means we're about halfway, right?" Clem reasoned. "So, if we go back or forward, we'll have to survive without gear for the same amount of time. At least if we're moving forward, we—"

"Unless…" Kiwi's eyes lit up.

"Unless what?" Clem salvaged her shirt from a nearby shrub.

"Unless we take Wek and Rea's shortcut." Kiwi picked up an empty jar floating by her feet. "Wek did say it started somewhere near this tree."

"You mean the shortcut Rea said would get us hopelessly lost or we'd break our necks on? That shortcut?" Clementine raised her eyebrows. It wasn't a bad idea, but it also wasn't good.

"Yup. But more important than breaking our necks, do you remember after dinner on our first night at Base? Rea said you could get to the swamp in two weeks 'if you know what you're doing.' She had to be talking about their shortcut. Fourteen days! If it took them eight days to get here, the swamp is only six days away. It would shave an entire week off our journey."

Six days to a dry, warm bed? Clem had to admit it was tempting.

"It can't be any worse than what we've already been through," Kiwi reasoned.

"Rea said it was poorly marked. Besides, how would we even know where to go from here? It could be anywhere."

"That's the best part. Wek thought we could do it. She marked it on the map. Then when Rea said no, she crossed it out… I watched her. Come, I'll show you!"

Kiwi dragged Clementine into a space beneath the ancient tree's roots and spread the map on the only dry patch of ground in Pangier. "See, right here!"

"Can you read it?" Clem looked skeptically at the crossed-out symbols.

Kiwi squinted and pressed her nose to the map. "Lower left arm of tohu'ala points to the first white blaze. Always locate the next blaze before proceeding, rocky something, blah blah, hand and foot, keep left, blah blah, dangerous… Turn right at the swamp and follow the Fringe to Wheku. Huh, seems pretty straightforward to me." Kiwi popped her head up, banging it on the underside of the root. "What do you think?"

"Seems too straightforward," Clem mumbled. "Tell you what. If we can find the first two blazes easily enough, we go. If not, we stick to the trail."

"Deal." Kiwi folded the map and tucked it back in her pocket.

Clem fashioned the spare shirt she'd found into a backpack and tossed in the jar, the book, and as many pan'a as she could fit.

They oriented themselves beneath the tohu'ala symbol, then followed its lower left arm into the forest. A single white smear stared back at them from a distant tree.

"Is that the blaze?" Clem asked.

"I guess so." Kiwi shrugged. "It's white. Ready?"

"Not at all. I don't think I'll ever be ready for what Pangier tends to throw our way."

CHAPTER 29

"Wek is certifiably insane," Clementine vented. "'Nothing the sure-footed can't handle'… Seriously?"

"It's a miracle we're alive." Kiwi handed her a leaf full of mush sprinkled with nuts and berries. "There's no way those two haul supplies up here. It would be impossible."

They'd been playing an adrenaline-filled game of Find the Next Blaze for five days. Mostly it involved free-hand climbing from ledge to ledge down the rain-slick rocks of a nearly vertical cliff.

"Totally. I'm glad we don't have our packs at this point. There's no way we'd have gotten them down that last stretch." Clementine rubbed her puffy ankle. Forget a pack; *she* almost hadn't made it down the last stretch.

Rea had been right: they shouldn't have come this way. They'd barely succeeded in not breaking their necks. The not-getting-lost part? Well, that was up for debate.

The fog had done an excellent job of blocking what Clem imagined was a terrifying view. However, it also made spotting white blazes on gray rocks impossible. Half the time, she couldn't even see Kiwi, who was usually only ten feet away. Clementine had to teach her Marco Polo just so they could keep track of each other.

Kiwi insisted she'd seen a blaze earlier in the day, but Clem suspected it was bird droppings. They knew if they headed north, they'd find the swamp, eventually. But how were they supposed to know which way was north when they hadn't seen the sun in over a week? Po's crash course in navigation had failed to cover cloudy skies.

"Thanks for finding dinner, by the way. Sorry I wasn't much help." Picking up her leaf, Clem took a big bite of mush. It tasted like banana and garlic mashed potatoes.

"No worries." Kiwi swatted at something over her head. "How's your ankle?"

"It'll be fine by morning, I hope. You didn't happen to find anywhere we could sleep while you were looking for dinner, did you?" They'd spent the previous night huddled in a tiny cave. Clementine was desperate for a decent night's sleep.

"Yeah, there might be a—" Kiwi dropped her dinner on the ground and batted wildly at the air. "Get away from me! Get away, get away, get away!"

"What is it?" Clem scanned the air around Kiwi, trying to figure out what was attacking her.

"The butterflies! Get them off of me!" Kiwi buried her head protectively in her arms.

"What are you talking about?! Kiwi, there are no..." Clementine's gaze fell to the leaf in her lap. "Oh no... Kiwi, is this noo'anga?"

"Are they gone?" Whimpering, Kiwi lifted her head.

"Was this noo'anga?" Clementine asked again.

Kiwi scanned the treetops, nodding.

"Was it blue or gray?"

"The butterflies?" Kiwi panicked. "They were black, with glowing red eyes and fangs! Why is it so hot here... It's practically night, and it's still a million degrees..."

"Kiwi, concentrate!" Clem snapped. "The noo'anga, was it blue or gray?"

"Gray, duh." Kiwi began aggressively batting at the air again. "Gray means it's ripe."

"Oh no..." Kiwi swam in and out of focus in front of her.

"The gray ones are overripe. Rea said if you eat them, you'll be seeing monsters for... How much did you eat?" Clem only had two bites. How bad could that be?

"They're back!" Shrieking, Kiwi jumped to her feet and bolted into the forest. Clem started to run after her, but a human-sized butterfly swooped down and blocked her way.

"You're not real. I'm not afraid of you."

The butterfly bared its fangs and hissed.

"No. You're not real." Clementine closed her eyes and tried to convince herself to run straight through it. It wasn't really there. But what if it was?

When she opened her eyes, Raveen hovered in the space the butterfly had been.

"Hello, Clementine," she sang. "Am I real?"

"I dunno... Are you?" Not wanting to find out, Clem turned and ran, Raveen and an army of black butterflies hot on her heels. Vines slithered up her arms. Leaf-like fingers clutched at her ankles.

"Let me go!" Clementine screamed. Ducking and weaving, she tried to escape the forest.

"Clementine? Clementine! Help!" The words ricocheted in the darkness, bouncing off the trees until it sounded like a million people screaming from every direction.

"Kiwi? Where are you? Kiwi!" Clem tried desperately to follow Kiwi's voice, but running with the ground rolling beneath her feet was like trying to climb the down escalator at the mall.

Raveen landed in front of her, wings outstretched like a spider web. Clem turned. Falk dug his long talons into the earth. Like bars on a jail cell, she was trapped beneath his feet. She didn't want to go back to hanging in a tree. She'd come so far. Not now.

"STOP!" Kiwi flew out of the forest, arms flailing. "Make it stop!"

"Kiwi, no! Run! It's a trap!" Clementine yelled. "Don't let them get you too!"

"Clementine?" Kiwi stopped dead in her tracks and stared wide-eyed in Clem's direction. "Don't let who get me?"

"Falk and Raveen." How Kiwi was not seeing her predicament was beyond her.

"I think you've lost your mind." Kiwi picked up a branch and held it like a bat. "Whatever you do, don't move. There's a ginormous butterfly right above your head."

"Kiwi, no!" Clementine ducked as Kiwi swung.

"Auuuggghh!" Kiwi kept running. Swinging the branch violently in the air, she disappeared back into the darkness.

Leaning against a tree trunk, Clem tried to pull herself together. She lay there with her eyes closed until the ground stopped rolling and the trees stopped screaming. Thankfully, she'd only eaten two bites. Letting out a deep breath, she opened her eyes. When it wasn't screaming at you, the forest at night was actually beautiful. Bioluminescent fungus and glowing eyes lit up the trees like Christmas lights. Clem poked a tiny purple mushroom.

"Hey, don't touch me!" The mushroom pulled its long, pointed beak out of the bark, spread its tiny wings, and glared at her.

"Oh, I'm sorry, little glowy hummingbird," Clem mumbled. "I thought you were fungi. Get it, *a fun guy*." Clem rolled on the ground laughing. "Guess what? I'm a hummingbird too, listen." Pulling the flute from around her neck, she blew.

"Shhh!" the hummingbird hissed. But it was too late. All the mushrooms rose from the trees and flew into the night sky.

The forest went pitch-black.

"Come back! Don't leave me alone!" Clem cried into the void. The vines slithered like snakes up her arms, wrapped themselves around her neck and over her mouth. Unable to move or scream, Clem watched helplessly as two red dots appeared in the darkness. The last thing she remembered was the purring of a cat and something cold and wet moving across her cheek.

Clementine's face made a slurping sound as she peeled it out of the mud. Overhead the sky was a cloudless blue. She was thirsty. Her mouth felt like sandpaper and tasted like rotten banana. After rubbing her cheeks, one hand came back muddy, the other covered in slobber. Was it her slobber? Gross.

Clem shook her head and tried to remember how she'd gotten there. Images of Raveen and Falk, butterflies, and glowing hummingbirds danced in her head. A cat? She was almost certain there had been an enormous cat with black spots and red eyes. Oh, and Kiwi playing baseball with a butterfly. Kiwi!

"Kiwi?" Clementine called. "Kiwi?"

"POLO!" came a distant reply, followed by hysterical laughter. "Po-LO! PO-lo! Marco POLO!"

"Hang on, I'm coming." Clementine stumbled in the direction of Kiwi's laughter.

Pushing her way through a tangle of vines, she landed in knee-deep water. The bush stopped abruptly. Deep, dark water spread out as far as the eye could see. Giant lily pads floated serenely on the surface, gently bumping into the roots of the massive swamp trees dotting the landscape.

"I think I found the swamp." Kiwi lay on a lily pad a few

feet from the shore. "We are not in Whaka'wai anymore...trust me."

Two dragonflies zipped, drone-like, over her head.

Thwack.

One of the fireflies vanished into thin air.

"What the..." Clem furrowed her eyebrows. Oh, right, the noo'anga. It was all coming back to her now.

"Did you see that dragonfly disappear?" Kiwi asked.

"Wait, you saw that too?"

"Oh, thank the gods," Kiwi sighed. "Some weird stuff has been going on in this swamp. I thought I was losing my mind. I had the craziest dreams last night."

"I don't think you were dreaming... Remember dinner? I think you might have picked an overripe noo'anga, which is poisonous and makes you hallucinate. I'm still unsure if what I'm seeing is real, and I only had two bites. Last night was brutal."

Thwack! A long, lightning-fast tongue shot into the air and pulled the remaining dragonfly out of the sky. Clem and Kiwi gazed in the direction the dragonfly had disappeared. Sitting on the root of a nearby tree was a frog the size of a compact car.

"How about that? Do you see that?" Kiwi asked.

Clem nodded. "Do you think it's safe to be standing in this swamp? I mean, what else lives in here?"

"Oh, what doesn't live in the Mutina'kol'e?" Kiwi slowly paddled her lily pad back toward the shore. "Nak'esa, pea'wai, every amphibian you can imagine, plus a million more you couldn't imagine. And a billion kinds of fish. Besides the canopy, the swamp and the Fringe are the most biodiverse ecosystems in Pangier. We studied the Mutina'kol'e in biology once. I did a whole report on the diet of alligators."

Clem leaped out of the water. She hadn't spent a month barely surviving the forest, only to be eaten by an alligator.

As they worked their way east along the Fringe, they stopped a dozen times to ask each other if what they were seeing was real. If they both saw it, they decided it must be. The giant spider was real. The shark trolling through the mud was not.

They spent the morning detangling themselves from vines that hung like webs across their path. Crawling on their hands and knees beneath thick brambles that scrapped and grabbed at their tattered clothes. Thankfully, they saw less and less weirdness as the day progressed.

"Hey, did I see you last night?" Kiwi asked.

"See me? You tried to knock my head off with a tree limb." Clementine wiped the sweat from her forehead. It was funnier now it was daytime.

"Sorry about that. I swear, this swamp is like walking through a greenhouse on the sun's surface." Kiwi wrang out her feathers.

A carnivorous ng'an'ua sprung out of nowhere, snapping at them as they passed.

"What the..." Clementine jumped. She hadn't seen anything abnormal for hours, but this couldn't be real. "You didn't see that, did you?"

"I did," Kiwi squeaked.

"What is it?" Clem poked the gaping green mouth with a stick. Its razor-sharp teeth snapped shut, breaking the stick in two. From a safe distance, Kiwi stopped to look it up in their book.

"Plants can eat you?" Her mouth dropped. "What kind of world do we live in?"

Eventually, the jungle became so overgrown even the

ng'an'ua were having a hard time moving. When the sun sank, the waemu, gratefully not much larger than the mosquitos back home, came out in full force. A shadow passed over. Clem looked up, terrified it was Falk. Kiwi looked up, scared it was a butterfly.

"This is the worst day ever," Clem groaned. "I don't want to spend another night out here, but my ankle and nerves can't take any more of today. Can we stop?"

"Yeah. My head is throbbing," Kiwi agreed.

Stopping on a pebbly beach next to a cascading waterfall, Clem and Kiwi used the last of their energy to build what they hoped was an alligator-proof shelter out of driftwood. They dragged a giant lily pad out of the swamp and pulled it over the top.

"It looks like a pancake." Clementine flopped on the beach. "Speaking of which, I'm hungry."

"I can go find us something to eat." Kiwi stood.

"No!" Clem grabbed her hand and pulled her back down. "I'm not hungry. I mean, I'm hungry, but I don't feel like eating. Thank you, though."

"More like you don't want me to poison us again?" Kiwi raised her eyebrows.

"Yeah, that."

"Hey, Clem"—Kiwi pointed up the Fringe—"I'm still seeing random butterflies and snakes, but those lights are real, right?"

"Holy ti'kea, yes! Is that Wheku?!"

"What else could it be?"

"I can't believe it."

"Yeah, if nothing kills us between here and there, we might make it by tomorrow." Kiwi sounded equally shocked. "Man, we're awesome."

"Yeah, we are," Clem said, smiling. "Clumsy, but awesome."

As the sun sank into the watery depths, Clem and Kiwi sat on the beach, dreaming of what awaited them in town.

CHAPTER 30

A sepia sunset ricocheted off the swamp, casting the world in an eerily beautiful orange glow. Clem and Kiwi waited on the outskirts of town until all the color had drained away. When darkness fell, they clambered onto the wooden boardwalk and headed into Wheku Whak'ani.

Lightning bugs in metal cages flickered to life as they passed, illuminating the way ahead. The broad boards creaked beneath their feet. Through the cracks, Clem could hear the water lapping at the shoreline. The smell of must and mold pricked at her nose and coated the back of her throat. A jumble of shabby hotels and clapboard shanties hugged the Fringe.

A ghostly dugout drifted by, the iridescent green of the swampman's face glowing in the moonlight. Wheku hung suspended in space, a billion stars twinkling overhead, their reflection mirrored in the dark water of the swamp. It was so surreal, Clem wasn't sure if she was still hallucinating.

"You know you reek when people can smell you over the dead fish and swamp mud." Kiwi tilted her head toward her armpit.

"Yeah." Clem smoothed her matted hair with her hand. "Maybe we should have had a bath in the swamp this afternoon."

She hadn't thought about how bedraggled they looked (or how bad they smelled) since they'd arrived at Wek and Rea's. Even the toughest-looking swampmen, busy loading and unloading boats on the dock, wrinkled their noses and turned their heads in disgust.

Two men stumbled out of a nearby saloon, fists flying. A small crowd gathered to cheer them on.

"What are you lookin' at, stinky?" one of the men growled as he landed with a thud at Clem's feet. Everyone stared. Clementine wished she could disappear beneath the dock.

"From what Dad said, Wheku's a pretty rough place. It's probably better we do stink." Kiwi yanked Clementine by the arm and pulled her into a narrow alley. "Maybe if no one wants to look at us, they won't notice you're…different."

Clem and Kiwi wove their way through the labyrinth of alleys crisscrossing the swamp. Untidy rows of dilapidated buildings jutted out of the ink-black water like a flock of sleeping storks. Wooden boats and dugouts drifted silently through the canals, stopping to offload goods and passengers as they went.

"Where are we going?" Clem asked as they clamored up a flight of rickety stairs. They'd taken so many turns she doubted she could ever find her way back to the Fringe.

"I don't know," Kiwi admitted. "I wanted to get away from the bright lights and people. I was so excited to get to Wheku, but now we're here, it's too much. I never thought I'd say this, but I miss the silence and stillness of the forest. Plus, everyone does business with the Amphi, even the Winged. I don't know who we can trust here. It's probably safest if we stick to the shadows until we find my dad."

"Well, how are we going to—" Clem was interrupted by a haggard woman standing next to a barrel of burning wood.

"What corner of the swamp did you poor creatures crawl outta? Come 'ave a bite to eat." She stretched her hand over the barrel and offered them a hunk of bread.

Clementine stared. She had to be Amphi. Her forked tongue darted out of a gaping hole between her teeth, reminding Clem of the giant frog they'd seen eating dragonflies in the swamp. Everything, right down to her toad-like skin, screamed *witch*. The woman stared back, her thin, slit pupils flickering back and forth in large gold irises.

"Sorry, it ain't much"—her tongue darted involuntarily out of her mouth as she spoke—"but it's all I got left this time of night. The others come home hungry, you know?"

"Thank you." Clem greedily took the bread and handed half to Kiwi. She felt guilty for thinking this woman was a witch. Then again, Hansel and Gretel were also given food by a witch.

The bread disintegrated like sand in her mouth. But Clementine was hungry. They hadn't dared eat anything since Kiwi's failed attempt at dinner. Maybe this is what her dad meant when he said, *Beggars can't be choosers*. Clem closed her eyes and tried to remember the last time she'd eaten real bread. Probably breakfast the day the key had arrived in the mail. She was more grateful for this stale piece of sandpaper than she'd ever been for freshly baked bread back home.

"I'm Borea, but everyone calls me Ma." The woman handed Clem a dingy cup of water. It tasted like it had been scooped directly out of the swamp, but Clem was grateful for it too. Anything to wash the sand from her mouth. "You new arrivals? Of course, you are. Ain't see you 'round before. Where's your roost?"

Clem and Kiwi side-eyed each other.

"Don't want to say? That's smart," Ma said, nodding. "Probably for the best. Lots in this town lookin' to take advantage of newcomers. Suppose you need a bed for the night? You're in luck. We still got one or two left…"

"Thank you, but we don't have money for a hotel," Clementine said sadly. A bed and a hot shower sounded like heaven. In her imagination, Kiwi's dad had been waiting for them, open-armed, on the outskirts of town.

"Ain't no hotel, just a safe roof over your head," Ma said with a sniffle. "You can help with the cleanin' come morn' if you want. You lookin' for work? Lots of people come from all parts lookin' for jobs in the swamp these days. I might be able to help you find somethin'. You two know your way 'round a boat?"

"We're actually looking for someone," Kiwi responded. "As soon as we find them, we'll be gone again. But thank you."

"I see. And what do we call you while you're 'ere?"

"I'm Wek," Clementine said quickly. "And this is Rea."

The woman's tongue flicked, then she turned and walked down the dark alley. Clem and Kiwi followed her to a thick, moss-covered door. Inside, two giant lightning bugs hung from the rafters. Their light flickered as they lazily bumped against the sides of their cages. Rows of shabby bunk beds, stacked four high, were crammed tightly along the back wall. Some of the beds were occupied; others were empty. A half-dozen Amphi and Wingless huddled around something on the bare wood floor.

No one noticed them enter.

"Winged? Don't call him that. I'm Wingless, and I still think that's an insult to Winged," Clementine heard one of the girls say. "Even if you weren't blind as a bat, you couldn't fly five feet with those pathetic things, could you, Myst?"

"Could you imagine?" a boy with glistening blue skin croaked. "He'd be like a lightning bug trying to escape its cage! *Thump! Thump!* Is this the exit? *Thump!*"

"Good one, Dart." The girl tilted her head back and laughed. "Honestly, it's a wonder Ma keeps you around, Myst.

You're useless."

"Not in my house!" Ma roared. "How many times have I told you, Kookie? If you can't be nice, you can sleep on the dock. This is your last warnin'.'"

"We're just playin', Ma," the girl sang sweetly. "Weren't we, Myst?"

Ma shook her head and turned to Clementine and Kiwi. "Find a bed wherever you can. It ain't much, but it is home. There'll be fresh bread and fish-head stew once the netters come home midmornin'.

"Everyone to bed now. Lights off in ten, Dart." Ma disappeared through a side door.

The group broke apart and silently drifted off to bed. In the center of the grimy floor, a small boy lay curled in a ball. His beady black eyes, nearly invisible beneath a tight shock of curly brown hair, stared blankly at the floorboards.

"Hey, are you okay?" As Clementine knelt, two tiny, paper-thin wings fluttered furiously in the air behind him. His left wing was tattered near the bottom as if something had taken a bite out of it.

"It's okay," she whispered. "I'm not going to hurt you. I'm…Clementine. Are you Myst?"

The boy nodded.

"Should we find beds before the lights go out?"

Myst shook his head.

"Okay. Are you hungry?"

Myst nodded.

"Here." Clementine held out the chunk of bread she'd been saving for later. In the blink of an eye, it was gone. Clem untied the shirt she'd been using as a backpack and draped it over his frail shoulders.

"Good night, Myst," she whispered and headed off to the

back of the room where Kiwi had already found a bed.

"You shouldn't have done that," Kiwi said.

"She's right. You shouldn't have." Kookie popped her head down from one of the upper bunks.

"Why?" Clem asked.

"You know perfectly well why," Kiwi huffed.

"Yeah, you know perfectly well why," Kookie mimicked.

"Don't say it," Clem said. "He's just a kid."

"He's a Winged." Kiwi tossed their book at the end of her bed and climbed beneath the covers.

"Well, that's being a bit generous." Kookie's laugh grated on Clem's nerves.

"Will you leave us alone?" Clem snapped.

"Lights out!" Ma yelled.

Grabbing a chain from the far wall, Dart hoisted the lightning bugs through the rafters. The room went dark.

"He's going to rat us out," Kiwi whispered. "You'll see."

CHAPTER 31

"He stole it," Kiwi said. "You shouldn't have given him the shirt. We literally had a shirt, a book, and a jar to our names. The book was the only thing we needed to survive, and now it's gone."

"Why would someone who's blind steal a book?" Clementine opened the door and swept a cloud of dust into the street.

Myst clung to Ma as she stirred a large cauldron of soup at the end of the cramped alley. With evident pride, he rolled up the sleeves of his new shirt. It hung past his knees, but he didn't seem to care.

Clementine felt extra protective of Myst. Maybe because he reminded her of Andro. Or at least what she pictured Andro to be like.

"Well, if he didn't take it, then who did?" Kiwi said.

"Who, indeed?" Kookie sang from her bunk.

"Who, indeed?" Clem put her hand on her hip and glared at Kookie.

"Surely you can't mean me," Kookie cooed.

Clementine waltzed out the door, slamming it behind her.

Without the stars and the lightning bugs reflecting off the inky-black waters, Wheku looked less dreamy and more "wild west." The city sagged in the moist heat. If any of the buildings had been painted, the paint had long since flaked off. Swamp vines climbed the walls, attempting to pull whole buildings into the murky depths. Clem wondered if the shabby city—suspended on its rickety stilt legs—had plumbing or if everything landed straight in the water.

The stew Ma had scooped into her bowl didn't look much different than the swamp water under the dock. Clem shuddered and tried not to think about it.

Kiwi emerged from Ma's with Kookie and Dart, laughing like she'd just heard the World's Best Joke. Ignoring Clementine, they sat in the shade of the buildings.

Clem took her bowl to the far side of the boardwalk and dangled her legs over the edge. A fish eye bobbed to the surface of her stew and stared at her. Clementine vowed to never complain about her mother's cooking again. Not even her meatloaf.

"Strigops?!" Kiwi yelled from behind her. "Holy ti'kea, Strigops!"

Clementine whipped around, spilling her soup in the swamp as she turned.

"Strigops?" Forgetting she was mad at Kiwi, Clem bounded across the boardwalk.

"Kiwi! Clementine! Well, aren't you two a sight for sore eyes?" Strigops dabbed his forehead with a hanky. "For weeks now, I've been making the rounds to all the usual places newcomers end up, desperate to hear any news of your whereabouts. Your poor Dad trekked halfway to the Anue'anue and back looking for you! Is the flu— Is it safe?"

"How'd you guys escape? Is Dad alright?" Kiwi's eyes sparkled. "Where is he?"

"Well"—Strigops paused—"he's gone on."

"What do you mean he's 'gone on'?" Kiwi's voice trembled.

"With Akylas hot on our heels and the s-rail out, it took longer to get here than we imagined. When we found the old bridge hanging in the gorge, we weren't sure if you girls were ahead or behind us." Strigops seemed frazzled, as he twisted his damp hanky between his fingers. "I told your dad, 'The girls will wait in Wheku.' He's been worried sick because Akylas has been relentless. A few days back, we got word someone saw a pair of girls matching your description on the far side of the swamp. Emos was convinced you weren't safe here and you'd crossed over. He took the boys to try and catch you. I told him he was chasing ghosts, but he was desperate. I couldn't talk sense into him. Told him I'd wait here, just in case. I sure am glad I did. Do you still have it?"

Clementine nodded.

"Good, good." Strigops furiously dabbed at his forehead as if trying to stop a leaky pipe with a wet rag. "They're no more than two days ahead. If we get tickets for the next crossing, we'll catch them before they leave Mau'una Kupuka. Quickly now."

"So these are the two you've been lookin' for," Ma said. "Guess that means you girls will be off now?"

"Yes!" Kiwi said enthusiastically.

"Wek and Rea, hey?" Ma winked her vertical eyelid. "Next time they're in town, I'll tell 'em you were here."

"Thank you." Clem smiled. Myst stood next to Ma, slowly shaking his head no.

"What is it, Myst?" Clem cocked her head to one side and furrowed her eyebrows. Before he could answer, Kiwi grabbed her elbow and tugged her into the crowd.

"Can you believe this?!" Kiwi went on. "One week! It only takes one week to cross the Mutina'kol'e. One week, and we'll be with Dad! We don't have to worry about Akylas, food, or shelter! No more getting lost. No more traps. We can have a bath. A real bath. With hot water!"

Clementine only half listened as she tried to remember their route. They wove through a narrow lane between houses built into the roots of a monstrous swamp tree. Over a bridge. Down a flight of stairs. Down one canal and up another. Too much to remember. If that optical-illusion guy she'd learned about in fifth grade built a town, Wheku would be it. What was his name? Escher? School seemed a million light-years away.

"Ah, here we are." Strigops came to a stop in front of a large two-story building. "In you go…"

They were back on the Fringe. The saloon the men were fighting in front of the night before was next door.

"What are we doing?" Kiwi demanded. "I thought we were getting tickets for the next crossing?"

"Oh, well, yes, of course. All in due time," Strigops panted. "Next crossing won't be until tomorrow now. I thought we'd stop at the inn so the two of you could clean up. They won't let you on the paddler smelling like you do. It's a proper boat. We'll wait out the heat of the day before we venture out for tickets and supplies. I've got some business to attend to next door. You'll be safe here. Run along inside."

Clementine spent an hour in the bath, scrubbing the dirt from between her toes and trying to untangle her hair.

"I think I forgot how you looked underneath all the grime," Kiwi said with a giggle when she finally emerged. "It's super obvious you don't have feathers now. Good thing Dad left a change of clothes with Strigops."

"I forgot how bouncy your feathers are when they aren't caked in mud." Clem tousled Kiwi's hair. "I feel so much lighter. Food?"

"Absolutely! Strigops said they serve 'all-the-food-you-can-eat' downstairs. Whatever it is, I'm hoping it doesn't involve fish-head stew."

"I'm hoping Strigops's supply list includes new shoes." Clem held up her holey sneakers and plugged her nose. "These smell worse than fish-head stew."

As luck would have it, fish-head stew was not on the menu, but nearly anything else they could think of was. They piled plate after plate with food until the proprietor shook her head in disapproval and refused to serve them more.

"That's not all the food I can eat, though," Kiwi said, burping in protest. "But it is the first time I've been remotely full in weeks. And it wasn't a bug, so I can't complain."

"I kinda like eating beetle." Clem smirked as the stuffy proprietor turned up her nose in disgust. "I mean, it's not as good as tarantula meat, but…"

Pushing their chairs back, they basked in the luxurious swirling air of a palm-leaf fan and fell asleep, waiting for Strigops to return.

"Blasted heat," he hiccupped when he finally stumbled through the front door.

"Sounds like he was conducting important business at the saloon," Clementine whispered.

Kiwi raised her eyebrows. "As long as he gets us to Dad, I don't care what he does."

"Don't know how the Amphi can tolerate these temperatures. Faster I get out of here and get home, the better. Let's go get our supplies." The sun had set, but Strigops was still sweating profusely.

"And tickets," Kiwi reminded him.

"Yes. Yes, of course." Strigops stumbled down the stairs and onto the boardwalk.

"Hey, Strigops, are you sure you know where you're

going?" Clementine asked. "This side of town seems a little sketchy."

They'd walked to the edge of the Fringe. Half the light cages were empty; the other half flickered like their inhabitants were about to go legs up. The buildings that hadn't fallen into the swamp seemed abandoned. If a swamp monster was going to eat them, it would happen here.

"Oh, yes. Looks far better in the daylight, I assure you." Strigops turned up a long pier toward a sad-looking warehouse. "The best goods at the best prices are on this side of Wheku!"

Strigops must have been the only man on the planet who knew about the "best prices" because the warehouse was deserted.

"Cane," Strigops said with a nod to the man behind the counter as they entered. The man's leathery brown head melded into his body like Jabba the Hutt's. It was impossible to tell if he'd nodded back.

"I'll grab us some food while you girls have a look around." Strigops picked up a woven basket. "Expedition-related goods are in the back, I believe."

Clem and Kiwi wandered the aisles. The few products on the empty shelves appeared to be for commercial netting. The only semi-practical thing they found was a heavy old tent.

Near the back of the store, a ghostly white man sat, mending nets. Clem wasn't sure what was more intimidating: his completely tattooed scalp or the long, frilled gill stalks sticking out of his neck.

"Excuse me," she asked, "where are the shoes?"

"Do I look like I work here, girl?" Something in the way his lidless blue eyes never blinked made her skin crawl. He snorted and spat out the gaping hole in the wall behind him.

"I don't like that guy," Clem said to Kiwi. "Seems off."

She and Kiwi scurried back to the front of the store.

"Find everything?" Strigops eyed the door.

"No," Kiwi said. "We need sleeping quilts, shoes, and packs, Strigops. Not nets and anchors."

"Ah, yes. Yes, I suppose you do." Strigops plucked a jar off the shelf and stuck it back exactly where he found it. His basket was empty. "Since yours got stuck up that tree and all."

"We never told you our packs ended up in a tree, Strigops." Clementine glanced at Kiwi, who shook her head.

"Well, you must have... I..." The man's hand rested on the shelf a second too long. "How else would I..."

"How did you?" Kiwi and Clem slowly backed toward the door.

"Wait! No, you can't go!" Strigops dropped his basket and lunged at them. Grabbing Clem by the shoulders, he pinned her against the wall.

"You can't... You don't understand..." he gasped. "They have my wife and son... Akylas said if I... He's coming... You just have to give it to him, and he'll let you go..."

"Liar!" Kiwi yelped. "It's a trick, Clem. He doesn't have a son!"

"You think you're so smart, like your dad. Don't you?!" Strigops spat at Kiwi. Enraged, he wrapped his fingers around Clementine's neck.

"Have you lost your mind?" Kiwi pulled at the man's stout arms. "Let her go, Strigops!"

"Your dad is constantly getting credit for everything." Strigops's perpetually startled face distorted into an ugly sneer. "*Emos, the Famous Explorer, Discovers a New Lost City!* Not this time. This is Strigops's moment. Headlines will read: *Strigops Discovers the Great Forgotten City of Kot'ani.*

Akylas has given me his word."

"Akylas's word m-means nothing," Kiwi stammered. "You know this. He's only saying what you want to hear to get what he wants."

"You know nothing," Strigops hissed. "Akylas has been my friend for years."

"Wait"—realization dawned on Kiwi's face—"you're the informant. You're the reason Akylas shows up the second Dad makes a new discovery, aren't you? You sent us on the old trail on purpose… Did-did you know they planned to blow the bridge on the s-rail?"

"Where is it?" Strigops spat at Clementine, ignoring Kiwi completely. Clem could feel his hot breath on her cheek as she gasped for air. "Give it to me!"

Strigops grabbed at the leather cord around Clementine's neck. Kiwi cracked him across the back of the head with the tent. He stumbled, releasing his grip just long enough for Clem to wriggle free.

"Cane," Strigops roared, "the door!"

The bulky man leaped over the counter with such agility, Clem couldn't help but be impressed.

Clem and Kiwi turned and ran for the back.

"Get 'em, Axol!" Cane yelled.

"Oh, they won't be gettin' by me." Axol cracked a piece of rope on the floor like a whip.

"We're trapped," Kiwi whispered.

As Strigops closed in, Clem and Kiwi hopped up on the long counter. It was the only place to go besides back into his clammy grasp.

"Where are you going to go now, little birds?" Strigops wiped his hand across his mouth. "Hang tight. Akylas will be here soon with a nice cozy cage for you."

Clementine glanced down the counter toward the large glass window. Catching Kiwi's eye, she nodded in its direction. They sprinted across the counter and hurled themselves through the glass.

Crashing onto the pier with a thud, Clem pulled Kiwi to her feet.

"Don't let them get away!" Strigops burst through the door. "You should've stuck to the plan and tied 'em up when I sent them back to you, Axol. You fool!"

Clem and Kiwi raced up the pier and onto the dimly lit boardwalk. Strigops they could outrun, but Cane and Axol were closer every time Clem dared turn and look.

As they neared the busy quarter of the Fringe, Falk and Raveen landed in front of them. Wings spread, they blocked the path. Clem and Kiwi darted into the tangle of boardwalks leading into the swamp. They swerved and turned, sticking to the narrowest canals so Falk and Raveen couldn't land. Clem had no idea where she was going, and she didn't care.

"Straight?" Kiwi guessed, breathing heavily.

They were at a three-way intersection. Clem didn't have time to disagree. It was the only direction with no stairs to slow them down. The footsteps behind them grew louder. How could a man the size of Cane move so quickly?

As they broke free of the houses, they could see lights shining brightly ahead. Music and laughter drifted across the water. A night market! They could disappear into the crowd if they could just make it that far!

Water lapping at both sides of the boards, she and Kiwi raced across an open stretch of boardwalk and up the side of a small bridge. They were so close!

Falk and Akylas landed at the far side, blocking their way. The blade of Falk's knife glinted in the moonlight.

Clem and Kiwi stopped short.

Axol, Cane, and Raveen raced up behind them.

"What now?" Kiwi panted.

Grabbing Kiwi with one hand and clutching the hummingbird in the other, Clem dove off the side of the bridge and into the murky, alligator-infested waters below.

"What was that?" Kiwi sputtered as they surfaced between two docked boats.

"What was what?" Clem choked out.

"That?!" Kiwi treaded water next to her. "You should have seen yourself back there! You jumped off the bridge like it was nothing! How did you know to do that?"

"I read about it in a book. Adriana James finds a jade talisman in the jungle. It's supposed to go to a museum, but this politician thinks it has mystical powers, so he hires these bad guys to steal it from her. In the book, she jumps off a bridge to escape them… And my mom said I'd never learn anything useful reading 'that trash.' Ha!"

Clem and Kiwi poked their heads over the top of the boat. In the distance, Akylas and Strigops were cursing and yelling at each other on the bridge.

"Adriana won in the end, right?" Kiwi asked.

"Yeah, eventually…" Something brushed up against Clem's leg. Alligators. There were alligators in the swamp.

"It was more fun reading about it than actually doing it," she added through clenched teeth.

Clem scanned the boardwalk, looking for a place they could get out of the water without being seen. Did alligators sleep? She wasn't sure, and she didn't want to find out.

"Hello, Clementine," a ghost-like voice whispered from the shadows.

The hair on Clementine's neck stood on end as she turned and scanned the dark. She could just make out a fuzzy brown head hanging from the underside of the boardwalk.

"Myst?"

"What are you doing in the swamp?" Myst swung himself upright.

"Trying to escape from the bad guys," Clementine answered. "What are you doing down here?"

"Going to the place I hide when people are mean to me at Ma's. Do you want to hide with me? Nobody will find us in my secret spot."

"Absolutely not." Kiwi's teeth chattered as she spoke.

Clem peeked back over the edge of the boat. The bridge was empty. Strigops, Cane, and Axol were searching the crowded market on the far side of the water. Akylas and Raveen were making their way up the boardwalk toward the boat. Falk was nowhere to be seen.

"We'd love to!" Clementine pulled herself onto the beam next to him.

"Clementine, no! We can't trust him," Kiwi persisted. "He's one of them."

"One of them? What does that even mean? Is Strigops 'one of us'? Because he betrayed us. And from the sounds of it, he's been selling out your dad for years. Kookie? Is she 'one of us'? Because our book is under her pillow. How about Ma? She's not 'one of us,' but she happily took us in, no questions asked. What about me? Am I one of you? There's no such thing as 'us' or 'them.' There are good people and bad people everywhere. Winged, Wingless, Amphi, feathers, no feathers…it doesn't make a difference to the kind of person you are. Remember when you said, 'We're kids. What can we do about it?' This is what we do. We choose to be better than our parents. We choose to trust each other." Clem stretched out her hand.

Kiwi squared her jaw and scowled.

"They can't have gotten far..." Akylas's voice drifted through the night.

The planks groaned over Clementine's head. Wide-eyed, Kiwi grabbed her hand and scrambled onto the beam beside her.

"Did you hear that?" Raveen's silhouette cast a long shadow across the water.

"I don't see anything, probably just an alligator." The beam of Akylas's light danced on the ripples. "I'm not about to get in there and find out. I hate water."

Myst tugged Clem's sleeve, nodding for them to follow him into the black space between the city and swamp.

"How does he even know where he's going?" Kiwi muttered under her breath. "I thought he was supposed to be blind."

"I'm not blind," Myst answered from ahead. "I just don't see the same way you do. It's more like I hear and smell where I'm going, which forms a picture in my mind. It's hard to explain. At night the picture is way clearer. The sun hurts my eyes. Where I'm from, we don't spend much time outside during the day."

"What about all the things that could eat you at night?" Clem shivered, thinking of all the growls and scratches she'd heard in the forest.

"Wingless are funny, so afraid they'll get eaten by the night hunters," Myst said with a giggle as he dropped off the beam and landed with a *thump* below them. "They're easily avoidable if you know what you're doing. Way less scary than being out in the day with the Wingless or other Winged. Are you guys coming down?"

"Down where?" Clem couldn't even see the beam they were crawling along, let alone anything else.

"Oh, right." Myst let out a low, shrill whistle. "I forgot, you can't see in the dark."

Myst whistled again. A giant glowing orb drifted toward him.

"Hey Thunder, how you been, buddy?" Myst cooed as a giant lightning bug landed with a thud beside him.

Clem blinked, her eyes adjusting to the sudden light. Below them, a decent-sized boat hung above the water from fraying ropes. Myst stood on the front deck.

"Well, what do you think?" he asked proudly as they dropped beside him. "I found it abandoned down here. I'm trying to fix it up enough to sail it home."

Clem looked around. It was a similar shape to an s-rail glider, only wider. Instead of being enclosed, the middle portion was covered with a mat of leaves. Under the cover, Myst had made a cozy space full of random things he'd salvaged from the trash.

"Very cool. I'm impressed, Myst." Clem ran her hand over the tight coils of newly braided rope tying the roof cover to the frame.

"It looks barely swampworthy."

"Kiwi!" Clementine huffed.

"I'm not trying to be rude." Kiwi shoved her hand through a large hole in the woven reeds of the hull. "One good storm and this thing will blow apart. I wouldn't trust it to get safely across Wheku."

"Well"—Myst sat on the deck and stroked the lighting bug's head absentmindedly—"I'm trying. I know I have a lot of work to do, but if I keep working on it, maybe one day it will get me back across the swamp."

"Across the swamp? In this? You can't be serious," Kiwi continued. "You'll never make it. I mean, it doesn't even have a sail. Why not buy a ticket for the paddler?"

"I'll never get home if I wait until I have enough money to buy a ticket on the paddler," Myst said, his shoulders slumped. "No one wants to hire me. Wingless don't trust me because I have wings. The Winged don't want to hire me because I can't fly anymore. The Amphi don't want to hire me because I can't day-see. The netters work at night but say I'm too weak to be useful. Ma's the only one who cares, but she doesn't have any money."

"Why did you even come here then?" Kiwi rolled her eyes.

"I didn't come here on purpose," Myst said, frowning. "I got caught in a storm and blown halfway across the swamp. The rain was so loud it was hard to hear where things were, and everything smelled like lightning. I crashed in the swamp, and then something tried to eat me, which is how my wing got all shredded. Some netters fished me out and promised they'd take me home, but instead, they made me work on their boat. I could feel myself getting farther and farther from home. I tried to fly away but didn't make it very far on my bad wing. When they hauled me back on board, they caged me, so I couldn't escape again. Ma saw me when we docked in Wheku and helped free me. I miss my family. I just want to go home."

"I'm trying to get home too"—Clem sank onto a pile of old tarps beside Myst—"and Kiwi's trying to find her dad."

"I know," Myst said.

"What do you mean, 'I know'?" Kiwi demanded.

"A few days ago, I heard Strigops ask Ma if she'd seen you around," Myst answered. "Ma asked him why he was looking for you, and he said you were his friend's daughter and his friend was beside himself with worry. I tried to warn Ma Strigops is a bad man, just like I tried to warn you guys. But she was busy and didn't pay attention. No one pays attention to me around here. Sometimes it feels like I'm invisible."

Clem knew the feeling all too well.

"I know what you mean. How did you know Strigops was a bad guy?" Kiwi sat cross-legged in front of Myst, giving him her full attention.

"I get feelings about people. When Strigops left Ma's, I followed him. I heard him talking to the scary Winged guy, who said someone had spotted you down swamp. 'Get that feathered idiot out of here by any means necessary,' he said. Strigops offered to feed him to the alligators, but the Winged guy said, 'Not yet. If she lost it, we might need him to lead us to Tua'mua Taup'aku, you fool. Just make sure he doesn't find the girls before we do.' Why are they after you, anyway?"

"They want this." Clem pulled the flute from beneath her shirt and held it in front of Myst.

Myst reached out and gently ran his fingers across the wings and down the beak. "They're chasing you for a bird whistler? Why? There are tons of these lying on the forest floor in Po'ana Rao'āwa. All kinds of bird shapes, too, not just hummingbirds. I've never seen one with musical notes inscribed on it like yours, though. Why don't you tell them to go get another one?"

"They only want this one," Clem started. The lightning bug flickered away, leaving them in total darkness. "They think it's magical—"

"Clementine," Kiwi interrupted. "Stop—"

"As I was saying," Clem interrupted back, tired of Kiwi telling her how Myst couldn't be trusted, "they think this one is magical and will lead them to the Forgotten City of Kot'ani,

Tua'mua, or the First Tree—or whatever they want to call it. So they can prove their superiority over the Wingless, Amphi, and everybody else, once and for all."

"That's stupid. Who cares?" Myst said. "That wouldn't change anything. Why don't you just give it to them?"

"Clementine!"

"I would, but I can't." Clem wished it wasn't pitch-black, so Kiwi could see the dirty look she was giving her. "You know how this boat is your only hope of getting home? Well, this flute is my only hope of getting home. I was brought here to find something important. This is supposed to be a clue, but until I figure out what it means—"

"Clementine! Stop talking and listen to me!" Kiwi barked. "Did you not hear what Myst said? He said he's never seen one with musical notes like yours!"

"What?"

"Did you not say," Kiwi asked Myst, "'I've never seen one with musical notes on it before'?"

"Yeah. They're right here." Clem felt Myst run his fingers across the underside of the tarnished wings. "These raised bumps are musical notes. It's too short to be a song, but it's definitely a tune. It's weird because I've found many of these while playing in the old forest, but I've never found one with notes."

"Can you play it?" Clem asked.

"Yeah, of course." Myst pressed the hummingbird's tail to his lips and blew. Before he finished the last note, something buzzed by his head and hovered to a stop inches from his nose.

"Can you see it?" he asked. "A hummingbird is hovering right in front of me."

"I can't see it, but I can hear it," Clem answered.

"This has to be the clue!" Kiwi said excitedly.

"Maybe." It was a neat trick, but...*the clue?* "Can you teach me to play it?" Clem asked, deciding it might be useful.

"Absolutely. I'll teach you tomorrow when you can see what you're doing."

"Hey, Myst?" Clem's question floated through the darkness from where she lay on the open deck.

"Yeah?" Myst mumbled.

"Where is Po'ana Rao'āwa?"

"It's my home." Myst sighed. "It's in the old forest, upriver from Mau'una Kupuka, in the shadow of the Central Pangian Range."

"No one lives past Mau'una Kupuka," Kiwi said with a yawn. "That's where you fall off the map."

"Lots of people live past Mau'una," Myst said quietly. "It's just nobody sees us. We are the people of the night."

CHAPTER 32

Disappearing early, Myst returned with breakfast courtesy of Ma.

"Kiwi and I are going to help you finish the boat, and we're all going to sail across the swamp together." Clementine dipped yesterday's bread in cold swamp meat stew.

"Come again? We're what now?" Kiwi's face went blank.

"Really?!" Myst yelped.

"No." Kiwi stuck her hand through the hole in the hull. "Remember this?"

"Yes, yes, yes!" Myst danced around excitedly. "We're going home!"

"Look," Clem said to Kiwi, "we need to get across the swamp. Akylas and Strigops will be watching the paddler and water lifts like hawks. Which doesn't matter because we have zero money for tickets anyway. Your dad said it would take six months to walk around the Mutina'kol'e, so that's a hard no. Myst has a boat. We're headed in the same direction. It's a win-win."

"The goal is to get across the swamp alive, though." Kiwi grimaced.

"It'll be fine," Clem assured her. "What needs to be done before we can leave, Myst?"

"We need a new sail." Myst pointed to the tattered pinwheel at the back of the boat. "When you spin the wheel, the flippers move like they're supposed to, but one of them is broken. Somebody probably hit a rock, or a gator bit it off. We should re-mat the sidewalls to have a dry place when it storms.

And I only have one oar so far. Two would be helpful. Otherwise, we just need trip supplies."

"Aren't you forgetting something?" Kiwi cleared her throat and pointed to the hole.

"Oh, and we need to patch the holes in the hull."

"Holes?" Kiwi shot back. "You mean there's more than one?"

"Oh yeah, you don't even want to see the one behind the counter," Myst said. "It's huge."

"Great," Kiwi sighed.

"Well, it's a boat, which is more than we had yesterday," Clem reasoned.

As they ate breakfast, she and Myst made a list of supplies they'd need to fix everything. Most of it could be gathered for free from the Fringe—new reeds for the hull, a lily pad for the matting, and vines for rope. The actual boat parts—a new pinwheel, a flipper, and another oar—they'd have to salvage from the boat graveyard.

Sticking beneath the city, they made one trip after another to the Outer Fringe, where the reeds grew thick and strong.

"How long do you think it will take us?" Clem dumped an armful of reeds on their lily-pad barge. "I mean, before we're ready to go?"

"Well, if all three of us are helping, we can do the work in a couple of days." Myst used his single oar to push them back beneath the city. "It's just finding the right parts and the money that's been problematic. I've been working on this for months."

"Well, we don't have months," Kiwi huffed. "My dad's already three days ahead. If we're lucky, he'll hang around Mau'una Kupuka for a while looking for us. We need to get this done as fast as possible."

"Your dad didn't leave three days ago. He left yesterday morning. Strigops lied to you. When Ma sent me to collect fish heads from the netters on the Fringe, I heard Strigops tell the Winged guy, 'I got him on the paddler this morning. The featherhead almost didn't go. He kept whining, "Kiwi wouldn't leave Wheku without me, Strigops."' Then Strigops told the Winged guy that you were at Ma's, and he was headed to get you immediately. After you left, Kookie wouldn't stop bragging about how much money she made for ratting you out."

"Ugh," Kiwi grumbled. "And to think I thought she was nice."

"But that's good news," Clem said. "If we hurry, we stand a chance of catching them before they leave Mau'una."

While they waited for the cover of darkness, Myst taught Clementine to play the tune on her flute. It wasn't difficult to learn: six notes, pause, six notes. As she played, hummingbirds danced in the shafts of light spilling through the cracks overhead.

"Are you sure this stuff is free?" Clem whispered as they stealthily paddled their lily pad through a gaping hole in the side of a half-sunk paddler and out the far side. The graveyard looked like a marina after a hurricane. Boats, pieces of paddlers, and ships were strewn everywhere.

"Look!" Myst whispered as they bobbed among the labyrinth of hulls. "Over there!"

In the pool of light cast by Thunder, the back of a reed boat jutted out of the water. Like the feet of a bobbing duck, its wooden flippers stuck straight in the air.

After paddling up beneath it, Clem and Myst worked to remove the left flipper. While they worked, Kiwi crawled onto the deck of a nearby boat and disappeared.

"Catch!" She tossed a coil of rope and an oar to Clementine.

"Great, all we need now is a pinwheel!" Myst got so excited he forgot to whisper.

"Who's there?" A light flicked on in a hut at the end of the dock.

Thunder's light went out. He buzzed back to the lily pad and buried himself beneath the coil of rope.

"Who's out there?" The outline of a man appeared in the doorway. Clem and Myst ducked as a lightning bug flew like a searchlight overhead and hovered to a stop above Kiwi.

"I see you! You're the kids those Winged guys are lookin' for, ain't you? Go get 'em, Cranky! Chomper! Be warned, I ain't fed 'em today."

"Cranky? Chomper? That doesn't sound good." Kiwi jumped onto the lily pad.

Two dark shadows slid off the dock and landed in the swamp with a splash.

"Gators!" Myst yelled.

"*Go, go, go!*" Kiwi screeched.

The water rippled menacingly behind them.

Clem paddled furiously with the second oar. A lily pad was not a speedboat, but a speedboat was what Clem wished for as they slowly bumped between the skeletal remains of long-dead ships.

"How do we get out of here?" Clem panted as they slid around a corner and paddled to a dead end. The water heaved behind them. Jaws rose from the inky depths. A giant set of teeth clamped onto the back of the lily pad, dragging them backward.

"We're trapped! We're going to die!" Kiwi screamed. She

ferociously pounded the gator on the head with the flipper until it let go. "I refuse to die like this!"

"Quick, lift the sides," Myst barked, squeezing the front of the lily pad into an impossibly narrow gap between two rusted barges. Clem grabbed the left side. Kiwi grabbed the right. Together they rolled toward the center. The lily pad folded like a taco with a bite missing and slid between the hulls.

Unfolding with a splash in the open swamp, they didn't stop paddling until they were back at the boat.

"That was terrifying." Kiwi flopped on the deck. "And to think I was crawling around in those boats, looking for things. What if there'd been gators in them?!"

"I thought you said this stuff was free?" Clem prized her white knuckles from the oar.

"I didn't say it was free," Myst said, shaking his head. "I said we could find what we needed there. And I was right. We did! Well, everything but the pinwheel sail. We'll have to try again tomorrow night."

"What?! No. There's no way I'm going back to the boatyard." Kiwi stood firm. "We can patch the pinwheel with that old tarp over there."

"That's my bed," Myst protested.

"Kiwi's right. We can't go back. That guy asked if we were the kids those Winged guys were looking for, which means Akylas and Strigops must suspect we're looking for another way across the swamp. If we go back, it's only a matter of time before they figure out what we're up to."

"But this is my bed!" Myst threw himself dramatically on the pile of musty tarps.

"We'll find you a new bed before we leave, I promise. But for now, I think we should lie low." Kiwi slumped against the side of the boat.

Clem lay awake, staring into the darkness. How were they going to get everything they still needed? They needed money. But how? She'd never had a job before. What would they even do? Could they fix the boat well enough to float, or would it sink like a rock when they cut it loose?

Kiwi, they discovered, was a boat-repair genius. Clem could barely tell where the holes had been when she finished weaving new reed into the hull. Kiwi also figured out how to remove the broken flipper, then patiently reconnected the new one while Clem and Myst held it in place.

Clementine and Myst cut the lily pad into long strips, which they wove into the walls until they were cross-eyed, and it felt like their fingers would fall off. Myst was the only one who ventured topside, disappearing just long enough to fetch food from Ma.

"What if we left this spot as a window?" Clem stretched her blistered fingers and looked at the foot-long section near the top of the wall that still needed to be finished.

"No." Kiwi expertly sewed Myst's bed into the pinwheel. "If the weather picks up, we're going to want a dry place to be. Plus, we don't need anyone passing by to see us when we're inside."

"But that's another whole afternoon of weaving," Clem whined.

"Then you'd better get back to it," Kiwi snapped.

"Yes, Mom." Clementine had to admit Kiwi was a great project manager.

"Now that you've chopped up my bed," Myst interjected, "when can I be expecting a new one?"

"That's the least of my worries right now," Kiwi said with a sigh. "I don't have enough tarp to finish the sail. We need more."

"And we need a week's worth of food, nets, backpacks, a tent, sleeping quilts, and new shoes. All without money and without being seen." Clem could stick all five toes through the hole in the front of her sneaker. Kiwi's shoes weren't in much better condition.

"And my bed." Myst folded his arms across his chest. "There's an Amphi, Komo, who owns a mercantile on the Fringe. Ma says he may let us work for what we need. He's a tough guy. She said we shouldn't expect sympathy or a deal, but he won't turn us in because he hates Akylas. Akylas did Komo dirty a few years ago on a business deal. Komo said if he ever saw him again, he'd pluck him clean to the bone. I heard one time Komo hanged a guy upside down over a gator pit because he owed him three taa'la—gator bit the guy's ear clean off."

"Yikes." Kiwi gulped.

"Sounds like a pleasant man." Clem pursed her lips. "I guess if he's our only option."

"There's only one small problem," Myst said, scrunching his nose. "It's near the inn, and we can't get to that part of the Fringe underneath the city. We're going to have to go topside."

"What? How are we supposed to get there without being spotted?" Kiwi stabbed the tarp with her needle.

"Carefully." Clementine pulled herself onto the beam beside Myst. "I'll keep my hood up and my head down. It's afternoon. Strigops will be in the saloon, hiding from the heat. It's not like the whole city's looking for us."

They hadn't been topside for five minutes when Kiwi yanked Clem and Myst off the boardwalk and into a narrow gap between two buildings.

"Holy ti'kea, the whole city is looking for us! Look!" Kiwi pointed at a wall full of posters. Clem's and Kiwi's faces stared back at them from every page.

"They put up Wanted posters? Are you kidding?" Even though she couldn't read them, Clem could tell it wasn't good. Beside her face was a feather with an *X* through it. The longer she stared at the wall, the harder she scowled. Ducking her head out of the alley, she could see Wanted posters fluttering in the breeze up the entire length of the boardwalk.

"What do they say?" she demanded.

"It says: *Kiwi and Clementine: Wanted for theft and illegal transportation of priceless antiquities. Two Wingless girls, aged thirteen. Wingless 'Kiwi' is average-looking, with drab gray hair and plumage. Wingless 'Clementine' is easily recognizable, with long dark hair and a birth defect leaving her noticeably featherless.* Average-looking? Drab gray hair? My hair is obviously silver, thank you very much," Kiwi muttered as she scanned the symbols. "*Artifact in question is a small copper-and-green flute in the shape of a hummingbird. The duo was last seen in the mid-swamp area. Wanted alive by the Joint Winged and Wingless Antiquities Protection Force, currently stationed at the Soggy Bottom Inn. 5,000 taa'la reward for their safe capture. 7,500 taa'la reward if discovered in possession of the stolen artifact.*"

"Is that a lot of money?" Clem bit her lower lip.

"So much money," Myst said, nodding. "It's enough money to buy a boat, fishing supplies, a new bed, and everything we need to cross the swamp. Plus, hire a crew to take us there."

Kiwi's eyes narrowed. "Don't even think about it."

"You know I wouldn't. I was trying to put it in a way

Clementine would understand," Myst huffed. "Even a Wingless would hand you over to Akylas for that much money. You know it's true."

"Joint Winged and Wingless Antiquities Protection Force, ha! Drab gray feathers! What a joke." Kiwi tore a fistful of notices off the wall and wadded them in a tight ball.

"Shhh, people are coming." Myst tugged Clem and Kiwi farther away from the boardwalk.

"Great!" Clem kicked at a nearby garbage barrel, which fell over, spewing garbage everywhere. "What are we supposed to do now?"

A stench worse than rotten fish guts steaming in Ferg's gym bag slapped her in the face. Clem puffed out her cheeks, half out of rage, half trying to keep from barfing. The garbage oozed between the planks and dripped into the swamp.

"Don't hate me, but I have an idea." Kiwi bent and grabbed a fistful of feathers from the trash.

"What? No, no way! Gross! Where did those even come from?" Clementine shook her head in disgust. Kiwi couldn't be meaning what she thought she was.

"From the amount of hair and feathers in this trash bin, there's probably a preener nearby. Everyone is looking for someone with long hair and no feathers, right? So if we tie up your hair and give you a little makeover?"

"With garbage feathers that came off someone's head?! That's disgusting! What about you and your drab gray hair?" Clem shot back.

"See this?" Kiwi kicked at a rotten piece of fruit. "It's pap'oni rarukia. It permanently stains everything it touches a violent shade of red. I'll do you if you do me?"

"Fine," Clem answered.

"Oh, this is perfect," Kiwi said after what felt like forever. "If I saw you on the street, I'd have no idea it was you."

Clem's forehead felt sticky from the trash ooze Kiwi had used as glue. A single feather slid down her eyebrow and covered her eye. Leaning around the building, she stared at her reflection in the window.

"I look like a great horned owl that's been crushed in the grille of a semi-truck." Clem wasn't sure if she was impressed or horrified by her reflection. She didn't want to hurt Kiwi's feelings, but she looked ridiculous.

"You do look like an owl!" Kiwi gasped proudly. "Perfection, right?!"

Picking up a piece of pap'oni rarukia, Clem squeezed it over Kiwi's head.

"When you said permanent, how permanent did you mean?" The red juice ran down Kiwi's beautiful silver curls. Rubbing it in until no silver was left, Clem rinsed it off with a bucket of swamp water.

"Well?" Kiwi asked. "Is it super-red?"

"Um, no. Not exactly." Clem stared at Kiwi's head. "It's more what I'd call Pepto-Bismol pink."

Kiwi ducked around the corner to look at her reflection.

"Oh. My. God." Her mouth hung open as she stared at herself. "I love it! We look so good! I wonder if my dad will let me keep this. I hope it lasts forever!"

"We look ridiculous," Clem mumbled. "Unrecognizably ridiculous."

With her feathers sliding down her face and Kiwi's shocking hair, Clementine was afraid they'd stick out like a sore thumb, but this was Wheku: everyone was weird.

Komo, the mob boss of lizard people, was no exception.

"How much work would we have to do for all of this?" Clem asked as Myst tossed a hammock on the heaping stack of goods they'd piled on the man's counter. A jar of food tipped over and rolled toward him.

"A month," Komo said with a finality Clem understood meant it wasn't open for negotiation.

"A month? With all three of us working?!" Kiwi choked out. "That's exploitation! If the three of us worked anywhere else, we could make enough money to pay for this in a week."

"Then go work elsewhere and come back with taa'la," Komo growled. "You think everyone will jump on the opportunity to hire two wimpy Wingless girls and a blind boy? Good luck. I'm doing you a favor. One month, sunup to sunset, and it's yours."

"That's not fair," Kiwi huffed.

"Keep running your mouth, and it'll be a month and a half, little girl."

"The thing is"—Clem cast a *shut up* glance in Kiwi's direction—"we're kind of on a tight schedule, and we can't spare a month. What could we get for three days' work?"

The man pointed at the tent and raised the green scaly humps where his eyebrows should be. Myst and Kiwi protested, but Clementine raised her hand in silence. She'd watched her grandma barter a million times. Not breaking the man's stare, she added Myst's hammock, the tarp, a backpack, two pairs of shoes, and a few cans of food to the pile.

"How about that?"

"Three weeks." Komo's forked tongue slid between his lips.

Clem put back the backpack and the tent.

"Two weeks," Komo said with a smirk.

"One week," Clementine countered, pushing the shoes out

of the pile.

"Still two weeks… Or this—" He grabbed Clem's wrist and ran a leathery finger over the turquoise stone in her bracelet.

"No deal." Clem pulled her hand back. "It's not for sale."

"Suit yourself," Komo said, shrugging.

Clem, Kiwi, and Myst made for the door. Clem's hand was on the handle when Strigops and Akylas stumbled out of the saloon and into the street. Stopping in front of the mercantile, Akylas held up a Wanted poster and began shouting. A small crowd gathered around him.

Their disguises were good, but not that good. Clem winced. They needed a distraction.

Looking at her wrist, she popped off her bracelet and paused. Clem marched back to the counter and slammed it down.

"Fine. You can have it, but I'm taking the shoes, two fishing hooks, and three more cans of food."

"Clementine, no!" Kiwi said.

"I like you, kid. You drive a hard bargain." Komo strung the bracelet around the chain hanging from his muscular neck. "You got yourself a deal."

"Thanks." Not looking at her bracelet for fear of crying, Clementine quickly tossed everything in the hammock and slung it over her shoulder.

"That guy's really causing a scene out there, hey?" She nodded toward the door.

Komo looked out the front window.

"Akylas," he hissed, a vein throbbing in his scaly forehead. "That arrogant, double-crossing, Winged son of a nak'esa! Wait till I get my hands on—"

Komo stormed out the door and into the street. Clementine

smiled as feathers and fists flew. In the commotion, they slipped across the Fringe and back to the swamp.

"That was so awesome!" Myst yelled. "Did you see Komo punch that guy? I could hear the feathers flying through the air!"

"That was pretty clever, Clem," Kiwi agreed. "Sorry about your grandma's bracelet."

"It's okay," Clem sighed. "She'd have understood. Besides, it was worth it to see Komo kick Akylas's butt."

"Hey, Myst, where've you been, buddy?" Dart popped out of a side street. "We've missed you at Ma's."

Clem looked around. In their excitement, they'd wandered into Mid-Swamp.

"Yeah, Myst, we've missed you at Ma's," Kookie parroted. "Who are your new friends?"

"Pepto and Semi-truck," Myst answered.

Snorting, Clem pulled her hood down.

"Where you from, Semi-truck?" Dart asked.

"None of your business," Clem said, trying to sound gangster like Komo.

Kookie and Kiwi stared daggers at each other.

"You lookin' for work?" Dart asked. "If so, have Myst bring you by Ma's. I'll let you know where to find the real taa'la."

"Yeah, sure," Clem said with a nod. The hammock was getting heavy. "We're kinda busy right now. Maybe we'll stop by later."

Kookie whispered something in Kiwi's ear as they walked away, but Clementine didn't catch what she said.

"Ugh, that was close." Clem dropped the hammock in the front of the boat. "Pepto and Semi-truck? You're hilarious,

Myst."

"I listen," Myst said, beaming. "Especially when people say weird things, and you always say weird things."

"Do those two know about this place?" Kiwi wasted no time getting back to work.

Myst shook his head.

"Have they ever seen you climb down here?" she prodded.

"I don't think so."

"We should cut the ropes and make sure this thing floats." Kiwi ran her finger across the blade of the knife she'd been using to cut the tarp.

"Lighten up, Pepto!" Clem smiled. "Of course, it floats."

"She knew it was me, Clementine," Kiwi said seriously. "Which means she knows we're with Myst."

"There's no way she—" Clem started.

"Kookie said she had a book she thought I'd be interested in reading. She gave me a look when she said it. Trust me, she knows. Besides, Komo was wearing your bracelet when he went after Akylas. You can't tell me Akylas won't recognize it. It's unmistakably yours. Nothing in Pangier looks like it. After their little run-in, Akylas is going to be out for blood. It's only a matter of time before they figure out we're down here."

In the distance, muffled voices skipped like stones across the water.

"You're right. It's time to go." Clementine shivered.

CHAPTER 33

"You think they've realized we aren't in Wheku anymore?" They drifted like a shuttle to Mars, floating through space with nothing but the twinkling stars to keep them company. Clem stared up at Orion, comforted by its familiarity.

Having narrowly escaped in the dead of night, they'd spent three days sailing under the cover of darkness and hiding beneath the arching roots of swamp trees through the day. She cowered at even the faintest shadow.

"Almost certainly," Kiwi said. "Do you think we're halfway?"

Clementine doubted it. They'd spent the first night rowing while Kiwi finished mending the pinwheel. The second night, they'd stopped early to fix a leak. This was the first night it felt like they'd found their groove, but then the wind died, and an eerily calmness fell over the swamp. The pinwheel spun slow, lazy circles behind them.

"Not even close." Myst steered the boat through a tangle of roots. Clem had to admit the kid had an uncanny ability to navigate through the darkness. "But the trees are starting to thin out—that's a good sign. There aren't trees in the middle of the Mutina'kol'e, just water for as far as the eye can see."

A pea'wai, the size of a rhinoceros, gently bumped against the side of the boat. In the moonlight, Clem could just make out its eight stout legs below its plump body. During the day, she liked watching the docile animals hoover up tree moss with their bear-like snouts.

"Do we have a plan for getting across the open swamp?" Kiwi asked.

"Don't get caught?" Clem offered.

"I was thinking we could take turns," Myst said. "Since you're night blind, I'll sail at night while you sleep. You can sail in the day while I sleep since I'm day blind. We can get across twice as fast."

The boat lurched forward. Clem and Kiwi looked at the pinwheel. It rotated and began to spin steadily in the sudden breeze.

"Storm's coming," Myst said. "I can smell the electricity in the air."

The wind blew at gale force; the swamp heaved. Water sloshed over the low sides of the boat. Even with Clem and Kiwi tugging on the tiller, Myst had difficulty keeping them on course.

Lightning flashed, outlining a single tree in the distance.

"There!" Kiwi yelled over the rumble of thunder.

Another flash.

"We're too far left," Clem yelled. "We're going to miss it!"

"Augh, I wish it would stop," Myst cried. "The lightning is ruining my ability to navigate. I can't see a thing."

The sky glowed yellow.

"We're going to hit it! Hard right!" Kiwi screamed.

Throwing their weight against the long tiller, they drifted sideways through the reeds and slammed against a massive tree trunk.

Kiwi fell headfirst over the tiller, barely grabbing Myst before he slid overboard.

Clem rubbed her shin. If she ever got home, she was never leaving her bedroom again. Andro could find the other three

Stones himself. Limping across the deck, she grabbed a rope and lassoed a gnarled root as they slid by. She and Kiwi pulled the rope as hard as they could, dragging the boat between the tree and a half-sunken log and into calmer waters.

"Well, it's not ideal, but at least we're anchored to something," she panted, ducking beneath the covered deck.

Too tired for breakfast, they threw themselves on the floor and let the waves rock them to sleep.

It was midmorning when Clementine awoke with a start to the steady splatter of rain drumming against the roof. Why was she awake?

Lifting her head off the floor, she scanned the room. Everything seemed to be in place. Myst hung in his hammock, fast asleep. Strigops leered at her through the section of wall they'd never had time to finish. Kiwi snored gently beside her, buried under a pile of tarp.

Wait, what? Clementine's head snapped back to the gap in the wall, but no one was there.

A loud crack of thunder rumbled across the swamp. That must have been what woke her. She closed her eyes. The boat thumped against the log.

"What is it?" Kiwi mumbled. "Is it time to get up?"

"No," Clem sighed. "The boat must have come unmoored in the wind. If you roll away from the door, I'll tie us back up."

Groaning, Kiwi scooted over, so Clem could squeeze out.

While they'd slept, a thick fog settled over the swamp. Clem could barely see the bow. She slid across the deck to test the line. It was tight. The boat was nowhere near the log. Weird.

Turning around, Clementine came face-to-face with Strigops. Every hair on her body stood on end, as if she were about to be struck by lightning. Clem slowly eyed the side of the boat. She could jump overboard, but where would that leave Kiwi and Myst? Besides, the fog was so thick, she'd never find her way back onboard. Clenching her jaw, she stared Strigops down. One of his eyes was black and blue, half of his lime-green feathers had been plucked out, and he appeared to be missing a chunk of his right ear.

"Clementine Lemons," he said, sneering through a swollen lip.

It must have been his boat she'd heard thumping against the log.

"What happened to you? You look terrible." Clem asked flatly. *She would show this man no fear.*

"Your friend Komo is what happened to me," he spat.

"I don't know what you're talking about." Clem made no effort to hide her amused smile.

"Well, when Akylas and Falk get here, I'm sure they'll refresh your memory."

"Oh, I'm not too worried. You and I both know Falk and Akylas aren't coming. Akylas is afraid of water, and Falk's a big baby who doesn't like to get his poor little wings wet. That's why they sent you, am I right?"

"What's going on out here?" Kiwi threw the door open.

Strigops lunged forward. Clementine ducked. She slid across the deck and sailed through the door, taking Kiwi with her. They landed with a thump beneath Myst's hammock. Strigops burst into the cabin. Grabbing Clementine by the hair, he dragged her toward the door.

"What's going on?" Myst yelped.

"We've got company!" Kiwi yelled.

Axol hopped over Clementine and reached for Myst.

"I'm not going back in that cage." Myst kicked and

punched Axol with his tiny fists.

"I don't want you, you tiny runt. You're useless, and there's no bounty on your head." Axol swatted Myst with the back of one of his giant fists. Myst flew across the room, landing in a crumpled heap against the wall. Grabbing Kiwi by her bright pink head, Axol dragged her out behind Clementine.

As Strigops pulled her onto the log, Clementine grabbed one of the oars and cracked him across the back. Screaming in agony, he dropped to his knees. Fumbling in the fog, Clementine searched for Kiwi.

"One of you fools, get down here and help me," Strigops bellowed.

"Yes, boss!" Clem didn't see Cane jump, but she felt it. The edge of the log lifted high in the air. The next thing she knew, she'd landed in the water.

"You fat fool!" Strigops growled at Cane. "I said help, not launch us into tomorrow."

"Where'd she go?" Axol yelled. "I can't see a thing in this blasted fog."

Clementine couldn't see the tree, reeds, or the boat. Everything was gray.

"Forget about her," Strigops spat. "As soon as Emos finds out we've got his girl, he'll lead us straight to the Forgotten City."

"But Akylas said if we wanted to get paid—" Cane croaked.

"We don't need Akylas," Strigops said with a snort. "When we get to the Forgotten City, you'll have more money than you could ever dream of."

An engine whirred to life, and the voices faded away.

"Kiwi? Clementine?" Myst's voice was distant and small.

"Myst?" Clementine gagged on a mouthful of swamp water.

"Where are you, Clementine?" he cried.

"I don't know, buddy. I'm in the swamp, but I can't see anything. Are you okay?"

"Yeah. Don't be scared, Clementine. I'll find you."

Not five minutes later, a tiny hand reached out of the fog and pulled her to safety.

"How you do that, I'll never know!" Clem wrapped Myst in the biggest hug. "You're amazing!" She rubbed his bruised cheek. "Are you okay?"

"Yeah." Myst wiped a tear from his cheek. "Those are the bad guys who put me in a cage. I hate them."

"Me too, buddy," Clem said. "Me too."

"Where's Kiwi?"

"Strigops took her. You think you can find them so we can get her back?"

Nodding, Myst stared blankly into the thick fog. Grabbing the tiller, he swung the boat around.

CHAPTER 34

"If I were you, I'd hold on to something." They'd been sailing for hours, and Myst hadn't said a word until now.

"What?" Clementine asked.

"Hold on to something," he repeated.

Looking at his determined face, Clem obeyed. Myst turned the pinwheel directly into the wind. The boat flew through the water at full speed.

"Ah, Myst," Clementine yelled as the broadside of a barge appeared out of nowhere, "slow down, buddy—there's something right in front of us!"

"Oh, I know." Skipping over a wave, Myst rammed the boat onto the deck. Like a dart hitting a bull's-eye, the tip of the bow nailed Cane right in the gut. Cane flew through the air and disappeared into the fog. A moment later, a thunderous splash sent spray arcing over their heads. Axol and Strigops stood there, stunned.

"Kiwi?" Clem didn't waste a second.

"Over here!"

Near the bridge, Clementine spotted her locked up, like an animal, in a cage. Probably the same one they'd locked Myst in. Clem skidded across the wet deck and crashed into the solid iron bars. Axol and Strigops ran toward them.

Grabbing a piece of rope, Myst skated in front of them.

"Give us back our friend!" he cried, pulling the rope taut.

Axol and Strigops tripped. Strigops crashed headfirst into a nearby barrel. Axol skidded across the deck, coming to a stop at Myst's feet.

"Where are the keys?" Clementine held the rusted lock in her palm.

"In there, I think." Kiwi pointed to a door about five feet away.

Axol jumped to his feet, plucked Myst off the deck by the scruff of the neck, and held him up until they were face-to-face. "Scrappy little thing, aren't you?" he growled.

Clementine looked at the door, then over at Myst and Axol. Strigops groaned and rubbed his head. Should she get the key or help Myst?

"Save Kiwi!" Myst swung his fists at Axol's face. "I got this guy!"

It didn't look like he "had that guy," but Clem made a mad dash for the door anyway. They needed Kiwi's help. Three against two gave them way better odds.

Clem blinked in the darkness.

"Ouch, you bit me, you worthless..." Axol yelped. One loud thump was followed closely by another.

"Where?" Clem frantically searched the messy room.

"On a hook next to the door!" Myst squeaked.

Clementine grabbed the keys and raced back outside. Myst had somehow gotten free and was kicking Axol in the kneecaps. As Clem darted toward Kiwi, Strigops tackled her.

"Kiwi, catch!" Clementine threw the keys toward the cage but didn't see where they landed. Kicking and screaming, she and Strigops rolled around the deck. As she struggled to find footing, she heard a splash.

Myst!

Clem tried to turn her head to see what was happening, but Strigops had her by the neck. Her head dangled over the side of the barge.

"Give me that!" Spit sprayed from Strigops's rabid lips as

he grabbed at the leather strap.

Clem clawed at his hands, but he was too strong. She couldn't breathe. As she glared at Strigops's angry, twisted face, he suddenly looked stunned, blinked once, and toppled over.

"That's for selling out my dad and locking me in a cage!" Kiwi stood above Strigops, looking absolutely deranged. Her bloodshot eyes bulged beneath her Pepto-pink feathers. In her hands, she held a fish club.

"Kiwi, you can't… I've known you since you were a little girl," Strigops said, sniveling and getting to his knees. "Please…I can explain."

Kiwi swung the club again and again.

"Kiwi, please. This isn't what you think. We were never going to hurt you, I swear."

"You want a headline? You want to be famous like my dad?" Kiwi wound up like she was up to bat at the World Series. "Here's a headline for you: *Strigops: First Wingless to Discover the Bottom of the Swamp!*"

Giving the club one last swing, she sent Strigops overboard.

"You are amazing." Clem rubbed her throat with one hand while Kiwi pulled her up by the other. "Terrifying when mad, but amazing. Where's…where's…Myst?"

"I'm here." Myst leaned in the doorjamb. Blood trickled from his lip. "I thought I was going to die, but I showed that guy who was boss."

"Good job, buddy." Clem fist-bumped him. "Speaking of dying, we'd better get our boat unstuck and back in the water before those three find their way back onboard."

Heaving the front of their boat off the barge, they scrambled on just as Cane clawed his way back onto the deck.

Myst swung their boat around. Without so much as a glance behind him, he sailed for home.

"You think they'll come after us?"

"They couldn't even if they wanted to," Myst said with a snort.

"Because we have the best navigator in Pangier, and they couldn't find a feather on their own heads with a mirror?" Kiwi tousled his hair.

"No." Myst blushed.

"Because you have superpowers that let you see what no one else can with such precision, you can knock a guy off a moving barge in whiteout conditions?" Clem asked.

"No." Myst giggled.

"Why then?" Clem and Kiwi asked.

"Because I stole their keys." Myst held a key ring over the side of the boat and dropped it in the swamp.

The fog and rain hung over them like a wet blanket. They sailed hard, eager to cross before the sun came back out. When they ran out of canned food, Kiwi fished. When Myst got tired, Clementine took over. The water was rough, but the wind blew them steadily toward their goal.

"Whoa." Clementine popped out of the cabin. The fog had lifted while she slept; the last of the rain clouds were smeared in long peach streaks across the morning sky. The trees grew dense along both sides of a wide channel. Moss, glistening gold under the rising sun, hung in long wisps from the branches.

"Amazing, right?" Kiwi tossed her fishing line back into the water.

"It's beautiful," Myst sighed.

"You can see this?" Clem was never quite sure what Myst

saw.

"No," Myst said, smiling. "But I feel it, and it feels beautiful."

"Where are we, exactly?" she asked as he turned off the main channel and into a narrower one.

"Home." Myst breathed deep. "It smells delicious, doesn't it?"

"Po'ana Rao'āwa? I thought we were headed to Mau'una to find your dad?"

"Yeah, Myst and I changed the plans while you were sleeping. Myst thought, and I agreed, that stopping in Mau'una would be dangerous. He's taking us home, where we'll be safe. Then he'll ask his dad to send out trackers to find my dad."

"And your dad's going to trust these trackers?" Clem raised her eyebrows and drew wings in the air with her fingers.

"I hadn't thought about that," Kiwi said. "Maybe I can send them with a note or something."

Clementine asked Myst if he wanted to stop and wait for sunset before they continued, but not even the midday sun could keep him from home.

Unstoppable, he snaked his way through the meandering channels of the Po'ana Rao'āwa Delta. The flat humid bush of the Fringe gradually gave way to the soaring forests nestled deep in the foothills of the Central Pangian Range. This was the edge of the old forest, the forest from which all other forests were born.

Around the bend, the limestone valley opened its enormous jaws and swallowed the river whole.

"Home," Myst whispered breathlessly as he headed toward a massive cave. "I'm home."

The boat was little more than a speck as it sailed through

the gaping arch and into the belly of the Earth.

Long shafts of light poured through the cave roof, illuminating the marbled rock walls and diving deep into the cold, turquoise water. Even if she spent a million years in Pangier, Clem would never stop being amazed.

"I'm home!" Myst's scream bounced off the walls. *"Home, ome, ome!"*

Heads poked out of square windows carved in the stone walls. Feet pattered across ancient walkways and down limestone steps worn smooth with time. Tiny black wings fluttered down from above. By the time they drifted onto the beach at the back of the cave, a crowd had gathered.

"Hi, everybody! I got a bit blown off course." Myst's bare feet hit the soft white sand. "But I found my way home."

"Myst!" His parents threw their arms around him. "Oh, Myst!"

The crowd closed in, everyone wanting to welcome back their lost son. Clem and Kiwi smiled at each other. Would Clem's family be this excited when she came home? She hoped so.

"We thought we'd lost you." His father wiped tears from his eyes. "It's been so long. I can't believe you're home."

"I would've never made it if it wasn't for my friends." Myst yanked Clem and Kiwi by their arms. "Dad, this is Clementine and Kiwi. Guys, this is my dad, Myo. Dad, I told them you'd be able to—"

"Kiwi?" Myo interrupted. "Emos's girl?"

"Yeah?" Kiwi's eyes widened.

"Emos!" the man yelled.

"Back here," a familiar voice called from behind the crowd.

"You need to get over here." Myo shook his head in

disbelief.

The crowd parted just enough for the girls to spot Emos's silver head.

"Dad," Kiwi whispered.

"Emos is your dad?" Myst questioned.

"You know my dad?" Kiwi squawked.

"Yeah, he comes here every summer. He's, like, our only Wingless visitor. Why didn't you tell me Emos was your—"

"What?" Kiwi looked like her head was about to explode. "What is he even doing here?"

"When your dad couldn't find you in Mau'una, he came here to ask for help," Myo answered as Emos made his way toward them. "We may be blind, but our tracking skills are second to none."

"You can say that again," Clem agreed.

"Oh, it's good to see you, champ." Emos ruffled Myst's fluffy brown hair as he wandered up. "What's up, Myo?"

Myo pointed at Kiwi.

"Dad!" Taking a flying leap, she landed in his arms.

"Kiwi?" Emos stared at the fluffy pink ball buried in his shoulder. "Kiwi! What? How? Where have you...? What happened to your hair?"

Kiwi pulled her head back and inhaled deeply. "You are not going to believe this, but..."

CHAPTER 35

"Breakfast this morning was one of the best expedition meals I've ever eaten," Casso said as they climbed uphill for the seventh day straight. "I never thought about setting night traps. Brilliant."

"Well, I learned from the best." Clem remembered how worried she'd been in Whaka'wai that everyone would think she was a fraud. Now they were calling her brilliant. It wasn't a word she was used to hearing, but she liked it.

If Clem was honest, she'd mainly set the traps to show off. She said it was because she wanted to help, but…Emos, Casso, and Auk were happy to take care of everything. She and Kiwi no longer worried about starving to death, getting attacked by butterflies, or getting hopelessly lost. Clem didn't worry about where they'd camp or if there was water ahead. She wasn't even worried about Akylas or Strigops.

Though Emos had been shocked to discover the extent of Strigops's treachery, he wasn't surprised. Emos had suspected Strigops was a snitch since the previous summer when Akylas had landed at a new site only five minutes after they'd discovered it.

"There was no way he could have known that quickly," Clem had heard Emos tell Myo. "We were weeks away from the nearest…" The rest of the story had been drowned out by Kiwi.

Due to his suspicions, Emos had never shown Strigops exactly where he thought Kot'ani was located. Strigops did, however, have a rough idea of the valley they were headed for.

How much Akylas knew was another story.

Before they left the cave, Myo had suggested they take an alternate route, one the Winged wouldn't suspect and likely wouldn't be watching.

It had been a week since she'd reluctantly hugged Myst goodbye, and they hadn't seen so much as a shadow. Clem secretly hoped Akylas had given up. It had been all summer. Surely, he had better things to do?

As they trudged uphill, Clementine tried to figure out how long it had been since she'd first met Raveen, left Whaka'wai, or last been home. All the days melted together like butter under the late summer sun. Emos had asked Myo to send word to the university saying he wouldn't be home in time for the start of the fall semester. Her best guess was that it was early September back home.

She wondered if Brook and Maddy had gone school shopping without her. They'd probably found desks next to each other in home room. Fergus had better not be getting special treatment because she was gone.

"Woohoo!" Kiwi howled from up ahead. "We've gained the ridgeline!"

Once they made the ridgeline and dropped into the valley to the west, they'd be a week away from knowing if Kot'ani was where Emos had drawn the X on the map. A week from knowing if she was going home or… Clem pushed the thought from her mind.

The dry brown grass rippled like waves across the open ridge. Stepping out of the forest, Clementine spun in a circle. How she missed open spaces!

Clem walked the ridgeline, the warm sun on her face, the fuzzy brown grass kissing her fingertips. It was as if she were standing on the fold of a crumpled piece of art paper, the emerald creases of Pangier spreading out around her. Ahead, the Central Pangian Range rose like a gray wall into the cloudless sky. Clem couldn't help but wonder what was on the far side. Behind them, the Mutina'kol'e sparkled all the way to the horizon.

"That's our valley." Kiwi pointed west as they walked. "If we find Kot'ani, we're going to be so famous when we go back to school! I bet they ask us to make a speech and everything. Do you want to talk when we do the speech, or should I? Because I'm happy to… Oh right, I forgot, if we find Kot'ani, you might not be here anymore…"

Clementine was conflicted. She was beyond excited at the idea of going home, even if that meant going straight to school. She dreaded the thought of waking up to a day with no birdsong, no green, and no Kiwi. As difficult as the journey had been, she didn't want the adventure to end. But if it didn't end, that meant she hadn't succeeded, and she'd let Andro down. Why couldn't life just be easy?

"Kiwi! Clementine!" Emos's voice drifted in the steady breeze.

Clem turned around. She hadn't realized they'd wandered so far. In the distance, Emos was jogging toward them, waving his hands.

"What's your dad doing?" Clem asked.

"Probably wants to stop for lunch."

"Lunch?" Clem yelled, but the wind caught her words and blew them over the ridge. "Can you hear what he's saying?"

Auk and Casso pointed into the sky. High overhead, a dozen Winged circled.

"Run!" Emos yelled.

Instinctively, Clem grabbed Kiwi's hand. At a dead sprint, they ran to the safety of the forest.

"Cut them off before they get lost in the trees!" Clem couldn't be sure, but it sounded like Akylas.

"I'm on it!" Raveen was so close Clementine could feel the rush of air from her wings.

"Every time you try, she gets away, Ravi," Falk said with a sneer. "Leave it to us!"

"Falk, no!" Akylas screamed.

A half-dozen fire-tipped arrows rained down from above. The grass at their feet exploded into flames. Fire leaped through the branches of the nearest trees. Clem's gaze met Akylas's for a moment, then the sky turned black, and she and Kiwi were alone.

Clementine couldn't see, couldn't breathe. The wind whipped up a wall of flames around them. Her eyes stung. What were they supposed to do?

Think, brain!

"Aargh, are you joking?" The Smokey the Bear fire song popped into her head.

A hand reached out and grabbed hers, pulling her downhill. Bits of burning debris drifted into the trees, lighting them up like candles.

"So this is how we die?" Kiwi choked out.

"Get under the smoke. Crawl if you have to!" Emos instructed.

On her hands and knees, at least the air was breathable. Kiwi and Emos were barely visible even though they were right beside her.

"Did you hear that?" Kiwi shouted.

"Hear what?" It was hard to hear anything over the deafening roar of the fire.

"That," Kiwi yelled.

Clementine stopped and listened. Had she heard

something?

"There, that!" Kiwi said again.

This time it was distinct—"Help!"

"Don't stop moving!" Emos yelled.

"We have to go back! Someone's in trouble!" Kiwi turned and ran back uphill. Clementine ran after her.

Her lungs burned.

"Kiwi, we need to go back," Clem choked out.

If Kiwi heard, she didn't answer.

At the edge of the treeline, they found Raveen, her wing pinned beneath a fallen branch. The fire raged around her.

Clementine grabbed Kiwi and pulled her back as the tree beside them exploded.

"We can't leave her!" Kiwi shrugged Clem off.

Clementine looked at Kiwi and nodded. If they were going to save Raveen, it was now or never. Dashing into the open, Clem grabbed one end of the branch while Kiwi grabbed the other.

"Clementine? Kiwi?" Raveen croaked. "What are you doing here?"

"Saving you…we hope." Clem and Kiwi leaned their weight into the branch.

It wouldn't budge. The new shoes they'd gotten at the cave smoked.

A branch cracked overhead and crashed to the ground in a poof of orange spark and flame.

"Go, Wingless!" Raveen shouted. "Or we're all going to die."

"No. We're not leaving you here." Kiwi leaned back and dug in with her heels. "Uuugghh!!!"

The branch snapped, freeing Raveen. Kiwi stumbled backward and landed in Clem's arms. Together they pulled

Raveen to her feet.

"Do you think you can fly?" Kiwi asked.

Raveen flapped her wings. She didn't make it a foot in the air before crumpling back to the ground.

"I think it's broken," Raveen moaned in agony.

Emos, Auk, and Casso burst out of the forest.

"She needs help, Dad. Her wing's broken." Kiwi breathed heavily, ready to pass out from the smoke.

"Think you can walk?" Emos asked, flames licking at his ankles.

Raveen nodded.

Auk and Casso grabbed Clem and Kiwi. Emos grabbed Raveen.

"Keep running downhill! And don't stop," Emos yelled as he and Raveen dodged a falling tree.

They ran until the embers stopped falling like rain and all that remained of the fire was the distant smell of smoke.

Throwing her blackened body on the cool, damp moss next to a babbling brook, Clementine stared at her barely recognizable reflection.

Her face was black with soot, her eyes were bloodshot, and her lips were shriveled raisins. She plunged her head into the cold water and held it there until her lungs screamed for air. Everything hurt, but at least they were alive.

"Holy ti'kea, are you okay?" Kiwi fell to the ground beside her. "That was so close! God, I thought we were really going to die that time…"

Emo leaned Raveen against a tree; one of her wings hung limply beside her.

"Why did you come back for me?" She stared at Kiwi and Clementine, her hands smoothing her singed feathers.

"Well, we wouldn't leave you to die," Kiwi answered.

"We're Wingless. We protect each other."

"But I'm not a Wingless."

"So?" Clem shrugged.

"Yeah," Kiwi said, smiling. "Wings, no wings, feathers, no feathers: what does that have to do with anything?"

Nodding proudly at his daughter, Emos said to Raveen, "You might not be Wingless, but if we don't take care of your wing, you won't be flying anytime soon. Shall we take a look?"

"Are you sure you aren't going to de-wing me?" Raveen flinched.

"I wouldn't dream of it." Emos held out his hand.

CHAPTER 36

"I still can't believe you guys came back for me yesterday," Raveen said as they followed a babbling brook upstream. "I probably wouldn't have done the same."

Emos, Casso, and Auk were in camp debating the fastest route back to civilization. With nothing better to do, the girls had gone exploring.

They walked until they found a short waterfall cascading down a mossy gap between two limestone cliffs. Beneath the cliffs, the water pooled in deep green wells, bubbling underground and popping up elsewhere. It didn't look like they could go much farther.

"Yes, you would have," Clementine disagreed. "You saved me from Falk." She stretched out on a mossy rock and debated going for a swim.

"Falk's completely batty." Raveen looked at her bandaged wing and singed feathers and frowned. "Some days, I can't believe we're even related. And just so you know, I only saved you because I wanted the flute."

"If you only wanted the flute," Clem said, smiling coyly, "wouldn't it have been easier to let me hit the ground? That would've saved us all a lot of trouble."

Clem watched a giant goldfish disappear from one pool and resurface in another. On second thought, she would not be going for a swim.

"If you die here, do you die in your world too?" Raveen asked.

"I dunno." Clem pulled the flute from around her neck. "I

guess so. I don't think this thing comes with a reset button."

"What exactly are you doing here again?" Raveen asked.

Clem wasn't sure if Raveen didn't get it or just didn't believe it. Probably the latter. It was, after all, a pretty crazy story.

"She's trying to be a rock that makes waves," Kiwi said, bursting out laughing.

"You're such a jerk." Clementine rolled her eyes.

"Well, I figured since you're going to be around until at least next summer, I'd try acting more like your brother. You know, so you don't feel as homesick."

"Thanks." Clem tried to smile, but the edges of her lips didn't want to cooperate. "We're really in the wrong valley, huh?"

"Yeah, Dad said that the fire pushed us over the wrong side of the ridge. We're really far east of where we should be. With the mountain still on fire and Raveen unable to fly, there won't be time to find Kot'ani this year. We need to get back to civilization. By the time we get out of here, Dad will have missed a crazy amount of work. Next year. We'll come back next year."

Clem spun the hummingbird by the leather cord. Next year seemed so far away.

"Do you ever wish you'd never pulled that thing out of the drawer?" Kiwi asked.

"Are you joking?" she answered. "Then I'd never have met you. My only regret is not telling Andro the key arrived. I'd rather he think I died trying to help than that I abandoned him. I guess I wish I'd hugged my family goodbye too. And I regret appearing in front of Raveen, not that I had any control over that."

"In my defense," Raveen said, "you literally appeared out

of nowhere. Who does that? It totally freaked me out! Sorry you aren't able to go home now."

"It's not your fault. Even if we'd found Kot'ani, who's to say the Stone is there? Or how long it would take me to find it." Clem fought the urge to cry. Ferg always told her she never won anything because she didn't try hard enough and gave up too easily. She tried so hard this time. She hadn't given up even when it got hard, and she really wanted to, and still, she'd failed. What was wrong with her?

To keep her lip from trembling, Clem put the flute to her lips and played the tune Myst taught her. A glint of gold flashed in front of her face, followed by a sparkle of purple. Clem kept playing.

"That's so cool." Kiwi smiled.

"Yeah, it's a pretty good party trick." Clem held out her finger and watched a hummingbird land on it. "Speaking of which, will your dad let us go to parties?"

"Not in our wildest dreams," Kiwi said with a snort. "He barely let us walk up this creek by ourselves. He's protective enough of me, but he'll probably want to wrap you in a down-filled air bubble since you're not his kid."

"Hey, you guys, look." Raveen pointed to the hummingbirds dancing up the rainbow spray of the waterfall. Near the top, they hovered around a large boulder shaped exactly like a...

"Is that a hummingbird?" Clem leaped to her feet.

"Holy ti'kea! It's a ruin!" Kiwi screeched. "Wait until Dad sees this!"

By the time Kiwi returned with Emos, Clementine and Raveen had scaled the waterfall.

"See anything else up there?" Emos called up.

"This hummingbird's beak points toward another statue,"

Clem called back. "That statue's beak points around the bend to another waterfall. That fall has a set of stone stairs carved into the rock beside it. We didn't go any farther, though."

Emos didn't need to hear more. In a flash, he was standing next to them.

Climbing the stairs, they discovered an even larger statue. The remnants of its once long, slender beak pointed north.

Stone bricks peeked out between moss and fern. An overgrown path, some of the cobble still visible, turned and followed the creek around the next bend.

Raveen picked up the stone tip of the hummingbird's beak and examined it.

"Do you think this could be it?" Raveen handed the artifact to Emos. "Tua'mua?"

As Emos reached to take it, an arrow whizzed past his fingers, embedding itself in the ground between their feet.

"Leave my daughter alone!" Akylas yelled. Landing between them, he shoved Emos out of the way.

"Dad, he—" Raveen started, but in his rage, Akylas ignored her.

"Leave your daughter alone?" Emos lost it. "Leave your daughter alone?! That's rich coming from the guy who spent his summer chasing my kid halfway across Pangier. How about you leave my kid—and her friend—alone!"

Emos clenched his fist and punched Akylas square in the jaw.

"Dad!" Kiwi's mouth dropped.

"Well, maybe you should teach your daughter not to hang out with filthy little thieves." Akylas wiped the blood from his lip.

"The raven calls out the magpie," Emos said, scoffing. "That's rich."

The two men stared each other down.

"Are you calling me a thief?" spat Akylas.

"Well, I'm certainly not calling you an archeologist." Emos glared at him.

"How dare you, you tam'iki a…" Akylas lunged at Emos.

"Dad, stop!" Raveen screamed, or maybe it was Kiwi. Clementine couldn't tell.

Auk and Casso attempted to break them apart, but Falk flew between them. The next thing Clementine knew, all five of them were brawling in the creek. Raveen and Kiwi tried in vain to break them apart.

Clementine followed them up the creek, unsure of what to do.

Falk and Auk crashed into Kiwi, giving her a bloody nose. Falk unsheathed his knife and pointed it at Auk. Casso snuck up from behind, grabbed Falk by a wing, and swung him into a nearby tree.

"You think I'd let you kidnap my daughter," Akylas said as he held Emos's head underwater.

"It's not what you think," Emos gasped, coming up for air just long enough to punch Akylas in the ribs. "She's with us by choice."

"Is this true?" Akylas stared at his daughter.

"Yes," Raveen cried as she desperately tried to pull his arms from around Emos's neck. "They saved my life. Please, let him go, Daddy."

"They only saved you so they could de-wing you. Emos can't stand the fact he's always losing to me." Akylas turned his attention back to Emos. "Isn't that right, Emos? Thought you'd kidnap my daughter as revenge?"

"Losing to you? You couldn't find a—" Emos's head went back into the creek.

"Dad, enough!" Raveen pleaded.

"These people aren't your friends, Raveen." Akylas pushed her out of the way. "One day, you'll understand."

Stumbling backward, Raveen tripped, banging her head on a rock. Blood trickled into the water.

Someone was going to be seriously injured, killed even. Clementine needed to do something, and quick.

"STOOOOOOOOOPPPPPPP!" she shrieked until she was red in the face. Reverberating off the canyon walls, the sound was deafening. "Have you lost your damned minds?"

Everyone froze.

"Look around you! What happened to you people?" Clem pointed up the canyon.

Akylas raised his head as if seeing the world for the first time. His hands fell from Emos's neck.

"Tua'mua…" he whispered as he stared at the towering stone statue of a Winged, its left arm raised above its head.

Picking himself up from the creek, Emos stopped dead in his tracks.

"Kot'ani," he whispered as he stared at the towering stone statue of a Wingless, its right arm raised above its head.

Between the two statues hovered a stone hummingbird, its outstretched wings resting on their mighty palms. Carved symbols ran across the length of its massive body.

"What does it say?" Clementine asked.

"It says," Kiwi and Raveen said in unison, *"Welcome to Kot'ani Tua'mua Taup'aku: Sanctuary to All."*

Together Clementine, Kiwi, and Raveen wandered beneath the outstretched wings and into the Forgotten City.

CHAPTER 37

"Hey, Raveen, this one looks like you." Kiwi brushed a curtain of delicate yellow flowers from a once-colorful mosaic.

"Holy ti'kea, it totally does," Raveen said with a whistle. "You should see the one over there. It looks like Falk kissing a feathered version of Clementine."

"Gross!" Clementine huffed. "In no reality would that ever happen."

"Oh, I've got to see this," Kiwi cooed excitedly as she followed Raveen around the corner. "Are you coming, Clem?"

"Absolutely not." Clementine shook her head. "Why would I want to see that?"

Sitting on the edge of a fountain, Clem surveyed the ruins of Kot'ani. They'd been wandering around all afternoon and hadn't even made it off the main street. There was so much to see.

Akylas and Falk wandered in and out of any structure with an opening, presumably looking for treasure. Emos, Auk, and Casso stood together admiring a long row of toppled columns.

"Hey, if you're going to start looting already, could you at least note what you took and where you found it?" Emos barked at Akylas.

Akylas glanced at the small statue in his hand and glared at Emos.

"Dad!" Raveen scolded.

Muttering under his breath, Akylas tossed it on the ground.

Well, at least they weren't trying to kill each other. Maybe

371

that was a start. Clem looked at the Winged and Wingless carved into the fountain blocks. It was hard to imagine them peacefully living together, even in this magical place.

What had driven them apart? Why had Kot'ani been abandoned? If anyone could piece the story together, it would be Emos.

Was Kot'ani already in ruins when the princess came here, or did time work differently for her? So many questions without answers. For the millionth time, Clem wished she had the chest so she could message Andro. Maybe he'd learned something new that would be useful.

Clem pulled the flute from around her neck, the copper flashing like fire in the long rays of the evening sun. Where would the princess have hidden the Earth Stone in this overgrown jumbled mess? And how long would it take to uncover it?

Emos and Kiwi had offered her a home in Whaka'wai. Emos promised they'd return every summer to continue the search. But Clementine would not be returning with them. She had already made up her mind. She would stay here for as long as it took. Clementine would never stop searching for the Stone. She would never stop trying to get home.

Pressing the flute to her lips, she played the tune and waited. A tiny hummer, its feathers as pink as Kiwi's, darted out in front of her.

"You'll keep me company, won't you, little friend?"

The bird chirped in response.

Clem put the flute back to her lips. More and more hummingbirds fluttered down from the treetops. Standing on the edge of the fountain, Clem played and played until the whole sky burst with color. This is what it would feel like to catch a rainbow.

On the last note, the shimmer drifted over the fountain and down the grassy street.

Not wanting the moment to end, Clem followed the rainbow around the corner and deeper into the ruins. They drifted to a stop at the base of a colossal tree.

"The First Tree…" Clementine whispered.

There was no mistaking what it was. Its smooth roots draped down the sides of an elaborate stone temple, swallowing it whole.

Slowly walking around the tree, Clem was stunned into silence. It was…the mother of all trees.

Around the back, a colossal stone hummingbird hung suspended in its tangled roots. Beneath its wings, a stone staircase led to what Clementine could only guess was once the temple's entrance. Its long beak hovered over the center of the stairs, nearly kissing the last mossy step.

Falk and Akylas raced up the stairs, Emos and Auk hot on their heels, both eager to be the first to "discover" what was inside. Clem shook her head. Even from where she stood, she could see it was pointless. The temple walls had long since caved in, crushed under the weight of the First Tree.

Clementine walked to the first step, her nose nearly touching the end of the statue's beak, and stared up at it.

"This is unbelievable…" Raveen breathed.

"Whoa." Kiwi pointed to the canopy where thousands of hummingbirds flitted between the flowers.

Mesmerized, Clementine brought the flute to her lips and blew. The First Tree erupted in chorus. As they hit the last note, the giant wings of the stone statue began to rise.

"Holy ti'kea, Clementine…what did you do?" Kiwi panicked.

"I don't know, I just…" The flute fell from Clem's hands,

landing on the mossy step at her feet.

As the wings rose higher, the lower portion of the long beak slowly tilted downward.

Plink.

Clem tilted her head and listened. Something was rolling down the open beak. She reached out with cupped hands and caught it.

Time slowed. The world went silent and still. Clementine exhaled.

In her palms, she held a perfectly round stone, the color of summer honey. Embedded in the center was the tiniest of seeds.

"You guys… You guys, we…we found it!" Clem called over her shoulder to Raveen and Kiwi.

Turning, she caught sight of the flute resting on the stairs by her foot. The most triumphant sentence she'd ever uttered, and no one had understood it! Figured. Picking up the little hummingbird, Clem turned and held the Stone victoriously in the air.

"You guys, we found it!" But when Clementine looked up, she was alone, standing in the middle of her boring old bedroom.

"Kiwi?" Her hand dropped to her side. "Raveen?"

"Clementine! Fergus! Dinner's in five minutes." Her mom's familiar voice wafted up the stairs.

Bewildered, Clementine glanced at her clock. 6:32. A whole summer of adventure had passed in under five minutes. How was that even possible?

Clementine shook her head as if waking from a dream.

She was…home.

"One of you, come set the table, please."

"N-not it!" Clem stammered, looking at her filthy, tattered

clothes.

That would buy her enough time to change and comb the moss and twigs from her hair.

"I did it yesterday," she added as Ferg began to protest. Had she, though? Yesterday felt like a whole other lifetime ago.

Ferg grumbled under his breath then slammed his door shut and thundered down the creaky stairs of their old house.

Home…she was home!

"Love you, Fergus!" Clem added, a huge grin spreading across her face. And she meant it. She loved him so much she might even give him a hug.

"Whatever, ugly!" Ferg yelled back from the kitchen. Maybe she wouldn't give him a hug after all. But still, it would be nice to see his obnoxious face again.

Clem turned to the chest. The key hung from the open drawer, exactly where she'd left it. She stared a moment at the hummingbird, wishing she could have seen the look on Kiwi's and Raveen's faces when she'd vanished. Kiwi! She hadn't even had a chance to say goodbye. She would never see Kiwi again. Her eyes welled up with tears. And yet, she had the biggest smile on her face. She was home! Overwhelmed, Clem locked the tiny hummingbird back in its drawer and strung the key around her neck in its place.

Clem stared a moment at the Stone. She'd done it… She'd actually done it.

The smell of dinner crept under her door. She was famished. Food! Not tarantulas and nuts—real food!

Pocketing the Stone, Clem grabbed some clean clothes off the floor and darted toward the bathroom.

Wait…Andro!

Andro would be thrilled!

Maybe she should give him the Stone. Yes, he'd definitely want it. He'd know how to keep it safe.

Clem ran back to her desk.

"Clementine!" her mom yelled.

Clem pulled out a pen and a piece of paper and wrote a quick note. The whole story would have to wait until after dinner!

"Coming!" Clem yelled back, grinning from ear to ear.

Gently placing the Stone in the chest, Clementine tossed in her note and sprinted downstairs.

She was home!

CHAPTER 38

Thwack.

The enforcer's whip cracked against the side of the ladder, narrowly missing Andro's ankle.

"Stop your daydreaming and get back to work!" the man barked.

Andro clenched his jaw and balled his cherry-stained fists. Ever since he and Ablikim had returned from the Last Library, he found it increasingly difficult to mask his hatred for the Regime. Every inch of him wanted to jump off the ladder and challenge the man to a fight. Even the switch from the rice fields to the cherry orchards, usually a favorite, had done nothing to soothe his anger. He longed to bust through the Outer Wall and run back to Daro and his mountain of books. But he didn't dare, not now. They were so close.

"Yes, sir," he muttered, plucking a handful of cherries from the branch, and depositing them in his empty bucket. From a nearby tree, Ablikim shot him a stern *behave yourself* glance.

How was he supposed to behave? To pretend there was nothing more important in life than picking cherries for the Bird? Andro rolled his eyes.

It had been ten days since Clementine sent the message saying she'd found the first key. Her note had been scribbled on a picture of an island called New Zealand, with a fuzzy gray bird in the corner. Ablikim had been busy translating the pages Clementine had sent about Princess Cyra and where the Stones were hidden. He'd told Andro to translate the shorter message himself. It hadn't been easy. Andro had understood *found key* and *far away*. The part he'd translated as *coming in the air* confused him. Was the fuzzy bird in the picture delivering the key? Maybe that was why it was taking so long; perhaps the bird had gotten lost. As the days passed, he'd become so familiar with the words *not yet* and *still waiting* he no longer needed to translate them.

Handful by handful, he filled his bucket. When that bucket was full, he descended the ladder and carried it to the express cart so the cartmen could whisk it away to Nimbina. Picking up an empty bucket, he started all over again. Why the elite were so obsessed with cherries, he'd never know. He was tempted to try one to see what the fuss was about, but he thought better of it.

As the day wore on, Andro stewed about the key. Was Clementine sure it was the right key? How much longer would it take to arrive, and what would she find in the drawer? Ablikim had translated enough of the long text that Andro knew it would be a clue. Whether or not they could solve it was a whole other worry.

Clementine said they might need to travel to a foreign country to retrieve the Stones. If only she knew how difficult it had been just to get to the Last Library and back. Andro doubted he'd ever see beyond the wall again.

By the time the records keeper had tallied his buckets for the day, Andro was in a mood.

"Patience," the old man said as they strolled home.

"How am I supposed to be patient?" Andro shot back. "I should be in the library helping search for information about the sword or helping Clementine hunt down the bird that lost our key! Or searching for the Stones! Not wasting time picking fruit I can't even eat. We're prisoners in our own city."

"Shhh!" Ablikim hissed. "All in due time, Andro. I know

you're excited and frustrated, but you must learn to be patient. One impulsive decision could destroy everything we're working toward. Word will arrive when there is word worth sending. For now, go home. Rest…

"…keep quiet, and practice your reading," he whispered so only Andro could hear.

Groaning, Andro turned up his street.

"I'm home," he said to no one as he stepped inside the door. Now the days were longer, Granny and Zari often spent their evenings working in the garden. Sighing, he set a pot of water to boil and stared a moment at the old chest.

"Not yet. Still waiting," Andro whined, throwing back the lid dramatically. Sure enough, in the center of the chest was a new note. Which one would it be? Andro's Coin was on *not yet*.

As he picked up the pink paper, his fingers grazed something cool and smooth. A perfectly round stone, the color of fresh cherry sap, rolled out from beneath his fingers. Hands trembling, Andro picked it up. The Stone glowed gold in the thin ray of summer sun shining through the tiny window. There was no doubt what he was looking at. Between his fingers, Andro held all his hopes and dreams.

He turned his attention to the paper. There weren't many words, but he couldn't understand them.

Ablikim would be able to—He needed to show Ablikim!

Andro darted out the door and ran blindly up the street. They were real! The Stones were real! And she'd found one! Clementine Lemons had found one!

Tearing around a busy corner, Andro tripped over a curb and crashed into someone.

"Oh, sorry, I…" Andro's eyes fell on the symbol of the Black Peacock, displayed proudly over the chest pocket of a familiar gray uniform.

He gulped.

"You again? Where do you think you're…" the enforcer roared.

Andro didn't hear the rest of the sentence. He was too busy watching in horror as the paper fell from his fingers and slowly drifted to the ground between their feet, the forbidden words *One down, three to go!* glaring up at him in bold, black ink.

Te Mut'ena | The End

If Clementine Lemons took you on an adventure you won't
forget, I'd love to hear about it! Leaving a review helps other
readers discover the story and means the world to me as an
author.

Thank you for being part of Clem & Andro's journey.

Up Next in the Clementine Lemons Series:

The Adventures of Clementine Lemons
& the Lost Stones of Dohi: *The Water Stone* – **Coming
2026!**

The Adventures of Clementine Lemons
& the Lost Stones of Dohi: *The Wind Stone*

The Adventures of Clementine Lemons
& the Lost Stones of Dohi: *The Fire Stone*

The Adventures of Clementine Lemons
& the Lost Stones of Dohi: *Aether*

**For more details, release dates, bonus content, or to sign
up for the newsletter visit clementinelemons.com.**

About The Author

IRELAND VON MUELLER is the author of middle grade and young adult fiction imbued with strong themes of connection, perseverance and resistance. Her fantastical settings are inspired by her extensive travels, and she is currently pursuing a degree in Environmental Science with a goal of preserving endangered wild spaces. She lives in the Okanagan Valley with her husband, Carl, and a rescue kitty named Rigby.